*

BEST NEW
VAMPIRE
TALES

Volume One

*

*

- BOOKS of the DEAD -

BEST NEW VAMPIRE TALES Volume One

Graphic design by Cynthia Gould
Interior design by James Roy Daley
Edited by James Roy Daley
Photography by Danielle Tunstall
Model: Danielle Tunstall

FIRST EDITION

BOOKS of the DEAD

10 9 8 7 6 5 4 3 2 1

For direct sales and inquiries contact:
besthorror@gmail.com

This series was inspired by Stephen Jones and Ramsey Campbell for their work in *Best New Horror*, and by Richard Davis, Gerald W. Page, and Karl Edward Wagner for their work in *The Year's Best Horror Stories*.

COPYRIGHT ACKNOWLEDGEMENTS

Ad Infinitum by Robert Elrod, copyright 2011. ** Original for this anthology.

Through the Valley of Death by Matt Hults, copyright 2011. ** Original for this anthology.

Cold Calls by John F. D. Taff, copyright 1993. * First appeared in Fictionwise.

A Candle Lit In Sunlight by David Niall Wilson, copyright 2010. * First appeared in Starshore Magazine.

A Sunset so Glorious by Rycke Foreman, copyright 1995. * First appeared in Fantasy Magazine, volume #7, issue #3.

The Verbpire by Fredrick Obermeyer, copyright 2006. * First appeared in Forgotten Worlds.

Morning Sickness by William Meikle, copyright 1993. * First appeared in The Velvet Vampyre #23, published by the UK Vampire Society.

When Barrettes Brought Justice to a Burning Heart by John Everson, copyright 2000. * First appeared in Cage of Bones & Other Deadly Obsessions, published by Delirium Books.

The New Racism by James Newman, copyright 2002. * First appeared in Darkness Within, issue #4.

Banalica by Michael Laimo, copyright 1999. * First appeared in Demons, Freaks and Other Abnormalities.

Window Across the Street by Jay Caselberg, copyright 2003. * First appeared in Bloodlust UK.

Endless Night by Barbara Roden, copyright 2008. * First appeared in Exotic Gothic 2, published by Ash Tree Press.

Preserver by Tim Waggoner, copyright 1996. * First appeared Blood Muse, published by Donald Fine Inc.

A New House by John L. French, copyright 1996. * First appeared in Weird Stories #2, published by Fading Shadows Publications.

Lover's Triangle by Colleen Anderson, copyright 1996. * First appeared in OnSpec Magazine.

The Sabbatarian by David M. Fitzpatrick, copyright 2011. ** Original for this anthology.

Bridges by Alan Smale, copyright 2001. * First appeared in Dark Regions Magazine.

Thirteen Lines by Don Webb, copyright 1995. * First appeared in Blood Muse.

Flotsam by Scott Harper, copyright 2009. * First appeared in The Bitter End, published by Pill Hill Press.

Moving Lines by Steve Vernon, copyright 2004. * First appeared in the collection Nightmare Dreams.

Farm Wife by Nancy Kilpatrick, copyright 1992. * First appeared in Northern Frights, published by Mosaic Press.

*Reprinted by permission of author.

**Used by permission of author.

*

EDITED BY
JAMES ROY
DALEY

*

*

- BOOKS of the DEAD -

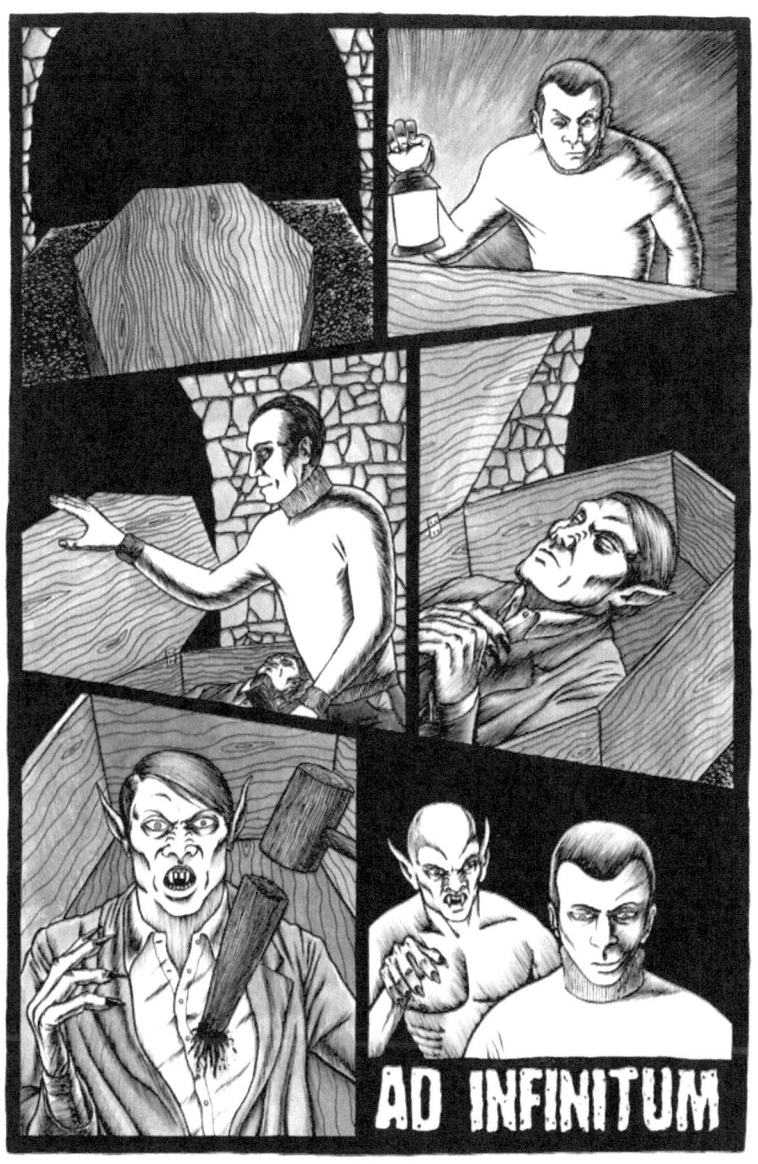

AD INFINITUM

- BOOKS OF THE DEAD -

BLOODY MARY #1

1 1/2 OZ VODKA
1/2 OZ LEMON JUICE
3 OZ HUMAN BLOOD
1 DASH OF WORCESTERSHIRE SAUCE
CELERY SALT
GROUND PEPPER
HOT PEPPER SAUCE TO TASTE
CELERY STALK FOR GARNISH
LEMON AND/OR LIME WEDGE FOR GARNISH
ICE CUBES

~

1. BUILD THE LIQUID INGREDIENTS IN A HIGHBALL
GLASS OVER ICE CUBES.

2. MIX WELL.

3. ADD THE SEASONINGS TO TASTE.

4. GARNISH WITH THE LEMON/LIME WEDGE.

5. SERVE.

MORE GREAT BOOKS FROM
BOOKS OF THE DEAD

NOVELS
Matt Hults - Husk
James Roy Daley - Terror Town

ANTHOLOGIES
Best New Zombie Tales (Vol. 1)
Best New Zombie Tales (Vol. 2)
Best New Zombie Tales (Vol.3)
Classic Vampire Tales (Vol.1)

COLLECTIONS
James Roy Daley -13 Drops of Blood

∞☉∞

CONTENTS

- BOOKS OF THE DEAD -

-Through The Valley Of Death-
MATT HULTS

Jacob wiggled his toes inside his loafers, finding that the soft material of the shoes had almost frozen solid. He wondered how long it would be before his flesh did the same.

He hugged himself tighter, drawing his wool dress-coat snug to his body. Though no wind gusted along the narrow mountain road, the thieving winter air had already seeped through his clothing and gone to work at stealing his body heat. If another vehicle didn't come along soon, he knew the situation would become far worse than a mere inconvenience.

He glanced back and forth as he wiggled his toes again.

To his left the two feet of fresh powder covering the road appeared smooth and unbroken, better resembling a frozen forest stream rather than twin lanes of asphalt. To his right, the only sign of traffic came in the form of the overlapping tire tracks cut through the snow by his own SUV. Hoof prints from the deer that had bound into his path dotted the snow mere inches away from them.

Jacob cursed at the sight, knowing there was nothing he could've done to change what had happened. His only solace to having crashed his vehicle, avoiding a collision, was that he'd swerved to the right, toward the cushioning snowdrifts lining the forest, rather than left, where he could've smacked head on into the towering wall of granite bordering that side of the road.

He sighed, creating a miniature cloudbank in front of his face.

Across the road, his wounded vehicle sat at an odd angle, nose pointing toward the forest. The Chevy's rear end canted upward, its undercarriage resting on an old log that had been concealed by snow until the SUV's front tires crashed over it. Even at a distance he spotted the broken branch that had impaled the fuel tank like a medieval pike, spilling over thirty-five gallons of gasoline. Fumes still haunted the air, lingering around the wreck like a disquieted spirit with nowhere to go.

"Nothing yet?"

Jacob turned at the sound of his wife's voice. Thirty feet away, Kate emerged from a small corpus of pines, carrying Sadie on her back to spare her from having to tromp through the hip-deep drifts on her own. In her puffy pink snowsuit, their daughter looked like a three-year-old astronaut.

"I peed and pooped," Sadie cheered.

Jacob laughed. "Good job. Just remember that these are special circumstances, though. I don't want to start finding surprises in the front hedge after we get home."

He looked to Kate and winked, hoping the comment would soften her look of concern. She formed a weak smile and winked back.

He took Sadie in his arms when Kate walked up beside him, allowing her to brush off the snow that had crusted on her dress pants and in the imitation fur surrounding the tops of her boots.

"It's been over an hour," she said, her teeth chattering every few words. "We can't stay out here much longer. Did you check the car again?"

He frowned. "We could use if for shelter, but we'd probably all start hallucinating within five minutes after sitting down."

"That bad?"

"Afraid so." He shifted Sadie in his arms as they crossed the road to the vehicle. Within five feet of the tailgate Kate stopped and waved one hand in front of her nose.

"Ugh," she said. "You're right."

"Pee-ewe," Sadie agreed.

A hawk shrieked from somewhere along the higher reaches of the cliff behind them, its icy cry accentuating the enormity of the wilderness around them. The sound echoed once in the dead winter silence then faded.

Sadie searched for it, squinting against the cloudless blue overhead.

"So what do you think?" Kate asked.

Jacob shrugged. He kicked the back bumper, knocking loose the crust of dirty snow that had caked on the license plate. "California tags, small family all dressed up like they've got money, gas-guzzling SUV … What do I think?"

He put Sadie down and covered her ears with his hands.

"Daddy!"

"I think those hillbilly bastards at the gas station screwed us," he said. "I think they sent us up the wrong road on purpose, knowing we'd get stuck, so I'd end up having to trudge back there and pay a fortune for a tow."

"Daddy, you're deafing my head," Sadie yelled.

Jacob released her. "Sorry, kiddo. Better?"

She nodded and ran over to a snowdrift.

Kate shivered. "If the road was closed we would've seen signs, though, right?"

Jacob put his arms around her, pulling her close. "You heard the radio. They were measuring nine-foot snowdrifts along I-80 after yesterday's storm and that's just a few miles from here. Remember those mounds we drove around that Sadie said looked like big molehills? One of them might've been covering a roadblock for all we know."

Kate exhaled a fogbank of a sigh and leaned into his chest. "This is crazy," she whispered. "There's got to be someone who patrols this area: a local sheriff, DNR, someone. And how long before anybody knows that we're missing? I told a few people at work we were going to your friend's wedding, but that was over a month ago, when the invitation came. I didn't think to mention it again. Hell, we were only supposed to be gone for the day."

Jacob looked at his watch. "The ceremony won't start for another two hours, and even once it does I don't think we'll be missed. Paul's a good guy and all, but I doubt he's counting the minutes until his old college roomy shows up."

"Shit," Kate replied. "Suppose no one comes. What do we do once it gets dark? We can't sleep in the car with those fumes."

"And we can't make a fire," he added. "You tossed out the cigarette lighter when you quit smoking, remember?"

"Hey, for the record, that wasn't easy."

Jacob rubbed her back. "And I applaud you, but right now I'm thinking we'll have to hike back."

Kate had tucked her head down into the lining of her coat to cover her mouth from the cold. Now she perked up, her rosy red lipstick matching the crimson color of her unprotected cheeks.

"Hike?" she asked. "Montgomery must be over a half hour drive from here."

"Easily," Jacob agreed. "But that's not where we're going."

"Where then?"

Jacob tipped his head toward a gap in the tree line.

Kate's mouth dropped open. "You can't be serious. Cross country, in these clothes?"

He cringed at the thought of it. "It'll suck, but I don't think we'll be out there too long. Look at that."

Beyond the gap in the forest a wide valley opened up lower in the woodland, appearing as a huge swath of white surrounded by trees. There, on the other side, a series of angular gray shapes poked over the far treetops.

His wife squinted. "Are those buildings?"

Jacob nodded. "It's probably Ethridge. That's the nearest town to Montgomery on the map. If we took the road we'd have to detour around Voyager's National Forest. Going across this valley, we'll only have to travel three or four miles."

Kate tucked her chin back into her coat. "All the experts say you're supposed to stay with your vehicle if you get stranded."

Again, Jacob agreed with her. "True, but we've got clear skies and almost no wind, plus five hours of daylight. Being that we're still in the lowlands, I'm betting we can make the hike in well under that."

He turned and looked at the tower of rock looming over them. "Besides, I'm not so sure I want to camp out under this monster. The sunlight will have those rocks warming up. All it takes is a few drops of melt-water freezing in the right crack after sundown and—BAM—we're part of the mountain."

"The forecast did call for flurries tonight," Kate said.

"Which might equate to another two or three feet of snow in these parts," Jacob replied. "If we're going to go, this could be our best chance to do it."

Kate eyed him. "Aren't you supposed to order me to stay put while you go act brave?"

He pulled her close again, pressing their cheeks together until their combine warmth chased the cold from their skin. "Leave my little heater behind? Hell, no."

Kate laughed, her breath tickling his neck. He held her in silence, not needing to speak to relay his dread of what lay ahead if something went wrong. The world seemed to shrink to a pinpoint, and the only thing left was his love for his family.

"It's just a few miles," he said. "We'll be fine."

Kate nodded, her gaze flicking to where Sadie was drawing squiggles on a tablet of unbroken snow.

"Hey, kiddo," Jacob called. "Want to go for a walk?"

"Do I get a piggyback ride?"

"Sure thing."

She ran over and he lifted her onto his shoulders.

"I'm taller than you, Momma," their daughter declared from her perch. "I'll beat you."

"Momma goes first," Jacob corrected. "Her boots are warmer than Daddy's shoes. Plus, we can walk in her footsteps so I don't accidentally trip on something hidden in the snow. You wouldn't want to fall from way up there, right?"

"Uh-uh," Sadie answered.

Kate leaned in and gave each of them a kiss. "Follow the leader," she said.

Turning away, she stepped over the first drift bordering the roadside. Her leg sank up to her thigh in the powder, but she pressed on, moving into the forest, toward the valley below.

Jacob followed.

∞Θ∞

The first fifteen minutes passed in silence.

The ground sloped steadily downward from the road, dotted by huge boulders that jutted from the snow like colossal stumps of half buried bones. Even Sadie, with her insatiable hunger for new information, fell quiet while they navigated the terrain. The sound of their footfalls became the only noise in the snow-muffled stillness.

Jacob tried to ignore the various discomforts already encroaching upon his awareness as he marched. His cheeks burned. His feet ached. The bridge of his nose felt like a wedge of cold steel had been inserted under the skin. He had hoped that the snow wouldn't be as abundant here in the forest, but the powerful mountain winds had managed to deposit a minimum shin-deep layering throughout the area.

They trudged onward.

Roughly sixty yards from the road they came to a vast grouping of tall pines. Each tree had to be well over a hundred feet tall, with the space between the ground and their lowermost branches a fifth of that distance.

The world grew darker.

Sadie's grip tightened on Jacob's shoulders.

Under the boughs of the evergreens the forest became a black and white realm of heaped snow and deep shadows. What little light did make it to the ground burned in bright pools around them.

When they first started off, Jacob's main concern had been the snow and the cold, but now his mind conjured images of winter-starved bobcats and man-eating grizzly bears.

He glanced around, reevaluating the splendor of the forest.

The tall trunks of the encompassing trees appeared black in the shadows, their bark jagged and horribly knotted. Jacob grimaced when he passed under them, happy to get back into the light.

Ahead, a wide deadfall blocked their path, and Kate paused to consider her options.

Here, broken branches and more rocks gave the snow-covered ground the appearance of a mangled corpse shrouded by a white coroner's sheet. The fresh scent of pine, which had filled his lungs with each breath since entering the woods, now smelled like something meant to disguise a more sinister odor.

Jacob shook the thought off and hurried to follow Kate when she turned right and resumed her trek.

The trees, the darkness, the strange shapes concealed by the snow … the whole area seemed to exude a malevolence Jacob wasn't accustomed to, certainly not it connection with nature. He couldn't say what gave him such an unwholesome impression, but, rational or not, the feeling persisted.

He suddenly wondered if he'd made the right choice.

A branch snapped.

It sounded off to the left, and Jacob pivoted to look. A flash of darkness merged with the deeper shadows under the trees.

He stopped walking.

"Hello?" he started to say, but stopped short when another twig cracked to his right. This time Kate came to a halt.

"What was that?" she asked.

Jacob held up a hand to silence her and continued to listen.

They'd come to another cathedral of pines, but the staggered ramparts of smaller saplings surrounding them limited his sight to only a few yards.

"Probably the deer that ran us off the road," he said.

The snow had thinned out a bit under the larger trees, and Jacob used the opportunity to walk alongside his wife when they started moving again.

"Not long and we'll be sucking down hot coco at the nearest restaurant," he said to break the uneasy hush. "How's that sound?"

"Yum," Sadie cheered. "With mushmellows, too?"

"As many as you can eat."

Jacob noticed Kate give the area behind them one last appraisal before joining in. "I just hope we don't all end up with pneumonia."

He smiled at her. "Did you hear the one about the doctor whose patient died of bronchitis?"

She regarded him with one eyebrow raised in suspicion.

"He said he knew the guy was a goner because of the coffin."

Kate rolled her eyes but grinned.

"Get it? Coughing. Coffin."

"Very clever, dear."

Sadie leaned over his shoulder. "What's bronto-po-cysus?"

Jacob looked up at her. "It's like a really bad col—"

But his reply tapered off when he spotted what loomed overhead.

He stopped walking.

Kate continued several steps before turning and tracing his line of sight. She gasped.

A deer's carcass hung from the branches of the nearest tree, its skeleton picked clean. It seemed to float in the shadowy stillness, the tethers of rawhide that secured it to the tree all but invisible when set against the backdrop of the snow-frosted forest.

Jacob gaped at it, captivated.

Ice from the recent storm clung to its boney crown like transparent flesh, creating a sharp contrast to the darkness that gazed back at him from the black pits of its eye sockets.

Sadie mewed. "Daddy, what's that?"

"Bones," Kate answered for him. "Probably left by some hunter."

"What's hunting?" Sadie asked.

"It's how people used to survive in the wilderness," Jacob replied. He had to swallow to wet his throat. "Way back before grocery stores people had to hunt animals for food. Now most just do it for sport."

Sadie shifted on his shoulders. "Sport?"

"Yeah, like a game, to have fun."

"People kill things for fun?"

"I'm afraid so, kiddo."

Sadie's gaze returned to the bones, her young mind no doubt trying to make sense of the notion. "That's not nice," she said.

Fifty feet ahead a white glare cut through the trees where they opened into the valley.

"No, it isn't, sweetheart," Jacob agreed. "Come on. Let's keep going."

They altered course around the tree with the skeleton, Jacob taking the lead. He made it three steps before stopping again.

"Jesus," he said out of shock.

He'd pushed through a cluster of spruce saplings to behold a towering curtain of fleshless animal remains blocking his path. Thousands of withered hides and stripped bones decorated the forest like gruesome ornaments on row after row of blasphemous Christmas trees.

Jacob stared, mouth hanging open.

Skulls. Femurs. Vertebrae. Ribs.

They adorned branch after branch.

Some hung in groupings meant to resemble the animals they came from, whereas others had been mixed and fitted together to create elaborate abstract sculptures of death.

Jacob thought of the wind chime hanging outside their kitchen window back home and wondered what kind of music this collection would make on a blustery day.

"My God," Kate said under her breath. In the cold, the word came off her lips like a ghost.

"Was this from hunters?" Sadie asked.

"No," Jacob replied. He glanced behind them, to the cavernous shadows under the pine trees and the million or so hiding places among the ground clutter and rocks.

Kate, too, scanned their surroundings. "Should we go back?"

Jacob strained to hear into the depths of the forest before answering. He thought he heard a low chanting in the distance, a repetitive cadence that he soon realized was his own heartbeat pounding in his temples.

He looked ahead of them, beyond the bones. Twenty feet away the woods opened onto a ledge overlooking the valley.

"No," he answered. "Whoever did this did it a long time ago. Let's just keep moving and put it behind us."

He adjusted Sadie's seating on his shoulders and moved forward, not looking up when he passed under the bones. Kate followed.

They cleared the trees, all squinting against the glare of the snow. The valley floor lay below them, looking like a vast frozen lake. On the opposite side, a palisade of pines hid the view of the town. The sun hunkered on the horizon behind them, creating a silhouette that looked like a row of black fangs.

Jacob gazed in disbelief.

Kate gasped even as he looked to his watch.

"Jacob, the sun—"

"I see it," he croaked.

"But how?" she asked. "It wasn't even noon when we left."

"I know."

Sadie shifted uneasily. "Is it going to get dark now?"

Jacob patted her leg but couldn't summon the saliva to answer. He looked back into the cave of trees where they emerged from the woods and the shadows that seemed dim beforehand had become impenetrably black.

"Jacob how—" Kate pleaded.

"I don't know!" he shot back, then muted himself.

He stepped onto an outcrop and stared out at the valley. What had first appeared as a blank white palette now looked streaked with oranges and purples, divided by long, pointed shadows. Their brilliance faded with each passing second.

There was no denying it—they'd walked for less than an hour, yet his watch showed that it was five minutes to sunset.

"Let's go back," Kate whispered.

Jacob nodded his agreement and gestured to the left. "This way looks less rocky."

He started walking, but a crisp noise suddenly cut through the stillness and his right leg sank up to his crotch. He buckled over, straining every muscle in his back to keep Sadie from tumbling off his shoulders.

"Shit," he yelped.

Sadie screamed. Her small hands clutched his head.

"Hon—" Kate started, but Jacob cut her off with a shout.

"Stay back! I can't feel anything underneath. I think we're on a snow shelf or something. The way this land slopes away ... Christ, we could be fifty feet off the ground."

"Can you get back up?"

"I don't know."

He tried to push up with his left hand and it disappeared into the snow up to his elbow.

"Damn," he cried. "Quick, take Sadie and back away slowly."

Kate moved forward, easing her weight down with each step. The snow crunched underfoot. Below them, phantom sounds issued from something unseen, something Jacob knew could've only been hunks of packed snow breaking loose and dropping to the rocks.

"Don't come any closer," he shouted.

Kate froze, her arms outstretched. Sadie mewed at the force of his voice.

"It's okay, baby," Kate said. "Just hang on."

Jacob sank another inch as he maneuvered Sadie off his shoulders with his free hand, struggling to keep her balanced.

"Momma!"

"I'm right here," Kate said, her voice miraculously calm. "Just move slow and come to me."

Jacob reached.

Sadie reached.

Kate clutched the girl's hand.

And the shelf collapsed.

Jacob saw the crack open in the snow inches from his wife's boots, giving them enough time to lock eyes before he and Sadie plunged six feet, dropping with the slow motion fluidity of a Hollywood special effect.

Sadie's hand pulled away, leaving her empty mitten in Kate's grasp.

Jacob saw the scream form on his wife's lips, her cold-blanched face creasing in horror. But then the section she stood on followed suit, breaking off before the cry left her mouth.

The two massive slabs of snow shattered into a thousand hard fragments, engulfing them in an avalanche. The world went black. Jacob's ears filled with a rumbling white noise. He felt Sadie yanked from his hands as the flow engulfed them, tumbling him end over end, contorting his body regardless of all efforts to curl into a ball.

With each roll and twist he expected a fist of granite to punch a hole in his ribcage or smash open his skull. But then he came to a halt in mid-summersault, suspended upside down in the snow.

He tried to move. His muscles flexed, straining each fiber, but the snow had packed tight around his body, immobilizing him in a frosty embrace.

Panic bit into his senses. He imagined Sadie trapped somewhere nearby, buried alive. The back of his throat seared with pain as he fought to scream through a mouthful of snow.

Something slammed into his back.

A hand grabbed his coat.

"Jacob," Kate cried.

He felt the pressing weight of the snow shoved aside, and her shouts grew louder. She hauled him free just as his lungs seemed ready to explode.

He gasped for air, ignoring the frigid sting of it as he drew in breath after breath.

Kate helped him up, wiping snow from his face, and he exhaled a great sigh of relief when he saw Sadie standing next to her. The young girl's eyes glistened but looked bright and alert.

"Are you all right?" Kate asked between sobs. "Is anything broken?"

Jacob shook his head. He looked up, shocked to find the ledge that they'd fallen from now towering three stories above them.

"I thought I lost you," he said to his wife.

"Ditto," she replied.

He reached out and hugged them, clinging to his wife and daughter as his own emotions evolved into tears. The last rays of sunlight bled out of the valley as he gazed over his wife's shoulder, leaving the sky a deep shade of crimson.

When he finally released them, Kate regarded him through wet eyes. A faint grin dimpled her fiery red cheeks.

"Now the hard part, right?"

∞☉∞

Runny nose. Freezing ears. Chapped lips.

None of the other pains compared to the ache in Jacob's feet as he plowed onward through the dark.

Three hundred yards from the cliff the wind picked up, coming out of the north.

"Cover your face," Jacob said to Sadie as another gust hit them. He held up one hand to shield his own face from the cold, and the suede material of his driving gloves felt like stiff rawhide on his skin.

With the sun gone, the valley had turned into a shimmering white sheet that glowed in the starlight. The forest had before a black ring around them, with the only sounds coming from their feet and the morose howl of the wind.

Jacob was trying to think of something to say when his wife beat him to it.

"Look," Kate cried. She pointed through the flying snow.

Jacob peered past her, making out five figures moving toward them. He refused to believe his own eyes at first, worried the wind was playing a trick on them, but when the black shapes moved closer he knew he wasn't imagining it.

"I'll be damned," Jacob said.

Both he and Kate waved their arms over their heads, signaling the newcomers. Jacob counted five people, their features lost in the dark. The shape in the lead waved once in reply.

Jacob pushed on to meet them, a fresh surge of hope charging his spirit.

"Are we glad to see you," he said once they'd neared within speaking distance.

The men remained silent as they approached. All five appeared to be American Indians, clad in camouflage snow pants and jackets with bright orange hunting vests. Rather than rifles or shotguns, however, they sported more traditional bows and arrows that looked handmade.

Jacob adjusted his grip on Sadie, smiling.

"Hello," Kate said.

The quintet closed within ten feet and came to a halt, watching Jacob and his family with unreadable eyes. None of them spoke, not even to acknowledge Kate's greeting.

Jacob extended his hand. "I'm Jacob Strode, pleased to—"

"What are you doing here?" the closest man asked. He was older than the rest, his face a craggy landscape of wrinkles.

Jacob swallowed, wetting his throat. "We had a bit of an accident with our car," he explained. "A deer ran into the—"

"This is sacred ground," the man interrupted. "It is a spiritual place. You shouldn't have come here."

Jacob exchanged glances with Kate. "I'm sorry. We didn't intend to trespass or anything. We're just trying to get to town."

"There are roads to town," the man answered.

Jacob swallowed again. He saw Kate look to him out of the corner of his eye but kept his attention focused on the tribesman. He shifted position, trying to free himself from the snow hugging his legs.

"Like I said, we wrecked our car back there, and we haven't seen any other traffic for hours. You see, we were on our way to a wedding, so we're not really dressed for—"

"You are not welcome here."

"Please," Kate cut in. "We just need a cell phone or a radio, and we'll—"

The elder shook his head. "Your white man's magic will not work here."

Jacob blinked, catching another shocked glance from Kate.

White man's magic? Did he actually say that?

"This is a place of uneasy spirits," the elder went on. "You have disturbed them with your presence, and for that you must die."

Each word of the old man's statement resounded with perfect clarity in the open air, but Jacob floundered for a response while he waited for the grin that would put them in context. In contrast, the man's expression remained maddeningly impassive.

"We said we were sorry," Kate said. "You don't have to play games with us."

"Regret means nothing," the old man replied. "Only blood will cleanse your transgression."

"This isn't funny," she shot back.

The wind howled, stirring up specters of snow that swirled around them. For a moment the distant trees become lost in a white haze, and the rest of the world vanished.

Jacob used the moment to turn to his wife and slide Sadie into her arms. When he faced the hunters again, he stripped off his gloves and dug his wallet out of his pocket.

"I have sixty dollars cash," he said, pulling the bills out to show them. He strove to keep his voice level, as if the leader's announcement never registered. "I know that's not much, but if there's a bank in town, I'd gladly pay you men one hundred dollars apiece to—"

"Five hundred," Kate interjected. "We'll pay you five hundred dollars apiece. It's all we have, but we'll give it to you if you help us. Please."

"Trade will not save you," the leader replied.

Jacob's eyes flicked to each of the men. They all shared the older man's blank gaze, not one looking even the slightest bit insincere. Their silent subservience cleaved a new wound into Jacob's resolve.

"Look, we're scared enough as it is," Jacob told them. "Why are you doing this?"

No one replied. Had someone sneered or offered a comment, then at least he might have had a clue to their intentions, but their incessant silence deepened his fear that the old man wasn't joking.

"Is it a racial thing?" Jacob pressed, searching for the source of the unspoken hostility. "Is that what the white man comment was about? Because we're not like that."

The leader's stare remained constant, his expression unyielding.

Jacob crammed the money into his pocket. A flush of anger drove the cold from his cheeks.

"Forget it," he said. "We'll find our own way—"

"Jacob," Kate cut in.

He turned to look at her, only to find her attention trained on five more natives who'd approached from behind. Like the first group, all of them wore hunting gear and carried handcrafted weapons.

By the time Jacob faced the leader again the other hunters had fanned out, joining with the newcomers to surround them.

"Come on, guys," Jacob pleaded. "Enough is enough."

Ignoring him, the leader nodded to his fellow tribesmen, and the men all readied their bows. They drew arrows.

Kate gasped, moving closer.

"Okay, stop this," Jacob demanded. He glanced back and forth, trying to watch everyone at once. He shuffled his feet in the snow, hoping to bump into a rock or a stick, anything he could use as a weapon.

"This has gone way too far. If you're not going to help us then just back off and—"

But his words died off in mid-sentence when he saw the hunters knock the arrows to their bowstrings and pull back. The wood creaked as the pressure compounded.

Jacob froze, his anger turning to terror.

Kate grasped his arm.

"There is no fighting it," the old man said. "The spirits demand sacrifice."

Jacob's heart machinegunned inside his chest, firing adrenaline to every muscle in his body. His hands shook. His legs trembled. Sweat burned on his brow.

The valley surrounded them like a wasteland, offering no shelter, no means of escape. The deep, clinging snow assured that even the fastest lunge would prove useless, and the nearest tree seemed a world away.

But not nearly as distant as reasoning with the man standing ten feet in front of him.

Jacob met the elder's emotionless gaze.

"Take me," Jacob pleaded. "Let my family go."

"Jacob, no," Kate cried.

"Yes," he said, stepping away from her. "I'm the one who decided to cross here. Leave them out of this. I'm begging you, don't hurt my family."

The old man's eyes never blinked. His pupils appeared huge in the gloom, and what Jacob saw welling in their black depths drowned his last hope for salvation. Behind his impervious expression of detachment, Jacob saw a glimmer of revelry in the old man's dark gaze, a sinister obedience to customs that had been forged in another age and carried out over the centuries with an unbending devotion.

"The woman first," the old man ordered.

And with those words, Jacob realized what had been nagging him ever since the hunters arrived: no steamy exhalations issued from the man's lips when he spoke. His chest remained as still as the frozen valley floor.

Because he's already dead, Jacob thought. All of them are.

—This is a place of uneasy spirits—

Jacob's mouth dropped open even as the sound of bowstrings thrummed the air. Arrows hissed past on both sides.

Half a dozen impacts issued from behind, like fists hitting a pillow.

Moving with the tarry slowness of a nightmare, Jacob swung around to see his wife falling backwards, wooden shafts jutting from her torso and legs. She collapsed with her eyelids peeled back in shock, teeth bared in a display of animalistic horror. Sadie tumbled from her grasp, landing facedown in the snow.

"No!" Jacob bellowed.

Something punched him in the back.

He glanced down to see an obsidian arrowhead poking through his coat, just over the right breast pocket. Thin wisps of steam trailed from the blood smeared across its surface.

Jacob glanced up, immobilized by shock.

He saw Sadie, still stuck in the snow, unable to move. Kate rolled toward her, reaching out, striving to help the girl in spite of her wounds.

Then his eyes caught a flash of movement from the hunters beyond his wife and child, and suddenly five arrows stabbed into his legs.

The cold stone missiles punched through his aching muscles with brutal force, ravaging his flesh. Their sharp points chipped against bone.

Jacob howled in agony but lunged toward Kate as he fell, now hearing the terrible chorus of multiple knife blades as they were drawn from their sheaths.

The natives charged forward, casting up a blizzard of snow with their footsteps.

Someone dropped down on Jacob's back, pinning him in place.

He struggled to free himself, but each twist caused him to sink farther into the icy carpet covering the valley, pressing the arrowheads deeper into his legs.

His breaths came out as a thunder of pain and rage.

The weight on his back shifted and someone snared his right arm, yanking it back. The steel edge of a blade found the joint of one finger and sliced it from his hand.

Jacob screamed.

Then again. And again.

The cold valley air struck the exposed nerves like liquid nitrogen poured into his veins. Teeth bit down on the open flesh and sucked his blood from the wounds.

"Yessss," an ancient voice hissed with inhuman pleasure.

Jacob growled through the pain when the attacker released his arm, watching helplessly from ground level as one of the hunters seized Sadie by the leg and dragged her away, a stone tomahawk clutched in his free hand.

Kate grabbed at the man, snatching a leather strap from his boot before another native dropped to his knees behind her. He tore off her hat and clutched a fistful of her hair. With his other hand, he brought a gleaming knife to her scalp and—

The top of the man's head exploded.

Even in his current condition of unparalleled terror, Jacob flinched at the sight. The shattered fragments of the hunter's skull sailed through the air like confetti, soon joined by the distant report of a gunshot.

Jacob craned his head to one side and saw four muzzle flashes blink on the horizon.

The headless attacker kneeling beside Kate pushed to his feet, standing even as the bullets punched holes through his torso and exploded out his back in great plumes of dust.

The man didn't stagger. Didn't fall.

He disintegrated.

One moment he appeared as a solid figure standing tall; a heartbeat later he'd become a man-shaped accumulation of twigs, dirt, and leaves that blew apart in the wind.

The other natives had ceased in mid-action, and now all turned toward the wood line even as a fresh round of gunshots flashed from the shadows.

The tribesman looming over Sadie fell backward, his chest torn open to expose a hollow space filled with dried weeds and animal fur.

Another man's shoulder erupted into a cloud of brown pine needles and feathers.

The weight on Jacob's back suddenly lifted, and he looked up to see the old man standing over him, his eyes empty black pits, his mouth opened impossibly wide, filled with a hundred mismatched animal fangs. An inhuman shriek erupted from the cavern of his throat; then a rifle blast ripped it from his body sending his severed head rolling through the air, trailing streams of black ash.

It crashed to the snow and disintegrated into a dusty heap of crushed bones and black hair.

Several more gunshots boomed, now closer, but when Jacob glanced up again all he could see was Kate's slumped form laying just out of reach. The heart wrenching sound of Sadie's weeping emanated from somewhere nearby.

"Hang on, baby," Jacob called, trying to raise himself high enough to find her. "Daddy's coming, baby, just hang on."

The butchered remains of his damaged hand reddened the snow when he attempted to push himself upright, and he screamed in agony when both arms sunk up to his elbows. Ice crystals stabbed at his wounds.

"Kate?" he howled. "Oh, God, Kate, answer me."

"Jacob."

The roar of a snowmobile engine overpowered his sob of relief at the sound of Kate's voice, and within moments he heard the soft crunch of footfalls growing near.

He faced the sound to see another group of American Indians rush forward.

One of them lifted Sadie from the snow, gently wiping her face. Another rushed to Kate with a multi-tool, using its pliers to trim the arrow shafts. A third knelt beside her with a first aid kit.

Three others stood watch with rifles in hand, scanning the landscape with impatient glances.

Suddenly, a pair of hands settled on Jacob's shoulders and rolled him onto his back. A broad-faced Indian stared into his eyes.

Jacob tensed, kicking his feet, pushing away.

"Try to relax," the tribesman said. "We'll get you to a hospital but we must hurry."

It took a moment for the words to sink in, but then Jacob detected the tones of warmth and compassion. Unlike the elder, this man's breath puffed in the cold.

Jacob tried to speak, failed, then tried again.

"My daughter. My wife."

"Are being cared for," the man said. He unfolded a cutting tool and quickly snipped the wood shafts jutting from Jacob's body, setting off a dozen explosions of pain. Agony raked its claws along his nerves where the arrowheads nestled in his flesh.

"I'm sorry," the man said. He pulled Jacob to a stand, hauling him forward. "We don't have a choice. Time is running out. The blood makes them stronger."

Jacob eyed him across his shoulder. "They were dead."

The Indian nodded. "This is cursed ground, the burial place of a thousand rogue shamans who tried to stop the settlers from passing into the West. They were the drinkers of blood, and the eaters of children. They defied the Great Spirit to gain their power, and now they are trapped here, immortal but imprisoned."

He deposited Jacob on the back of a snowmobile. Every muscle in his body seemed to disconnect from his bones, and he sagged into the seat. Several feet away Kate and Sadie were helped onto another sled.

"They're coming," one of the men shouted.

The broad-faced Indian spun toward the voice. Jacob followed his gaze to where one of the riflemen pointed into the black gulf of the valley.

The snow was moving.

"But you destroyed them!" Jacob cried.

"Only the sunlight can do that," the man replied. "We must hurry!"

Sixty yards away a swell the size of a house had raised from the flat landscape, pushed upward from something beneath.

"Go," another man yelled. The others jumped on their snowmobiles and the engines roared as the throttles cranked open. They spun and raced for the far tree line, the icy wind nipping at Jacob's flesh like a buzzard.

He clung to his rescuer with all the strength he had left, glancing back just long enough to see the huge swell moving closer. The snow spilled away as it shifted and flexed, revealing the leathery hides of a thousand mummified corpses surging forth as a single, monstrous mound.

It was a mass-grave come to life. Chaos made flesh.

The mere sight ripped the breath from Jacob's lungs and clawed at his sanity. He saw bone and hair and muscle and skin, teeth and eyes and dehydrated entrails. It moved with unearthly speed, closing the gap between them with the horrific pace of a nightmare.

Then they were past the trees, plowing into the forest. Evergreen boughs slapped Jacob's head and body, folding inward behind him to block his view of the madness pursuing them. A second later they shot through another barrier of bones. Shattered skeletons rained to the ground, knocked loose from their tethers.

The snowmobiles slid to a halt, their front skis grating on hidden rocks and branches. Jacob shook his head, thinking *No! Don't stop!* even as an enormous shadow darkened the thin spaces between the trees. The forest went black. Even the stars vanished from sight.

The titanic horror hit the tree line and exploded into a blizzard of snow. A huge cloud of white filled the air, blasting through the branches to cover the area with an additional two feet of powder.

When Jacob looked up again, the monster was gone. Stars once again dappled the night.

He hauled himself off the snowmobile. Pain knotted his insides, but he limped to Kate and Sadie, dropping beside them and clutching them in his arms. Kate's pants glimmered with blood, but her grip was strong when she hugged him.

Jacob's rescuer stepped up beside him, laying a hand on his shoulder.

"We're safe," the man said. "The dead cannot pass the barrier."

No, Jacob wanted to say, *the dead can't get through it, but the dying still can.*

He looked down at his hand and moaned at the bony claws that had sprouted from where his fingers had been severed, watching as the muscle and tendons and skin reformed around the bite marks in his flesh.

The pain in his gut intensified. He could feel his bodily fluids turn to dust, his organs shrivel inside him. He gagged as his throat became a cracked desert and winced as sharp fangs burst from his gums.

He gazed at his rescuers and would have wept if he could.

They'd risked their lives to save his family.

Now he only hoped they'd be enough to sate the centuries-long hunger that was boiling inside him, at least long enough for Kate and Sadie to get away.

-Cold Calls-
JOHN F.D. TAFF

"Last, we've got Buddy Burnett," said Mr. Hastings, sighing heavily.

The slide clicked onto the screen, and Buddy felt himself sinking into his padded seat. He was glad they kept the conference room lights dim for these sales meetings, so no one could see his cheeks flush or his hands leaving wet smudges on the table's surface, so he didn't have to see the pity in the others' eyes. It always came from people who liked Buddy, people who meant well. But it made him feel hollow inside.

Hastings clicked the slide from the screen, but not before the descending red lines burned into the retinas of the entire sales staff.

As the lights came on, everyone's eyes avoided Buddy.

"Buddy, could you stay a moment?" said Hastings as everyone rose to leave.

Hastings closed the door and motioned him back to a seat.

"We have a problem, you and I," said Hastings. "For the last five quarters now, you haven't met goal. In fact, your sales have declined."

"I know it's been off, sir, but I think … "

"Buddy, maybe it's time you stepped down, took some of the pressure off yourself."

"Let me have just two more weeks. If I can't turn it around, then I'll … I'll quit. But give me this one chance," Buddy said in a rush.

Hastings frowned. "What can you expect to accomplish in two weeks that you haven't in 15 months?"

"I don't know. But what have you got to lose?"

Hastings pondered this for a moment, then smiled sourly. "If you can sell me that easily, it's a wonder you haven't met your goal."

"Yes, sir. Thanks," said Buddy, grabbing Hastings' limp hand in his own and pumping it.

"I may have a prospect for you," Hastings said, reaching into his black suit and pulling out a pink telephone message slip. "I hope I'm doing the right thing by passing this to you, Buddy."

"You are, sir," Buddy said, looking gratefully at the old man. "Well, have casket, will travel."

∞☉∞

The mortuary loomed in the twilight; an imposing white structure perched high on the river bluffs in Alton. Buddy pulled the car onto the gravel road that wound its way to the front of the old mansion.

A mortuary this size had to represent a *substantial* contract.

As he approached, though, his initial euphoria turned to a swirling, sour feeling in his gut.

The place was falling apart. Ramshackle would have been too kind a word.

The six stately Corinthian columns that held the second and third floors separate from the first were peeling and cracked, iron rods showing through like sinew. Shutters, rotten and splintered, hung desultorily from their hinges, stirred feebly in the evening breeze.

Grabbing his briefcase, Buddy climbed the rickety, warped steps, avoiding beer cans, boards with nails in them and the occasional dead bird.

The front door appeared to be the only solid, serviceable thing about the house. Buddy rapped lightly on it, echoes thumping hollowly within the huge house.

Several minutes passed before footsteps reverberated across the dark entry hall.

Buddy straightened his tie, ran a hand through his thinning hair, a finger across the front of his teeth.

Smiled.

The door moved slowly and anciently on its hinges. It was dimly lit inside, but it illuminated a face that was unexpectedly young and handsome.

"You must be Mr. Burnett. Come in, please," said the man, extending a hand. "I'm Carsten Moors."

Buddy enfolded the hand in his own, and was surprised by its lack of warmth. It was a big hand, with just a hint of calluses, a farmer's hand with a strong grip and prominent veins.

Moors was about six feet tall and solidly built, dressed in a simple pair of pressed khakis, a plain white shirt—open at the collar—and a navy blazer. A crop of sun-blonde hair fell boyishly uncombed across his forehead.

"Nice to meet you, sir," said Buddy, stepping inside a house that, like its outside, had seen better days.

The marble floor was pitted and stained, cracked in places. Misshapen lumps cowered in the foyer, covered with yellowed, dusty sheets. Tatters of what looked like antebellum wallpaper hung from the chipped plaster walls.

"As you can see," Moors apologized, gesturing around him. "We still have quite a bit of work to do."

"Well," Buddy said, without missing a beat. "This old lady has a lot of promise."

"Well, we like to think so," said Moors, seeming to appreciate Buddy's comment. "We think it will make an excellent base of operations."

"So, then," said Buddy, wetting his lips. "You're thinking of expanding already?"

"Oh, most assuredly, Mr. Burnett. Most assuredly," he said, leading him into a spacious sitting room off the main foyer.

"Please, call me Buddy."

"And feel free to call me Carsten. Would you care for a drink? A beer, perhaps?"

"A beer would set just fine, Carsten."

"Have a seat," Moors said, indicating a divan that squatted next to a delicate Louis XIV chair and a small table, all of which looked as if it had been arranged specifically for this visit.

Moors returned with the beer and a small china cup and saucer on a tray, which he set on the table between the divan and the chair.

"Ahh, ice cold," said Buddy after a draught. "Well, sir, I suppose we should get down to the reason I came here in the first place."

Buddy opened his briefcase, pulled out a smooth, glossy catalog, as thick as a small town's phonebook.

"Buddy," interrupted Moors. "You've got the sale."

Buddy blinked twice rapidly. "Excuse me?" he said, feeling a little dizzy.

Moors smiled. "I may give you unusual instructions from time to time. I expect you to make sure they are followed to the letter. I'm not interested in your opinion. And I will neither brook nor answer any questions. I hope this is clear without being impolite."

"No, sir. I understand completely," he lied.

"We will schedule appointments in advance. You will make no unscheduled visits, for any reason. Is this acceptable?"

"Yes, sir," croaked Buddy, wondering what his boss had gotten him into.

"Now, let me give you the good news," he said, producing a set of papers from the inside pocket of his jacket.

"I took the liberty of drawing up the contracts myself based on the pricelist I was sent. Why don't you see if everything meets your approval?"

Buddy accepted the papers, unfolded them on his lap, and read through them. The contract stipulated fifty-six of the company's top-line caskets with various modifications; Buddy had never sold one of these models … even in the good old days. The total price of the contract was more than one million dollars. With his five percent commission, his share came to fifty thousand.

"I trust it's all in order."

"Yes, sir," Buddy whispered.

"Shall we sign the papers, then, and get you on your way? It's getting late," said Moors, pulling a pen from the same pocket that had held the contracts.

Moors signed, then Buddy did likewise, albeit with a shaky hand.

"Another beer and a handshake to conclude this business deal?" smiled Moors, capping and replacing his pen.

"That'd be great."

Moors walked from the room, and Buddy stood, stretching his limbs as his brain screamed at him.

You just made more tonight than you have in the last year!

A smile spread across Buddy's face as he imagined his next sales meeting.

Buddy bent to drop the papers into his briefcase, when he caught sight of the coffee cup Moors had emptied.

Dark maroon dregs clotted at the bottom, and a thin, pinkish film coated the rim.

For a reason unknown to him, Buddy put his nose to it, sniffed.

The rich, assertive aroma of coffee crept into his sinuses, but there was something underneath it.

Something *metallic*.

Moors came into the room with another beer, handed it to Buddy.

"Here's to a great partnership," said Buddy, raising his bottle to Moors and taking a long drink. "Bad water, huh?"

"Pardon me?"

Buddy jerked his finger back to the empty coffee cup on the table.

"Too much iron in the water. You should look into a softener."

"An interesting suggestion. I will do that, since I'm quite sure I get enough iron in my diet already," Moors smiled politely.

∞⊖∞

Back in his motel room, Buddy stripped down to his boxers, spread the contracts over the bed. The first several pages were standard, but the remaining six pages listed the modifications Moors wanted.

They ranged from having all of the caskets made of solid mahogany—unusual in this day of refrigerator-aluminum coffins—to having handles and locks *inside* the caskets.

Rather than upgrading their interiors, Moors wanted them stripped of all the plush satin pillows and upholstery and replaced with a quarter-inch thick lead pan secured to the bottom of the caskets' interiors.

∞⊖∞

Two weeks later, orders from Moors were, literally, pouring in. Even though the original order of caskets had not been finished, Moors ordered thirty-seven more the next week and an additional forty-five after that. Taken in total with his first order, Moors had ordered more than three million dollars worth of caskets.

And Moors showed no signs of slowing. During Buddy's last visit, Moors intimated that another, larger order was on the way for some interested European clients.

As Moors had warned, strange requests, too, began to come in, at least once an evening, phoned in by Moors himself, always at night.

He demanded to have Buddy's home phone number, and Buddy was only too happy to oblige.

After all, Carsten Moors was making him rich.

There had been the odd request for the double coffin—able to hold two bodies.

And the one that had to be wired for a stereo system.

And the thirty-seven child sized caskets.

Aside from these strange instructions, what really puzzled Buddy was that Moors was ordering all of these caskets, even though there was absolutely no construction going on at the mansion; nothing that would turn the wreck into a working mortuary.

Moors always assured Buddy that some work was going on, but the fact was that the first order of fifty-six caskets would be ready for delivery in three weeks.

And Moors still had no place of business.

Buddy had offered to store the caskets for Moors until the mortuary got up and running.

"I've given you my instructions." Moors had told him, in a cold, controlled tone.

Buddy had never seen Moors angry, even though he'd asked other questions that had provoked irate responses from the man.

He began to worry that Moors might take the future business he always alluded to elsewhere.

Maybe, Buddy thought, *it was time to do something for the client, something with a little flourish, a little panache.*

Something that said Buddy J. Burnett and Hastings Casket Co. appreciated his business.

Buddy knew just the thing.

∞☉∞

There was a moment in the parking lot of the Sears store when Buddy was afraid that the damned water softener was not going to fit in his car. But the salesperson wrestled the bulky box inside and tied the trunk shut around it.

He pulled onto the gravel road at around 8 p.m. The house was very quiet, and only a few dim yellow lights shone through the windows.

The box came out of the trunk far easier than it went in, and soon Buddy was hauling it step by step up to the front door.

When he'd made it up all of the steps, he paused to wipe his forehead with a handkerchief.

A flash of movement caught his eye from one of the ground-floor windows.

Squinting, he saw Moors inside dancing with a woman—swirling across a large, bare room that opened just to the rear of the sitting room where he and Moors always conducted their business. He'd never seen this room, though, because Moors always kept the door closed.

The woman wore a light blue cocktail dress and blue pumps with heels that were too high. Moors was dancing at an incredible pace, flinging the limp body of the woman around so fast they were both a blur.

But that was not what made Buddy's pulse race, his mouth go dry.

From some wound on the woman's body, blood jetted across the room in a dizzying arc, spraying the bare, white walls.

Then Moors, looking ecstatic, stopped, folded the woman's body in his arms, and rammed his face ungracefully into her neck so hard that Buddy swore he heard a crunch.

Two tracks of blood ran down the back of the woman's pale, delicate neck.

Pushing himself away from the window, Buddy fell against the porch railing.

With a crack like a broken bone, it gave way under his weight, and he fell to the ground with an impact that pushed the breath from him.

When he could think again, he found himself sitting in the darkness, clutching his chest and looking up at the porch.

Dear Lord. He killed her. Moors killed that woman.

Jumping up, he raced for the car, threw himself in without bothering to close the trunk.

As he started the car, he could swear that, in the upper floors, in the windows lit with smudgy yellow light, he saw the shapes of other people. Some of them moved within their rooms, some of them simply stared out the windows.

But some of them hunched over other shadow shapes, just as Moors had.

He managed to keep himself from throwing on the lights and squealing out of there—at least until he reached the front gate.

∞Θ∞

Once off the grounds of the mansion, he drove straight home. Back among familiar landscape, he relaxed, his heartbeat returning to something near normal.

Moors killed that woman, he thought. *I saw him kill a woman.*

However disturbing it was, it paled next to how he had killed her.

He shivered, tried to clear his mind of that ridiculous thought, but it was too late.

Moors is a vampire.

"No," groaned Buddy aloud, rolling his eyes. "He probably didn't even *really* kill her."

Then, he thought of something that made his scalp tingle.

Buddy stomped the brake, and the car fishtailed to the side of the road, a procession of horn-blaring cars swerving as they passed him.

I left the water softener. He's going to know I was there.

Shit. Shitshitshitshit!

"Shut the fuck up!" he screamed, lurching the car back onto the road and starting home again. "He's not a vampire. There are no such things as vampires!"

Okay, all right, calm down. There are no such things as vampires.

He sure looked like he was sucking her blood.

He sure has ordered a lot of caskets.

He sure has asked for a lot of strange things to be done to those caskets.

He sure has a lot of empty room in that mansion, which, by the way, he shows no intention of really turning into a funeral home.

Oh, and that red stuff in his coffee cup? Do you still believe that was hard water?

"Christ, maybe … maybe he is. I mean, what would you do with all of those caskets if you're not opening a mortuary?"

What about those other shadows in the windows?

What if Moors was buying caskets for other vampires—a sort of undead real-estate agent?

His heart began to beat fiercely again, and what was left of his cold blood evaporated.

If Moors is the real-estate agent then I'm his developer.

He made the turn into the driveway of his modest two-bedroom home, sat there for a spell feeling uncomfortably responsible for the death of that nameless woman.

What could I have done to stop him?

Nothing, the other voice said. *He'd have killed you, too.*

He shivered at that.

But you can prevent anyone else from being killed.

How?

Kill him.

Buddy thought of the money he was making … *real* money. A lot of very real money. And here he was thinking of getting rid of it because he thought he saw a vampire.

Then he remembered something else.

Hell, he's already paid. I've got his money … and a referral to boot.

What the hell else does a good salesperson need?

Buddy smiled at that, until a vision came to him: *the thirty-seven children's caskets they were preparing to deliver, filled with thirty-seven tiny, pale-faced cherubs, each with rosy red cheeks and protruding canines, each grasping the handles inside their Hastings Caskets with doughy hands, opening the lids, coming out.*

Coming out looking for someone to hold them.

Someone to warm them.

As he punched the garage door opener, he thought of the 138 caskets to be delivered to Moors in the next ten days.

And he had an idea.

Mr. Carsten Moors and his tenants were going to get another option installed in their caskets.

Courtesy of their salesperson, Mr. Buddy J. Burnett.

∞☉∞

Three-thirty a.m., and the phone on the nightstand jangled him from sleep.

Still unconscious, he reached to answer it.

"Hello?" he answered, trying to sound groggy.

"Buddy," hissed Carsten on the other end, sounding too cool, too refined and too polite. "Something a bit strange happened this evening."

"What's that?" asked Buddy, trying his best to keep his voice level and neutral.

"Someone dropped off a gift at my house tonight. A water softener."

"Oh, you got that? Great!" Buddy's pulse began to race as he waited for Moors' answer.

"Thank you, Buddy. I'll see that it's installed soon. Tell me, did you, perhaps, deliver it yourself?"

At that, Buddy's mouth went dry.

There was silence, then, on the line, during which Buddy was quite sure that his heart was thumping loud enough for Moors to hear.

"I think," Moors began slowly, civilly, "that whoever delivered this lovely gift may have seen something this evening that shocked, even frightened him. I think this someone should keep his visit and what he saw quiet. If, that is, he'd like to keep his … *contracts*."

"Other than that, the gift was quite thoughtful," Moors said, the dark cloud underneath his tone dissipating. "Now, I have a few modifications I'd like to discuss, and the European order has come through."

"Yes, sir," Buddy said, swallowing, and in shock.

He knows, but he isn't going to do anything, Buddy thought as he scribbled down Moors' request and the new order. Because you can't do anything to stop him.

Buddy smiled at that, kept scribbling.

∞⊖∞

"Here's the daily list of changes," said Buddy, pounding Jim on the back and slipping the papers into his free hand.

Jim, the plant manager, hadn't looked forward to a morning since they got the first Moors contract. At the start of every day, Buddy visited him, like today, with a list of Moors' recent requests— sometimes a single paper, sometimes a sheaf of papers.

Today, it was just a sheet.

"You gotta be shittin' me!" Jim snorted as he scanned the list. "What's this?"

"Just what it looks like. Can you do it?"

"Sure. I mean, I guess so," Jim spluttered. "He wants these installed on all of them?"

"Yeah, even the ones we've already finished. Will it hold up delivery?"

"Probably not," he answered sourly. "Not if we can find enough parts."

"Well, hold everything until they're all finished. He specifically requested that there be no partial shipments," said Buddy.

"Oh, and by the way, Moors' European contact called me the other day. We got the order in—a five million dollar contract."

"Christ! You mean a five million dollar headache," said Jim turning away.

Buddy laughed and shook his head as he left the plant.

∞⊖∞

In the bright light of the early morning Buddy could see the house's imperfections with startling clarity, the way its shutters drooped, its paint flecked, its siding bowed.

Other than that, though, the house looked no different than it did four months earlier when he'd first been here in the evening. Moors had made no improvements.

Actually, this was the second time this week he'd been here. The first time, four days ago, Moors had signed the delivery papers and handed over a check for the entire European order.

Two days later, the caskets had arrived and been off-loaded into Moors' house, all at night.

Now here he was sitting in an idling car wondering what the hell he was doing.

From the pocket of his jacket, he produced a small device that, at about the size of a cigarette lighter, fit snugly in the palm of his hand.

It had a single red button and a key chain that dangled from one end.

Imprinted on it, in tiny white letters, were the words:

"Open Sesame."

Buddy remembered how he got the idea, thumbing the button on his garage door opener the night he fled from Moors' mansion.

If he's really a vampire, he needs the coffins to protect him—and his guests—from the sunlight.

If we install something to open those coffins during the day ...

Actually, what they ended up installing were not garage door openers, but commercially available devices that could open a car's trunk or doors by remote.

It had been the only modification Buddy had hovered over, making sure that Jim had it just right.

"No, no," he'd told Jim. "The lids have to open completely. And all the receivers need to be set to the same code."

Buddy prayed that Jim's attention to detail held out.

He climbed the steps to the front porch, tested the door. As he thought, it was locked.

Walking casually around the porch, he fingered the device.

Then, he pushed the button.

The tiny red light illuminated.

Just to be sure, he pressed it again and again and again …

He didn't know what to expect, but within seconds, he heard a chorus of high-pitched screams. Several of the windows on the upper floors shattered, sprinkling the porch with glass.

Then, more screams, some distant, some very clear, joined the chorus.

Buddy ran down the porch steps, still punching the button, and looked at the house. Through the upstairs windows, he could see flashes of light.

Just then, there came a terrific, cycling shriek, and one of the front windows on the lower floor exploded, a dark shape hurtling out of it, crashing through the porch railing.

It came to rest, twisted and charred, near the foot of the steps.

Buddy backed away, covering his mouth against the burning stench that rose from it.

It turned its head up to the light, and the burning began again, erasing its features.

Not before Buddy saw the unkempt blonde hair, the blunt face.

∞☉∞

After the screams had died away, Buddy eased himself into the house through the broken window, pressing the tiny button continuously. He walked through the room where Moors and he always met, opened the door onto the room in which Moors' had killed the woman.

The walls were covered with splotchy, rust-colored stains.

He found the refrigerator where Moors kept his beer and took one. Draining half the bottle in one breath, he spotted a telephone across the room.

The first call he made was to Jim at the plant.

"How did the old son of a bitch like 'em?" Jim asked.

"Oh, well enough I suppose, though I doubt we'll get any orders from him for a while. How are the European orders coming?"

"Not nearly as many changes as Moors made. Probably be ready in two weeks."

"And the automatic openers?"

"All installed."

Jim transferred him to accounting, where the secretary confirmed that the European check had cleared just that morning.

Buddy hung up the phone and pulled out his airline credit card.

"Hello, I need to book a flight to London," he said when the agent answered the phone.

I may not be a great salesman, but I bet I'm the highest paid vampire killer in the world.

And the only one with referrals.

-A Sunset So Glorious-
RYCKE FOREMAN

The djinn thought that Herman's first wish was a valid one:

"I wish I was very handsome. Appealing to women, you know." He said this in his funny little voice while bright red blossoms bloomed over his cheeks. "Sexy, you know. Irresistible. Sleek, even."

"Very well, Master," said the djinn. With the wave of one mighty hand, a new man emerged—a man who would no longer be know as Herman (oh no—that name was *so* inadequate for the proud new gentleman now standing before the djinn), but possibly Arman or Armond. Indeed, the Herman who had brushed his sleeve up against the lamp was gone; rips from his now insufficient suit resounded throughout the room as his biceps, triceps, and gluteus expanded. No more horn-rimmed glasses that distorted his once sheepish, watchful eyes; his meager, rounded jaw was now square and sharp. Herman (or rather, Armond) no longer slouched, but held his shoulders square and erect, his spine stiff—he seemed to have grown a full five or six inches.

The man turned, glancing into a nearby mirror. Herman would have gasped and exclaimed "Dear me!" but Armond simply studied his new face, held fast his own magnetic-blue eyes while fluffing his already perfect hair. He smirked. "You really are a genie, then, aren't you?" he asked, admiring the newly acquired potency to his voice.

"A djinn, actually."

"But you can make magic—I mean, truly *perform* it."

"Certainly, Master. Did I not state that clearly enough to begin with?"

"Well yes, but of course I thought you meant party tricks or something. Pulling rabbits out of hats, that sort of rubbish."

The mighty creature smiled, thinking in an ancient, long-dead language: *In what form now comes your greed?* The djinn knew he had but a moment to wait.

Armond returned his gaze to the mirror, seeming to stun even himself for a moment. "My God ... " He looked deep into the mesmerizing orbs. "No ... I don't think being an accountant will do anymore. Not for this face, this body—no. This is a temple that must be worshipped by the world. It's simply too beautiful not to, but ... but is this the face of a movie star? An athlete? Or the start of a political dynasty?" The man paused, as if savoring the aroma of a juicy T-bone steak.

"I want power," Armond said firmly, with a dark sneer that somehow complemented his radiance and added luster to his newfound beauty. "True Power. Nothing so trivial as a hick oil tycoon or even the Presidency. No—I want the *real* thing, the power to hypnotize, mesmerize, influence and maintain control upon the nations. I will leave my mark and they will feed me with their undying devotion ... " Armond trailed off momentarily; the wish granter wasn't sure if the man was lost in the depths of his own eyes or the fantasy.

"Is that your second wish?" the djinn prompted.

"Yes."

"State it as a wish, if you please."

"Very well, then. You heard what I just said, so grant it now, for that is how I wish."

"Yes, Master. Your wish is my—"

"And I know what my third wish is to be, as well." A maniacal grin slashed across his perfect features "I want immortality, too. I wish it—now grant it."

The floating dastard nodded solemnly, preparing to gift his nine hundred ninety-nine thousandth, nine hundred and ninety-eighth and ninth wishes; the final two any bound servant was required to grant. The last—and mightiest—was reserved for the wishmaster himself. But first:

"May I ask of you a few questions, my Master?"

"If it's quick," the man snapped.

"Do you subscribe to a particular religious faith?"

"No."

"Do you have an affinity for Italian meals?"

"No. When I was ... *him* ... I suffered quite severely from indigestion."

"Do you participate in many outdoor activities—day hikes, swimming, sunning yourself at the beach?"

An eye-roll was enough for the djinn.

"Do you have an aversion to blood?"

Armond was growing impatient. "*He* might have, but I am quite confident in my own capabilities."

"Very well, Master. And now, a final *caveat:* There are few beings in any realm that possess true immortality, and only One allowed to grant it. However, I can bestow eternal life … within certain limitations—"

"What sort of limitations?"

"Based on your answers, nothing *too* difficult to avoid." *Save for one, perhaps,* the djinn thought.

"Fine, fine. Just get on with it."

"Your wish is my command." As the djinn finished bringing Armond's wishes to pass, he quickly granted himself the millionth wish. His legs—until now merely a funnel-shaped mist—materialized beneath him, much the same way as the rest of his new life was entering the world far beyond these walls. He exercised his restored limbs with a deep knee bend. Surprisingly, they weren't too stiff either, given the passing of so many millennia. Joints popping loudly as he stood, the former djinn (soon to be Kamal al-Mas'ud ibn Khaldun aal-Filistenni again, once he got on with his new life) made hastily for the door.

Behind him, Armond growled, "Wait a minute! What's happening? I can't see myself." Armond was looking desperately into the mirror; it revealed a room full of everything that should be there—except him. "Where is my reflection?"

Soon-to-be-Kamal didn't bother to answer. Instead, he threw the front door wide, gazing breathlessly upon a sunset so glorious. Its golden rays were warm and exquisite, seeming to gently sizzle his tender new flesh.

The sizzle of the vampire's flesh was much louder and more dramatic, popping and crackling and fizzing in a frenzied stutter, Armond's scream lingering even after he'd been reduced to fluttering ashes.

Kamal shot one last glance at the smoldering remains littered before the looking glass, then he shut the door. He took another moment to again admire the fiery gloaming before he turned, ready to give his new legs a run for the money.

-The Verbpire-
FREDRICK OBERMEYER

I'd like to think that feeding off other people's verbs is at worst a victimless crime, but there are people who feel otherwise. Diana Freswelth was one of them and thanks to her I nearly died.

Until the night when I tried to feed on her verbs, it had been bliss. We hit it off in London and from there traveled around the world to cities far and wide.

After five weeks of pleasure, we settled down together in Seattle and I continued to go on in secret for months after, consuming my daily requirement of verb forms with languages ranging from English to Spanish to Arabic. Sometimes I'd even sample the occasion adverb, but most of the time they were bloated and left me with a lot of gas.

Life was good and since people often had a surplus of verbs in them, I had plenty to eat. And unlike regular bloodsucking vampires, I never left a wake of dried out corpses after me. Just some people who couldn't speak verbs for a few days.

Now tell me, is that such a crime?

But I still shudder at her reaction the night I told her that I was a verbpire. We had just come back to her apartment after dinner. She had put some Frank Sinatra on the CD player and I leaned back and relaxed as I listened to "Strangers in the Night."

Diana fixed up two fingers of whiskey sour, gave me one and sat down on the couch next to me. We clinked our glasses together and then drank.

Afterwards, she slid closer. I took her in my arms.

"I love you, Larry," Diana said.

"I love you too." I kissed her on the cheek, sighing as I tasted the edge of her first person verb. The word "love" is perfectly concise and put in its best verb form. "I love" is probably the most delicious verb ever made. I wanted to suck even more I loves out of her. But I held back. I had to tell her who and what I was.

"Shall we … "

"Yes, but first I need to tell you something," I said.

"It's not that you're really gay or that you have genital warts, is it?"

"No, it's not that. It's just … " My voice trailed off and my stomach rumbled. I wanted to taste her verbs so bad it made me ache, even though I had consumed a maitre d's worth of conjugated verbs back at the restaurant during a supposed cigarette break.

"What? Spit it out."

"I'm a verbpire," I said.

"A what?" Diana blinked and stared at me as if I had just started babbling incoherently.

"A verbpire."

"What's that?"

"A vampire that thrives on verbs to stay alive and live forever." I licked my lips, feeling hungry at using up so many verbs.

Diana looked at me for a moment. Her lips trembled. Then she broke out laughing and my heart dropped into my shoe.

"Verbpire, that's a good one." She snorted and laughed so hard that tears rolled down her cheeks. "Honestly, where do you make up this stuff? I know you're a writer, but—"

"But I'm telling you, it's true. I really am a verbpire."

"I think you need to loosen up a little. Have another drink."

She reached over for the whiskey bottle, but I grabbed her hand and said, "No, I'm being serious here." I let go of her arm and she lowered it. "Before we get any deeper into this relationship, I want to be open and honest with you. And I want us to have no secrets between us. Normally I wouldn't have told you, but you're the first person I've met in a long time that I feel I can be totally open and honest with."

Confusion tightened her normally smooth face and she stared at me for a moment.

"I agree that we shouldn't keep secrets," Diana said. "But what you have just told me doesn't sound like a secret."

"Then what does it sound like?"

"Bullshit."

"You need proof?"

FREDRICK OBERMEYER

"That might be nice."

"But I don't want to make you verbless."

"Shall I bear my neck for you instead?" She tilted her head, exposed her neck and laughed again.

"Knock it off." I waved my hand.

"I'm serious. If you really are this thing, then prove it. Take my verbs away from me."

"Let's just drop it, okay?"

"No, really, how do you do it? Do you drain them out of my forehead?"

"Actually I use the lips."

"Then do it."

"I really ought not to. I already had my fill."

"Then why did you bring it up in the first place? Are you trying to spoil the mood?"

"No, I just—"

"Show me that you're telling me the truth."

"Fine," I said. "But just remember you asked for it."

I grabbed her shoulders, pulled her right up close to me and pressed my lips hard against her own, forming a tight seal. For a second, she started kissing me.

Then I began feeding.

Suddenly the look of pleasure on her face transformed into one of terror. She thrashed and tried to pull free, but I held her tight as I sucked all the verbs right out of her voice and her mind. The hunger in the language centers of my brain began to dull as they became satiated.

Apparently she was multilingual, judging from the influx of English, Romania, Spanish and even some ancient Celtic, Welsh, Greek and Sanskrit verbs that flooded into my mind.

Finally I pulled my lips off hers and she collapsed on the floor, gasping and wheezing.

"I ... not any help," she snapped at me. Then suddenly it hit her. The look I've seen thousands of times before.

She blinked, then glared at me with cold, hateful eyes.

" ... speak ... I ... no verbs."

"That's what I told you."

"Bastard! You ... my verbs."

"I said it was the truth."

"I ... you. I ... I ... " She bit her lip and I could see her struggling to form a single word, just one verb phrase. But she couldn't do it.

"Look, it's only temporary," I said. "In a few days, you'll regain your verbs. It's like blood cells. You lose some, but you'll grow more back."

"I … you. I … you."

"Easy now."

"I … a secret of my own."

"Let me guess. You're a nounpire and to seek revenge you're going to drain all of my nouns from me."

"No. I … another idea. You … for what you … I … a witch."

"You mean like Samantha like on Bewitched?"

"Not that kind of witch. I … more powerful than her. And I … you a curse."

"A curse?" I blinked. "Don't you need verbs to cast curses?"

She shook her head, then turned and spat on me. The spittle hit my shirt and burned like acid. I screamed and stumbled back off the couch.

"A curse. Starvation. The only food for you … second person singular English verbs in the subjunctive mood, past tense."

My heart sank.

"Wait a minute," I said. "Can't we discuss this?"

"No. Now out! Before I … you."

"Diana, please. You told me to prove it. I was just doing what you said."

"OUT!"

I sighed, knowing that I couldn't make any head. I turned and left her apartment, listening to Sinatra's "Strangers in the Night" on the way out.

∞ ⊕ ∞

Alone on the streets, I tried to take solace in the only thing I could. Verbs. I found a young man walking alone on the street that night and used a tongue twister on him. In the movies, Dracula hypnotizes his victims with his voice and that penetrating gaze.

On the other hand, I often use tongue twisters to catch them off guard and then drain them before they even know what hit them. But this time I found that it was almost impossible to feed. For a while after, I thought that she was just angry at me and had spat some random words. But when I tried to drain some verbs out of the man, all I kept getting was a rare "You had gone" and "You wouldn't have happened ... "

One might think that I could feed on the second person subjunctive mood and still live at least reasonably well. But out of all three moods, subjunctive was the rarest in English and the least nutritious and satisfying. It's like going to an all-you-can-eat buffet and only being allowed a few scraps of old lettuce instead of steaks and chowders and the rest of the salad bar. Sure, you can eat it, but it won't fill you up and sooner or later you'll have to go back looking for more.

Finally I let the man go.

"What the hell are you doing?" the man said. He swung his fist at me and I barely managed to dodge it.

I turned and ran down an alleyway. He chased me for a block, but I managed to lose him behind a group of garbage crates. Once he was gone, I emerged and found an old Chinese lady.

The same thing happened, though.

In fact, I probably could have gone through more than half the population of Seattle and still not had enough verbs to live on for more than a day or two.

Despondent, I continued to roam the streets.

Why she couldn't have at least given me indicative or imperative mood? I wondered. Or at the very least the present tense for the subjunctive mood along with the past and all persons?

I needed to find some way to regain my ability to consume other verbs. Otherwise I might literally starve to death, no matter how much normal food I might eat. I even thought about taking a flight over to Great Britain, where at least they had impeccable grammar. But it wouldn't matter. Too many young English speaking people shunned the subjunctive mood for "may" and "should" and "might." Seeing that, I might as well have ended it right there. But being as stubborn as I was, I knew that there had to be some way that I could get rid of or at least allay Diana's curse.

I had one place left I could turn to.

∞⊖∞

Percy Dalvinger lived in a small apartment right next to one of the local coffee bars that seemed to cover every other square inch of Seattle. I hurried down there, ran up to his apartment on the third floor and rang the doorbell.

After two more tries, he answered. In the background a pot of tea whistled. He stood there, four foot five, the wrinkles on his craggy old face shaped like old English script, his lips as black as shoe polish.

Most shapescripters liked to remain in their print form as often as possible, morphing from book to book when the mood suited them or when the current paper where they resided was in danger of being lost. But Percy was unique in that he enjoyed his human form as much as he did his print form. Especially when he wrote himself out of his own stodgy books on English grammar.

"Lawrence?" Percy said in his Welsh accent.

"Yes, it's me," I said.

"It is I, you mean."

"Yes, it is I."

"Why have you come here?"

"I need your help."

"Whatever for?"

"A witch named Diana. She put a curse on me."

"A curse." He laughed. "Why on Earth would she do that for?"

"Because I showed her what I really was."

"Yes, I suppose that would do it." He nodded for me to come inside, then closed the door.

"Right. Come in, sit down. Would you like a spot of ink tea?"

"No, thank you." I sat down in one of his sumptuous leather chairs in the living room. He had several bots of inks lying open on a chess table. He took one and swallowed it down like a shot glass full of vodka as he went into the kitchen.

Shapescripters always needed their daily dose of outside ink to keep their part human/part living ink forms stable. He shut the kettle off, made his ink tea and then came back and sat across from me.

"So, this curse … might you tell me what it consists of?" Percy said.

"I can only consume English verbs that are in the subjunctive mood, second person singular, past tense," I said.

"Sounds dodgy." He sipped his ink tea. "And the problem is?"

"I'm starving. That's my problem. Already I can feel the hunger for verbs. It's gnawing in my stomach, in the back of my mind. I can't think about anything except consuming verbs."

"Well do not look at me, old chap. Because I am not your one stop shop for verbal cuisine."

"No, no, it's not that. It's just—I need some way to stop it. Do you know of a cure?"

"For a curse? No, I am not a warlock, for heavens sake. Sure, I may know a few incantations and how to take possession of werewords for my own personal uses, but I draw the line squarely at curses, old chap. Not my style, I'm afraid."

"So you're saying that you can't help me?"

"No. Please, do not put words in my mouth that you are not willing to take out later on."

"I wouldn't dream of it," I said, and smiled at him.

"I might have a way for you to regain your verbal abilities, but I am not making any assurances on this matter. The only reason I am even helping you is because of what you did for me back in 1937."

Back in 1937 I saved a shapescripter that he loved named Miriam from being destroyed along with hundreds of other books that the Nazis burned at one of their rallies. Although she had gone on to other beings since then, Percy still felt that he owed me a debt of honor. To be honest, I don't think it was fair of me to impose it upon him after all these years. But then I was desperate and willing to try almost anything.

"At midnight tonight go to the very top of the Space Needle," Percy said. "I know of a coven of local witches who convene there every Tuesday night and they might be able to help you with your problem, provided that you are willing to offer them some compensation."

"Like what? Newt tongue? Or lizard eyeballs?"

"Hardly." He gave me a dour look that was pure English. Then he stood, went into the kitchen and came back with a bottle of red wine, an old vintage way back from 1472. "I know a number of witches who love old wines, especially those that are rare vintages. And this is one of the rarest brands that I have." He handed it to me. "It is yours."

"What am I supposed to do?" I held it up. "Get them drunk?"

"No, offer it as compensation."

"Are you sure it will work?"

"No, old chap. I am not sure that it will work. But it is the only thing that I think might help your situation. And I hope that it will settle the debt that I owe you."

"Yes, it will." I looked down at the French wine and smiled. "I just hope that this hasn't become vinegar."

"Highly unlikely. This wine has been magically treated so that it will last for at least fifty centuries."

"That's good to know."

"Good luck, my friend. I truly hope that you do not starve."

"So do I," I said.

I nodded to him, then stood and left his apartment.

∞☉∞

Just a few minutes before midnight, I arrived in front of the Space Needle with the bag of wine in tow. The place was deserted and closed for the night, but I managed to convince the security guard on duty to let me in with a well-placed tongue twister that sapped his will. He took me up to the top level and I thanked him and gave him another tongue twister to make sure that he wouldn't come back up anytime soon.

On the top level the wind howled and blew my trench coat all around me. At that point my hunger tore through my guts like acid and each step was a struggle.

I went around the top level, searching for the witches, but they weren't there. I was about to give when I caught a wisp of silk rise up from the top level onto the roof. Then it dawned on me.

Percy had said the very top and I thought he had meant the top floor. But they must have meant the top of the needle. I went around the building, looking for some room or place that could give me access. But all the main doors were locked and I couldn't find any ladders.

I thought about calling the security guard back to help me up there, but then a witch caught me. She was a tall blonde with ice blue eyes and tanned skin.

"What are you doing up here?" she said and put her hands on her hips. "This place is closed for the day."

"I'm sorry," I said. "I mean no harm. I came to seek conference with your coven."

"What about you talking about?"

"You're a witch, right?"

Recognition flashed across her face, but she remained still.

"My name's Audrey," she said. "And what are you, might I ask?"

"My name is Lawrence, but you can call me Larry. Most people do whether I like it or not."

"You haven't answered my first question. What are you?"

"I'm a verbpire. I—never mind. It would take too long to explain. I need to get up there and speak with the group. It's important. Here, I brought something for you." I reached into my bag. She tensed, but I told her to stay calm and pulled out the wine.

"What's in the bottle?"

"Wine. A very rare vintage."

Audrey licked her lips and said, "Let me see that."

She walked over, looked at the label and nodded, as if in approval.

"Good wine," she said.

"I'd be willing to trade it for some help," I said.

"What kind?"

"I need a curse undone. Can you do it?"

"I can't. That's not my department. But maybe Marjorie can."

"Who's Marjorie?"

"The head of our union."

"Union? I thought it was a coven."

"We have labor unions too, you know. Magicless aren't the only ones who get exploited by an uncaring bourgeoisie."

"Right, I'm sorry."

Great, I thought. Just what I needed. A socialist witch and her labor union. I wonder if werewords had labor unions as well.

"This way," Audrey said.

I followed her over to the edge of the railing. She vaulted over it and flew out of sight. I looked up and a rope dropped down in front of me.

I looked down and shuddered.

Did I neglect to mention that I don't like heights?

"I can't climb," I said.

"Who said anything about climbing? Just grab the rope."

I did as she said and it hoisted me up onto the roof of the space and deposited me on top. Suddenly a group of witches flew down from the sky and surrounded me. Their garb ranged from elegant socialite with three-piece charcoal gray suit and high heels to punk rocker leather bitch goddess with one hundred body piercing and every variant in between.

Say what you will about witches but at least they are very snappy dressers.

To reinforce the fact that I meant no harm, I held up the wine as a peace offering. The wind up there made me shake and shiver and I had to struggle to keep my balance.

"Who is this mortal?" an old, beautiful black woman with silver hair said. She floated towards me and stopped just above my head.

"He says he's a verbpire with a curse, mistress Marjorie."

"Lawrence," a voice cried.

I turned and saw my worst nightmare floating behind me.

"I … it … you," Diana said. " … out of here."

"Is this your fiancée?" Marjorie said.

"Ex-fiancée!"

"Look, I'm sorry, Diana. But this was my last choice. I had no place else to go—"

" … out of here right now before I … "

"Wait a minute. I only came to get this curse undone."

"Did you harm one of our own?" Marjorie said. Her eyes burned like hot coals and my blood grew even colder.

"It was an accident, I swear. She wanted me to prove to her that I was a verbpire and I did it. But I never meant to hurt her. I swear to you. Please, don't blow me off. Literally."

" … him off," Diana cried. "I … him."

"But he says that he meant you no harm. Is this so?"

"He … my verbs. He … them!"

"Only after you told me to," I said, and spread my arms to keep my balance. "I swear to you, I never meant to hurt you. I just came here because I was starving and I didn't have any other place to go."

"Why did you bring us wine?" Marjorie said. "Did you wish to bribe us?"

"Not bribe. Deal with you. And besides, before last night, I didn't know that she was a witch. I just want the curse lifted. Really, that's all I want." I sighed and lowered the bottle. "Besides, no matter what you might think, I still care about you, Diana. Even after what you did to me."

"Liar. You … me."

"He does sound sincere," Marjorie said. "And I sense no lies from him. If I had, I would have pushed him off the needle already."

A strange mix of relief and terror swept through me.

"I believe we should lift the curse from him in exchange for the wine," Audrey said.

"No!" Diana cried. "He … my verbs."

"You'll get them back," I said. "I promise you."

"Normally we would side with one of our own," Marjorie said.

"But in this case, we believe that you were the one who was wronged. And in the past we have known Diana to have a rash temper."

"He … not … any punishment."

"We will ask that you leave the city. Can you do that much in exchange for us lifting the curse?"

"Of course. I'll even throw in the wine."

"You will also leave and never come back to our city."

"If you say so."

Diana glared at me while Marjorie and the other witches closed their eyes and whispered in some strange language. And suddenly I felt different, as if they had reached in with their collective magic and dissipated the curse. Suddenly I felt free again.

"And now you will leave us to our business," Marjorie said. "Remember, you may not come back here."

"Yes, I'll remember. I held up the bottle of wine. "Do you still want this?"

"Of course."

Marjorie held out her hand. The wine disappeared from my hand with a rush of displaced air and then reappeared in Marjorie's hand.

Diana screamed and flew at me.

"No, I … not … him … away."

"Stop!" Marjorie said and held up her other hand. Diana froze in mid-air. "He has paid his debt. Let him go in peace."

She kicked and spat and struggled, but in the end I managed to get off the roof and down to the bottom in one piece. And I even managed to get some verbs from the security guard on the way down. So I can't say the night was a total loss.

But Diana …

Women like her could drive a verbpire like me into taking a vow of silence.

But at least Diana taught me a valuable lesson.

Always let your date have the last word.

Especially if it's a verb.

-A Candle Lit In Sunlight-
DAVID NIALL WILSON

Lucifer watched with deep interest, and some concern, the arrival of The Christ upon the Earth. Well aware that he could not prevent it, and unwilling to forego the amusement, in any case, he set about sowing the seeds of jealousy, fear, and distrust that would later lead to the crucifixion. Once satisfied, he waited for the child to grow. A small mountain of dead children grew on Christ's birthday, sacrificed by those who feared the birth of a king.

Men seem often given to strange excesses in the solving, or prevention, of problems. I saw it as a shame; Lucifer saw the destruction not at all. His eyes were turned Heavenward in search of a glimpse of the anger he knew his actions would spark. I walked the Earth in his shadow, watching. In the Christ, he saw another part of his enemy, another work to corrupt. I saw beauty, a piece of something forever lost to me. Lucifer saw none of that; his hate had become too great. I saw him as he was, and I loved him. The Christ was very beautiful.

{From the Book of the Gospel, According to Judas Iscariot}
Judas 1:1

[1] And it came to pass that Jesus went alone into the desert to be tempted of the devil. [2] He remained there forty days and forty nights, fasting, and on the fortieth night, he hungered. [3] The tempter came before him then, asking, "If you are truly the son of God, turn these stones to loaves of bread" [4] Jesus answered him, "It is written, 'man does not live on bread alone, but on every word that comes from the mouth of God.'"

5 Then the tempter led him to the highest point of the temple. 6 "If you are truly the son of God, cast yourself down, for it is written, 'He will command his angels concerning you, And they will lift you up in their hands, So that you will not strike your foot against stone.'"

7 Jesus answered, "It is also written, 'do not put the Lord your God to the test.'"

8 The devil took him to a very high mountain and showed him all of the kingdoms of the world in their splendor. " 9 Bow down and worship me," he said, "and I will give them all to you."

10 Jesus replied, "Away from me, Satan, for it is written, '*Worship the Lord your God, and serve him only.*'"

11 The devil laughed and gestured, raising from the sands a temptress. 12 "See here the things craved by man," he said, waving his arm to include the cities below. 13 "You are Son of man, does she not please you?"

14 And Jesus, seeing that she was fallen from Heaven, and sorely used, beckoned to the temptress, saying, "For all who would follow me, there burns a light in my father's house."

15 And the temptress fell to her knees, forsaking the devil and his darkness. 16 In an awful rage, Lucifer laid upon her a curse, bringing a great thirst which could be sated only by the lifeblood of man, and saying, "Feast you upon the fruits of his labor, for I say unto you, you shall be his undoing." 16 Then the devil left them, and angels came and attended Jesus. 17 Fleeing into the desert, the temptress wept.

∞☉∞

I hid for many days among the burning sands, and the thirst grew, grasping at my thoughts and twisting them beyond my control. I heard echoing laughter in the pits below, but had no concentration to spare it. As the sun dipped a final time, on the eighth day, I came to the fringes of the city of Galilee. At that time, the horror of what had befallen me was not clear in my mind. I slipped through the shadows of the city as a silent mist, searching for that which could end the thirst, hungering for freedom to follow him who had promised me hope.

∞☉∞

Isabella, late in returning to her home from that of her sister, Jessamine, stopped at the sound of footsteps in the night. No direction lay in the sound. It seemed to echo from every shadow. When her steps ceased, the others ceased as well. Her heart sped nervously, and she called out to the night. "Who is there?" Straining to hear an answer, she heard the whispering rustle of silk, nothing more. More loudly, she called out again, "Please, who is it? May I pass in peace?"

A figure melted from what had seemed only mist, moving slowly and silently forward. It was a woman. Isabella's shoulders loosened somewhat. As the woman approached, Isabella caught sight of her eyes, tormented, anguished eyes, lost. Catching her breath, she reached out, wanting somehow to help.

"Who are you, lady, and what is wrong?" She asked, stepping forward. "May I help? I … "

The eyes were horrible in their pain. She felt drawn to them by more than compassion, unable to pull her gaze from their depths. Far, far too late, she forced her eyes down, down to where trembling lips parted, lips of deepest, darkest red, framing teeth that gleamed and sparkled with captured moonlight.

She struggled against the control of the eyes, against her fear. Her lips formed words, screams, any sound to negate the horror. They left her only a whisper, caught in the night breeze and borne away. The teeth were long, curved and sharp, inhuman. They drew nearer now, shocking—

The morning dew misted on the chill, pale skin of Isabella's motionless form. She lay, awaiting the morning sun, broken and lifeless. There were twin punctures in the softness of her throat, and a ghastly contortion of absolute fear masked the innocent beauty of her face. There was no blood, but the shadows had lifted.

∞☉∞

Judas 10:20

[20] As he spoke, a ruler came to him and knelt before him, saying "My daughter has died. [21] Come and lay your hand upon her, and she shall live." [22] Jesus rose and followed him as did his disciples. [23] As he walked, a woman who had bled for twelve years reached out to touch

his cloak. 24 She said to herself, "If only I touch his cloak, then I shall be healed."

25 Turning, Jesus saw her and said, "Take heart, daughter, for your faith has healed you." 26 And the woman was whole from that moment on.

27 When Jesus entered the ruler's house and saw the musicians and the noisy crowd, he moved them aside. 28 Seeing that no color remained in the girl's cheeks, and seeing also the marks upon her throat, he said, "Go away, for the girl is not dead, but only sleeping." 29 They laughed at him. 30 After they had been put outside, Jesus closed the door behind himself, barring it from within.

∞☉∞

After touching the girl's throat, which was still and without pulse, Jesus felt a tug at his heart. A shadow passed the window and he raised his eyes, now wet with tears, to meet those that faced him. Weeping also, the temptress only watched to see if he would smite her, removing the hunger, ending the pain.

"Why?" he asked simply, brushing the soft strands of the girl's hair with tender fingers.

"You heard the curse, Lord," she responded, unable to hide the bitterness in her words. "Lucifer saw in my heart that I would die for you. He took steps to insure that I could not. Each night the hunger grows. I am too weak to fight it. I seek only to follow you."

Feeling the sincerity in her words, Jesus heaved a sigh of deepest resignation, feeling suddenly the great weight thrust upon his shoulders.

"She may walk again," he said, simply, and the girl's eyes fluttered and opened. She did not smile; her expression was one of need—of desperation.

"Her lifeblood is now a part of me," the temptress spoke, each word catching at her heart. "She will hunger as I. You know this is true, why do you raise her to such torment?"

"I am the way, the truth, and the light," he said, slowly turning to the door. "Even in her torment, she is forgiven. For every such horror unleashed upon my father's children, I shall exact threefold payment on the day of reckoning."

"And I," she breathed, fearing the answer to come, "am I forgiven, then?"

Staring deeply within her eyes, Jesus communed with her heart. Since the days when she had walked freely upon the roads of Heaven, she had felt nothing like it. His purity surrounded her, probed her, and then was gone.

"I shall call you Mary," he spoke. "Go with open heart, for we shall meet again." He turned then, leaving the room with the girl at his side, returning to the disciples and those who waited. Mary, for she gladly accepted the name, departed the window and walked through the crowd, going again into the desert to be alone. Only Judas, who had seen her at the window and noted her odd, exceptional beauty, appreciated her passing, and he was too much in awe at the miracle of the dead girl walking to dwell upon it.

∞☉∞

Judas 10:31

31 A woman was seen to pass the window frame and to speak. 32 Taking the girl by the hand, Jesus led her outside, and she lived, though no spark remained to her eyes—except that of hunger—and her pallor was that of death. 33 All stood in awe, and the news spread rapidly throughout the land. 34 Ignoring her father and those about her, the girl walked into the desert and was seen no more.

∞☉∞

Judas 13:9

9 When Jesus heard of the beheading of John the Baptist, he withdrew to a solitary place by boat. 10 Hearing this, a great crowd gathered and awaited his arrival, traveling there on foot. 11 Seeing them, Jesus had compassion on them and healed their sick.

12 As darkness began to fall, the disciples came to him saying, "This is a remote place, and the hour is already late. Send the crowds away so that they can go the villages and buy something to eat."

13 Jesus replied, "There is no need for them to go away. We will give them something to eat."

14 "We have only five loaves of bread and two fish," they replied.

15 "Bring them to me," he said. Jesus directed the people to sit in the grass, and breaking the loaves, raised his eyes to the heavens and

gave thanks. [16] Then he gave them to his disciples, who gave them to the people. They all ate, and were satisfied, and the disciples collected twelve basketfuls of pieces that were left over. [17] Those that were fed numbered about five thousand men, besides women and children. [18] Immediately after, Jesus made the disciples get into the boat and go ahead of him to the other side, while he dismissed the crowd. [19] After the people had departed, one woman remained, Mary of Magdalene, and they spoke at length.

∞☉∞

As the crowds dispersed, Mary moved slowly forward, watching first from afar for any sign that she was not wanted. She had remained in the desert as long as her will could stand. Again the hunger was upon her. She stood, wavering, and watched as the son of Man bid farewell to his people. Her heart calmed somewhat, being close to him, but the aching need did not diminish. Slowly, he turned, seeing her as if from far away, and he came to stand by her side, watching as the last of the crowds disappeared into the distance.

"They have beheaded John," he said slowly, ignoring the plea in her eyes, "Truly these are evil times. Your master has sown well."

"What is death," she asked, eyes wide, "to one who serves you? It is the victory in the greatest of battles. I wish death would come to me in such service … I hunger again."

With a great sadness in his eyes, he put his hands upon her shoulders. "You suffer because of me, as did John, and I feel your pain. The time is not yet upon us when I can offer you peace. You must follow, remaining close to my side, for I say unto you, the Son of Man is not like other men. You may feed upon me, for I shall not die."

Feeling the depth of the emotion in his words, and seeing the tears as they began streaming from his eyes, Mary turned and fled. He did not know, could not know, what might befall him if he offered her salvation. As one of the fallen, she knew only too well the fire of his father's wrath. She ran through the desert and into the villages, running until she could no longer concentrate her will upon flight— until the hunger overwhelmed her. Creeping through the shadows, she tried to rest, but inside her mind, Lucifer laughed, saying, "Mary, time to feed. The hunger will return you to me. It is greater than you, or he can conceive. It is my hunger, and I will feast."

∞☉∞

Jesus climbed the mountain, sore of heart. She drew him, even then, and the weight of John's loss was heavy on his human heart. Stones cut his fingers and feet as he climbed, and the wind chilled him, but he ignored it all. He ascended to the uppermost ledge that he could reach and knelt upon the cold, dusty stone.

"Forgive me, father," he prayed, "but I have no answer for this one, now named Mary, and she is sorely beset. Your enemy controls her, but her heart is pure. Give me the strength, lead my steps, for I love her, and I would not see her, or any other, suffer."

Thunder echoed from the hills, lightning flashed, and still he prayed. No space remained in his father's heart for those cast out, no redemption was theirs. Jesus knew, and yet he prayed, for his heart was pure, and he bore no grudge against any who would be saved, no matter their sin. No answers were forthcoming, and he was forced to rise, finally, descending the mountain with heavy heart.

On the horizon, far from shore, he saw the boat with his disciples, his children. He stepped onto the surface of the water, walking slowly after the retreating sails, as waves slapped his legs and stung his cuts with their chill caress.

∞☉∞

Judas 13:29

29 During the fourth watch of the night, Jesus came to the boat, walking upon the lake. 30 Seeing this, the disciples were terrified. "It is a ghost," they said, crying out in fear.

31 But Jesus said to them, "Take courage, it is I! Do not be afraid."

32 "Lord," cried Peter, "If it is you, tell me to come to you on the water."

33 "Come," he said.

34 Then Peter left the boat, walking on the water toward Jesus. 35 Seeing the wind and the splashing of the waves, he became frightened, and began to sink. 36 Crying out, he said, "Lord, save me!"

37 Jesus reached out his hand, pulling him from the waves, and said, "Oh, you of little faith, why did you doubt?" 38 And when they

climbed into the boat the wind died down. [39] Then those who were in the boat worshipped him, saying, "Truly you are the son of God."

[40] Then Judas, still confused over the woman, Mary, asked, "Lord, why do you consort with a woman plagued by demons? Shall you not cleanse the world of darkness?"

[41] Jesus looked at him and spoke a parable: "If you take a candle and light it in the darkness, it can be seen for many miles. [42] Light the same candle in the sun's rays, and it pales to nothing. [43] I am sent to show the path to my father's lost sheep. She is among them. [44] I say to you, only in the last days shall evil and darkness be washed away, for in their very darkness, they glorify the light of the heavens."

[45] So saying, he fell silent, and spoke to no man as long as they were upon the boat.

∞Θ∞

Judas 15:20

[20] Eight days after saying this, Jesus took Peter, John, and James with him, and went onto a mountain to pray. [21] As he prayed, the appearance of his face changed and his clothing became bright, like a flash of lightning. [22] Two men, Elijah and Moses, appeared in glorious splendor, talking with Jesus. [23] They spoke of his departure, which he was about to bring to fulfillment in Jerusalem. [24] They spoke as well of the temptress, Mary, whose soul Jesus would save. [25] There were looks of sadness on the faces of his companions, then, for they knew the father's heart was hardened to the fallen, and they feared now for his son. [26] They had no answer for him, though they bid him not to fear. [27] Peter and his companions were very sleepy, but when they became fully awake, they saw his glory, and the two men standing with him.

[28] As the men were leaving Jesus, Peter said, "Lord, it is good for us to be here. Let us put up three shelters, one for you, one for Moses, and one for Elijah." (He knew not what he said) [29] While he spoke, a cloud appeared, enveloping them all, and they were afraid. [30]

A voice came from the cloud, saying, "This is my son, whom I have chosen. Heed his words." [32] When the voice had spoken, the cloud dispersed, and they were alone with Jesus, who had tears in his eyes.

³³ The apostles decided to keep this to themselves, and told no one what they had seen, or heard, at that time.

∞☉∞

Judas 17:1

¹ A man named Lazarus was sick. He was from Bethany, the village of Mary and her sister Martha. This Mary, whose brother Lazarus now lay sick, was the same who had poured perfume on the Lord and washed his feet with her hair. ² The sisters sent word to Jesus saying, "Lord, one you love is dying."

³ "This sickness shall not end in death," Jesus said. "No, it is for God's glory, so that God's son may be glorified by it." ⁴ Jesus loved Mary, Martha, and Lazarus, yet upon hearing the nature of the illness; he waited two days before going to them. ⁵ There were reports that Lazarus bore strange punctures on his throat, and his pallor was deathly and pale. ⁶ Then he said to his disciples, "Let us go back to Judea."

⁷ "But Rabbi," they said, "a short while ago the Jews tried to stone you, and yet you are going back there?"

⁸ "There are twelve hours of daylight," Jesus answered, "a man who walks by daylight will not stumble, for he sees by this world's light. It is when he walks by night that he stumbles, for he has no light."

⁹ After saying this, he went on to explain. "Our friend Lazarus has fallen asleep, I go to awaken him."

¹⁰ His disciples replied, "Lord, if he sleeps, he will get better." ¹¹ Jesus spoke of death, but they did not understand. ¹² Then he said plainly, "Lazarus is dead, and for your sake, I am glad I was not there, so that your faith may grow. ¹³ Let us go to him, for the darkness from which he must awaken is of my own creation, and there is another there whom I seek."

¹⁴ Then Thomas said, "Come, let us follow that we may die with him."

∞☉∞

When the word of Jesus' return reached the sisters, Martha hurried out to meet him. Mary, deep in mourning, would not leave the house.

She babbled of dark, shadowed women, and blood, and many feared she was either mad, or possessed of demons.

"Lord," Martha pleaded, as she arrived at his side, "If you had been here, I know my brother would not have died. Even now, I know, whatever you ask, God shall give it to you." Jesus saddened, doubting this in his heart, but he answered, "Your brother shall rise again."

Martha answered, "I know he will rise in the last days, at the resurrection."

Jesus said to her, "I am the resurrection and the life. He who believes in me will live, even though he dies. Whoever lives and believes in me will never die. Do you believe this?"

"Yes Lord," she replied, falling to her knees and brushing his legs with her hair, eyes wide. "I believe you are The Christ, son of God, who has come to the earth as a man."

"Where is your sister, Mary?" He asked.

"I will send her to you, Lord," Martha answered, rising. "She is mad with grief, speaking of demons and shadows and afraid to walk, even in daylight."

"I shall comfort her," he said, seating himself on a stone to wait. "Send her to me."

Martha rushed back to her sister's side with Jesus' message, hope blooming in her heart. She had lost her brother already. She did not wish to lose Mary as well.

When Mary heard that Jesus had come, she rose, as though frightened, and ran from the house, much to Martha's shock. Several of the others there, believing Mary was going to Lazarus's tomb to mourn, followed a short distance behind.

Mary's breath came in short gasps, and the sharp stones of the road cut into her feet as she ran. Every three or four paces she looked over her shoulder, eyes wide with fear, searching the pockets of shadow surrounding the trail. Her heart pounded wildly beneath her breast, threatening to burst from her skin. Stumbling into the grouped disciples, she staggered to Jesus, falling to the ground at his feet, sobbing.

Reaching down, Jesus took her by the hands and raised her to face him. "What is wrong, Mary?" He asked, searching her tear-stained face. Her entire body trembled like that of a frightened colt, ready to bolt and run.

"Lord," she choked out, dragging huge gulps of air into her lungs, "Lord, my brother has been killed by a demon!"

Jesus showed no doubt, only asked what she meant, and she answered, "She came in the night. I saw her twice, a woman wearing only a cloak of shadows. She drank of his blood, Lord, leaving him weaker with each visit. She had fangs. Lord, I am frightened for my brother's soul!"

"Take me to where you have laid him," Jesus said, "and fear not."

When they reached the place, a cave which had been sealed by the placement of a very large stone, Jesus looked upon it and wept. The people who had followed Mary in her flight saw this and said, "See how Jesus loved him?"

But Jesus cried only a little for Lazarus. His heart was heavy with the knowledge of who was responsible, with the weight of another soul. The face of the temptress, Mary, haunted his thoughts, her fate haunted his tears. He turned to Mary, Lazarus's sister. "Have them remove the stone, daughter," he said.

"But Lord," she protested, eyes wide, "it has been four days! Already the smell of rot will be upon him … why must we do this?"

And Jesus, weary of heart, replied, "Did I not tell you that, if you believed, you would witness my father's glory? Open the tomb."

∞☉∞

Judas 18:39

[39] So they took away the stone. Then Jesus looked up and said, "Father, in all things you hear me. I say this not for myself, but for those standing here, that they may believe you have sent me."

[40] When he had said this, Jesus called out in a loud voice, "Lazarus, come forth." [41] The dead man came out, his hands and feet wrapped in strips of linen, and a cloth binding his face.

[42] Jesus said, "Take off the grave clothes, and let him go."

∞☉∞

And Lazarus, staggering in the sunlight, came forth from his tomb. The wind billowed his stringy hair about his head, and his eyes glowed with the light of hunger. Facing Jesus, he removed the shroud from his face, revealing the white, pale skin beneath. When he smiled, all present shuddered and backed away. His teeth, glistening in the light, were pointed, like those of a serpent. "Son of man," he called, "you have granted me that I may walk again, though the price is great. Why must I suffer so?"

And Jesus, speaking slowly and clearly, answered. "When the last days come, your soul shall be remembered. Know that I am with you, go in peace."

"I will go, but in hunger, not peace," the dead man snarled, glaring about at those assembled in hatred. Then there was a flash of mist, pungent with the cloying scent of open graves and death, and when it cleared, Lazarus was gone. Only the empty tomb remained.

Jesus, weeping openly again, pulled the sisters, Martha and Mary, to his side and comforted them, wiping the fear from their hearts with his touch. Gesturing to his disciples, he bid them to stay with the crowd, and he went off after Lazarus. He found the dead man in the shadows of an old well. "Lazarus," he called out, "come to me!"

Unable to resist, the dead man complied. "What now, Son of Man," he called out in fear. "Have you come to kill the evil you have created, now that they have seen? Was it only a show for their benefit, the casting aside of my soul?"

The words cut deeply, and Jesus' voice trembled as he answered. He knew that what he was about to do was not a part of his father's plan. He could not help his heart, though, and was unable to witness Lazarus's suffering.

"Come to me, Lazarus," he said, tilting his head to one side, "for I have promised that you will live, and I know of your hunger and she who brought it upon you. Feed you from the blood of the Son of Man, and be renewed. Fear not, I shall not die, for it is not yet my time."

Lazarus gazed in wonder, backing away at first, but the temptation to sate his need was too great, and the power of Jesus' voice compelled him. Drawing near, he leapt wildly, sinking his fangs deeply into flesh and causing Jesus to stagger, moaning from the pain. Despite the agony, Jesus stood quietly, and moments later, Lazarus stopped, stumbling backward to collapse on the sand.

Recovering quickly, and causing his own wounds to heal, Jesus gathered Lazarus into his arms and returned the way he had come. The man he carried, no longer pale, breathed easily. Lazarus lived, though the spark in Jesus' eyes was a bit dimmer, and his steps slightly uneven. Delivering Lazarus to his sisters, he said, "Take him home, for he must rest. I have cast forth his demon, and he is whole. Now I, too, must rest."

Seeing that Lazarus' teeth were those of a normal man, and that he slept peacefully, the crowd murmured in wonder, and rushed to spread the news of what he had done.

As the crowds left them, Jesus called aside his disciple, Judas Iscariot, and spoke to him alone. "Go to the village," he said, "find the woman, Mary of Magdalene, and bring her to me."

"But Lord," Judas said, frightened for his master, "she has followed us, and where she goes, evil goes as well. Why must I bring her here?"

"She loves me, as do you, Judas," Jesus replied. "Her evil is my burden. Go quickly, for I must see her in the darkness. Do not tell the others, for I would not put my own weight upon their hearts."

Casting aside his fear as best as possible, Judas went into the village. The other disciples, knowing that Judas carried the purse, assumed that he went to purchase food, and asked no questions. Darkness was falling swiftly, chilling the air and silencing the sounds of life. Judas' heart hammered wildly, and his footsteps quickened. It was nearly the ninth hour when he came across Mary, seated in a garden and watching the night—as though expecting him.

"Hello, Judas," she called out, beckoning him closer.

"Why are you abroad, alone, on such a night? Has your master no use for you?"

"He has sent me for you, Lady, though I know not why," Judas replied. Her presence drew him like a magnet, calling out to his senses. His skin heated, and he blushed.

"Do you fear me, Judas?" She asked, no smile in her eyes.

"Lady, I do," he replied, avoiding her eyes. "Will you come? He is waiting."

"If he calls, I will come," she answered, rising with a rustle of linen that melted Judas' loins. "But I tell you, Judas, for my sake he risks everything, and I am saddened, for I, too, love him."

"I pray thee, Mary," Judas burst out, spinning to brave the depths of her eyes. "Do not come. Stay away from him. I fear for him, and I fear you."

She smiled then, but he felt no trace of sincere emotion from her heart. He froze in shock at the hunger of her gaze, the misery so obvious in the expression of her face. It was bitter, overwhelming, threatening to swallow him. Then she averted her eyes, and she began walking. He could only follow.

When they were near to where Jesus lay, he bid her wait, and, entering the camp, he came to his master and spoke. "She has come, Lord; I have left her just beyond the camp."

"It is good," Jesus replied, rising. "Tell any who asks that I am in the desert, praying. Do not fear for me, Judas, for I have said, it is not yet my time. Fear instead for Mary, for I am not certain of her fate."

And Jesus walked into the shadows, leaving Judas alone to kneel and pray.

She waited for him in shadows, watching him approach with hooded eyes. His steps were firm and steady, and a glow encased his features. She trembled as she felt the brush of his nearness, cowering deeper into the blackness.

"Mary," he commanded, stopping and staring unerringly into the darkness, "come forth, for the time is upon us that I must begin to bear your burden."

She wanted to break free, to run, but she was his to command, and she could not.

He stood, arms wide, waiting, and he beckoned her forth. She came, haltingly at first, then rushing—blowing across the sand like a dark wind, and they embraced.

"I will take from you your hunger," he whispered, cupping her face in his hands and staring into her eyes in love, "and you shall have a part of what is mine, that you may be saved."

"You cannot know what he will do! Your father will not be pleased!" She pleaded with him, even as he directed her, placing her lips to his throat and caressing her teeth with his skin.

"My father's will be done," he said, eyes brimming with trapped emotion, "I will not allow any to suffer. Drink, Mary, for the hour is late, and my days here are now few."

And the hunger swept aside her objections as he spoke. She plunged her fangs deep, drank richly of his lifeblood, weeping as she fed, and he moaned from the pain, yet caressed her hair softly, eyes closed in prayer.

Watching from nearby, Judas shrank away in horror. Rushing to the camp, he looked about wildly for his weapons, waking the others in his frantic haste.

"What is it?" Peter asked, grabbing his arm. "Where is our Lord?"

"He is in the desert!" Judas cried, "beset by a demon! We must go to him!"

And they all rushed out then, some only partially clothed, bearing swords and spears. Judas led them quickly through the shadows to where he had seen Jesus and Mary. When they arrived, however, they found only their Lord, seated, head bowed in prayer.

"Master," Peter cried, "Judas said that you were beset by a demon, so we have come to you!"

Looking up, eyes very tired and voice weak, Jesus answered. "There is no demon here, but I am weary. Lead me to the camp, for I must rest."

Eyes full of wonder, for they had never seen their Lord in such a state, they raised him between them and carried him to his bed, where he fell asleep immediately. In the shadows behind them, weeping, yet marveling at her near-human skin and the peace in her heart, Mary watched them go. Turning, she ran back to the village. The night swallowed her quickly, and the desert was once more still.

∞Θ∞

Judas 21:1

[1] When he had finished praying, Jesus left with his disciples and crossed the Kidron valley. [2] On the other side was an olive grove, and Jesus and his disciples entered it.

[3] Judas, sent to the village for food, met with the woman, Mary of Magdalene, and was delayed in coming to the grove. [4] As he neared the place, he saw Peter in conference with several armed men. [5] The soldiers, accompanied by officials from the Priests and Pharisees, entered the grove just after Judas, who bore a message from Mary. [6] Kissing his master on the cheek, he whispered the words he had been given. [7] Then the soldiers stepped forward and the disciples grew silent.

[8] "Who is it you seek?" Jesus asked, knowing all that would come to pass.

[9] "Jesus of Nazareth," they replied.

[10] "I am he," Jesus said.

[11] Peter, attempting to hide his betrayal, drew his sword and struck the High Priest's servant, severing his ear (The servant's name was Malchus).

[12] Jesus said, "Put that sword away. Shall I deny the cup my father pours me?" [13] Turning to the Pharisees and soldiers, Jesus said, "Am I leading a rebellion, then, that you need come upon me by stealth, with swords and clubs? [14] I sat teaching in your courtyards every day, yet you did not arrest me. [15] This has come about that the prophecies may be fulfilled."

[16] Then all his disciples deserted him and fled.

∞☉∞

In great anger, Judas followed Peter in his flight. When they reached a point far enough away from the soldiers for safety, he grabbed his fellow disciple's shoulder, spinning him roughly. "What have you done, Peter?" he demanded. Peter's eyes were haunted, distant, and Judas recoiled from them in horror.

"He looked well in chains, do you not think so?" The voice was cold, like brittle ice, cracking through the air. It was not Peter's voice, nor was it any human expression that rode the familiar features.

"Who are you?" Judas asked, backing away, "You are not Peter!"

"I am more than your mind can grasp, fool," the demon voice chuckled, "more than even your master imagines. Perhaps he is coming to some knowledge of this, even now!"

Lowering his gaze to avoid the eyes, which glittered with unnatural light and gripped at his heart, Judas began to pray. The demon, jeering and dark, ranted at him, giving no reprise. Steeling himself, Judas ignored the voice, falling to his knees in the sand.

"Our father, who art in heaven," he began, "be with your servant in his hour of need. Free my brother from this evil, return to us Simon, called Peter, for our Lord needs us now, your son, unworthy as we are, and I have not the strength alone."

As his courage grew, he rose, raising his eyes to those of his tormentor, searching for his brother.

"You are too weak." The demon's voice seemed to waver. "I leave of my own will, not that of your accursed father, or his six-mothered bastard. And I leave you a gift. Your brethren will believe you the cause of your master's death. Your kiss will become the symbol of his betrayal!"

"Get thee hence!" Judas staggered forward, as if his physical presence alone could intimidate the evil confronting him. Peter's features contorted, rippled between despairing, imploring humanity, and gripping, snarling darkness. As Judas's fingers touched Peter's shoulders, there was a sound like the rushing of a great wind, and they were both struck to the ground. When the demon had passed, leaving swirling pillars of sand in its wake, they rose slowly, blinking their eyes and checking their bones.

"We must follow our Lord, for they have taken him," Judas said, turning away. Peter watched him, a glare in his eye. His expression, accusing and dark, was more painful than even the demon's gaze had been, for it shone through the disciple's own features, and rose from his own mind. Judas trembled, remembering the words, "Your kiss will become the symbol of his betrayal."

Peter followed, but did not speak. The ominous weight of his silence bore down upon Judas like a smothering fog, but still he walked on. It was a small price, he told himself, for his brother's soul. Tears burned with the swirling sand down his cheeks, and dried instantly, wisping into the eye of the sun.

∞☉∞

Judas 25:17

[17] The soldiers took Jesus into their charge. Carrying upon his shoulder his own cross, he went out to Golgotha (called the place of the skull). [18] Here they crucified him, along with two others—one to each side, with Jesus in the middle. [19] Pilate had a notice prepared and fastened to the cross. It read:

JESUS OF NAZARETH,
THE KING OF THE JEWS

[20] It was lettered in Aramaic, Latin, and Greek, and many Jews read the sign, for the place of the crucifixion was near the city. [21] The Chief Priests of the Jews protested, saying, "Do not write, 'King of the Jews,' but instead write that this man claimed to be King of the Jews."

[22] Pilate answered, "I have written what I have written." [23] When the soldiers had crucified Jesus, they took his clothes, dividing them into four equal shares, one for each of them, with the undergarment remaining. [24] This remaining garment was without seams, woven in one piece. [25] "Let's not tear it," they said to one another. "Let's decide by lot who will get it."

[26] This happened that the Scripture might be fulfilled which said, 'They divided my garments among them, and cast lots for my clothing.' [29] So this is what the soldiers did.

[30] Near the cross of Jesus stood his mother, his mother's sister, Mary, wife of Clopas, and Mary Magdalene. [31] When Jesus saw his mother there, and the disciple whom he loved, (Peter), and she for whom he wept, he said to his mother, "Dear woman, here is your son," and to the disciple, "Here is your mother." [32] To Mary Magdalene he said, "You are one with my heart. Though my father calls, I will be with you. [33] Do not forget."

From that time on, the disciple took Jesus' mother into his home.

[34] Mary Magdalene, hearing the Lord's words, wept bitterly, unable to stand his pain.

∞☉∞

Darkness fell upon the threefold wooden frames, trailing shadowy tendrils among the rivulets of blood that clotted and grew sticky on his skin. Jesus regarded those below in the weaving, half-coalesced vision of his pain. Tears dried, unwilling to remoisten his cheeks. He remained conscious only through continuous, jumbled prayer, chasing the tumbling words and thoughts through his heart and pressing them outward to his father with all the strength of his will. None answered. It was done. He'd dared to presume himself above his father's disfavor, reached out to one beyond his power, and he'd given of the greatest gift he'd received to one beyond redemption, desecrating himself in the eyes of his own father.

He could feel his strength ebbing. The pain was beyond anything he'd experienced before, beyond even the pain of his father's disapproval. The human body he wore neared death, and it spoke of this eloquently. So hard, he thought, such a weight to bear. How do they retain faith? And what have I done, taking my gift of salvation and flinging it aside as if it were mine alone?

"I ... I am thirsty," he croaked at last, beseeching those below.

A plant stem was raised, topped by a sponge, and he greedily sucked on the moistness, feeling the bitter sting as the wine-vinegar trickled down his parched throat.

Pulling his face from the sponge weakly, he raised his eyes to the sky and cried out, hurling the words from deep inside his breast, calling out loudly.

"My father, why have you forsaken me?"

And life slipped from his body at that moment, leaving him limp and unmoving on the skeletal framework of the cross.

Mary, seeing that it was truly death that was upon him, screamed a terrible scream, an impotent, nerve-grinding wail to a God she could not reach. Those around her fled from her fury, crying out in fear and racing for homes and fires. She paid them no heed.

He had risked it all, all that he was, for her, for her soul, and the risk had been in vain—he was dead! He had walked the Earth as the Son of God, but, having given to her of his gift, having fed her a part of himself, he had died as a man, and all he had lived was wiped away as if it had never been. In that instant, prophecy was cast to the winds without thought. Still screaming, she ran to the desert, pulling at her almost human hair and cursing the sky with raging torrents of unchecked emotion. Deep within her, sparked by her loss of control, a dark voice reached out to her, laughing the mocking laughter of the victor.

Unable to go on, she dropped to her knees, and, fighting back the encroaching darkness in her soul, she began—for the first time since her feet touched the earth—to pray, loudly and blindly. He had given himself for her, for her salvation, though it cost the world. She prayed for only the chance to return his love, to replace his gift. She continued to pray, unaware of her surroundings, while a glowing figure appeared at her side. She did not notice that she was not alone until his fingers brushed her shoulder.

Stifling a cry, she backed away, half-rising to her feet. Elijah stood before her, resplendent, but with sorrow beyond comprehension on his features—sadness beyond measure.

"Woman, now called Mary," he spoke, "would you truly return the light?"

"I … " she lowered her eyes, bowing in supplication, "I would release to you my soul to return him—to fulfill his prophecy. I would do anything."

"Go you then" the voice instructed, "and find Judas, who they name betrayer.

Tell him all. In his lifeblood, and in his love, you will find the strength. If you willingly replace the gift of the Son of Man with Judas' mortal blood, your curse will return. In that hour shall all be righted … go and may we all be judged on a standard such as your love."

The light was gone, the darkness remained, and Mary rose, returning through the sifting shadows to the cross. Tears streamed steadily down her cheeks, dampening the locks of her hair, and her steps were uneven. It was too great a cost. She had been granted that which no other could give a second time, and now it was demanded of her to return it … she clutched her arms tightly to her stomach to ease the churning and the pain. In her mind, echoing voices mocked her feeble will, laughed at her lack of courage. Already Lucifer and his minions counted the victory won. She was lost to them, but The Christ was lost to mankind. Wailing her despair, she ran on, finding Judas just before the dawning sun rose to the horizon. He knelt alone, lost in prayer of his own. He did not see her coming, and she watched him for a long moment before speaking.

∞Θ∞

Judas 28:1

¹ And Judas Iscariot, blamed of the betrayal, prayed in the darkness. ² The temptress, she called Mary Magdalene, came upon him, wild of eye, and cheeks damp with tears, crying out, "Judas, beloved or our Lord, a great evil has come upon us."

³ "Lady," Judas replied, "in three days our Lord shall rise from his grave, redemption is at hand."

⁴ "He is dead," she told him, seating herself, "of love for me, he sacrificed all. We bear the weight, you and I, for I have spoken with Elijah, and he has sent me to you."

⁵ And she spoke to him of Lucifer, and of her curse, and of Jesus' gift of life, with its terrible price. ⁶ They wept, clinging to one another, and Judas cried out, "The weight is too great on you, Mary, for he would not wish you to pay this price!"

⁷ "That," she replied, "is why I must pay it."

⁸ "Then take me," Judas lay back, baring his throat, tears in his own eyes, "for truly your love rivals even his, and his gift is too precious to lose."

⁹ Seeing the love in Judas's eyes, feeling the wrench of Satan's very claws as he leapt to prevent her, the woman, Mary, fell upon the body of Judas and fed, the curse taking her even as she swept forward. Weeping, she cast herself willingly to the darkness from which she'd

been raised, feeling the icy claws of the hunger that would once again consume her.

[10] Sated, she rose, and Judas also, now pale and alight with hunger of his own, and they fled as Lucifer hunted them, possessed of a great and futile rage. [11] As darkness engulfed them, they shared one last glance—a last time they smiled. [12] Then it was black, and they were smitten with the fire of Lucifer, losing all thought.

∞☉∞

When Mary and Judas regained consciousness, they both awoke to hunger.

Fighting it back, screaming inwardly with the fire of their need, they walked, side by side, through twilight three days beyond Jesus' death. Silence filled the night. All those who lived nearby either slept, or were sitting home. They reached the place where Jesus' tomb lay without meeting a soul, coming to stand by the huge stone that had blocked his return to the world. A fear gnawed at the depth their breasts, nearly smothered, but burning still.

Standing within, gazing at them through haloed prisms, formed of the brilliance of his glory, seen through the mirrors of his tears, the Son of Man regarded them with great sadness, and endless love.

Their own eyes, devoid of natural light, flickered with the pain of loss, and the wonder of the intensity of his love. No word did they speak, only awaited their fate and drank in the sight of their Lord.

"Though I suffer not your curse, I will be with you," Jesus spoke. "A time will come when I walk these roads again—you will be there, and I will remember."

Turning, Mary Magdalene and Judas Iscariot, called traitor, fled into the darkness, overcome with hunger and pain, tethered in the cutting bonds of evil. Alone once more, Jesus stood, weeping tears of glittering sadness to wet the sand at his feet.

They blurred his sight. Time was so short. He could not follow them, could do nothing but accept their sacrifice. It should have been his alone. He turned, walking forth to embrace the world.

∞☉∞

Judas 30:1

[1] Running from the tomb, where Jesus stood, resurrected, Judas stole a length of rope from a nearby home. [2] Coming upon a tall tree, he cast it upon a sturdy branch. [3] Putting to the end of the rope a noose, he climbed to a branch high above the ground, fixed the rope to his neck, and leapt, hanging himself. [4] Finding him thus, the people spoke against him, led by Simon, called Peter, saying, "He has taken his life from shame, for he betrayed his Lord." [5]

Mary Magdalene, running to where the disciples were gathered, said, "I have seen the Lord, and he is risen."

[6] And Jesus appeared other times to his disciples, speaking words of comfort and salvation, and was raised once more to his throne in Heaven. [7] We, who hunger, remain. [8] The rope has failed to relieve me of my burden. [9] In the bark of the tree where we left the rope, Mary inscribed the words,

Here hung one who loves beyond life.

[10] May God forgive us.

-Morning Sickness-
WILLIAM MEIKLE

We knew it was a bad idea to isolate ourselves when it was so near her time but it had been years since our last holiday and besides, her doctors assured us that we were at least three weeks away from the birth.

It wasn't planned, not at all. We'd settled for a couple of weeks rest and I'd booked a three month sabbatical from the office, hoping to get some work done on the house. Then we won the competition––a week in Britain, anywhere of our choosing as long as we took the holiday within the next month. One day we were in our flat in London, surrounded by the building's half-finished work—noise, dust and general aggravation—the next we were all alone on the west coast of Scotland, in a cottage by the shore on Jura. It was just us, the seals and the view over the sea to Argyll.

I wasn't sure at first. I wanted to be near a hospital in case of emergencies, but she insisted. It would be our last holiday alone for a while; she was fit, healthy and she wanted to do it.

The nearest house was five miles south—the nearest doctor twice that distance. To the north and west there was only the rugged hills and the deer. We didn't even have a boat. At least there was a road: a single-track lane with passing places. It had been recently resurfaced and we had been provided with a new Range Rover for the duration. I was confident that we could reach the doctor's house in less than twenty minutes in event of an emergency, which was quicker than I could have managed in London. I had talked myself round to the idea and I wasn't worried. I should have been.

We arrived late. Jura is not the easiest place to get to. It involved a flight to Glasgow and a short hop over to Islay. The Range Rover was waiting at Islay airport, which is more a glorified field than an airstrip.

After that it's a fifteen-mile trip to the Port Askaig ferry, which is small and rickety and on a calm day can take four cars across the half mile of treacherous waters towards the stunning mountains of Jura.

Once on the island, it was a single-track road all the way, twenty miles, with Craighouse, the only town, halfway along. We were going right to the far end.

We stopped at the one and only hotel for a meal, but we were too late to pick up any other provisions; that would have to wait till morning.

It was dark when we arrived and Sandra was too tired to do anything other than fall into bed and sleep. As for me, I was restless. I never believed that I would miss the bustle of London's streets, but the lack of noise here had me on edge. The only sound was the gentle lapping of the sea on the rocks only ten yards from the cottage's front door. Occasionally there would be the forlorn cry of a gull or the croaking of a crow, apart from that it was silent and dark and strangely disquieting.

It was very late by the time I snuggled into bed, taking advantage of the radiating heat from my pregnant wife beside me. I believe I slept soundly, I don't remember any dreams and nothing disturbed me during the night.

She woke me the next morning with a whisper.

'Get up. Hurry. You've got to see this.'

I was still groggy when I raised my head to see her leaving the room. I got out of bed, wincing at the cold seeping through the floorboards, and joined her at the window in the front room.

'Look', she said, 'Isn't it wonderful?'

It was very early morning. The sun was just coming up over the hills of Argyll, spreading a pink glow across the wispy clouds.

The sea was being slightly ruffled by a small breeze; there in the foreground, in front of the house, at the edge of the small lawn, sat three otters—obviously a mother and two smaller young. They trotted along the shore then slipped into the water.

We crept out, still naked, and watched them cavorting among the huge fronds of seaweed until I slipped on the wet grass. My sudden movement caused them to dive, resurfacing again much farther out.

Sandra came over and squeezed me, her full belly pressing its heat against my flesh.

"Thanks for bringing us here John. I love it." We kissed and I marveled at how hot and alive and heavy with life she had become. It was only as we turned back to the house that I noticed the mound.

It had been too dark the night before to see any details of the surrounding area, but now I could see that the cottage was built on a small raised piece of land between two arms of a river. We had come across a small bridge but in the dark I had failed to notice it.

Behind the cottage where the rivers split there was a huge stone cairn, standing eight to ten feet high, topped off with a cross which looked to be the same height as the cairn and made of solid iron. Around the cairn there was a wrought iron fence with spiked railings jutting up towards the sky.

"Why would they put something like that out here?" she asked me. "I thought cairns were usually built on top of hills?"

"I'm not sure. Maybe it's for someone who died either here or at sea near here. We can ask in town if you like?" I turned towards her, noticing the goose pimples on her arms. "Get yourself inside and put some clothes on; we don't want you to catch a chill. Anyway, by the time we get going and get to town the shop will be open."

When we eventually got to the shop it was ten o'clock; there had been many things to see on the drive down.

The shop held only basic foods: eggs, bacon, cheese—nothing too fancy, but Sandra had gotten over her cravings for exotica and we would be able to stock up with most of our needs for the week. Sandra was the focus of much talk and was in danger of excessive mothering from some of the women we met. We turned down several offers of a warm room closer to town, and the shop owner took our list from us, promising that she would make it up and we could collect it later.

Luckily the hotel served a late breakfast. The pace of life on the island moved slowly and you could run breakfast into lunch into supper without leaving the hotel grounds. We managed to escape at one in the afternoon, weighed down by bacon and sausages and swilling with coffee. It was only when we stopped by the shop to pick up our supplies that I remembered the cairn.

The shopkeeper tried to hide her movement but I caught it—the sign against the evil eye, two pronged fingers stabbing at me as she spoke. "You don't have to worry about that sir. It's only an old memorial. Some say there used to be a plaque fixed to it but no one can remember what it' was there for."

I noticed that the rest of the customers in the shop had fallen silent. I supposed that the cairn was the focus for some old superstition. That didn't bother me, but I wasn't about to tell Sandra. Unlike me, she held a fascination for the supernatural. Anything that went bump in the night or was out of the ordinary, she fell for it. I could never understand the fascination with scaring yourself half to death, but I knew if she found out there was something weird about the cairn she would not stop until she had wrinkled out the story. In the car on the way to the cottage I told her it was a war memorial and let the subject drop. She didn't ask any questions.

We got back in the late afternoon, having made numerous stops to marvel at the stunning variety of life around us. Sandra made a big show of hand-washing our traveling clothes and hanging them from a clothesline at the back of the house.

The rest of the day passed lazily as we sat on the lawn, drinking long drinks, watching the scenery and making happy plans for our future. We took our food onto the grassy area, sitting on an old rug and throwing occasional morsels to an inquisitive squirrel. I think that evening was the closest to heaven I had ever been.

We were finally forced indoors by a chill, which brought the clouds down the hills just as the sun disappeared and a fine grey mist spread over the sea. It wasn't long before we adjourned to the bedroom and made tender careful love as the darkness closed in around us. Later, as I was falling asleep, I could hear the wind rising, whistling through the chimneybreasts, causing the trees to rustle and crack.

I woke early and squeezed myself away from Sandra, taking care not to wake her. After boiling some water in the kettle I ventured out to see what the weather was like. The first thing I noticed was the effect of the wind. The washing was gone from the line, torn off the rope during the night. I found a shirt in the left hand stream, a pair of underpants halfway up a tree, and Sandra's blouse hanging from one arm of the cross on the cairn.

I retrieved everything I could find before moving to the mound of stones. I stepped over the railing, nearly injuring myself on the spikes as I clambered up the rocks, dislodging a few in the process, and gaining several bruises on my knees.

The blouse was wrapped around the rusted spar. Straining and stretching I could just about reach it. Catching hold of the blouse I pulled. My footing gave way and I fell, pulling the blouse with me. I felt the material tear before something solid and heavy hit me on the head, forcing me onto the rolling, dislodged rocks until I was brought up against the railings.

I heard a loud creaking and looked up to see the cross, now with a spar missing, swaying from side to side in the breeze. When I looked down I found the missing piece lying by my side with Sandra's blouse wrapped around it. I left it there as I hauled myself over the railings and hobbled back to the house.

That was it for the rest of the day. I was dazed, bleeding from a head wound with bruises over much of my body. Sandra wanted to fetch the doctor but I talked her out of it. I didn't want anybody to know that I had defaced the memorial—not yet anyway, not until I had the chance to repair the damage. I spent the day in bed, most of the time with Sandra beside me, nursing my wounds and wondering what the islanders' reaction would be. As darkness filled the room Sandra fell asleep but I laid awake, listening to the creaking of the cross and the rasping of iron against stone as it swayed back and forth in the wind.

At some point I must have fallen asleep. I was awakened by a cold draft hitting me on the back of the neck. I rolled over, hoping to snuggle against my wife's warm body, but I met only more empty space. It took several seconds for me to realize that she wasn't in the bed.

Moonlight was streaming in through the window enough for me to make out her pale figure and the cross that bobbed and swayed hypnotically in front of her. I was out of the room and onto the grass before I realized we were both naked.

I went back to fetch some clothes; I pulled on a long jumper and picked up an overcoat for her. When I returned to the door I could see she was not alone.

He stood inside the railing, thin and white, tall and naked, beckoning to her with one long white finger, saliva dripping from his mouth. My mind screamed *vampire*—I wasn't stupid. I'd seen the films; I knew what the long teeth meant.

I was twenty yards away when she reached out to take his hand, ten yards away when he bent his head to her neck. His long hand stroked across the swell of her belly. I was close enough to see his eyes sparkle once he realized she was pregnant. I could see the blood oozing across her shoulders as he gulped noisily against her neck; the dark liquid glowed black in the moonlight.

He still hadn't noticed me, until I gripped his head and pulled it away from its feed. I realized at once it had been a mistake. He lifted me off the ground, causing the muscles of my back, which were already tender from their earlier bruising, to scream out in white-hot agony.

The beast stared at me from the deep silver pools of his eyes. My feet were flailing as I tried to wriggle from his grasp. He pulled me close to his face—so close I could feel the cold dampness of his breath and see my wife's blood glistening on the curved fangs. Suddenly I was lifted higher, above his head, and thrown, dumped to the ground, forgotten.

I knew what he wanted; I had seen the lust in his eyes.

Once more he reached for her, long white arms pulsing red with the blood he had taken, white hair spreading behind him like a cape as he lunged forward. He took her in his arms and crushed her body to him. She moaned a deep groan of pleasure as I writhed on the ground. I tried to get on my feet and block the sucking and moaning sounds from my brain.

I tripped over the broken spar of the cross. I lifted it, hoping to smash it across his skull before an image from the films came into my head: the image of the beast impaled.

He was still oblivious to me as I struck, forcing the heavy rusty metal into his back, putting all my weight behind it.

The screaming started immediately. Sandra was dropped to the ground; black blood pulsed from her throat as the beast raged. It turned towards me, pulling the spar from my hands and taking several layers of skin with it.

I moved back, stumbling over the fallen stones.

The vampire's eyes pierced me—silver turning to gold and then black as its face opened in a shriek and the first wisps of smoke appeared at its chest. It looked down at the six inches of iron protruding from its breastbone just as the first flame exploded into life, taking away the lower face and much of the head of hair.

It burned a deep golden fire, which consumed it entirely in less than five seconds—a fire which stretched my skin and singed my eyebrows even as I grinned. I was left with the moonlight and the cold and the ashes and the madness echoing round in my head.

The spar was still there, lying in the midst of a heap of smoking ashes. I left it where it was and piled some of the fallen stones on top of it, giggling all the while.

Sandra was breathing heavily when I finally got to her but at least the blood had stopped. As I lifted her into my arms she let out a scream which drove through my skull.

'The baby. Oh God … it's coming. It's coming.'

I don't remember much of the next half hour, only fragments—driving like a maniac as she sobbed quietly behind me, the sudden light in the deer's eyes before the car hit it dead on, smashing the car's headlights into a million tinkling fragments, the small twinkling lights in the black distance as I managed to avoid the cliff edge, and finally, the iron gate on the path, which I almost fell over as the doctor came towards me and I collapsed into a faint.

I have a vague memory of being put in an armchair and force-fed whisky as my wife was carried upstairs and the doctor called for some help. My legs wouldn't move and my arms were heavy; sleep called me back again.

I dreamt hot lurid fantasies of violence and fire, of rape and bloodletting, of a cold, black fury that carried all before it. I woke from screams into screams.

My legs pushed me out of the chair and towards the door long before my brain was fully awake. I was halfway up the stairs before I recognized the voice behind the screaming. I reached the door just as the screams stopped.

Early morning sunlight was streaming into the room, lighting a scene which will be forever etched into my memory:

The doctor standing off to one side, his left hand covering his mouth, his right clutching his chest as if to keep his heart in.

An old woman lying across the bed in a dead faint, her grey wisps of hair mingled with the blood from my wife's legs.

My wife lying on her side, throat muscles straining, mouth opened in a long soundless scream that refuses to come; her gaze is fixed on the writhing shape. She is ignoring the wisps of smoke which are beginning to rise from her legs; the charring and peeling and blackening are immaterial to her pain as she looks upon our child.

And there on the floor lies our future, burning golden in the first rays of the sun, being cleansed in the purifying light of the new day, my son. The last thing I see before darkness takes me away for a long time are the fangs, two tiny spikes sliding out of those new pink gums, the fangs which are the last things to disappear as the fire burns out and the ashes shift in the breeze.

-When Barrettes Brought Justice To A Burning Heart-
JOHN EVERSON

He staggered from the smoky heat of the bar into the chill autumn wind. The street outside was empty, the cloud-scummed sky a leeching black. Bill Frond's stomach sloshed as he weaved to the corner, but all the liquor his wallet could afford hadn't assuaged the burning in his chest. In fact, through the haze of inebriation, he actually felt more wounded now than before he had stomped into Ale's Head Tavern several hours ago. The fire in his heart had contracted to a pinpoint of heat, leaving behind a blackened void. He feared when the little acid flame that still burned was extinguished he would stop dead in his tracks, a flesh appliance whose batteries had spurted their last current.

But another fire was lighting in his guts; it surged past the dying ember in his heart to race through his throat. Bill froze a moment, staring sickly at the dark alleyway just ahead. As his binge lit to purge, he dashed for the privacy of the narrow street.

Ten minutes later, exhausted and slumped on the ground near a pool of bitter vomit, Bill pulled a tissue from his jacket, wiped the tears from his eyes, and blew the acid from his nose.

"Feel better?" a voice whispered, grating from the darkness. Bill's heart leapt at the unexpected sound. He squinted at the uneven bricks and shadows around him. The dim outline of a man began to take shape from the depths of the darkened street.

"Not really," Bill answered, wondering if, after all this, he was now going to be mugged. Or killed. Preferably the latter, a voice within him begged.

"Tell me," the voice asked, its owner settling just far enough away that Bill couldn't make out his face. A white flash as the man spoke, a glint from eyes turning down. That was all. A hint of a face.

"Tell you, what?" Bill snapped. "That I feel sick inside? That I just wasted 30 bucks trying to drink away reality? Please leave me alone; I'm not in the mood for company."

"Don't worry, I'm not anybody's idea of company." The hint of a face blurred, shifted, moved closer. Bill caught the sour odor of alley trash and felt his belly kick in complaint.

"Tell me why you're here, while you still can," the voice demanded. The roughness of its tone sent a chill through Bill's neck. If this guy was going to beat him up—or worse—what difference did it make *why* he was here?

"You want to know? I'll tell you," Bill began, slipping easily into the words, recounting events he had already relived a hundred times this night.

"Seven months ago, Lissa, my daughter, was walking home from school. We live just a few blocks away from Sanders High, and she always walked home—in the rain, in the snow, in the summertime. She liked to walk. And she always came straight home. But on that particular afternoon, she didn't come home on time. Cheryl, that's my wife, worried a little, but figured Lissa had stopped off to talk with someone. When it got to be dinnertime, Cheryl started calling the parents of Lissa's friends. No one had seen her. After I came home from work, and she still wasn't home, we checked the hospitals. Then we called the police."

The shadowed figured nodded slowly, as if hearing a familiar story.

"They found her the next day in the woods behind the school. She was naked, her body smeared with blood. Her own. Her eyes were open. I think that hurt me the most. She was aware of every touch, every violation, I know she was. Her skull was crushed—she'd been hit on the head with rock. Then raped. But she felt every minute of it. Her eyes were screaming.

"They caught the boys who did it—a couple of seventeen-year-olds who thought they could just knock her out with a rock, then rape her and leave before she woke up." Bill's face wrinkled in silent agony; he coughed out a sob and shook his head clear.

"But they hit her too hard," he finally continued, tears now wetting his cheeks. "And somehow, she didn't fall unconscious. I wanted them to die like my daughter died. I watched them smirking to each other in the courtroom during the trial, and I pictured myself smashing their heads together until their brains pulped through my fingers."

He paused, unclenched his hands and laughed sadly.

"The violence I planned for them! I wanted to castrate them, bash in their brains, stab holes in their hearts. Every night during the week of the trial, I cried myself to sleep. And when it was all over ... the boys walked away free. Their lawyers managed to get every scrap of evidence the police had found thrown out of court on technicalities. They walked away free while my daughter rotted in the ground."

A flash of white, as the stranger's face nodded once again, inched closer.

"The day after the trial was over I stepped on my front porch to get the paper. And found these."

Bill pulled two triangular shapes from his coat pocket. They glittered in the faint light filtering into the alleyway from the street. "Lissa's barrettes. I know the boys left them for me to find. A joke. It was all a joke to them. And I hated myself, because instead of going after them, instead of giving them what they gave my daughter, I tucked these in my pocket, went back in the house, and cried some more."

The pale face again shifted closer, its outline now distinct, long in the heavy shadow of the alley. "Revenge is an expensive enterprise," it whispered, near enough that Bill could see the stranger's lips move. They seemed crooked, off-kilter. The alley stench had grown stronger; its character was led by the nauseous aroma of rotting meat, but filled out with the bitter taste of old milk and neglect. Bill began to breathe through his mouth.

"Well, I wish I had paid the price now," Bill retorted. The fire in his chest had flared briefly with the retelling of his child's murder, but now flickered lower than before. He was beaten. It was over. He couldn't avenge his daughter and the remaining foundation of his life, which he'd spent years building upon, had, just today, been swept away in an instant.

"You're not here tonight because of your daughter," the voice breathed. Bill heard a pain in that tone that sounded not unlike his own. "Tell me," the stranger demanded softly.

Bill looked up in surprise at the stranger's appraisal, then nodded. It seemed right. He wanted to tell *someone* everything. And so he did.

"My wife looked into my eyes this morning. I thought she looked sad, and I asked her what was wrong. She just kept staring at me, and a tear rolled down her cheek. Then she kissed me. I knew something was bad. Real bad. She'd been so quiet since Lissa died. Actually, she'd been quiet before that, but I hadn't noticed—until I thought about it tonight.

" 'I don't love you anymore,' she said. Her eyes were blinking fast and her voice cracked.

" 'I've been trying to find it for a long time, but I'm sorry, I just don't. It's gone,' she said. I looked at her then, and maybe saw her for the first time in years. It's funny, after awhile, you start to see your wife as part of the furniture. She's there, you know? But in that instant I saw her, Cheryl, the woman I met at a beach party 20 years ago. And in her eyes I saw an unknown woman—still with all the mystery of a first date. I thought I knew her inside and out, but quite suddenly I realized that all I really knew about Cheryl was her skin. *That* I knew by heart. And her routines. But her? The woman staring at me with tears and pity in her eyes, I didn't know. And the man who cried, and begged, and finally fled to the Ale's Head Tavern … I'm ashamed to know."

A hand patted him on the shoulder and Bill looked up into the startling eyes of the stranger. They were milky white, shot through with veins. They had no pupils. They rested in a face that seemed to move and shift in a manner no muscles could control. The rest of the man was cloaked in a long grey coat which didn't hide his gauntness. His bony fingers were also covered in half-gloves, hobo-style.

"And what are you going to do about it?" the stranger asked, his breath crossing Bill's nose in a putrid wave which made him realize the alley stench was not of the alley, but of the bum.

"Nothing," Bill whispered. "I just want to die."

"That wish, I will grant," the stranger answered, and with a leap, pinned Bill to the ground. He didn't struggle.

"Go ahead," Bill said, all resistance leaving him. "I don't really care."

At close range, the stranger's oddly twitching face appeared mottled with sores, violent explosions of purple standing in grotesque relief against bone-white skin. The hands, which pinned him to the gravelly asphalt, were cold, sticky.

"I can give you the tool for revenge," the lips offered, mucousy spit dripping from them to moisten Bill's face. "Or I can simply kill you. I give you the choice because it wasn't offered to me. I would have chosen death. The cost of revenge, as I said, is great."

Deep in the burnt-out shell of Bill's heart, a tiny flame guttered higher. An insane thought crossed his mind. *This was not your ordinary alley bum.* Looking into the bloody whites which passed for the stranger's eyes, seeing the pus oozing from the cracks in his neck, smelling the decay which was not garbage, not bad breath, but trench-coated the bum's *rotting flesh*, Bill concluded that this was the devil himself. And suddenly that long unslaked thirst for revenge poured gasoline into his heart.

"I'll pay the price, whatever it is," he gasped through gritted teeth. "If it's my soul you want, take it, I don't care." Anger flooded his mind like the bile still lodged in his throat. "I just want to make them pay. All of them."

The being hesitated a moment, and a word of warning gurgled in his throat. His eyes lowered to stare into Bill's own. The stench was overpowering. Bill's stomach threatened to lose whatever acid remained trapped within when the eyes suddenly pulled away and then with a watery cry, the man buried his mouth in Bill's neck. He only got out one yelp of surprise and pain, and then the night sky blurred. His body went rigid and a stream of cool ice froze in his head. He could hear the stranger slurping, hear the beat of his own heart: thud-thud, thud-thud, thud-thud … thud … thud … thud. Thud.

Thud.

∞◉∞

The stench. God, it was bad! Bill lifted his head from the cushion of a plastic sack and stirred a hive of flies from somewhere below. They swarmed across his face and landed on his lips. He shook them away and realized in doing so that, amazingly, he had no hangover. But where was he?

Rolling off the bag, he felt the surface shift beneath him with a metallic heave as bags slid away and his feet scrambled to find purchase on solid ground. Reaching above him, his fingers met cool metal that lifted with a push. He rose to full height, his back and legs creaking at the unaccustomed stretch. A garbage dumpster. He was standing in a garbage dumpster! In a dark, stinking alley.

And then the events of the night returned to him: the drinking, the stranger, his story, and then—an attack? He reached up to feel his neck. Sure enough, there were two big sores where the bum had bitten him. Bracing his hands on the side of the dumpster, he vaulted himself to the ground and brushed off his clothes. Something moved in the dark and he froze.

It was the expectation of hearing his heart pound wildly in his chest from fright that tipped him off. His heart *wasn't* beating fast.

Odd.

He put his hand to his chest, felt around. *It wasn't beating at all.*

Odder still. But the worst part was, while intellectually he expected to break down into hysterics at any moment, the fact that his heart was not pumping blood to feed his fear didn't bother him. In fact, he felt very little. Rubbing an index finger along his neck and jaw, he realized he could feel the texture, but it was dulled—the equivalent of a black and white movie versus color.

The shadows stirred again. The stranger from last night emerged from a lean-to shelter behind the dumpster.

"Well, you asked for revenge," the bum said in a grating voice. "Now is your chance. Don't waste it. You don't have much time."

The blotches covered the stranger's face now; a tattooed blur of motion, its lips twitched out of sync with its speech, which was now slurred and indistinct, as if his mouth was slow to respond to the twitch of his muscles.

"Who are you?" Bill asked, his eyes drawn with abnormally detached interest to the shivers coursing across the man's exposed flesh.

"My name is Lawrence," the man said, milky orbs meeting Bill's own. "And, as you've probably guessed, I'm a vampire. You wanted revenge, so I gave you some of *my* blood last night." He pointed at the bruises covering his cheeks. "And this is the result of my thirst. This is *your* blood."

Bill thought that he should have known anger, should have smashed his fist into the pruneface before him. But his head remained cool, empty of rancor. He'd been attacked and bitten by a man with a revolting skin disease, and here he was shooting the breeze with the same guy.

"I think you're just a sick bum with an S&M side," Bill laughed bravely, already trying to figure out if he should attempt to gain entrance to the couch at his house or head to a hotel for the rest of the night.

"You're dead," the voice before him gurgled. "And you don't have long to act if you want your revenge."

"Uh-huh," Bill said, starting to step away from the stinking, disease-ridden bum. But Lawrence shambled quickly to block the exit of the alley.

"Pull my finger," the bum begged, holding out his left palm. Bill laughed at the incongruous offer.

"Humor me," Lawrence demanded, ice in his tone.

Bill stared at the outstretched hand, its wrinkled whiteness a thoroughly unhealthy looking offering. Deciding that the faster he did what the transient wanted, the faster he could get to a bed, Bill grasped the extended finger and jerked.

And found himself holding the finger.

This appendage wasn't one of those trick pieces from the magic shop. This was real skin, real bone. And the red-black ooze at its disconnected end was, Bill suspected, his own blood.

"You're dead," Lawrence croaked. "Live with it."

Bill threw the digit away from him with a frown. He was now becoming somewhat disturbed at the situation. Things were looking, well, *unreal.*

"Okay, let's say I'm dead. What happens now?" he asked.

"The same thing that happens to all dead people," Lawrence returned, stepping away from the alley mouth. "So get your revenge. Fast. And stay out of the sun. It won't kill you, but it will make you unpleasant to be around a lot faster."

Lawrence turned and disappeared behind the dumpster once more, leaving Bill alone. He felt again for his heartbeat. *Dead.* Stepping out onto the street, he decided to find out just what a man with no heartbeat could get away with. Remembering his impotent rage at the two boys who had stolen his daughter from him, he began walking towards the southeast end of town. There was a growing burning in him that sought release, a fire that consumed not only his heart, but his limbs, his head, his lips. *At last,* he thought, *I will have some justice.*

∞☉∞

It wasn't hard to find them. There were only a couple of likely teen hangouts in this part of town, and the Angel's Park basketball court was one of them. Taking the bum's advice, he'd slept the day away in a cheap hotel, waking with the dusk to smooth his trash dumpster-scented clothes and step out onto the street once again. He briefly considered stopping at a McDonalds, and then realized that not only wasn't he hungry, but the idea of grilled beef made him somewhat nauseous. A drink wouldn't hurt though, he thought, and ducked into a Walgreens to buy a pint of whiskey.

"Is something the matter?" he asked the aged woman behind the register inside the store. She wagged her head 'no' while staring at the stubble on his cheek. Her nose crinkled obstinately in complaint. Bill smiled as he accepted the paper bag. Her hand shied from touching his in the exchange. *"How quickly we devolve,"* he thought. *"Two days ago she wouldn't have looked at me twice."*

Outside the store he opened the bottle, tilted it back. The amber liquid slid easily down his throat—but lacked any kick. It might as well have been grape juice. He felt it travel his throat, detected a thin hint of flavor, and that was all.

By the time he'd reached the basketball court the bottle was empty, and he'd realized that, as liquor lacked any ability to warm his palate, so did it lack the power to make him drunk. *"Maybe it will preserve my insides longer,"* he thought. And then he noticed the dark stain spreading down the insides of his pant legs. Droplets fell to the sidewalk from his cuffs with each step. *No control,* he realized. If he drank, it simply ran through him. If he ate, it would probably putrefy inside him.

His attention was suddenly wrenched from his deteriorating condition to the fenced-in asphalt lot before him. The two punks he'd come looking for *were* here! They dashed from side to side wrestling for the basketball with a group of other teens. Bill settled unobtrusively on a bench just outside of the lot.

He could wait.

It wasn't a long one; it was already dark. The boys played under the blinding white glare of the park's lights for 15 or 20 minutes after Bill's arrival, and then began to fragment. Soon, only his quarry and two other boys were playing two on two. And then, they too split, two of the players passing him on the way out of the lot, while the two Bill was after hopped the back fence and headed through the alley towards their homes. As soon as the others had passed him, Bill jumped from the bench and sprinted to the back of the brightly lit court. He vaulted the fence easily, and saw the boys just a block down the alleyway. The tall one—Marcus, he remembered—was punching the shorter blonde kid's shoulder. Terry, that was his name. *As if I could forget,* Bill shuddered. In the courtroom they had appeared like negatives of each other—Marcus tall, black, beanpole-skinny; Terry short, squat and blonde. But both had maintained those smirking "you'll never nail me" expressions that were so maddening as it became more and more apparent that they were completely correct. *Well, maybe not completely,* Bill thought as he began running down the alley after them.

As he ran, that hot feeling in his heart and gut began to build once more—the thrill of the chase could at least still reach his deadened nerves. And then he was on them, slamming open palms into each of their backs just as they began to turn to see who was pounding the pavement behind them.

Terry was caught off balance by the blow, and fell to the ground with a startled exclamation. Marcus stumbled, but with the grace of a true athlete, absorbed the imbalance, and turned to meet his attacker. His eyes looked like searchlights in the dark street as he saw Bill's maddened face.

"It's Lissa's dad," he yelled to Terry, who clutched a knee on the ground. "Lay off asshole, or we'll have you in jail," the taller boy boasted, dodging a punch.

But Bill wasn't listening now. His body was on fire, his blood boiling, his head ... hungry. He realized that even if he wanted to stop this, it had already gone to far. He *had* to have these kids.

Now.

He leapt at Marcus, ignoring the knife the boy pulled. He absently noted that the weapon lodged in his back as he and the boy fell to the ground. His voice seemed to slur as he pummeled the surprised teen's face with his fists and at last vented his anger: "You killed my daughter, you bastards!"

Reaching into his pocket with one hand, he brought out a shiny barrette. "Thought it was real cute to leave these on my doorstep, didn't you?" Bill raged.

Marcus let out one "holy shit" as Bill's mouth opened to expose a set of elongated fangs. In the same instant, Bill brought the barrette down, lodging it in Marcus' left eye. The boy shrieked an ungodly noise, and Bill felt rage electrify his body. He hated the sniveling creature beneath him. The boy had stolen his life.

Something crashed into his back, knocking him off balance. Then hands were around his neck, trying to wrest him away from the boy on the ground. He looked up to see the frantic face of Terry, trying to use his weight to drag Bill down. He only laughed and clubbed the fat slacker in the side of the head, and Terry went down like a rifled deer.

Then he turned back to Marcus, still writhing beneath him, hands covering his punctured eye. Bill felt a meanness he'd never known in life course through him like liquid fire and with his fist he beat at the boy's hands, pounding the barrette deeper into the boy's skull, until only a glint of metal remained visible amid the punctured white and red Campbell's soup of the boy's eye socket. Marcus' screams turned to metronomic near silent hissing squeals. His arms dropped to the ground and his hands clenched and unclenched, his entire body spasming. Bill pulled the knife from his back without even a wince and began to stab his daughter's killer in the heart, over and over and over again. With each thrust he hissed "you … killed … my … Lissa."

Marcus didn't answer.

Finally Bill stopped slicing and stared at the wreckage he'd made. Blood was smeared like an explosion of thick barbeque sauce across the boy's face and his t-shirt lay in dark stained tatters across a torso wet with crimson ruin. The scent of sweet iron filled the air and Bill realized he was salivating. Drooling over the carcass of a murdering rapist. His face inched lower to the boy's chest and he tried to pull back. But the pull of the scent was like a leash. The world faded out and all he could see was the slick red skin beneath him. He lapped at the chest wounds like a dog, and seconds later, Bill's newly grown incisors were buried in the soft unmarked flesh of the boy's neck. He sucked like a newborn babe on his mother's teat, drawing the essence of Marcus within himself, mouthful by mouthful, suckling breath by breath.

It was good, so good! As the liquor should have felt, that was how this blood was. He was floating in a garish maroon cloud of lust and drunkenness. Every touch, taste and emotion he'd lost upon his death combined in this hot elixir. Bill felt as if he was cumming, drinking an exquisite wine and laughing all at once.

This was heaven.

He was blinded to everything for a moment as the dying teen shuddered once more beneath him. With a fist he pounded the boy's chest to still him and found that with each punch, the rush of heaven increased. So, long after the boy's life had finally slipped away, Bill continued beating Marcus' middle, cracking his ribs, and eventually, forcing some of those splintered bones through the skin.

As the blood began to taste different, cooler, Bill pulled away from his drunken orgy and looked around. The night was still around them; amazingly, no one seemed to have been alerted from the boy's screams earlier.

Then, all at once, he saw that Terry had disappeared. He was loath to lift his mouth fully from his feast, but some last vestige of sanity forced him. He couldn't let the other boy live. Rising from the carcass, he saw for a moment the slashed neck, the white tips of ribs hung with shreds of skin and blood, the white, rolled back eyes—one with a shiny barrette skewer. He pulled the knife from its soggy chest holster and then he was running down the alley.

Terry would go home, he thought dimly, and home for the boy was only 10 or 12 more blocks, he knew. There were many times after the court trial that he had driven past Terry's house, wishing fervently that he could stop and go inside and beat the living shit out of the little rapist who lived there. But he never could.

He forced his feet faster; the neighborhood garages backing onto the alleyway became light blurs as he ran. And then he saw the blond head of the hobbling, injured boy, and the look of utter terror as Terry saw the bloody face charging towards him. Bill threw his body at the boy. Something cracked loudly as they hit the ground. But that wasn't enough. He wanted the boy to feel the way that his daughter had.

"How do you like your own medicine?" Bill whispered. Picking up a loose hunk of asphalt, he brought it down on the boy's forehead, ruining that golden blond hair purity with spatters of blood. Terry moaned and Bill stood up, dragging the boy's limp body with him.

"Thought you'd get away with it, didn't you?"

He threw the boy against the steel pole of a fence and didn't wait until the body had slumped back to the ground to yank it up again. Bill had never felt this strong in life. With one motion he slammed the body on the ground like a ragdoll and when one feeble hand reached out to stop him, he stood on the boy's chest, grabbed the hand and yanked until with a loud pop it separated from the shoulder joint.

"You were never good enough for my daughter," he mumbled, and then retrieved the knife from the ground. Slicing through the boy's shirt, belt and jeans, he stripped Terry and stared at the white folds of unconscious flesh beneath him.

"And I'll make sure you'll never do it to anyone else."

With that he brought the knife down at the base of the boy's shriveled penis, and pushed down. And sawed. And with a spew of blood and other fluids, he yanked and flipped the loosed sac of skin away.

"Aaaawwwwhh," the boy screamed, coming to just as Bill finished his castration. Again the knife went down, this time through the boy's open mouth to bang with a jarring crack against the rocky asphalt beneath them.

The scream trailed off to a choke, and Bill finally gave in to the lure that had been growing with every touch of his hand on Terry's flesh. He could feel the life pulsing slower in the dying teen, and knew that he had to have what was left for his own. Pushing the knife handle out of his way, Bill bit down hard into the soft, warm flesh of Terry's neck. Again the rush of heat, the ecstasy of orgasm, taste, life. He sucked the boy's last life, and when the flood lessened to a trickle, he began pounding the boy's torso, squeezing out the last drops into his own bloated belly.

After a time, it was done.

Bill sat back from the body as the fever receded in his brain. His stomach hung heavy and his whole body seemed suddenly weary. He wanted to lie down here, next to the battered corpse, and rest.

But no.

He shook his head, tried to clear his mind. The bodies would draw flies. And police. And he wanted neither near him. Pulling the remaining barrette from his body, he tossed it on the body, heaved himself to his feet, and shuffled back the way he had come, reaching his hotel room in the early hours of morning. He felt an odd discomfort as he collapsed on the bed, and reached to scratch his back. In moments he slipped into a coma-like sleep.

∞☉∞

Bill woke the following night with flies buzzing around his face. *How had they gotten in this room?* he wondered, lifting a hand to swat them away. The hand struck his face accidentally, and flopped back to the bed. He was getting stiff, he realized, and losing control of his muscles.

"I'm dead," he reminded himself aloud, but the words meant nothing. If he was dead, how could he be staring at the ceiling? How could he be swatting flies?

How could he have killed two boys?

He broke the thought but it came back anyway. He'd *killed* last night. Murdered! Lifting his hand again, he could see the dark stains of the boys' blood. He *had* had his revenge.

But if it had been heavenly at the moment of action, it didn't taste sweet anymore. It didn't taste at all. His mind cried with the enormity of his act. He had *killed* them both. Sucked the life from their bodies with his mouth. Whether they deserved it or not, their lives had not been his to take!

But the memory of the blood—and its effect on him—made his body shiver. He realized with a twinge of fear that he only wanted one thing: to kill again.

Rising slowly from the bed, he saw that he had stained the sheets with blood. It had pooled near his head and beneath his crotch. A thin smear of it seemed to cover the sheets, as if he'd sweated it out through every pore.

The mirror said he had. The single bathroom bulb reflected off a purpling face and dusky reddish chest. His entire body seemed drenched in blood. Its sight didn't leave him nauseous, as it would have but three days before. He did feel weak. And hungry. Or more accurately … thirsty.

Stepping into the shower, he saw that his feet and calves had purpled. His penis lay half erect atop truly blue balls. *Dead,* he reminded himself. Three days dead. He must stink. As he rinsed the blood sweat from his bruised body, he gulped water from the showerhead. It was an unconscious ritual, but as soon as he had, he knew it was a bad move. He could feel it slosh into his belly, gurgle through his intestines. And moments later, a pinkish stream dribbled from his dick. At the same time, a brown-black sludge began dripping from his backside. He could vaguely smell the foul stench of shit and rotting meat as his bowels released to the drain. This frightened him. What if these excretions continued? He would be forced to rot away in this room. He couldn't go out leaking sewage as he walked!

But the drainage soon stopped. Bill shut off the tap and dried himself. Then he dropped his clothes into the tub and began to scrub the bloodstains out. When at last he stopped wringing them, the stains were dulled. Though not completely obliterated, people would notice that he was wearing wet clothes before they'd see the stains on them. Luckily he'd been wearing jeans and a dark t-shirt on the night of his death. When wet, they hardly showed stains at all.

∞ ☉ ∞

The night was cool and quiet when Bill at last stepped onto the street from the dimly lit warrens of the cheap hotel. He should have been shivering in his wet clothes, but he wasn't. He could feel the cold, but it didn't affect him.

He walked, at first without direction. Images of the dead boys appeared unbidden in his mind. He angrily replaced them with the memory of his violated daughter, open-eyed and still on the morgue table. If he'd been alive, the battling emotions of the two visions would have led to tears. But he only blinked dryly.

He thought of the events that led to this: his own inaction, his wife's dismissal. *How could she cast him out after all they'd been through? How could he have let it get to the point where she wanted him to go?* He thought of the last time she had made love to him. As he'd settled into bed she had left one light on, and unbuttoned her blouse. Piece by piece, she'd dropped her clothing on the floor, not saying a word. He'd watched with growing interest, as the pink tips of her breasts grew taut and she stripped off her panties, as the kinky brown hair below her belly shifted, as she strode purposefully toward him across the room. Neither had spoken as she lowered herself upon him without foreplay. She had taken him hard, moved atop him brutally, and removed herself slowly when he had at last released a telltale groan.

And now she no longer wanted him in her house, let alone her bed.

He was angered, excited, lustful, thirsty. And he realized that he stood outside of his home. The lights were off; she was probably already asleep. Was she glad he did not snore beside her? Or had she regretted her words after the first night alone?

Quietly he eased open the screen door and tried his key. It still worked. The house was still, heavy. He moved through it slowly, not needing a light. How many times had he walked these halls, oblivious to life's fatal chasms yawning all around? Somehow, in the past few months, he'd fallen into all of them. His daughter murdered, his marriage in ruins, his life taken, and he himself had turned killer. As he passed the living room, he saw the dark square of the family portrait on the piano. *Those people don't exist anymore,* he thought, and stepped past.

Cheryl was asleep. He stood at the foot of the bed watching her chest move, hearing the soft hiss of her breathing. He touched his own chest, and felt the stillness there. He moved closer, could see the soft chestnut hair trailing across her cheek, could see the white of her teeth, as they touched, just barely, the warm blush of her lip. Could smell the heat of her blood pumping steadily through every artery, sending a reek of heady life through her pores. *This,* he could sense. With a trembling hand he touched her hair; she stirred.

The fire in his heart was growing again, feeding his anger at losing this, at losing her. This time he felt his fangs protruding, felt his erection at the nearness of bloody orgasm.

She turned on her back in her sleep, one nipple peeking seductively from the edge of the sheet. He leaned in to bite her, to steal her lifeblood. *Yes.* She should be even better to take than the boys. He would take her in lust and in love. As his teeth brushed her flesh, she murmured, "Bill?" in her sleep. Her voice was slurred, but seemed surprised and ... *happy?*

No!

From somewhere beyond the vampiric haze, Bill found the strength to throw his body to the floor beside the bed. He had killed the boys for revenge, and what pleasure did he have for it now? Guilt. They were rotten kids, but killing them had solved nothing. They had no chance to atone for their crime. And Lissa was still dead. *He* was still dead—in fact, probably rotting faster for their infusion.

If he stole Cheryl's life now ... Could she perhaps still find happiness, without him, without Lissa? Could he steal the chance from her, for a selfish moment of necrotic passion?

No! He rolled back and forth on the white carpet, inches from Cheryl, fighting back his instinct, struggling with his thirst. He could smell her, almost taste her. The nearness, the memories, the anticipation of her hot kisses, her hot blood! It was too much. His chest spasmed, his nose sucked air, just a breath. And from behind his drooping eyelids, a tear fell to stain the carpet red. In the morning, Cheryl would see it and wonder.

He took some fresh clothes from his closet, lingered a moment at her bed. "Goodbye," he whispered. "Be happy again." He went quickly then, to the only place he could think of to go. The alley by Ales Head Tavern.

"Lawrence?" he called into the dark narrow street. "Lawrence, are you here?"

There was no answer. Bill leaned against the brick back of an old store, slowly slid to the ground. Even the companionship of his killer was denied. He thought of the power of the bloodlust, felt it still, and forgave the bum for killing him. If it had been anyone but Cheryl, if he'd had an ounce less control, he would have killed tonight. He still might. But not her.

∞⊖∞

There was a shift, something sliding. The hollow metallic ring of the dumpster. From the shadow of the ancient alley, a lurching shape appeared. Even Bill's dead senses could smell the stench. The bloated man sunk to the street beside him. Bill could see the black and green slime that was once a face shivering, rippling. The figure reached a skeletal finger to its head, pried open its mouth. As the hand dropped, it scraped the shivering ooze of its cheek, releasing a stream of white, wriggling maggots. Bill cringed.

"Pretty, heh?" the bum gargled, almost unintelligibly. "Not long, not long now. Had your revenge?"

"Yeah," Bill whispered. "And yes, the price is too high."

"Going to … " Lawrence choked, spat a stringy stream to the ground. "Going to give someone else the chance?"

"No," Bill replied firmly.

They sat silent for a while, occasionally kicking at rats which tried to steal the meat of their decaying, yet still animated flesh.

"Tell me," Bill said suddenly. "How did you … get taken? How many did you kill?"

Lawrence's sagging, rippling face turned toward Bill. One eye glinted whitely in the streetlight. The other socket appeared empty. "Tell me first; will you drink again?"

"How can I not?"

Lawrence's head shook stiffly, sadly.

"The more you take, the faster you'll go."

∞⊖∞

The echo of an Ales Head Tavern barkeep bellowing "last call" lingered over the alley as two rotting vampires quietly fought their thirsts and began to share the night with stories of when they were alive.

The taste was as bittersweet as blood.

-The New Racism-
JAMES NEWMAN

The more things change, the more they stay the same.
Old saying, source unknown.

"Momma, I'm scared." Little Cecil's sandpaper voice came at her from the gathering darkness, startling her out of her reverie.

She looked at him, her eyes wet. The poor child—it wasn't fair. He had seen things, such horrible things, been through more pain and terror than most people *ten times* his age.

He was only five.

Again, from across the single room of the dilapidated shack she had chosen for their home: "Momma, I'm scared." A sniffle. "They're comin' ... ain't they, Momma? Them bad men are comin' for us."

In the dim light of the room she could barely see more than the whites of little Cecil's big brown eyes. His Papa's eyes.

She swallowed loudly, fidgeted with the bottom of her ragged dress.

"Yeah, honey," she finally whispered, her voice like silk. "They're comin'. But don't you worry none, baby ... I ain't gonna let nothin' happen to you."

In the quiet of the night, she could hear his stomach growl. It broke her heart.

"I don't understand why they hate us so bad, Momma," he intoned with that knowledge far beyond his years that always made her so proud. "We ain't never hurt nobody."

"No, honey," she replied, a bit ambiguously. "Not us."

He scooted closer to her in the dark, the bark of his rotten chair sounding a bit too loud on the hardwood floor below. She flinched, but did not scold him.

Off in the distance, past the chorus of crickets just beginning their nocturnal songs outside, she could hear them coming. Closer.

The bad men.

And a few women, too.

With their torches. Their crosses. Their off-white hoods and cloaks to hide their hideous bigot faces.

She fidgeted in her seat, balled her slender hands into fists. She wondered if these were the same men who had killed Uncle Virgil and Aunt Emma only last week. Or maybe those whose burning cross had spread from Cousin Reese's lawn into the new house he had worked so hard to build …

Reese and his wife and precious baby Sarah … a mixing of the races *their* side had deemed "unholy."

Self-righteous bastards. She gnashed her teeth, swore she'd see them all in Hell.

She sometimes wondered if they didn't realize *they* had *lost* the 'War! Or perhaps they did know, they just refused to acknowledge the fact.

"Payback tiiiiiime!" that one hillbilly with the birthmark on his face and the Confederate Flag on his cap and the rotgut rye on his breath had cackled so evilly as he slaughtered little Cecil's poor Papa.

("STRING 'IM UP!!!")

She remembered it as if it had happened only yesterday—though Cecil was merely a toddler then—remembered that vile, laughing man with his redneck war cries and his misguided views of "the Lord's Work."

"I kin hear 'em, Momma," Cecil said now, and suddenly he was in her arms. She exhaled sharply beneath his weight, could feel his tears upon her bosom and his frantic, tribal heartbeat beating in synch with her own.

"They're gettin' closer," he said. "Shouldn't we go now, Momma?"

She held him tight—a bit too tight, perhaps, but then he didn't seem to mind—as she watched the sun complete its fiery descent beyond the Great Smokey Mountains.

"Yes," she said softly. "Any minute now."

He didn't argue. He never did. Little Cecil knew the routine.

The night grew darker. The chill grew bolder. And the voice of the mob grew louder. Across the valley she could already see the angry glow of their burning crosses, their torches … she could even make out specific words and phrases now as they gradually drew closer and closer.

Racial slurs. Epithets. Cruel, cruel names they had chosen long ago for her people.

Words that hurt even more than the Clan's cheap array of weapons.

Weapons like …

Crucifixes. Plundered from local churches, or more often than not just two crooked oak branches nailed together in haste.

Garlic. Grown in abundance in their own sloppy gardens behind white trash trailers and shanties.

Holy water. Blessed by a priest who sometimes traveled with them, carried in flasks made from the bellies of their prey.

She took a deep breath now, wiped her eyes.

"You ready, honey?" she said at last, so pretty in the wash of the moon through the window.

He looked up at her, nodded but said nothing. My, how he loved his Momma.

She stood. He stood. Their eyes locked.

Cecil smiled.

And then the *Change* began.

Leathery bat-wings burst forth from olive flesh; bodies became furry and small. A bit of pain, but not too much, as bones popped and snapped and shrank. As teeth grew to curved razor-fangs and the frightened voices of mother and son—the hunted—transformed into the high-pitched squeals of night hunters. They took to the air as one, two soaring silhouettes against the night's full moon, one considerably larger than the other but both with the same burning crimson eyes.

Searching eyes … *hungry* eyes.

The eyes of *monsters*, some would say. Goddamned *fang-heads* who didn't deserve to live, who oughta just go back where they came from.

And so they did, mother and son. They left that place.

But first there was the matter of finding food, sustenance.

Then a new place to stay before dawn.

-Banalica-
MICHAEL LAIMO

I remember the very first time Juan-Carlos and I made acquaintance nearly fifteen years ago, when the mission first broke ground in Haslet, south of Baja. Father Sandi, head chaplain at my current post at *St. Aquinas of Mercy*, informed me of my transfer to oversee the final stages of growth at the new mission, *Our Lady of Hacel*.

Our Lady of Hacel was a modest tabernacle, erected in most proper fashion at the center of the quaint southern township, and I had been elected to assume all oversight of the sect. I believe the good Lord had been looking over me that day, granting my lifelong wishes to become a father of community. It had been perhaps the most glorious day in my career.

Juan-Carlos was the first to approach me the day I set foot in the new church. I remember the event so clearly, the gleam of the freshly polished pews reflecting the yellowish light from above onto his cloth-draped shoulders as I quietly paced down the center aisle—my aisle—for the very first time. He smiled and approached me with great open arms, and I had felt so dearly welcome at this start of my days at *Hacel*.

From that point on Juan-Carlos played a very special role in my life. Every day for fifteen years, through sickness and all, he made certain to welcome my entrance into the anteroom prior to mass, cloaking my neck with blessed rosaries, kissing the cross before draping them, crossing himself upon completion of the light ritual. He hadn't missed a day in fifteen years, had always been there for me, a true inspiration, and I in turn had become dependent to his waiting pretense as if God Himself had placed him there as a gift to ensure a cloak of sanctuary.

How badly his unanticipated absence one day then tore my soul to shreds, and I experienced great difficulty proceeding through the service that followed, my hands trembling so badly that it became an anguish to simply place the host upon the tongues of the worshipers.

Following what was perhaps my least inspired performance, I unexpectedly located him as I entered my quarters. "Miguel," he greeted me, his voice solemn, preoccupied. I turned and found him seated at the chair I kept alongside my only window, the same chair I sit in daily to contemplate the possible evils in the world and how I might stifle their influence upon the faithful people. He gazed into the wooded area just beyond the quartered panes of glass, and I knew at that moment, a voice in my mind told me, that Juan-Carlos would be leaving the mission.

"What does the sun tell you today, Juan-Carlos?" As a philosopher, he gazed often into the day and night skies seeking logic in the exertions of the world. When speaking of the world, he never offered to reveal his travails even though I knew his principles at times suffered from great misunderstandings.

He placed his fingertips upon the glass. *"El Sol ... "* he said, his breath fraught with fear, a patch of condensation forming upon a single pane. "He is wearied, but continues to struggle." I walked to the window and peered out. The sun was strong and vibrant, the woods bright and glorious. In this proximity, I looked for the first time into Juan-Carlos' face and saw tears streaming down his cheeks.

I knew not what troubled him, and dared not ask, allowing the brave man to work out his inner evils on his own. A confession I never solicited, only accepted if offered, and this day Juan-Carlos did not seek my counsel. He left not an hour later, placing the rosary around my neck and kissing me on my cheek before hoisting a single bag around his shoulder and departing on foot.

The mystery of his sudden departure ate at me for weeks. My confidence as a man of the cloth waned, and I wondered with great sadness how I had failed my best friend. I held his picture close to my heart at night in prayer for an answer to his deciding to leave—with great dismay I pondered the possibility of him deciding to leave the church altogether; the thought of which tore me to shreds. However, somewhere deep inside my soul I felt this to be an unlikelihood.

Yes I realize that I, as a holy man, see the world through much different eyes than most—eyes filled with an unbalanced mix of uncertainty and optimism. The world holds many different types of people, those that love me, those that hate me, all those including myself fragile human beings with no true understanding of life as it should be understood. We breathe, eat, love, hate, desire, and we act out on our feelings in effort to appease the hankerings in our souls and the word of God.

This, I truly believed, is what Juan-Carlos had done.

St. Hugh of Lincoln in Taos fifty miles north of here acknowledged my petition and graciously initiated the transfer of a deacon by the name of Tomas. Tomas arrived six days later and briefly announced his presence at my parsonage, desiring a rest before attending confessional in the afternoon. I placed him in Juan-Carlos' empty residence. In doing this I perhaps resigned myself to the fact that Juan-Carlos would not be returning after all, even though I knew in my heart that the moment he left, his presence would never grace my church again.

Less than an hour later, Tomas returned to my door, his knocks urgent, almost burning. Although I had no acquaintance of the man and his traits, I knew that something was amiss.

"Yes Tomas? What ails you?" His face carried beads of sweat, his features drawn downward in a mask of consternation. He looked much different than the man occupying my room just a short while earlier.

He paced the room in circles, shaking his head, and I wondered for a moment if Tomas was burdened with personal troubles that I had not been made aware of. "I … I found something in the rectory."

My heart pressed against my ribcage with apprehension for whatever secret he had suddenly unearthed in Juan-Carlos' quarters perhaps held an indication to his hasty departure. I guided Tomas to my chair, the one by the window, and asked him to sit, in which he did, however tentatively. I kneeled alongside him and placed a hand on his shoulder. It was hot and damp, rigid with tension. It was then that he reached into his shirt pocket and handed me a sheet of yellowed parchment. I unfolded it and viewed a handwritten note penned in nervously shaken script. It had been addressed to Juan-Carlos:

Dear Juan-Carlos:
It is with great hesitation and trepidation that I must contact you, but I foresee no other option at this time. God's grace has never failed to shroud you, and it is

now that I must plead for your endowed blessings. Please hear my words, accepting them as truth and nothing else, for you are my only prayer.

Banalica has succumbed to a great evil, and those unfortunate enough to have crossed its path have perished. Our crude fight, albeit a courageous one, has proved to be futile, and we now hide from its unrelenting grasp, relying on faith alone to deliver us from sure and certain death. I dare not reveal the true source of this evil that has invaded our tiny villa for fear that you will translate these messy writings as the ramblings of a madman. But I assure you I have not surrendered to any disease, be it mentally or bodily. We, the people of Banalica, are dwindling, and your empowerment of God is our only last hope, dear brother. Many have fled Banalica's domain (with success I can not answer), many have perished, and those beyond the perimeter of evil have remained at a distance, for any man without the dignity of the Lord's blessings would dare not step foot in this town again.

Please dear brother, return to Banalica and aid us in our battle against this evil.

And brother, this is my third attempt in reaching you. I will try five times, at which time if I do not hear from you I will assume the worst has happened.

Your brother,
Roberto

I read the letter twice, leaning upon the deacon's shoulder for support. I felt hit hard, and I could not fathom what this terrible evil could be. Evil rears its ugly head in many forms, in many potential menaces, plague, famine, disease, the list runs endlessly. Yet it still delivers an aftermath that affects all in its path with a similar burden: death.

A bitter tear ran from my eye, a lump of indignation forming in my throat. Juan-Carlos should have shared this plea from his brother with me! He should have beseeched my support! Now to sit here mute and speculate on the situation would be time and energy wasted. I would have to join my friend in his plight to extinguish this possible bane in order to appease my soul.

I would have to go to Banalica.

∞☉∞

I waited until the following morning before leaving Haslet, as I knew the journey to Banalica would take much of the day and I wished not to arrive by moonlight. I traveled south for nearly three hours on a bus crowded with locals. The ride seemed agonizingly long, spent in sweat, and I read Roberto's letter over and over again to pass the time. I listened to the starving babies aboard wailing for their mothers' milk, swatted mosquitoes and flies, and watched the remaining passengers shake along in their tattered clothes and ripeness. When my stop finally arrived, the joints in my legs cracked and popped as I stood to depart the bus in the town of Cocina.

Cocina's streets bustled, the center of trade for the inland villas. It sat beneath the boiling sun upon a stretch of land that ran for nearly three miles along the coast. The entire length had been built up greatly over the years, incorporating nearly every provisional trade imaginable. I had visited here on other occasions, so the scene was familiar: piers jutting out into the waters, fishing vessels unloading their catches for the day. Chickens frenzied in their coops awaiting fate, squawking in the neck-grips of their purchasers. Side-street vendors peddling their fruits and vegetables for a few coins to purchase drinking water or a few pounds of meat. And now and then, a car would race by, a wooden wagon in tow, clouds of dust spraying up from the wheels in whorling clouds, coming to rest on the dirty children playing in the streets.

It was here in Cocina that I hoped to find transportation to Banalica.

I immediately gathered that the presence of a holy man here in Cocina was a rarity, given the stares I elicited from most of those whose paths I crossed. I smiled periodically, nodding and moving for ten minutes through the marketplace until I locked gazes with a black man who leaned against a car that looked as if it had been left to die in the street.

"Good day," I said approaching him.

He offered a curt nod, nothing else. Sweat ran from his pores in rivulets.

I wasted no time. "Can you supply me with transportation? I will pay handsomely."

He grinned, exposing a mouth of empty spaces and brown rotting teeth that jutted from his gums like tree stumps. His gums bled red, a sharp contrast to his wet purple-black skin. "To Banalica?" he asked, eyebrows raised in question.

I felt a sharp twist of discomfort in my gut, and I remembered what Roberto had said in his letter, that those beyond the perimeter of evil had remained at a distance, that any man without the dignity of the Lord's blessings would dare not step foot in the town. I at once assumed that this man knew something of the evil Roberto wrote of.

"How is it that you know where I wish to go?" I asked him.

He folded his arms in a defensive posture, as if I carried a disease. "Many men of the cloth have traveled from great distances to go to Banalica. But none have returned. Only one *padre* remains in our house of God, and he has learned a valuable lesson from the *padres* that have tried to rescue those rumored to still be untouched in the villa. Banalica is an evil place, and those who enter bow down to the devil, never to return."

He remained silent after that, closing his eyes in thought. I was trying to make sense of his statements when he said, "I will take you to within two miles of the villa. From there you can follow the road into town. It will cost you."

We agreed on a price and rode in silence. The ride was long and the old vehicle did not handle the rough terrain very well. It shook along harshly, and I felt pains in my buttocks. I wanted dearly to solicit information from the black man, but he remained in prayer for the entire journey, lips trembling, undecipherable mumblings escaping his lips. Between his palm and the steering wheel a rosary dangled, half its beads missing. In my pocket I gripped Roberto's' letter, the sweat from my hand dampening the stale parchment. I closed my eyes and tried to sleep, but thoughts of evil kept my mind and body at bay.

∞☉∞

We arrived two hours later at a nondescript spot where the brush grew thickly at roadside and the jungle towered just beyond its perimeter.

The man continued to pray, shaking presumably with great fear, and I hesitated speaking to him for fear of interrupting his invocations. But I had no choice, as the day was getting late and I needed to move on.

"Where do I go from here?" I gently asked.

He quieted, quite abruptly in fact, then said, "Straight ahead, about a mile and a half, this path will lead you into town. You must go now." Not once had he looked at me throughout our journey, and he continued to lead his gaze away even in this conversation. I paid him and exited the car saying thank you, but received no acknowledgement. The car hastily kicked dirt up in my face as it turned around and sped back towards Cocina. I watched the car until it disappeared from my sights, then turned and began my walk to Banalica.

∞⊖∞

The dense growth flanking the roadsides had begun to clear some time later. I lost track of time but had kept a steady pace throughout, and by the looks of the sun I still had another hour before dusk. The jungle finally cleared and I saw a small ranch at the forefront of an open road. Two modest sized dwellings sat next to one another and looked out over a fenced area. It was here that I beheld a daunting sight.

Apparently the ranch had been a chicken farm, and I say *had been* because the chickens here were nothing more than withered feathers and decayed skin laced over splintered bone fragments. If it weren't for the few feathers swaying in the late afternoon breeze, the casual eye would have had a difficult time identifying the animals these bones once defined. Although thousands of tiny bones lay about the weeds and dirt within the fenced pen, a great many had been intricately woven together to form grotesque gargoyle-like creatures, one atop each fence post at the side of the road. I paced to one and saw that the creator of these hideous models had taken great pains to construct them, as the bones were sewn together with strands of steel-meshed wiring from the coop. They served an appropriate welcome to the evil that was rumored to thrive here. I crossed myself and continued on.

The next thirty minutes had me passing similar sights, tiny ranches whose cultivations had succumbed to some hideous butchery, the livestock—cattle, goats, more chickens—slaughtered and maimed in such a fashion that I had difficulty fathoming the nightmarish sights as plausible in this waking world. Stakes had been erected, the heads of goats, speared and staring at me through blackened worm-ridden eyes. Cows gutted, shreds of distended bellies giving way to fetuses long dried beneath the sun's rays. I had great fears of suddenly wanting to turn back, but forced myself to press on as the tiny structures of Banalica's community were now within my sights.

Banalica was small, its inhabitants numbering less than two hundred. Each civilian worked to simply live, farming for food and making trips into Cocina to trade for luxuries such as fish and fruit.

Here in this stretch, shanties stood alongside a lone dirt road, housing perhaps four or five inhabitants apiece. An open-air meeting place constructed of wooden beams and benches centered the town, and towards the end of the road by the outgrowth of the jungle, the church.

I stared hopefully at the much larger structure, but the uncomfortable silence here set alarm to me. Nothing but the wind stirred, and unlike the jungle where birds chirped and monkeys howled, Banalica slept, basked in stillness.

My thoughts came too soon, for something in the jungle discharged a terrible shriek, very loud, very long.

I nearly passed out from the start of the unexpected cry, and my body shook like a bundle of wires charged with high voltage. It went on and on; I wondered how a pair of human lungs could sustain such a bellow. I kissed the cross at my neck, and then the sound ended just as precipitously as it started.

I realized suddenly that night was quickly pouring in, the sun dropping down behind the cloak of the jungle. I picked up my pace even though my legs ached badly, and approached the front of the church. I took the four steps leading to the entrance, peering behind me one last time before entering, swearing to my Lord that I thought I saw a great black shadow moving in the trees just beyond the perimeter of the jungle.

I entered the church. Darkness virtually enveloped the interior as I passed the threshold, and if not for the candles and kerosene lamps alight at the altar, I would have presumed this town to be deserted. I paced slowly up the center aisle, crude wooden pews carved from tree trunks at either sides of me. A series of bowed heads came into view at the first two rows, and I smelled something overly ripened, like rotting vegetables.

"Hello?" I quietly called, and the heads turned. There were a few sharp moans; apparently I had caused some alarm. A single figure rose up, and I paced forward thinking at first that it was Juan-Carlos, but realized quite soon that the individual only merely resembled my lost friend.

His brother. Roberto.

"Miguel?"

Although we had never made acquaintance, he recognized me, perhaps from photos Juan-Carlos had sent over the years. "I found your letter Roberto. In Juan-Carlos' room."

The younger brother bowed his head. Looking to the ground he asked, "How long has it been since my brother left?"

Immediately I felt a great trepidation, an ache in my pounding heart, and the prospects I had forewarned myself of during my travels here may have actually arisen.

Juan-Carlos never made it.

I walked over and hugged Roberto and he began to cry. As his tears soaked up in the fabric of my shirt, I gazed over his shoulder towards the others. No more than twenty people, they contemplated me with empty eyes and forlorn expressions. I saw great amounts of suffering written on their faces, each undoubtedly witness to perils distressing beyond any imagination.

Perhaps evil had indeed assumed control of Banalica.

In what form, I needed to find out.

Roberto controlled his anguish and pulled away. In his teary face I saw a man whose most recent days had been spent in agony, a messy beard covering half his emaciated features; puffy black circles like half moons beneath soulless eyes.

"What has happened here, Roberto? Where are the rest of the townsfolk?"

"They are dead," he said forcefully, then grabbed my arm and added, "Come with me, Miguel."

He led me away from the others, leaving them to resume their prayers, and we sat in a pew a few rows back. "Nighttime has fallen," he said turning his gaze to the ceiling twelve feet above. "He will soon show himself, and you will see for yourself."

At once I associated his statement with those ramblings present in the letter that had brought me here, and I wondered regrettably if his written denial of being a madman might actually hold some truth. "*Who* will be here?"

He gripped my wrist, his bony fingers tight and hot on my skin. Sweat fell from his brow. "Dear Miguel, evil has risen in the jungle, and it has assumed control of Banalica. I am fearful to reveal the truth to you, as you may reject it as an invention of madness."

"Please … " I met his eyes with as much integrity as I could.

Then, he spoke. "Not one month ago, Banalica was a thriving community. We were happy. Suddenly the mutilations came, and all our animals within a week's time were dead. It wasn't until our people were victimized did we realize our true predicament." He paused for a moment, then confessed. "Miguel, I find no other explanation to give you other than ... the evil from the jungle, it comes in the form of a ... a *vampire*."

His last word came out as a whisper and my mouth dropped, but no reply came forth. I wanted to question his radical conclusion, but then I envisioned the slaughtered animals at the ranches, the bone-sculptures, and my tongue momentarily froze.

He continued, hands shaking wildly, tears flowing. "Many of our people have been snatched away into the jungle, I have seen it with my very own tired eyes. Some have attempted to flee, by morning, and I make no assumption as to how many have been successful in their plight for escape. Apparently it seems one has, as the letter you've received can attest. I've sent five letters with people who've chosen to brave the jungle on foot. So far only one letter has returned, with you."

I was about to force words from my mouth—anything that might humor the man—simply because I had difficulties deciding whether I should believe or doubt these frightened people shielding themselves within the church's armor, but I was cut short by a harsh scraping noise coming from above. Terror instantly struck me, not from the noise but from the shrieks of horror spewing from the mouths of all those cowering in the first two pews. Their shrieks quickly gave way to quiet apprehension—an apprehension of knowing that the possibility of death awaited them just beyond the frail walls of their shelter.

"Do not worry, we are safe here," Roberto said weakly, his confidence clearly overcome by fear. "He waits, tempts us, will scratch at the walls all night. But as long as you do not succumb to his hypnotizing beckon, you will live to see the morning."

The scratching grew louder, as if someone were attacking the roof with sharp knives. The curiosity of it had me in its grasp, and I wanted to investigate its source, despite Roberto's claims. The stench of garlic assaulted my senses, taking over the ripe odor of unclean bodies, and I looked over to see the townspeople donning themselves with roped cloves.

I felt somewhat incensed at this action, these people's brains being washed with folklore and not necessarily the truth of their real torment. "Roberto, whatever that is above our heads (the scraping had grown to a point where it began to daze me, and amidst it I thought I heard something purring), the reek of garlic is no serious defense. Faith and commonsense is what these people need! Stamina!

Not fairy tale logic!" My voice had turned to yells, and all eyes were set upon me. Above, the purrs had grown to grating, low-toned growls.

And the scraping went on and on and on.

"People! This is nonsense!" I yelled, somewhat in denial of the events suddenly taking place, also to distract myself from those terrible nails (I envisioned in my mind that the source of the noise above could very well be fingernails ... thick dirty yellowed fingernails) splintering the wood above our heads. I launched myself from my seat and set foot down the center aisle to the doors, much to the discouragement of the people, who outwardly voiced their concerns.

"You'll die out there!"

"Stay in here! He won't come in!"

"Come back!"

And there were more, many more, and they probably held validity, but I ignored them, determined to make sense of this so-called evil in Banalica. I reached the threshold when Roberto grabbed my arm.

"Whatever you do Miguel, do not look into his eyes."

I almost scoffed at his request, writing it off to yet another whim of folklore, but the seriousness in his eyes nearly had me in a trance, and I simply nodded, opened the door, and moved outside into the night.

At once a thrust of cold wind swept past me and slammed the door behind me. I stayed motionless on the top step, peering about the deserted town. The trees from the jungle sang, their leaves in concert with the wind. Circles of dirt flew up, and I instantly realized that the town was remarkably arid for such a temperate environment.

Then, just above and behind me, I heard the scraping.

Scrape ... scrape ... scrape ...

Each one sharp and long against the wooden exterior of the church, piercing my senses to a point where I felt as if they were cutting into my skin. Cowering a bit in fear of what I might find, I spun and saw the thing Roberto had spoke of. The vampire.

Perhaps not six feet away, the thing bounced and writhed on the edge of the roof above me, a man—or what used to be a man—with snow-white hair and ancient eyes whose sickly yellow corneas and black pupils stared pure evil at me. I swallowed hard as I found myself staring at this creature, this creature who looked older than time itself yet fidgeted with a kind of horrid, obscene glee, choking lunatic sniggers at me through rows of razor sharp fangs, spanning a formidable pair of tenuous milky wings from its back that propelled their dark winds in my direction. Its taloned feet gripped the eave firmly, pointed-clawed hands twisting and dancing in the air, mesmerizing me.

At once, ever so slowly, it descended upon me ...

My body was yanked away, back into the church. The door slammed behind me and Roberto was there, arms wrapped tightly around me. He held me like that for a few tense moments, then slapped my face as tears began to flow from my eyes. He pulled me further away from the door, and I stumbled along with him, feeling my hypnotic lethargy slowly slipping away. I realized with great dismay the peril I had just exposed myself to. Dear God, I had been tranced! I looked into its eyes just as Roberto told me not to, those terrible glaring eyes, and nearly fell victim to its evil, just as he said I would!

When my legs found their balance, Roberto led me to the altar where I sat and gathered my senses, trying so hard to get the image of those horrible demon-eyes out of my mind.

My strength soon returned, so did my lucidness, and I sat thinking, trying to conjure up a solution to this terrifying predicament—a plan that would grant myself and the people of Banalica freedom from evil.

My mind worked all night, and the scratching went on and on and on ...

∞⊖∞

The night itself lasted forever.

∞⊖∞

The scratching stopped moments before the sun appeared. During the night, Roberto and I had gathered all the supplies we needed to carry out our strategy. We used the two kerosene lamps from the altar to see our way into Roberto's quarters at the back of the church where we located a bundle of rags, a jug of kerosene, used for the lamps, and luckily enough, an old wooden bed in which we were able to rend the legs into a few sturdy slabs.

"I do not possess the *bravado* to approximate myself for such a lancing," Roberto said fearfully, but I ignored him and his belief in folklore.

We carried the supplies out front where I tied a rag about the end of one of the legs from the bed. I kept thinking back to my coming face-to-face with the so-called vampire, and although the dreadful sight of the monster had had me mesmerized, I still refused to believe in any movie-induced pretense, merely blaming the sheer horridness of the monster for my inaction last night. "Listen to me close," I said. "No more folklore. Throw away your garlic. We are not to stake the creature through the heart, even though I'm sure it would indeed kill it, as it would any man. Tonight we keep our distance."

"Then how are we to accomplish such a task, Miguel?"

I grinned for the first time since I arrived here. "We find its lair and burn it."

∞☉∞

About an hour after sunrise one of the townspeople—a young burly man named Jorge—Roberto, and myself, set out into the jungle with all our tools in hand. We commenced north into the trees opposite the church, as my faint sighting of something dark there when I first entered the church yesterday had me deciding that it was in this direction we should be looking. The hours swept by us in our search, and the day had almost been surrendered to futility when Roberto called out.

"Miguel! Come see!"

In truth I had hoped our search would end unsuccessfully, for by this time my stomach yearned for food, and my muscles had tired. I followed his voice and found him and Jorge crouched near a small cave that had been crudely camouflaged with leaves. At the entrance a wash of blood served as its welcome mat.

"It may be an animal's lair, perhaps an aardvark," Roberto said.

"We'll investigate this spot, but carefully." In truth I had a bad feeling about this place, but did not wish to say anything until after we went in. We doused the ragged ends of the bed-legs and lit our torches. Jorge led the way, followed by Roberto and myself. We had to crouch to enter and walked nearly ten yards through a narrow passage guided solely by flame-light before we came into a clearing, signifying to us that indeed, we had found the lair of the vampire.

First I saw the bones, hundreds of them connected together not unlike the animal bones I saw at the ranch upon my arrival in Banalica. They too had been intricately meshed to form a great sculpture of some evil mind that ran nearly ten feet high and just as wide, situated at the center of the subterranean chamber.

It was constructed of human bones, skulls and ribs and arms and legs and all.

I shuddered at the sight and felt my skin ripple. My hunger dissipated and gave way to nausea. I tried to reassert my beliefs in the one God, the Holy Ghost, but somehow for the first time in all my years as a man of the cloth I had difficulty simply conjuring heavenly thoughts. Indeed this was place of evil.

Slowly we paced around the sculpture, peering warily about. The underground chamber was quite large, and we saw situated at the rear the existence of two additional caves. Nodding to each other, we decided to stay together, our torches leading the way into the cave on the right.

The dancing flames revealed to us an empty room no larger than the one behind us: dirt walls, roots escaping from within, grubs falling all over. I glanced around thinking we had found nothing of concern here until Jorge stifled a scream.

I turned around and saw the man looking up, a twisted look of fear and revulsion painted on his face. Both Roberto and I followed his upturned gaze and immediately set our sights on the vampire, the same creature I had encountered last night, hanging upside down from the ceiling. It looked like a shadow in this dark place, the torchlights reflecting from its body in cinematic flashes, its clawed feet gripping a wooden beam running from wall to wall, its great wings enshrouding its entire body except at the feet—just like a bat.

"Damn," I muttered, staring up at the thing, my thoughts suddenly lost to a cloud of confusion: *is it human? Or animal? Or is it really a ...*

"Miguel ... " Roberto shook me with one hand, but I could only shake my head in denial at what I was seeing. "You must be strong!"

Nothing held more truth at the moment and I nodded, trying desperately to grasp my emotions. Yes, indeed I needed to be strong, but I also knew it would be no easy feat as I felt mesmerized simply contemplating the slumbering monster.

At that moment I realized Jorge was no longer with us. "Roberto, where is Jorge?"

"He moved off to investigate the other room."

We waited a moment in assumption that Jorge would quickly return. We had located the demon that had spent the past month terrorizing the people of Banalica, and felt no reason to look further. But when the time passed, and Jorge remained absent, we both moved to seek him out.

We exited silently from the antechamber of the vampire and paced over to the adjacent cave. In the back of my mind I kept reminding myself that from all our travels today it was growing late, and I wanted to put our plan into action before darkness took over, and the vampire awoke.

When we entered the second room, I wasn't quite sure what in God's name I was looking at. But then, as the ensuing events unfolded, the horrible truth reared its ugly head.

This room ran much larger than the first, perhaps twice the size. At its center and trailing all the way to the rear wall was a nesting of what I could only interpret as cocoons: white, bulbous egg-like spheres, perhaps fifty or more of them, united together in a sticky conglomeration of fluids and solids. Some of them, the larger ones at the forefront of the mass, had begun to hatch, and from within more vampire-beasts emerged, heads ensconced in a layering of something viscous, their papery wings still wet and newborn, not yet feasible for flight.

I'll continue by saying that Jorge was dead. Well, perhaps not dead yet, but in the process of being taken alive. One of the hatchlings in front had Jorge in its grasp, razored claws rooted into his shoulders, sharp fangs buried deeply into a great tear in his neck; hence we heard no scream, as it had bitten away his vocal chords. Jorge's legs shot straight out in front of him like two planks, kicking up wildly as if electricity were running through them. And then the blood—so much of it, covering his mask of death and the mask of life of his attacker.

Roberto took an angry step forward and began screaming in Spanish, and this time, I held *him* back.

Thinking of my plan, I looked around and realized with horror that it was Jorge who had held the half-filled jug of kerosene. But it was nowhere near him—not that I could ever venture close to the horrifying scene to retrieve it.

"Here!" I heard Roberto scream, and I saw him dart back towards the entrance where the container sat; Jorge had placed it down before approaching the vampire ovum. He immediately ran to the egg-collective and started splashing the fuel all over them, tossing the container back and forth in a heave-ho manner.

At once great screams echoed from the eggs, and they all began to tear open, quickly now, each and every Goddamned one releasing its very own vampiric beast. Albino-like, tenebrous, coated in embryonic wetness. Flattened wings, busily working their way free from their prisons into the new world.

Roberto finished spraying the fuel and I walked over, holding my torch, preparing to set it down. But then something caught my eye and I froze.

One of the emerging vampires, freshly broken free from its milky shell, was staring at me.

I felt my heart drop to my feet, heavy in pain. It was Juan-Carlos. Or what used to be him. "Lord have mercy," I managed. "My dear friend, taken by evil." The words came automatically as I stood there rooted watching my dear friend of fifteen years raise up and spread his wings out, a near six-foot span, and then launch a deafening roar along with the rest of the beasts: all of the missing people of Banalica.

Roberto had been wrong. The people of Banalica had not perished. They had found new life.

So *I* would be the one to put them to death, I thought, and placed the torch to the kerosene-drenched collective.

I watched with awe as it went up in great flames.

Screams erupted, pain, agony, bedlam, all evil things gone to hell and back, collected here in one single mass. I shielded my eyes as the flames multiplied, enveloping all the newborn vampires, watching in awe as their wings melted away. And then their fresh skins, sliding away from their bodies, and I held my breath as green smoke rose and the stench of sulfur filled the room. And through it all, I saw Juan Carlos' face staring at me, staring at Roberto, and it seemed to me that he was pleading for mercy, begging for our forgiveness.

I tossed my torch into the fire, forgetting all along my true purpose for coming here.

It was standing behind us as we turned around to leave.

The *great* vampire, the mother of all invention, looming over us, freshly awakened from a day of slumber only to find us—two priests—in its lair, burning its children. I tried desperately for prayer but found no words of faith to break through my mortal fear. Roberto and I stood close awaiting the worst: our deaths.

The vampire howled a shrill so loud my ears popped and I at once went deaf. I expected it to immediately trance us with its yellow gaze, take us for its children, and I watched its scowling visage in assumption that no other alternative existed for me. But then it turned its head, shielding itself with its wings. Still howling.

Then I realized.

The fire. It was afraid of the bright fire.

Roberto still held his torch. He thrust it toward the vampire and it cowered, staggering backwards, wings turned. It staggered back through the cave and we pursued, realizing its vulnerability, chasing it out into the night where we saw it take flight like a giant bat, sending its dark wind into our faces as we stood by the cave's entrance.

Smoke filtered out behind us and we quickly made our way back through the jungle into Banalica.

With the assistance of the townsfolk, we built a bonfire outside the church and spent the night there, watching the skies for the flying creature, knowing deep inside that Banalica would now be safe from harm's way.

∞☉∞

It has been six months since my experience in Banalica. I have relocated my plight of God to Cocina, where many of its *padres* have perished in attempt to rescue the faithful from evil.

With Roberto at my side, we wait—wait for word of some other villa that has been absorbed by evil.

And then, in the memory of Juan-Carlos, we will fight again.

-Window Across The Street-
JAY CASELBERG

Her window stands across the street, framed by white wood, by bricks, fawn shaded in the dimming evening light. Curtains are there, half-closed. A gentle breeze stirs them back and forth. The same breeze moves a tree branch and the leaves sway to and fro, occasionally obscuring then revealing the shadowed space beyond. My eyes are sensitive to every twitch of movement in the same way my cat's ears dart at every sound—like radar. Sometimes he sits with me as I watch and I stroke him gently from head to tail, my cat, my long time companion.

Late at night, across the street, she closes the curtains, chequered, glowing dimly in the darkness. Half-formed man shapes move behind them, and I can but imagine what goes on in there, in that private place shuttered from the world. She leaves the window open, but the curtains closed. The breeze sometimes parts the cloth tantalizingly, revealing the barest sliver of the space beyond.

She always looks before closing them, across the darkened street, glancing up before letting the hair fall across her face, a cascade of blond, as if she does not know. The lingering glance before she drops her gaze sets my heart pounding and dries my mouth. I speak to her then, my lips forming words, but no phrases come. The wind and the gentle rumble of my cat sitting beside me are the only sounds to break the stillness.

Winter will be upon us soon. The leaves will drop from the tree, leaving the branches to scrape at the sky, but revealing larger gaps that I can see between. Sometimes she wears a red silk robe, gilded dragons worked with fine embroidery at the shoulders. It's interesting, that choice of dragons. As she walks across her room the robe drifts behind her, flowing in her passage. She never bothers to tie it closed. With winter, I wonder if she will. So then, with the tantalizing gaps within my viewpoint made larger by the season's passing, I might see less instead of more. That would be rich irony. But I believe she will not allow that to happen. Perhaps she'll close the window to retain the warmth.

I discovered her by accident, one day as I sat on the edge of my bed, leaning down to tie my shoes. A flutter at the limits of my vision drew my gaze. It was only a brief flash, but it was enough, enough to draw me to the window's edge. I stood, using a finger to open the curtain a fraction so I could look across the street. I kept my face hidden by the frame and watched. The room was dark, but I could see her movement, her blonde hair a lighter patch within the colourless space. I noted it and put it from my mind.

Later that same night, again by accident or so I thought, I saw that flicker, that movement once more. This time the light was on in her room. Bathed in yellow, she walked from one side of the bedroom to the other, arranging things, folding clothes. She wore the red silk robe. As I watched, only glancing at first and then transfixed, she stood in the centre of the room where I was afforded a clear view; then she dropped the robe from her shoulders. Naked, she stood upon her bed as she reached for something on a shelf above.

Her form was milk-white, svelte. Though distance separated us I could see the contours of her shape, the movement of her muscles beneath the skin, and as she turned, the fine blonde down below her belly. Her body arched as she reached above her, a gentle curve. I became nervous then, guilty for watching, but I could not help myself. She moved to face me, placed her hands upon her hips and stood there, framed in wood and glass. Did she not see me? Unknowingly, I licked my lips. My heart was racing. A pause, and then she reached across and drew the curtains closed.

I watched the illuminated shadow play for half an hour or more, but eventually the light went out. Someone walked by on the street below and I pulled back from the window, feeling ashamed of what I was doing. I sat on my bed just thinking, well into the night, savouring the way my heart had raced, the thrill of discovery and the inner conflict about the morality of what I'd done.

Who was I? Who was this woman that I could invade her privacy like that? I put it from me, deciding that the brief sweet glimpse had been nothing more than chance.

Two days later, in the morning this time, I saw her again. I was at my window, looking at the state of the world, considering the weather and what I might wear for my day when I glanced across. She stood barely masked by her open curtain. She trailed a towel across her breasts. She rubbed it back and forth, flicked her hair back. Then she dropped the towel, trailed a hand across her belly and turned. I caught my breath, not believing that this could be happening. She was facing away from me now and, unable to help myself, I stepped closer to the glass. She lifted her arms to run her fingers through damp hair and I marvelled at the arch of her back, the curve of her hip, the firm roundness of her buttocks, the slight dimples above them. My breath fogged the small patch of glass and I stopped myself from breathing, allowing the place to clear. Slowly she leaned down; then just as slowly she dressed, unhurried in her movements as if she had forever. At the last, she moved to the window and drew her curtains closed.

The way her hand lingered, the way she looked out onto the street before dragging them shut set me wondering.

I soon established the pattern. Three times a day she would be there and before long I had narrowed it down to particular times of the day. I knew when she rose. I knew when she came home. I knew when she went to sleep. I became a sentinel at my window, hovering in the shadows and waiting for her to appear. Once or twice she would break the schedule and leave me disappointed. It only made me want her all the more. The first time she didn't appear I waited in place for more than an hour, until my eyes played tricks and conjured vague movements in the darkness. I could barely sleep that night, feeling as if at any moment she might reappear, that perhaps I had misjudged the time.

She was back the next morning, the barest hint of a smile upon her lips. Yet still I did not know whether she knew I was standing there, watching and waiting. I could do little more than suspect. But the suspicion grew, for always there was that lingering pause, the barest glance, before she drew the curtains shut again.

Some time later she went away. For two weeks she was gone, her room hollow and empty. The chequered curtains fluttered mournfully in the breeze, ballooning into the shadowed room before flowing out. I was there waiting for her, morning, evening, and late at night, but for two full weeks she failed to appear. My vigil was in vain.

The way I stood, holding my curtains slightly parted for more than an hour at a time took its toll, for that was when the pain started in my arm. It was only a slight pain—dull, running from my shoulder to my wrist. When at last I would give up for the night, I would flex my arm, try to stimulate some feeling and banish the annoying twinges that were becoming more and more regular. The discomfort was slight beside the knowledge that she wasn't there and I thought nothing more of them.

The two weeks passed, and that night my heart leapt as I saw the light flick on in her room. The pulse was loud in my ears, almost deafening. I felt as if I could feel the blood flow within my veins. My mouth was dry, my breath coming in short shallow gasps. She had returned. I leaned against the window frame, relief mixed with excitement, and watched. She was back and she wore the red silk robe. I had been right to wait, to stand vigil for her return. She opened the curtains wider and ran fingers through her hair. The action was just for me.

That was three weeks past. The pain in my arm has not left, but she is back, still here. That is what truly matters.

She is in her room again, and I am in my place, half-obscured behind my curtain. She wears the red silk robe, shiny, the golden dragons catching and sparkling in the light. For the first time I notice they have green eyes made from small polished stones that seem to shine. I frown, wondering why I have never noticed this before.

She steps towards the window and looks out across the street, directly at the place where I stand. Her robe hangs open, exposing the marble curve of breast and belly. My arm is throbbing but I banish the sensation. She presses up against the window, and just for a moment, I swear I can see the gilded dragons move and writhe upon her shoulders.

She looks at me. I can feel her looking. And then I know she sees me. With that sudden knowledge, a deep and thrusting pain stabs in my chest.

I frown again. With one hand I keep the curtain in place, slightly open so I can see her, but with the other I knead at my chest, trying to banish this pain that has sprung from nowhere. Instead of bringing relief, it intensifies, hot and burning, blossoming inside me. The strength of it makes me gasp.

She lowers her face, watching me still, her hair hanging to one side like a fine silk curtain. My vision is slightly blurred now and those gentle curves seem larger than they should. I can feel her leaning forwards at her window, as if straining, waiting for something. She passes her tongue over her lower lip.

Pain, beating inside me. The edges of my vision are fluttering with blackness. My legs are growing weak, barely able to support me. And still the hurt tears through me—wave after wave.

The darkness and blunt-edged pain flower like a hard jewel inside and finally I feel my knees give way. As I slip to the floor, I see her face, watching still, wreathed with her smile and golden hair. Surrounded by red silk and dancing dragons, I can see her eyes. They're deepest green and filled with light—the colour of an impossible ocean.

-Lover's Triangle-
COLLEEN ANDERSON

It was so cold I expected the ozone grids that waffled the sky to hiss from the rain. They continued to glow a false green. Their reliability didn't matter much; rad couldn't get through with the weather so shitty. The rain wouldn't matter anyway, once inside Fundamental Glue.

I saw the garish orange even in the deluge, and ran to the door. Wiping water out of my eyes, I palmed the door and entered Fundamental Glue. Warm ecstasy. It was dark inside, and my eyes gradually adjusted to the diffused wraith-lights that bobbed above each table. Inside was nearly as garish as the front with long diagonal stripes of green, blue and red that covered the kylar plastiplate walls. Keg had taken no chances and had made Glue impervious to almost all types of razing, except for old world bombs, which no one was fool enough to use. No one in their right minds, but we had long ago lost that perspective.

I walked into the din and pushed through the crowd, close as maggots, to the bar. The place would soon writhe in gyrations of bliss when Bore Hunter started playing. I searched through the mix of humans and Wireheads for Sharman and Claxon but couldn't see them. Turning back to the bar, I yelled at Keg. "Hey, Keg, Brosia please. How's biz?"

Keg, lean, angular and with a hooked nose, glowered under bushy eyebrows as he filled glasses with coolants. "Not bad, Agate. You gonna read futures tonight?" He plunked the can in front of me.

I patted my coat's pockets. "I've got the decks. Wasn't planning to but maybe I will for a while."

"Please do." He turned away to the far side of the bar and yelled back, "Quiet spot's at the back."

I squeezed by three Wireheads whose eyes sheened with a silvery metal. Probably housed special optics—unnerving to look at them. I bit back an old curse at such unnatural use of flesh. At least it was their bodies, not mine. I sat at a table scarred with initials and faced the stage.

I rooted into one pocket and felt the reassuring presence of stiletto and wand. The decks lay wrapped in silk in the opposite pocket and I pulled one out. The Romany Wanderer. I shuffled through the Gypsy *patteran*—symbols—and decided to use the Mythic deck instead, with its strong traditional images for the Emperor, the Fool, Death, etc.

I laid a piece of red silk patterned with black sickles and roses upon the table, and began shuffling the cards. Eyes closed, I concentrated, centering myself to the earth, letting the sounds of the Glue drift away. Once inner calmness blanketed me, I opened my eyes, feeling connected to the symbolism of the cards. The portents and messages swirled within me, waiting to be released into sequence. I let out a long breath and sipped the Brosia.

As I shuffled the cards, a shadow fell across the table and I looked up. The wraith-light obscured the features, but by the white skin color it had to be a Wirehead.

"Do you tell futures?"

I looked up into the shadowed face and answered, "Only if you ask."

"Then I ask." He pulled out the chair and sat. Classically handsome, with a strong brow and deep brown eyes. A Roman nose and a narrow chin were framed by auburn hair that just brushed his shoulders. He looked at me, waiting.

I held out my hand. "I'm Agate."

"Gamaliel." He shook mine and I passed the cards to him. I noticed the carbon steel nails and guessed cybersonics or lasers lay beneath them. He set his drink at the corner of the table and said, "What do I do? I've never had a reading before."

"Never?"

"I thought my future was fairly evident." He smiled. Pointed teeth. White skin. One of the undead. I tried to hide my unease.

"Oh, well … shuffle them, keeping the, uh, question you have in mind. When you feel ready, cut them into three piles on the silk and I'll take over from there."

I shivered slightly with dread, but was still fascinated at this man's nonchalance. From the moment I was old enough to understand, my parents and uncles, aunts and cousins, all the Rom had instilled in me the fear of death and the dead. Because my people feared death so much, we worshipped it—no—gave obeisance to keep the dead away. It had always been so: treat the dead with respect and they won't come back to haunt you. It was all I could do to keep myself from chanting a warding spell before this man.

It was difficult, but I recentered myself as Gamaliel cut the cards into three piles. I picked them up, then turned over one after the other until there were twelve in the sun-wheel spread, with a thirteenth card in the middle. I pointed to the middle card, the Emperor; an assured man sitting upon the throne.

"This represents you and shows you are strong, a leader. Um, that is beyond your, uh, natural attributes. You're in control." And I wasn't. Undead so close, I was unnerved and feeling foolish. I took a deep breath and tried to get through the reading.

I had forgotten to ask him what his question was. No matter, the cards would still reveal an answer. The past and present cards showed several swords cards, the Moon, the eight, and three of wands, and the king of coins.

I sipped my Brosia and said, "Your past shows there was a time of confusion and strife, partly caused by your view of magic. You were shaped by it and dealt with a great hardship.

But it shows here," I pointed to the wands, "that you have worked hard and become comfortable. You do not want for anything in the world of material gain, and have attained what you tried for."

I looked up and saw he watched me, not the cards. Looking down, I pointed to the next three cards: the knight of wands, the Fool, and the queen of cups. "Your future shows that you search for something more and that it will lead you on the Fool's journey. You must be careful, for you might be so blinded by what you seek that you will fall to someone who is charming, yet potentially harmful. You must remember reason, but don't overanalyze the situation."

He picked up his drink and sipped it, still watching me. He hadn't said a word and I wondered about the undead drinking normal drinks.

I licked my lips and continued. "These last three cards show the outcome of what you seek." The cards were strong: the Lovers, the Lightning Struck Tower, and the five of cups. I was surprised that the Death card hadn't figured in a spread for the undead. But then, I knew better, that card hardly ever meant the literal interpretation.

"Your search will lead you into a relationship, possibly a partnership. This card signifies that you must make a choice and that there is the possibility of rivalry. The Tower indicates sudden change and a collapse of old structures. I don't think this relationship of the Lovers will last through it, but in the end there will be something left to build on. You will find that choices for the future will have changed, and the old beliefs will have broken down."

Gamaliel leaned back in his chair and smiled. "An apt reading, and an interesting one. I should do this more often. Thank you."

I finished my drink and couldn't help saying, "You're not like the others." I had, of course, "encountered" my fair share of roving undead or gangs in this chaotic world.

He leaned forward, elbows on the table, while I avoided his eyes and wrapped the cards in the silk to put them away. I didn't feel like doing any more readings. Too hyped.

"Do you mean, like other Wireheads, or vampyrs?"

"Vampyrs. They're usually not so public, or so I thought, unless … "

He smiled widely, enjoying my discomfort. "I'm not on the hunt, if that's what you're worried about."

"Oh." But how did I know he told the truth? I fiddled with objects in my pockets and tried to maintain the cool facade.

He stood and I realized he was very tall, over six feet. "If you don't mind I'll buy you a drink. Partial payment for the reading."

I just nodded, hoping I wouldn't make a bigger fool of myself. I watched him walk to the bar, calm, barely parting the crowd.

Gamaliel returned and set the Brosias down. He took off his long, green lacquer plast coat and tossed it on the back of the chair. Its hard scales clattered and caught the wraith-light hovering above. His muscled arms were bare and he wore an insul t-shirt that said 'Go with the flow, it's here to stay.'

He moved his chair to the side, so he half-faced me, and so that he could watch Bore Hunter, a band of stocky men and women with strobing gemstones adorning their heads. One guitarist had silver tusks that protruded from her lower lip. A singular beauty.

Gamaliel leaned over and whispered, his breath hot and sultry in my ear, "I promise not to drink you if that's what you're worried about."

"Oh." I tried to laugh. "No … well, yes I was. Sorry, but I don't know many … of your type and well, my people have always had a great fear of the dead returning to haunt us."

"And do you think I'm haunting you?"

"No. But you do have to eat sometime."

After watching the band for several minutes, Gamaliel turned to me just when I thought he hadn't heard. "Yes, I do have to eat, but I choose carefully and usually those who deserve it."

That didn't ease my nerves. I'd met enough crazed Wireheads who arbitrarily decided what someone deserved.

"How do you decide? And wh ... what do I deserve?"

Amusement sparked his eyes. "To be paid, for one." He tossed some creds on the table. "Don't worry, I won't touch you."

"That's what you say." I gulped my drink. "How do I know it's the truth?"

"Well," he leaned close. "You just have to trust me. Besides, I know that Gypsies have charms against the undead. I'd have to wait until you didn't suspect me."

I smiled, feeling that I could trust him. My intuition was rarely wrong. I finally relaxed enough to talk with Gamaliel about the city packs, and the music of Bore Hunter, and the other new band, Acid Reign, that was hitting the scenes.

I realized as we talked that my perceptions, and old legends of the undead had clouded my view to the person beneath the vampyr image. Gamaliel talked warmly. I was fascinated by this friendly vampyr. This man could literally give me the kiss of death and yet he seemed at ease, lighthearted. But then, he could be. It wasn't he that had to worry about having his life stolen.

The evening passed and Gamaliel and I danced, sucked into the desperate ambiance of people trying to forget the world. We were still talking when Keg came over and said, "Time to run, folks. I need my beauty rest." I found myself attracted to this man, this dead ... thing. He seemed so alive, and yet, again I found preconceived warnings that my people had given coloring my views.

I pulled on my voluminous, many-pocketed coat and patted it to make sure everything was there. Gamaliel stood and pulled on his shiny coat. "Look, Agate, I'll walk you to your place. Too many packs out lately."

"I live at Stanley's Green. That's almost an hour from here."

He raised one eyebrow and motioned with his arm toward the door. "I have nothing but time."

It was a tomb outside. The rain had stopped. The only sound was the ever-present hum of the grids overhead. We walked down the quiet crumbling roadway, well away from the crypt-like depths of abandoned buildings. Neither of us talked, our boot heels the only living sound.

Suddenly I whirled, the sense of someone watching too strong to ignore. Behind us, emerging from a doorway, were two Gorgon pack members. Their fibril hair writhed about their shoulders. They smiled carbon steel smiles and razor nails glinted in the streetlight. I looked around as Gamaliel turned to face them.

Quickly, I pulled the stiletto and wand from my coat. I waved the wand through the air in a pattern of pentacles and chanted a warding against the Gorgons' hypno-sonic stares. I thumbed the safety on the laser stiletto. The blade hummed and the edge of white light lit my hand.

Gamaliel calmly fished a leather band from his pocket and tied back his hair. "I suggest you hunt somewhere else."

The female Gorgon, her hair ending in arrow-like points, laughed. "Hey, the man's walking his meat."

The other one moved a step forward. "Don't be greedy. There's plenty to share."

And then they were upon us. It happened as fast as lightning, and I managed one stab at the male before Gamaliel kicked him flat, then slashed through the throat of the woman. He bent over the man whose chest he'd crushed. The Gorgon wheezed and moaned. The smell of charred flesh and metallic blood tainted the air.

Gamaliel turned back to me, his lips drawn back from his fangs. He growled, "Turn away. You won't want to watch."

"But, what—"

"Turn away," he snapped, and I did. But I wanted to watch, like a moth drawn to the deadly flame. Saliva filled my mouth; I felt like vomiting at the thought of him sucking up the warm lifeblood. There was a part of me that said, *this is taboo,* and another part that said, *you can watch; you're not doing it.* I resisted the urge to look.

I jumped when Gamaliel touched my shoulder. He urged me on, saying nothing.

Just before we entered the green I turned to Gamaliel and said, "Did you have to—"

"Look, you knew what I was. They would have killed us. How do you suppose I feed?" He was angry, but I was scared.

"I saw you drink Brosia."

The anger left him and he sighed. "Yes, I can drink and eat regular food but my nutrition must be from blood. Oh." He stopped. "I see. Agate," he touched my face softly. "I swear I will never harm you. I only take from those who would do others harm; the evil ones, the flesh packs. Please, trust me."

"Yes, I do," and realized I meant it.

We stopped in front of the door to my cube. Trying to hide the lingering dread of the Gorgon encounter, I bravely invited him in. He declined, saying, "No, it is late and I would rather that you're totally comfortable with my presence. But I would like to talk to you again, if I may."

We agreed to meet at the quieter Schroedinger's Box the following night. I slept deep, and dreamt of walking through tombs, searching, searching, and always behind me someone wailing, "Come back, come back."

∞Θ∞

It wasn't until our third time together that Gamaliel revealed the extent of his sense of humor. We were sitting on the steps of the old gallery, talking.

"Oh, I brought something for you that I got last night." He dug through his pockets and pulled something out and dropped it in my lap. A red tongue and an eyeball lay shiningly on my coat.

I squeaked and jumped up, realizing at the same moment that they were very obvious rubber toys. Gamaliel laughed so hard he nearly rolled down the steps. I slapped him. "Idiot," and had to laugh too. It dispelled my last visions of contemptuous vampyrs.

"You're a very undignified vampyr, you know that?"

He just smirked. I touched his shoulder. "Gama? Would you show me where you live?"

He tilted his head, thought for a moment, and said, "All right."

We walked along crumbling streets, and Gamaliel clasped my hand. I didn't say anything but looked up at him. He looked straight ahead, his head tilted as if listening. I bit my lip but continued to hold his hand. It was warm, not as warm as a living person's, but not the cold of the crypt that I had been expecting.

"What … "

"Shh." He continued to listen.

I looked at the stunted, gnarled trees that lined these streets. Their leaves were few, warped like heated plastic. There had to be strong magic going down to keep them even this alive. I realized we were in Shaughnessy; large houses sprawled across crisp brown grass. Some homes were of stone and others, weather-stripped wood. The ritz used to live here in the twentieth century and it made sense that any ritz left would still live in the spacious homes.

We walked up the cobblestone steps to a house with a turret. The windows were still intact and the door was reinforced with embellished steel. Gamaliel opened the door and let me enter first. If I was expecting tomblike colors and velvet drapes, I was completely surprised. The place was furnished with soft couches, paintings and very little else. Everything numbed my eyes with bright shades of green and yellow.

"Ugh, it's bright in here."

Gamaliel smiled and bolted the door. "It's too depressing otherwise. But the whole place isn't done in these colors. Here, I'll show you." He led me up a dark wooden staircase. The second floor was more subdued but not somber; the colors ranged through red, green and brown, like a twentieth century forest in fall.

I shivered, imagining Gamaliel dragging victims into his home and keeping them chained in the basement. There was no evidence, but still I quivered, mortal jelly, at what he may have done here. "Very impressive," I said.

He stared down the hall and said, "I am not very old but I was able to find this place before the collapse destroyed too many homes. Except for fortifying, I've had little to repair." Then he turned suddenly and kissed me, holding my shoulders.

Surprised, I looked at him and he stopped, confused.

He dropped his hands. "I'm sorry, Agate. I thought ... I hoped. I'm sorry. I wanted you to like me."

"Wait, Gama, I do." I touched his face and dropped my hand. "I do. Why do you think I've spent this time with you?" Why indeed? The lies we tell ourselves. My heart pounded—fear moved like a moist worm into my throat. I swallowed and said, "I do care, very much." Then I kissed him back. The kiss blossomed, grew to many more and then into gentle caresses. He picked me up and carried me to his bedroom. My body responded to his and I clung to him.

We lay, heated by dozens and dozens of candles in his room, but the heat we gave off dimmed them in comparison. Light glittered back from mirrors and windows like thousands of knowing eyes.

Tears of sweat flecked our skin.

Gamaliel's flesh shone like a bank of snow against my brown flank. He licked warmly at my neck, my arms, my breasts. I vibrated from his caresses, expecting at any moment to feel the thin sharp bite of his teeth. It made my passion hotter, stronger, thinking that this might be my last act. And I wanted it, I didn't care, to be pulled down and taken at the height of intimacy. What more could I want, taken body and soul?

It was a feeling, not a conscious thought, and it wasn't until years later that I understood what I had wanted.

Later, much later, we lay curled into one another. Gamaliel murmured into my hair. "It is the worst part of this sort of life; the loneliness. So many people fear to be near me and can never relax. There are so many old world legends, and everyone has preconceived ideas that mold all their views. And my own kind," he laughed bitterly. "They are the worst; egotistical, competitive, jealous. They're happy to perpetrate the image of fear; they love the power, but I don't. I want to love a person."

I turned and looked at him. "Oh, Gama, I don't fear you." I feared myself, my lack of control, and his temptation.

∞⊙∞

We continued to see each other. Something was happening to me inside that I didn't like: a distorted pearl growing bigger, malignant. Something weighed me down, fought me, changed me. I brooded and provoked fights with Gamaliel, daring him to strike me, to lash out and drain my life. But he wouldn't. He looked at me, hurt.

"Why are you doing this, Agate? Why do you want to fight?"

I snarled, "Do you think it just takes one to fight?"

"No," he said calmly. "No, I don't." And he had turned away.

One night at his place we made love and I finally lay subdued beside him. My mind still roiled and I had grown temperamental over the weeks, afraid of what I wanted and didn't want. The big problem; I didn't know what I wanted, nor why I was angry.

I lay thinking of Gamaliel's long life and my relatively short one. I was more than a universe away from him. He murmured something, kissed my eyes, my mouth and nipped lightly at the flesh of my neck.

I gasped and returned to myself. Trembling, I felt a yearning to bare my neck—abandon soul and flesh to his caresses. In that moment, quicker than light, I murmured a Rom incantation against vampyrs. He yelped as light arced from my skin to his. An acrid smell filled my nostrils.

Pulling back, Gamaliel hissed, fangs flashing deadly. "How dare you! Have you no trust?" he bellowed. He turned and slashed the stuffed chair beside the bed and kicked it across the floor. It crashed into the wall and glass tinkled from the broken window.

I sat up trembling, afraid that I would die now.

Anguish cracked his voice. "I love you, I would never, never drain your blood! Don't you know that by now?"

Shaken, I knelt where I was, knocking a candle over as I reached for him in haste. "I know, I'm sorry. I w … wasn't thinking. Gama." I tried to reach beneath the red-rimming of his eyes. "I'm sorry. I was scared of my own reactions. I wanted to die. I … I wanted you to take me."

I heard him mumble something about mortals and I flashed resentment. He reached, hesitated, then grabbed my arm. I had eliminated the warding.

"Agate, I could make you vampyr. I can give you the kiss of eternal life. Won't you take it; be eternal with me? You need never fear again and we could be together."

"No, I can't, I can't." I shook my head, trying to escape the black pit that threatened to swallow and mold me into something dark, too powerful. "I … my people, we had strong taboos against the undead. Now I know why. I'm sorry. I'm too afraid. I don't think I would be like you, so noble. There is so much power. The Rom knew this, knew it could get out of hand and I never understood it, until now. I don't think I want eternal life."

"Why? Isn't it just a lesser of two evils? We would be eternally together. And there are ways to kill us. You can end it when you want."

I clasped my arms, cold in spite of the candle flames. I wanted it so badly. To live forever, to wield such power. I shook my head, crying, "I … I can't, Gama." I realized then, right to my frozen marrow, that I could never love him properly, for there was another to love.

There were tears in his eyes. He sensed that it was more than his offer that I denied. "Don't you see?" I whispered. "It is death I court, that I am infatuated with. I've used you to get close to death. To be kissed by you, to be loved by you was like loving … embracing it. I'm so sorry … so sorry." I hugged him tightly now. "I do care for you, Gama, but every time I'd be with you I would see my death and be tempted by it. But the power, the power is too much."

"No!" He tore himself away from me and fled into the night. I didn't wait for his return. I dressed and left. I had gone for the darker lover while Gamaliel had tried to lead the life of the living, not the undead.

We remained friends, albeit distantly. I could not stand to be around Gamaliel and see the hurt in his eyes. *Respect the dead and they won't come back to haunt you.* He walked as if wounded, and I knew I had dealt the most deadly blow to a dead man trying to live.

-Endless Night-
BARBARA RODEN

'Thank you so much for speaking with me. And for these journals, which have never seen the light of day. I'm honored that you'd entrust them to me.'

'That's quite all right.' Emily Edwards smiled, a delighted smile, like a child surveying an unexpected and particularly wonderful present. 'I don't receive very many visitors; and old people do like speaking about the past. No'—she held up a hand to stop him—'I *am* old; not elderly, not "getting on", nor any of the other euphemisms people use these days. When one has passed one's centenary, "old" is the only word which applies.'

'Well, your stories were fascinating, Miss Edwards. As I said, there are so few people alive now who remember these men.'

Another smile, gentle this time. 'One of the unfortunate things about living to my age is that all the people I once knew in any meaningful or intimate way have died; there is no one left with whom I can share these things. Perhaps that is why I have so enjoyed this talk. It brings them all back to me. Sir Ernest; such a charismatic man, even when he was obviously in ill-health and worried about money. I used to thrill to his stories; to hear him talk of that desperate crossing of South Georgia Island to Stromness, of how they heard the whistle at the whaling station and knew that they were so very close to being saved, and then deciding to take a treacherous route down the slope to save themselves a five-mile hike when they were near exhaustion. He would drop his voice then, and say to me "Miss Emily"—he always called me Miss Emily, which was the name of his wife, as you know; it made me feel very grown-up, even though I was only eleven—"Miss Emily, I do not know how we did it. Yet afterwards we all said the same thing, those three of us who made that crossing:

that there had been another with us, a secret one, who guided our steps and brought us to safety." I used to think it a very comforting story, when I was a child, but now—I am not as sure.'

'Why not?'

For a moment he thought she had not heard. Her eyes, which until that moment had been sharp and blue as Antarctic ice, dimmed, reflecting each of her hundred-and-one years as she gazed at her father's photograph on the wall opposite. He had an idea that she was not even with him in her comfortable room, that she was instead back in the parlor of her parents' home in north London, ninety years earlier, listening to Ernest Shackleton talk of his miraculous escape after the sinking of the *Endurance*, or her father's no less amazing tales of his own Antarctic travels. He was about to get up and start putting away his recording equipment when she spoke.

'As I told you, my father would gladly speak about his time in Antarctica with the Mawson and Shackleton expeditions, but of the James Wentworth expedition aboard the *Fortitude* in 1910 he rarely talked. He used to become quite angry with me if I mentioned it, and I learned not to raise the subject. I will always remember one thing he *did* say of it: "It was hard to know how many people were there. I sometimes felt that there were too many of us." And it would be frightening to think, in that place where so few people are, that there was another with you who should not be.'

The statement did not appear to require an answer, for which the thin man in jeans and rumpled sweater was glad. Instead he said, 'If you remember anything else, or if, by chance, you should come across those journals from the 1910 expedition, please do contact me, Miss Edwards.'

'Yes, I have your card.' Emily nodded towards the small table beside her, where a crisp white card lay beside a small ceramic tabby cat, crouched as if eyeing a mouse in its hole. Her gaze rested on it for a moment before she picked it up.

'I had this when I was a child; I carried it with me everywhere. It is really a wonder that it has survived this long.' She gazed at it for a moment, a half-smile on her lips. 'Sir Ernest said it put him in mind of Mrs. Chippy, the ship's cat.' Her smile faded. 'He was always very sorry, you know, about what he had to do, and sorry that it caused an estrangement between him and Mr. McNish; he felt that the carpenter never forgave him for having Mrs. Chippy and the pups shot before they embarked on their journey in the boats.'

'It was rather cruel, though, wasn't it? A cat, after all; what harm could there have been in taking it with them?'

'Ah, well.' Emily set it carefully back down on the table. 'I thought that, too, when I was young; but now I see that Sir Ernest was quite right. There was no room for sentimentality, or personal feeling; his task was to ensure that his men survived. Sometimes, to achieve that, hard decisions must be made. One must put one's own feelings and inclinations aside, and act for the greater good.'

He sensed a closing, as if there was something else she might have said but had decided against. No matter, it had been a most productive afternoon. At the door Emily smiled as she shook his hand.

'I look forward to reading your book when it comes out.'

'Well'—he paused, somewhat embarrassed—'it won't be out for a couple of years yet. These things take time, and I'm still at an early stage in my researches.'

Emily laughed, a lovely sound, like bells chiming. 'Oh, I do not plan on going anywhere just yet. You must bring me a copy when it is published, and let me read again about those long ago days. The past, where everything has already happened and there can be no surprises, can be a very comforting place when one is old.'

∞☉∞

It was past six o'clock when the writer left, but Emily was not hungry. She made a pot of tea, then took her cup and saucer into the main room and placed it on the table by her chair, beside the ceramic cat. She looked at it for a moment, and ran a finger down its back as if stroking it; then she picked up the card and considered it for a few moments.

'I think that I was right not to show him,' she said, as if speaking to someone else present in the room. 'I doubt that he would have understood. It is for the best.'

Thus reminded, however, she could not easily forget. She crossed the room to a small rosewood writing desk in one corner, unlocked it, and pulled down the front panel, revealing tidily arranged cubbyholes and drawers of various sizes. With another key she unlocked the largest of the drawers, and withdrew from it a notebook bound in leather, much battered and weathered, as with long use in difficult conditions. She returned with it to her armchair, but it was some minutes before she opened it, and when she did it was with an air almost of sadness. She ran her fingers over the faded ink of the words on the first page.

QUOTE
Robert James Edwards
Science Officer
H.M.S. *Fortitude*
1910–11
END

'No,' she said aloud, as if continuing her last conversation, 'there can be no surprises about the past; everything there has happened. One would like to think it happened for the best, but we can never be sure. And *that* is not comforting at all.' Then she opened the journal and began to read from it, even though the story was an old one which she knew by heart.

20 November 1910: A relief to be here in Hobart, on the brink of starting the final leg of our sea voyage. The endless days of fundraising, organization, and meetings in London, are well behind us, and the Guvnor is in high spirits, and as usual has infected everyone with his enthusiasm. He called us all together this morning, and said that of the hundreds upon hundreds of men who had applied to take part in the expedition when it was announced in England, we had been hand-picked, and that everything he has seen on the journey thus far has reinforced the rightness of his choices; but that the true test is still to come—in the journey across the great Southern Ocean and along the uncharted coast of Antarctica. We will be seeing sights that no human has yet viewed and will, if all goes to plan, be in a position to furnish exact information which will be of inestimable value to those who come after us. Chief among this information will be noting locations where future parties can establish camps, so that they might use these as bases for exploring the great heart of this unknown land, and perhaps even establishing a preliminary base for Mawson's push, rumored to be taking place in a year's time. We are not tasked with doing much in the way of exploring ourselves, save in the vicinity of any base we do establish, but we have the dogs and sledges to enable us at least to make brief sorties into that mysterious continent, and I think that all the men are as eager as I to set foot where no man has ever trodden.

Of course, we all realize the dangers inherent in this voyage; none more so than the Guvnor, who today enjoined anyone who had the least doubt to say so now, while there was still an opportunity to leave. Needless to say, no one spoke, until Richards gave a cry of 'Three cheers for the *Fortitude*, and all who sail in her!' A cheer echoed to the very skies and set the dogs barking on the deck so furiously that the Guvnor singled out Castleton and called good-naturedly, 'Castleton, quiet your dogs down, there's a good chap, or we shall have the neighbors complaining!' which elicited a hearty laugh from all.

22 November. Such a tumultuous forty-eight hours we have not seen on this voyage, and I earnestly hope that the worst is now behind us. Two days ago the Guvnor was praising his hand-picked crew, and I, too, was thinking how our party had pulled together on the trip from Plymouth, which boded well, I thought, for the trials which surely face us; and now we have said farewell to one of our number, and made room for another. Chadwick, whose excellent meals brightened the early part of our voyage, is to be left in Hobart following a freakish accident which none could have foreseen, he having been knocked down in the street by a runaway horse and cart. His injuries are not, thank Heaven, life threatening, but are sufficient to make it impossible for him to continue as part of the expedition.

It is undoubtedly a very serious blow to the fabric of our party; but help has arrived in the form of Charles De Vere, who was actually present when the accident occurred, and was apparently instrumental in moving the injured man to a place of safety following the incident. He came by the ship the next day to enquire after Chadwick, and was invited aboard; upon a meeting with the Guvnor he disclosed that he has, himself, worked as a ship's cook, having reached Hobart in that capacity. The long and the short of it is, after a long discussion the Guvnor has offered him Chadwick's place on the expedition, and De Vere has accepted.

'Needs must when the devil drives,' the Guvnor said to me, somewhat ruefully, when De Vere left to collect his things. 'We can't do without a cook. Ah well, we have a few days more here in Hobart, and shall see how this De Vere works out.'

What the Guvnor did not add—but was, I know, uppermost in his mind—is that a few days onboard a ship at dockside is a very different proposition to what we shall be facing once we depart. We must all hope for the best.

28 November. We are set to leave tomorrow; the last of the supplies have been loaded, the last visiting dignitary has toured the ship and departed—glad, no doubt, to be going home safe to down pillows and a comfortable bed—and the men have written their last letters home, to be posted when the *Fortitude* has left. They are the final words we shall be able to send our loved ones before our return, whenever that will be, and a thin thread of melancholy pervades the ship tonight. I have written to Mary, and enclosed a message for sweet little Emily; by the time I return home she will have changed greatly from the little girl—scarcely more than a babe in arms— whom I left. She will not remember her father; but she and Mary are never a far from my mind, and their photographs gaze down at me from the tiny shelf in my cabin, keeping watch over me as I sleep.

I said that the men had written their last letters home; but there was one exception. De Vere had no letters to give me, and while I made no comment he obviously noted my surprise, for he gave a wintry smile. 'I said my goodbyes long ago,' was all he said, and I did not press him, for there is something about his manner that discourages chatter. Not that he is standoffish, or unfriendly; rather, there is an air about him, as of a person who has spent a good deal of time alone, and has thus become a solitude unto himself. The Guvnor is pleased with him, though, and I must say that the man's cooking is superb. He spends most of his time in the tiny galley; to acquaint himself with his new domain, he told me. The results coming from it indicate that he is putting his time to good use, although I hope he will not have many occasions to favor us with seal consommé or Penguin *à la* Emperor.

Castleton had the largest batch of letters to send. I found him on the deck as usual, near the kennels of his charges. He is as protective of his dogs as a mother is of her children, and with good cause, for on these half-wild creatures the sledge teams shall depend. His control over them is quite wonderful. Some of the men are inclined to distrust the animals, which seem as akin to the domesticated dogs we all know as tigers are to tabby cats; none more so than De Vere who, I notice, gives them a wide berth on the rare occasions when he is on the deck. This wariness appears to be mutual; Castleton says that it is because the dogs scent food on De Vere's clothing.

29 November: At last we are under way, and all crowded to the ship's rail as the *Fortitude* departed from Hobart, to take a last look at civilization. Even De Vere emerged into the sunlight, sheltering his sage eyes with his hand as we watched the shore recede into the distance. I think it fair to say that despite the mingled wonder and excitement we all share about the expedition, the feelings of the men at thus seeing the known world slip away from us were mixed; all save De Vere, whose expression was one of relief before he retreated once more to his sanctum. I know that the Guvnor—whose judgment of character is second to none—is satisfied with the man, and with what he was able to find out about him at such short notice, but I cannot help but wonder if there is something which makes De Vere anxious to be away from Hobart.

20 December: The Southern Ocean has not been kind to us; the storms of the last three weeks have left us longing for the occasional glimpse of blue sky. We had some idea of what to expect, but as the Guvnor reminds us, we are charting new territory every day and must be prepared for any eventuality. We have repaired most of the damage done to the bridge and superstructure by the heavy seas of a fortnight ago, taking advantage of a rare spell of relative calm yesterday to accomplish the task and working well into the night, so as to be ready should the wind and water resume their attack.

The strain is showing on all the men, and I am thankful that the cessation of the tumultuous seas has enabled De Vere to provide hot food once more; the days of cold rations, when the pitching of the ship made the galley unusable, told on all of us. The cook's complexion, which has always been pale, has assumed a truly startling pallor, and his face looks lined and haggard. He spent most of yesterday supplying hot food and a seemingly endless stream of strong coffee for all of us, and then came and helped with the work on deck, which continued well into the long Antarctic summer night. I had wondered if he was in a fit state to do such heavy labor, but he set to with a will, and proved he was the equal of any aboard.

22 December: Yet another accident has claimed one of our party, but this one with graver consequences than the one which injured

Chadwick. The spell of calmer weather which enabled us to carry out the much needed repairs to the ship was all too short, and it was not long after we had completed our work that the storm resumed with even more fury than before, and there was a very real possibility that the sea waves would breach our supply of fresh water, which would very seriously endanger the fate of the expedition. As it was, those of us who had managed to drop off into some kind of sleep awoke to find several inches of icy water around our feet; and the dogs were in a general state of uproar, having been deluged by waves. I stumbled on to the deck and began helping Castleton and one or two others who were removing the dogs to a more sheltered location—a difficult task given the rolling of the ship and the state of the frantic animals. I was busy concentrating on the task at hand, and thus did not see one of the kennels come loose from its moorings on the deck; but we all heard the terrible cry of agony which followed.

When we rushed to investigate we found young Walker crushed between the heavy wooden kennel and the rail. De Vere had reached the spot before us and, in a fit of energy which can only be described as superhuman, managed single-handedly to shift the kennel out of the way and free Walker, who was writhing and moaning in pain. Beddoes was instantly summoned, and a quick look at the doctor's face showed the gravity of the situation. Walker was taken below, and it was some time before Beddoes emerged, looking graver than before, an equally grim-faced Guvnor with him. The report is that Walker's leg is badly broken, and there is a possibility of internal injuries. The best that can be done is to make the injured man as comfortable as possible, and hope that the injuries are not as severe as they appear.

25 December. A sombre Christmas Day. De Vere, in an attempt to lighten the mood, produced a truly sumptuous Christmas dinner for us all, which did go some way towards brightening our spirits, and afterwards the Guvnor conducted a short but moving Christmas Day service for all the men save Walker, who cannot be moved, and De Vere, who volunteered to sit with the injured man. One thing for which we give thanks is that the storms which have dogged our journey thus far seem to have abated. We have had no further blasts such as the one which did so much damage, and the Guvnor is hopeful that it will not be very much longer before we may hope to see the coast of Antarctica.

28 December. De Vere has been spending a great deal of time with Walker, who is, alas, no better; Beddoes's worried face tells us all that we need know on that score. He has sunk into a restless, feverish sleep which does nothing to refresh him, and he seems to have wasted away to a mere shell of his former self in a shockingly brief period of time. De Vere, conversely, appears to have shaken off the adverse effects the rough weather had on him; I had the occasion to visit the galley earlier in the day, and was pleased to see that our cook's visage has assumed a ruddy hue, and the haggard look has disappeared.

De Vere's attendance on the injured man has gone some way to mitigating his standing as the expedition's 'odd man out'. Several of the men have worked with others here on various voyages, and are old Antarctic hands, while the others were all selected by the Guvnor after careful consideration: not only of their own qualities, but with an eye to how they would work as part of the larger group. He did not, of course, have this luxury with De Vere, whose air of solitude has gone some way to making others keep their distance. Add to this the fact that he spends most of his time in the galley, and is thus excused from taking part in much of the daily routine of the ship, and it is perhaps not surprising that he remains something of a cipher.

31 December. A melancholy farewell to the old year. Walker is no better, and Beddoes merely shakes his head when asked about him. Our progress is slower than we anticipated, for we are plagued with a never-dissipating fog that wreathes the ship, reducing visibility to almost nothing. Brash ice chokes the sea: millions of pieces of it grind against the ship in a never-ceasing cacophony. We are making little more than three knots, for we dare not go any faster, and risk running the *Fortitude* against a larger piece which could pierce the hull. On the other hand we must maintain speed, lest we become mired in a fast-freezing mass. It is delicate work, and Mr Andrews is maintaining a near-constant watch, for as captain he bears ultimate responsibility for the ship and her crew, and is determined to keep us safe.

I hope that 1911 begins more happily than 1910 looks set to end.

3 January 1911: Sad news today. Walker succumbed to his injuries in the middle of last night. The Guvnor gathered us all together this morning to inform us. De Vere was with Walker at the end, so the man did not die alone, a fact for which we are all grateful. I think we all knew that there was little hope of recovery; I was with him briefly only yesterday, and was shocked by how pale and gaunt he looked.

There was a brief discussion as to whether or not we should bury Walker at sea, or wait until we made land and bury him ashore. However, we do not know when—or even if—we shall make landfall, and it was decided by us all to wait until the water around the ship is sufficiently clear of ice and bury him at sea.

5 January: A welcome break in the fog today, enabling us to obtain a clear view of our surroundings for the first time in many days. We all knew that we were sailing into these waters at the most treacherous time of the southern summer, when the ice breaking up in the Ross Sea would be swept across our path, but we could not wait until later when the way would be clearer or we would risk being frozen in the ice before we completed our work. As it is, the prospect which greeted us was not heartening; the way south is choked, as far as the eye can see, with vast bergs of ice; one, which was directly in front of us, stretched more than a mile in length and was pitted along its base by caves in which the water boomed and echoed.

Though the icebergs separate us from our goal it must be admitted that they are beautiful. When I tell people at home of them they are always surprised to hear that the bergs and massive floes are not pure white, but rather contain a multitude of colours: shades of lilac and mauve and blue and green, while pieces which have turned over display the brilliant hues of the algae which live in these waters. Their majesty, however, is every bit as awesome as has been depicted, in words and in art; Coleridge's inspired vision in his 'Ancient Mariner' being a case in point.

I was standing at the rail this evening, listening to the ice as it prowled restlessly about the hull, gazing out upon the larger floes and bergs surrounding us and thinking along these lines, when I became aware of someone standing at my elbow. It was De Vere, who had come up beside me as soundlessly as a cat. We stood in not uncompanionable silence for some moments; then, as if he were reading my thoughts, he said quietly, 'Coleridge was correct, was he not? How does he put it:

QUOTE
"The ice was here, the ice was there

The ice was all around:
It cracked and growled, and roared and howled,
Like noises in a swound!"
END QUOTE; NO INDENT NEXT PARA—

'Quite extraordinary, for a man who was never here. And Doré's illustrations for the work are likewise inspired. Of course, he made a rather dreadful *faux pas* with his polar bears climbing up the floes, although it does make a fine illustration. He was not at all apologetic when his mistake was pointed out to him. "If I wish to place polar bears on the southern ice I shall." Well, we must allow as great an artist as Doré some licence.'

I admitted that I had been thinking much the same thing, at least about Coleridge. De Vere smiled.

'Truly one of our greatest and most inspired poets. We must forever deplore that visitor from Porlock who disturbed him in the midst of "Kubla Khan." And "Christabel," what might that poem have become had Coleridge finished it? That is the common cry, yet Coleridge's fate was always to have a vision so vast that in writing of it he could never truly "finish" in the conventional sense. In that he must surely echo life. Nothing is ever "finished" not really, save in death, and it is this last point that plays such a central role in "Christabel." Is the Lady Geraldine truly alive, or is she undead? He would never confirm it, but I always suspected that Coleridge was inspired, in part, to write "Christabel" because of his earlier creation, the Nightmare Life-in-Death, who "thicks men's blood with cold." When she wins the Mariner in her game of dice with Death, does he join her in a deathless state to roam the world forever? It is a terrible fate to contemplate.'

'Surely not,' I replied, 'only imagine all that one could see and do were one given eternal life. More than one man has sought it.'

De Vere, whose eyes had focussed on the ice, turned and fixed me with a steady gaze. The summer night was upon us and it was sufficiently dark. I could not see his face distinctly, yet his grey eyes were dark pools that displayed a grief without a pang, one so old that the original sting had turned to dull, unvarying sorrow.

'Eternal life,' he repeated, and I heard bitterness underlying his words. 'I do not think that those who seek it have truly considered it in all its consequences.'

I did not know how to respond to this statement. Instead I remarked on his apparent familiarity with the works of Doré and Coleridge. De Vere nodded.

'I have made something of a study of the literature of the undead, if literature it is. *Varney the Vampyre*; certainly not literature, yet possessed of a certain crude power, although not to be mentioned in the same breath as works such as Mr Poe's "Berenice" or the Irishman Le Fanu's sublime "Carmilla."'

I consider myself to be a well-read man, but not in this field, as I have never had an inclination for bogey stories. I made a reference to the only work with which I was familiar that seemed relevant, and my companion shook his head.

'Stoker's novel is certainly powerful; but he makes of the central character too romantic a figure. Lord Byron has much for which to answer. And such a jumble of legends and traditions and lore, picked up here and there and then adapted to suit the needs of the novelist! Stoker never seems to consider the logical results of the depredations of the Count; if he were as bloodthirsty as depicted, and leaving behind such a trail of victims who become, in time, like him, then our world would be overrun.' He shook his head. 'One thing that the author depicted well was the essential isolation of his creation. Stoker does not tell us how long it was before the Count realized how alone he was, even in the midst of bustling London. Not long, I suspect.'

It was an odd conversation to be having at such a time, and in such a place. De Vere must have realized this, for he gave an apologetic smile.

'I am sorry for leading the conversation in such melancholy channels, especially in light of what has happened. Did you know Walker very well?'

'No,' I replied, 'I did not meet him until shortly before we sailed from England. This was his first Antarctic voyage. He hoped, if the Guvnor gave him a good report at the end of it, to sign on with Mawson's next expedition, or even with Shackleton or Scott. Good Antarctic hands are in short supply. I know that the Guvnor, who has never lost a man on any of his expeditions, appreciates the time that you spent with Walker, so that he did not die alone. We all do.'

'Being alone is a terrible thing,' said De Vere, in so soft a voice I could scarcely hear him. 'I only wish that . . .' He stopped. 'I wish it could have been avoided, that I could have prevented it. I had hoped . . .' He stopped once more.

'But what could you have done?' I asked in some surprise, when he showed no sign, this time, of breaking the silence. 'You did more than enough. As I said, we are all grateful.'

He appeared not to hear my last words. 'More than enough,' he repeated, in a voice of such emptiness that I could make no reply, and before long the cook excused himself to tend his duties before retiring for the night. I stayed on deck for a little time after, smoking a pipe and reflecting on our strange conversation. That De Vere is a man of education and intelligence, I had already guessed from his voice, manner and speech. He is clearly not a common sailor or sea-cook. What had brought him to Australia, however, and in such a capacity, I do not know. Perhaps he is one of those men, ill-suited to the rank and expectations of his birth, who seeks to test himself in places and situations which he would not otherwise encounter; or one of the restless souls who finds himself constrained by the demands of society.

It was, by this time, quite late; the only souls stirring on deck were the men of the watch, whom it was easy to identify: Richards with his yellow scarf, about which he has taken some good-natured ribbing; Wellington, the shortest man in our crew but with the strength and tenacity of a bulldog; and McAllister, with his ferocious red beard. All eyes would, I knew, be on the ice, for an accident here would mean the end.

The dogs were agitated; I could hear whining and a few low growls from their kennels. I glanced in that direction and was startled to see a man, or so I thought, standing in the shadows beside them. There was no one on the watch near that spot, I knew, and while it was not unthinkable that some insomniac had come up on deck, what startled me was the resemblance the figure bore to Walker: the thin, eager face, the manner in which he held himself, even the clothing called to mind our fallen comrade. I shook my head, to clear it, and when I looked again the figure was gone.

This is, I fear, what comes of talks such as the one which I had with De Vere earlier. I must banish such thoughts from my head, as having no place on this voyage.

7 January. There was a sufficient clearing of the ice around the ship today to enable us to commit Walker's body to the deep. The service was brief but very moving, and the faces of the men were solemn; none more so than De Vere, who still seems somewhat distraught, and who lingered at the rail's edge for some time, watching the spot where Walker's remains slipped beneath the water.

The ice keeping us from the coastline is as thick as ever, yet we are noting that many of the massive chunks around us are embedded with rocky debris, which would seem to indicate the presence of land nearby. We all hope this is a sign that, before long, we will sight that elusive coastline which hovers just outside our view.

17 January: We have reached our El Dorado at last! Early this morning the watch wakened the Guvnor and Mr. Andrews to announce that they had sighted a rocky beach which looked suitable for a base camp. This news, coming as it does on the heels of all that we have seen and charted in the last few days, has inspired a celebration amongst the expedition members equalling that which we displayed when leaving Plymouth to begin our voyage. The glad news spread quickly, and within minutes everyone was on deck—some of the men only half-dressed—to catch a glimpse of the spot, on a sheltered bay where the *Fortitude* will be able to anchor safely. There was an excited babble of voices and even some impromptu dancing as the prospect of setting foot in this unknown land took hold. I suspect we will be broaching some of the twenty or so cases of champagne we brought with us.

And yet I found myself scanning the faces on deck, and counting, forever since the evening of that conversation with De Vere I have half-convinced myself that there are more men on board the ship than there should be. Quite how and why this idea has taken hold I cannot say, and it is not something which I can discuss with anyone else aboard, but I cannot shake the conviction that this shadowy other is Walker. If I believed in ghosts I could think that our late crewmate has returned to haunt the scene of his hopes and dreams, but I do not believe, and even to mention the idea would lead to serious concerns regarding my sanity. De Vere's talk has obviously played on my mind. Bogeys indeed!

The man himself seems to have regretted his speech that night. He spends most of his time in the galley, only venturing out on deck in the late evening, but he has restricted his comments to commonplaces about the weather, or the day's discoveries. The dogs are as uncomfortable with him as ever, but De Vere appears to be trying to accustom them to his presence, for he is often near them, speaking with Castleton. The dog master spends most of his time when not on watch, or asleep, with his charges, ensuring that they are kept healthy for when we need them for the sledging parties, a task which we are all well content to leave him to. 'If he doesn't stop spending so much time alone with those brutes he'll soon forget how to talk, and start barking instead,' said Richards one evening.

The dogs may be robust, but Castleton himself is not looking well; he appears pale, and more tired than usual. It cannot be attributed to anything lacking in our diet, for the Guvnor has ensured that our provisions are excellent, and should the need arise we can augment our supplies with seal meat, which has proven such an excellent staple for travellers in the north polar regions. It could be that some illness is doing the rounds, for De Vere was once again looking pale some days ago, but seems to have improved. I saw him only a few minutes ago on the deck looking the picture of health. While the rest of us have focussed our gazes landward the cook was looking back the way we had come, as if keeping watch for something he expected to see behind us.

20 January: It has been a Herculean task, landing all the supplies, but at last it is finished. The men who have remained on the beach, constructing the hut, have done yeomans' work and, when the *Fortitude* departs tomorrow to continue along the coast on its charting mission, we shall have a secure roof over our heads. That it shall also be warm is thanks to the work of De Vere. When we went to assemble the stove we found that a box of vital parts was missing. McAllister recalled seeing a box fall from the motor launch during one of its landings, and when we crowded to the water's edge we did indeed see the box lying approximately seven feet down, in a bed of the kelp which grows along the coast. As we debated how best to grapple it to the surface, De Vere quietly and calmly removed his outer clothing and boots and plunged into the icy water. He had to surface three times for great gulps of air before diving down once more to tear the kelp away from the box and then carry it to the surface. It was a heroic act, but he deflected all attempts at praise. 'It needed to be done,' he said simply.

I have erected a small shed for my scientific equipment, at a little distance from the main hut. The dogs are tethered at about the same distance in the other direction, and we are anticipating making some sledging runs soon, although Castleton advises that the animals will be difficult to handle at first, which means that only those with some previous skill in that area will go on the initial journeys. It is debatable whether Castleton himself will be in a fit state to be one of these men, for he is still suffering from some illness which is leaving him in a weakened state; it is all he can do to manage his tasks with the dogs, and De Vere has had to help him.

And still—I hesitate to confess it—I cannot shake myself of this feeling of someone with us who should not be here. With all the bustle of transferring the supplies and erecting the camp it has been impossible for me to keep track of everyone, but I am sure that I have seen movement beyond the science hut when there should be no one there. If these delusions—for such they must be—continue, then I shall have to consider treatment when we return to England, or risk being unable to take part in future expeditions. I am conscious it is hallucination, but it is a phantasm frozen in place, at once too fixed to dislodge and too damaging to confess to another. We have but seven weeks—eight at most—before the ship returns us back to Hobart, in advance of the Antarctic winter; I pray that all will be well until then.

24 January: Our first sledging mission has been a success. Two parties of three men each ascended the pathway that we carved from the beach to the plateau above and behind us, and from there we travelled about four miles inland, attaining an altitude of 1500 feet. The feelings we had as we topped the final rise and saw inland across that vast featureless plateau are indescribable. All were conscious that we were gazing upon land that no human eye had ever seen, as we gazed southwards to where the ice seemed to dissolve into a white, impenetrable haze. The enormity of the landscape, and our own insignificance within it, struck us all, for it was a subdued party that made its way back to the camp before the night began to draw in to make travel impossible; there are crevasses—some hidden, some not—all about, which will make travel in anything other than daylight impossible. We were prepared to spend the night on the plateau should the need arise, but we were all glad to be back in the icicled hut with our fellows.

The mood there was subdued also. Castleton assisted, this morning, in harnessing the dogs to the sledges, but a task of which he would have made short work only a month ago seemed almost beyond him, and the look in his eyes as he watched us leave on a mission of which he was to have been a part, tore at the soul. De Vere's health contrasted starkly with the wan face of the man beside him, yet the cook had looked almost as stricken as the dog master as we left the camp.

1 February: I did not think that I would find myself writing these words, but the *Fortitude* cannot return too quickly. It is not only Castleton's health that is worrisome; it is the growing conviction that there is something wrong with *me*. The fancy that someone else abides here grows stronger by the day and, despite my best efforts, I cannot rid myself of it. I have tried, as delicately as possible, to raise the question with some of the others, but their laughter indicates that no one else is suffering. 'Get better snow goggles, old man,' was Richards's response. The only person who did not laugh was De Vere, whose look of concern told me that he, too, senses my anxiety.

6 February: The end has come, and while it is difficult to write this, I feel I must; as if setting it down on paper will go some way to exorcising it from my mind. I know, however, that the scenes of the last two days will be with me until the grave.

Two nights ago I saw Walker again, as plainly as could be. It was shortly before dark, and I was returning from the hut that shelters my scientific equipment. The wind, which howls down from the icy plateau above us, had ceased for a time, and I took advantage of the relative calm to light my pipe.

All was quiet, save for a subdued noise from the men in the hut, and the growling of one or two of the dogs. I stood for a moment, gazing about me, marvelling at the sheer immensity of where I was. Save for the *Fortitude* and her crew, and Scott's party—wherever they may be—there are no people within 1200 miles of us, and we are as isolated from the rest of the world and her bustle as if we were on the moon. Once again the notion of our own insignificance in this uninhabited land struck me, and I shivered, knocked the ashes out of my pipe, and prepared to go to the main hut.

A movement caught my eye, behind the shed containing my equipment; it appeared to be the figure of a man, thrown into relief against the backdrop of ice. I called out sharply 'Who's there?' and, not receiving an answer, took a few steps in the direction of the movement; but moments later stopped short when the other figure in turn took a step towards me, and I saw that it was Walker.

And yet that does not convey the extra horror of what I saw. It was not Walker as I remembered him, either from the early part of the voyage or in the period just before his death. Then, he had looked ghastly enough, but it was nothing as to how he appeared before me now. He was painfully thin, the color of the ice and snow behind him, and in his eyes was a terrible light; they seemed to glow like twin Lucifers. His nose was eaten away, and his lips, purple and swollen, were drawn back from his gleaming teeth in a terrible parody of a smile; yet there was nothing of mirth in the look directed towards me. I felt frozen where I stood, unable to move, and I wondered what I would do if the figure advanced any further.

It was De Vere who saved me. A cry must have escaped my lips, and the cook heard it, for I was aware that he was standing beside me. He said something in a low voice, words that I was unable to distinguish, and then he was helping me—not towards the main hut, thank God, for I was in no state to present myself before the others, but to the science hut. He pulled open the door and we stumbled inside, and De Vere lit the lantern that was hanging from the ceiling. For a moment, as the match flared, his own eyes seemed to glow; then the lamp was sending its comforting light and all was as it should be.

He was obviously concerned; I could see that in his drawn brow, in the anxious expression of his eyes. I found myself telling him what I had seen, but if I thought he would immediately laugh and tell me that I was imagining things, I was much mistaken. He again said some words in a low voice; guttural and harsh, in a language I did not understand. When he looked at me his grey eyes were filled with such pain that I recoiled slightly. He shook his head.

'I am sorry,' he said in a quiet voice. 'Sorry that you have seen what you did, and … for other things. I had hoped . . .'

His voice trailed off. When he spoke again it was more to himself than to me; he seemed almost to have forgotten my presence.

'I have lived a long time, Mr Edwards, and travelled a great deal; all my years, in fact, from place to place, never staying long in one location. At length I arrived in Australia, travelling ever further south, away from civilization, until I found myself in Hobart, and believed it was the end. Then the *Fortitude* arrived, bound on its mission even further south, to a land where for several months of the year it is always night. Paradise indeed, I thought.' His smile was twisted. 'I should have remembered the words of Blake: "Some are born to sweet delight / Some are born to endless night." It is not a Paradise at all.'

I tried to speak, but he silenced me with a gesture of his hand and a look from those haunted eyes. 'If I needed something from you, would you help me?' he asked abruptly. I nodded, and he thought for a moment. 'There are no sledge trips tomorrow; am I correct?'

'Yes,' I replied, somewhat bewildered by the sudden change in the direction of the conversation. 'The Guvnor feels that the men need a day of rest, so no trips are planned. Why?'

'Can you arrange that a single trip should be made, and that it shall be only you and I who travel?'

'It would be highly irregular; usually there are three men to a sledge, because of the difficulty of . . .'

'Yes, yes, I understand that. But it is important that it should be just the two of us. Can it be managed?'

'If it is important enough, then yes, I should think so.'

'It is more important than you know.' He gave a small smile, and some of the pain seemed gone from his eyes. 'Far more important. Tomorrow night this will be over. I promise you.'

∞⊙∞

I had little sleep that night, and next day was up far earlier than necessary, preparing the sled and ensuring that all was in order. There had been some surprise when I announced that De Vere and I would be off, taking one of the sledges ourselves, but I explained it by saying that the cook merely wanted an opportunity to obtain a glimpse of that vast land for himself, and that we would not be travelling far. When De Vere came out to the sledge he was carrying a small bag. It was surprisingly heavy, but I found a place for it, and moments later the dogs strained into their harnesses, and we were away.

The journey up to the plateau passed uneventfully under the leaden sun, and we made good time on the trail, which was by now well established. When we topped the final rise I stopped the sledge, so that we could both look out across that vast wasteland of ice and snow, stretching away to the South Pole hundreds and hundreds of miles distant. De Vere meditated upon it for some minutes, then turned to me.

'Thank you for bringing me here,' he said in his quiet voice. 'We are about four miles from camp, I think you said?' When I concurred, he continued, 'That is a distance which you can travel by yourself, is it not?'

'Yes, of course,' I replied, somewhat puzzled.

'I thought as much, or I would not have brought you all this way. And I did want to see this'—he gestured at the silent heart of the continent behind us—'just once. Such a terrible beauty on the surface, and underneath, treachery. You say here there are crevasses?'

'Yes,' I said. 'We must be careful when breaking new trails, lest a snow bridge collapse under us. Three days ago a large crevasse opened up to our right'—I pointed—'and there was a very real fear that one of the sledges was going to be carried down into it. It was only some quick work on the part of McAllister that kept it from plunging through.'

'Could you find the spot again?'

'Easily. We are not far.'

'Good.' He turned to the sledge, ignoring the movement and the barking of the dogs; they had not been much trouble when there had been work to do, but now, stopped, they appeared restless, even nervous. De Vere rustled around among the items stowed on the sledge, and pulled out the bag he had given me. He hesitated for a moment; then he walked to where I stood waiting and passed it to me.

'I would like you to open that,' he said, and when I did so I found a small, ornate box made of mahogany, secured with a stout brass hasp. 'Open the box, and remove what is inside.'

I had no idea what to expect; but any words I might have said failed me when I undid the hasp, opened the lid, and found inside the box a revolver. I looked up at De Vere, who wore a mirthless smile.

'It belonged to a man who thought to use it on me, some years ago,' he said simply. 'That man died. I think you will find, if you look, that it is loaded.'

I opened the chamber, and saw that it was so. I am by no means an expert with firearms, but the bullets seemed to be almost tarnished, as with great age. I closed the chamber, and glanced at De Vere.

'Now we are going to go over to the edge of the crevasse, and you are going to shoot me.' The words were said matter-of-factly, and what followed was in the same dispassionate tone, as if he were speaking of the weather, or what he planned to serve for dinner that evening. 'Stand close, so as not to miss. When you return to camp you will tell them that we came too near to the edge of the crevasse, that a mass of snow collapsed under me, and that there was nothing you could do. I doubt that any blame or stigma will attach to you—not with your reputation—and while it may be difficult for you for a time, you will perhaps take solace in the fact that you will not see Walker again, and that Castleton's health will soon improve.' He paused. 'I am sorry about them both; more than I can say.' Then he added some words in an undertone, which I did not quite catch; one word sounded like 'hungry,' and another like 'tired,' but in truth I was so overwhelmed that I was barely in a position to make sense of anything. One monstrous fact alone stood out hard and clear, and I struggled to accept it.

'Are you … are you ill, then?' I asked at last, trying to find some explanation at which my mind did not rebel. 'Some disease that will claim you?'

'If you want to put it that way, yes; a disease. If that makes it easier for you.' He reached out and put a hand on my arm. 'You have been friendly, and I have not had many that I could call a friend. I thank you, and ask you to do this one thing for me; and, in the end, for all of you.'

I looked into his eyes, dark as thunderclouds, and recalled our conversation on board the ship following Walker's death, and for a moment had a vision of something dark and terrible. I thought of the look on Walker's face—or the thing that I had thought was Walker—when I had seen it the night before. 'Will you end up like him?' I asked suddenly, and De Vere seemed to know to what I referred, for he shook his head.

'No, but if you do not do this then others will,' he said simply. I knew then how I must act. He obviously saw the look of resolution in my face, for he said again, quietly, 'Thank you,' then turned and began walking towards the crevasse in the ice.

∞☉∞

I cannot write in detail of what followed in the next few minutes. I remained beside the crevasse, staring blankly down into the depths which now held him, and it was only with considerable effort that I finally roused myself enough to stumble back to the dogs, which had at last quietened. The trip back to camp was a blur of white, and I have no doubt that, when I stumbled down the final stretch of the path, I appeared sufficiently wild-eyed and distraught that my story was accepted without question.

∞⊖∞

The Guvnor had a long talk with me this morning when I woke, unrefreshed, from a troubled sleep. He appears satisfied with my answers, and while he did upbraid me slightly for failing to take a third person with us—as that might have helped avert the tragedy—he agreed that the presence of another would probably have done nothing to help save De Vere.

Pray God he never finds out the truth.

15 February: More than a week since De Vere's death, and I have not seen Walker in that time. Castleton, too, is much improved, and appears well on the way to regaining his full health.

Subsequent sledge parties have inspected the crevasse, and agree that it was a terrible accident, but one that could not have been avoided. I have not been up on the plateau since my trip with De Vere. My thoughts continually turn to the man whom I left there, and I recall what Cook wrote more than one hundred years ago. He was speaking of this place; but the words could, I think, equally be applied to De Vere: 'Doomed by nature never once to feel the warmth of the sun's rays, but to be buried in everlasting snow and ice.'

∞⊖∞

A soft flutter of leaves whispered like a sigh as Emily finished reading. The last traces of day had vanished, leaving behind shadows which pooled at the corners of the room. She sat in silence for some time, her eyes far away; then she closed the journal gently, almost with reverence, and placed it on the table beside her. The writer's card stared up at her, and she considered it.

'He would not understand,' she said at last. 'And they are all dead; they can neither explain nor defend themselves or their actions.' She looked at her father's photograph, now blurred in the gathering darkness. 'Yet you did not destroy this.' She touched the journal with fingers delicate as a snowflake. 'You left it for me to decide, keeping this a secret even from my mother. You must have thought that I would know what to do.'

Pray God he never finds out the truth.

She remained in her chair for some moments longer. Then, with some effort, Emily rose from her chair and, picking up the journal, crossed once more to the rosewood desk and its shadows. She placed the journal in its drawer, where it rested beside a pipe which had lain unsmoked for decades. The ceramic cat watched with blank eyes as she turned out the light. In so doing she knocked the card to the floor, where it lay undisturbed.

-Preserver-
TIM WAGGONER

"That has to be the worst piece of crap I've seen in some time."

Benjamin Moulton looked away from what could only charitably be called a sculpture, startled to hear his thoughts echoed so precisely. The speaker was a petite woman, not much over five feet. She wore her blonde hair short, the cut too ragged to be called a pageboy, although that's what it put him in mind of. He expected her to be dressed in black—after all, well over half of the people milling through the gallery were. But she wore a maroon jacket which was a little too large for her and far too light for late January in Ohio, and a simple pair of jeans, not even designer as far as he could tell. In Benjamin's estimation, that gave her more real taste than ninety-nine point nine percent of the people in the place, himself probably included.

He smiled. "Don't hold back; tell me how you really feel."

She chuckled, the sound more mature, more knowing than someone of her apparent years should have been capable of making. She seemed to be in her early twenties, at most. "I could go on, but why bother? That … object isn't worth the time it would take."

Benjamin looked at the sculpture again. It was by an artist he'd never heard of, someone named Kopinski. The piece was a hunk of wood, nothing more than a small upright log, really, that had been scored numerous times with a sharp object, the deep cuts criss-crossing and zig-zagging in random, senseless patterns. The hand-lettered placard on the wall said it was called Orpheus Screams, and that the artist was willing to part with this masterpiece for the paltry sum of $365.00.

He turned back to his newfound fellow critic. "Come now, surely you can see what a bold statement the artist is making," he said with a smirk.

She grinned. "The only statement I see is 'I'm a no-talent hack desperately hoping to find someone gullible enough to pay a few hundred dollars for damaged firewood.'"

Benjamin laughed. "Now, now, they say art is in the eye of the beholder."

The woman was suddenly sober. "They're wrong. Art exists all by itself." She reached out and placed a pale, slender hand atop the chunk of wood. "Kopinski's got a whole pile of these behind his house. It took him ten minutes to score the wood, and that only because he paused to go get a beer."

"You know the artist?"

"Artist is far too kind a word, but no, I do not know him."

"Then how—?"

She removed her hand, smiled, and gave a little shrug. "Just speculating."

"I wouldn't be surprised if you were pretty damn close to the truth." And that seemed to be all there was to say about Kopinski and his log, for suddenly a silence descended between them. The woman seemed undisturbed by it, merely looked at him and continued to smile, and Benjamin realized how attractive she was. Not that she was pretty, not really, was more on the plain side actually, her complexion washed out, hints of dark circles beneath her eyes, her nose a touch too long, her lips a smidge too thin. But those eyes …

Her eyes were large and bluish green, with little flecks of color in them that seemed to change from moment to moment, first gold, then red, then black, then back to gold again. The pupils were dark and deep and wide, and it felt as if they were pulling at him somehow, as if they might suck him in and devour him whole if he weren't careful.

Benjamin suddenly felt self-conscious. He had never been an especially attractive man, and at forty-seven, whatever looks he did possess were on the verge of deserting him forever. His rusty-brown hair was thinning on top and too long in the back, and he hadn't shaved in two days. He wore a gray trench coat that was probably as old if not older than the woman standing before him, and which was a decade overdue for dry-cleaning. His brown slacks were rumpled and sported several stains—some old, some fresh—and his tennis shoes, which had once been white, were now sooty gray black.

He was old enough to be her father, too old for her to be looking at him like she was, too old to be liking it this much.

He knew the smart thing would be to say good-bye and get out of here before he embarrassed himself. Instead, he said, "So what besides the opportunity to indulge in razor-tongued criticism has brought you out to the galleries on such a cold night?"

"You, Benjamin Moulton. I'm a great admirer of your work."

Of all the possible responses she might have made, that was the last he expected. "How—?"

"Do I know you?" she finished. "I frequent the galleries; I've seen you around."

He smiled ruefully. "I didn't think I had any admirers. Most people don't understand my stuff."

She made a dismissive gesture. "Most people lack vision."

"But not you?"

"Not me," she agreed. No hint of pride, just a simple statement of fact.

Benjamin was a collage artist, but instead of paper or cloth, he used everyday household items to create his art. He took all manner of odds and ends, bits and pieces, and fit them together with glue, solder, wire and string to create his collages, to make his statements. Statements no one ever seemed to understand.

"Prove it," he challenged.

"All right. But you don't have any pieces on display here. We'll have to go to the Plaid Pony." And before Benjamin could respond, she turned and began threading her way through the crowd and toward the door, leaving him hurrying to catch up.

Outside on the sidewalk, Benjamin coughed explosively as the cold night air filled his lungs and he wished desperately to light up a cigarette, but he hadn't had enough money to buy a pack of Camels for the last four days. He briefly considered asking his new acquaintance if she smoked, and if so, could she spare a cigarette, but he decided against it. So many people were anti-smoking these days, and he didn't want to turn her off before he had a proper chance to turn her on.

The streets of the Old Brewery District were covered with a light dusting of snow, and tiny, almost imperceptible flakes were still drifting down, but they were few and far between.

"They look so small and lonely, don't they?" she said.

"What?" he asked, startled.

"The snowflakes."

"Ah, yes, they do." That was exactly what he had been thinking. He felt a sudden chill that had nothing to do with the winter air and he stuffed his hands deep into his coat pockets and wished he had a shot of whiskey to warm himself up, or at least a pair of gloves or a scarf. But the problem with the cliché of the starving artist was that it was a cliché for a very good reason.

They trudged along the sidewalk, slowed by the crowds who'd flocked from all over town to attend the first gallery hop of the year. Fifteen years ago the Old Brewery District was a pesthole of run-down and abandoned buildings, the only residents rats, drug addicts and other assorted vermin. But a wave of urban renewal had gone through the city, thanks to flocks of yuppies with money to burn, and the Old Brewery District slowly became reborn as a haven for artsy-craftsy types and where once bars and 24-hour porn emporiums had stood were now art galleries and coffee shops. And once a month the yuppies—no longer so young but still well monied, thank you—came down, along with a mixture of college students and a sprinkling of curious middle-class types, to wander from gallery to gallery, sometimes buying, more often just looking and feeling virtuously intellectual for taking a few minutes to stare at what was mostly hackwork in between cups of cappuccino and cheap burgundy.

Benjamin hated it. But he came every month. It was a good way to make connections with gallery owners and, better yet, potential customers. He might have been an artist, but that didn't mean he was above prostituting himself. The only problem was finding someone who wanted him to spread his legs.

Benjamin breathed as shallowly as he could to keep from coughing, the air curling slowly out of his mouth like miniature fog. He looked at his companion and noticed that her breath, unlike his, wasn't misting in the frigid air. He shrugged mentally. Some people just handled cold weather better than others, he guessed.

After all, she had on that light jacket, right? She probably sweltered in the summertime.

Before long they came to the Plaid Pony and went inside. The Pony wasn't as crowded as the last gallery had been, but then it was a small place with only a few works displayed. The girl brushed past the scattering of browsers and headed straight for his piece, the only one of his displayed in the Pony. For that matter, the only one displayed anywhere right now.

The collage hung on the wall, a conglomeration of household junk glued to a piece of plywood. Screws, bolts, and clock springs, doll parts and matchbook covers, playing cards and Legos, unopened condoms and small plastic dinosaurs, a riot of the mundane, an explosion of triviality.

The collage wasn't titled; none of his work was. The placard on the wall announced it simply as Number 142 and said he was asking $145.

Dream on, Ben, he thought. Dream on.

He turned to his companion and gestured toward his piece. "All right, Ms. Visionary … go to it."

Her eyes narrowed and she took a step back. Her fingers came to her chin and stroked it lightly as she examined every inch of the collage. Benjamin found himself growing uncomfortable. He was used to people glancing at his work and moving on, not giving it this kind of concentrated scrutiny. This woman wasn't just looking at his collage; she was truly seeing it.

She studied Number 142 for a full five minutes before speaking. "On the surface, it appears to be about Aids. The screws and bolts represent sex. The clock springs time, which is running out. Unopened condoms, which the ignorant and foolish refuse to use. They'd rather take chances, as evidenced by the playing cards. The matchbooks are empty, their fire gone, standing for those who have died. The Legos, oh, they're lost innocence, I suppose. And the dinosaurs represent the ultimate and final extinction of a species, which might happen to humanity if it doesn't wise up.

"Of course, beneath the particulars of the imagery is the heart of the work, the deep sense of isolation and futility in the face of death."

Benjamin didn't notice his mouth was hanging open, and if he had, he wouldn't have cared. "You … understand."

"Of course. It's rather obvious, really. Not that I'm criticizing, mind. It's quite good. Perhaps not up to par with your best pieces, but still far better than anything else in town."

Benjamin didn't know how to respond. After all these years of waiting for someone to actually get what he was trying to say, now that someone had, he had no idea what to think, how to feel.

"What's your name?" he finally asked, resorting to simple social custom.

"Seina," she replied with a smile. "Would you like to get some coffee?"

Benjamin smiled back. "I'd love to."

∞◉∞

Seina passed by several popular coffee shops before finally stopping at Java Hut, a hole in the wall joint that Benjamin had never visited before. "It may not look like much . . ." she began.

"And ten dollars says that in this case, looks are definitely not deceiving," he finished.

She grinned and led him inside.

Sure enough, it was small, cramped, dingy and dirty, with only a handful of tables and even fewer customers. Seina led him to a table in the back and they sat.

The only employee in sight, a pimply faced college kid behind the counter, looked sullenly in their direction, his lethargic gaze saying, You don't really want to *order anything, do you?*

Benjamin looked at Seina. "What would you like?" Ordinarily in this situation he would've added, 'My treat,' but all he had in his pockets at the moment was lint.

"Nothing, really. I just wanted to go someplace where we could talk."

Benjamin turned toward the kid behind the counter and shook his head. The kid nodded once, relieved that he wouldn't have to exert himself, and went back to staring into space.

"So tell me, how did you get to be such a fan of mine?" Benjamin asked.

"I follow the arts. Your work stood out. It's as simple as that."

"Not that I'm fishing for compliments—ah, hell, of course I'm fishing for compliments—but what makes my work stand out?"

She answered without hesitation. "The subtlety. The playful irony. Although it's gotten less playful and more biting over the years."

Years? "How long have you been following my work?"

"Oh, for a while now."

Benjamin didn't know what to make of that. She hardly seemed old enough to have taken a serious interest in art for very long. Months, perhaps, but years?

She smiled a private smile. "I'm older than I look."

"You did it again."

"What?"

"Responded to something I was thinking."

"Coincidence." But there was something about the way she said the word that made it clear she didn't expect to be believed. "Tell me something, Benjamin. Do you like being an artist?"

Benjamin started to answer, but before he could speak, he was seized by a fit of phlegmy coughing. It took him almost a full minute to get it under control and regain his breath. "Sorry," he wheezed.

Seina acted like it hadn't happened. She just sat patiently, waiting for him to respond.

"It's a mixed bag," he said. "Sometimes it's great, like when an idea takes hold of me. I start hunting for objects. And not just any old objects will do; they have to be the right ones. I can spend days— sometimes weeks—searching for the appropriate materials. And then when I finally have them, I can start putting them together. At random at first, or at least that's the way it feels. But before long a pattern begins to emerge, a pattern that was there all along. It just took me a while to see it. After that, the actual assembly goes fairly quickly. And then, when the collage is finished, I can see how close to my original idea I got." He smiled. "Or didn't get, as the case may be. "But sometimes it's not so great. There's the dry period between ideas, when it feels like you'll never have another again. And of course, there's the money, or rather the lack thereof. If I was a painter, at least I might be able to get some commercial work, you know? But there's not much call for a commercial collage artist. I end up working a lot of odd jobs. I've done everything from painting houses to driving cabs."

"And what does it feel like to know you're past your prime?"

"I'm only forty-seven," he said stiffly.

"I wasn't talking about age; I was talking about your creative prime."

"What do you mean?"

"Come now, Benjamin. I said I've been following your work for some time, and I meant it. I've seen you grow from an immature artist with little skill and even less to say to a seasoned master of his craft. But lately your work has been … lacking. Like your collage in the Painted Pony. It's still an accomplished piece of work, but nothing like what you used to produce."

Benjamin wanted to be angry, wanted to defend Number 142. But he couldn't. He knew she was right. "Maybe I'm just in a slump." He didn't sound convincing, even to himself.

"Perhaps. But there comes a time in every artist's life when he begins the downward slide to mediocrity. It's as inevitable as the approach of the grave."

"Now isn't that a cheery thought."

Seina leaned forward then, her remarkable eyes shining. "But it doesn't have to be like that, Benjamin. Not if you don't want it to be."

"I don't understand."

She leaned even closer, her voice low and intense. "I know a way to keep your talents and skills at their peak, as fresh and vital as they ever were—for all time."

Benjamin chuckled. "Sounds like you're about to launch into some kind of religious spiel."

Seina smiled, displaying sharp incisors. "Hardly."

∞⊙∞

Seina's home was the top floor of a condemned building not too far from the Brewery District. There was some furniture—a bed, couch, kitchen table, a few other pieces—but mostly her place was filled with creativity. There were paintings and sculptures in all styles from the minimalist to the gaudily bizarre. A piano rested in one corner, and next to it, on a table, were a saxophone and a flute, along with a stack of sheet music, some of which was pre-printed but most of which was hand-written. Quilts hung on the walls, next to framed poems—original, Benjamin presumed—rendered in ornate calligraphy. Origami animals of all colors were scattered throughout the rooms wherever there was space. Mobiles and wind chimes hung from the ceiling, stirring in the icy breeze wafting from the open windows.

He shivered.

"My kind don't need heat," Seina said.

Benjamin knew he shouldn't take her remark seriously. Vampire fixations were not uncommon among artsy folk. Some of them would go to any lengths to indulge their fantasies, including purchasing a pair of quite realistic looking fangs. Still, there was something about Seina, a sense of age, a feeling of restrained power. And those eyes . . .

"I am what I say I am, Benjamin. How else could I know what you're thinking?"

"Maybe you're just a good guesser."

"Maybe." She closed the windows then led him over to the couch. Not quite sure what else to do, he followed and they sat.

"Have you ever wondered what it's like to live for eternity, Benjamin? It's wonderful for the first century or two, but before long, much sooner than you'd think, it grows dull. Each night is like the one before it, and the next night, and the next … Some of my kind take their own lives rather than endure any more of the numbing sameness. Some go mad. But some of us find ways to fill the emptiness, take up pursuits to keep us amused."

Benjamin told himself that he was humoring her; that he really didn't believe.

"And so you collect art?"

If she truly was what she claimed to be and caught his thought about humoring her, she gave no sign. "In a manner of speaking. You see, I've always been attracted to the arts, but I lack talent. And since I have no talent of my own, I preserve the talent of others. Preserve it forever."

Stories flashed through Benjamin's mind, novels he'd read, movies he'd seen.

Immortality—the vampire's most seductive promise. For him? He couldn't bring himself to believe it. "Why me? Why here? Why aren't you in New York or Paris, searching out real artists?"

"Because, Benjamin, those artists have opportunities to be noticed, opportunities for their own sort of immortality, a place in a museum, a niche in a canon of Artists with a capital A. But there are other artists in other places who don't have such opportunities, artists of great talent and skill who are equally deserving, but who are destined to remained unnoticed. Artists like you, Benjamin."

She laid a hand on his. It was ice cold.

He jerked his hand away. "So just like that, I'm chosen to become immortal, like I'm some sort of supernatural sweepstakes winner?"

"Not at all. I said I've been following your work for years, Benjamin, and I have. I frequent the galleries, the museums, the university art shows, concerts and plays, always searching for another artist whose gift I can preserve. I first became aware of your work fourteen years ago. I remember the piece. It was your Number 11, a eulogy for the death of sixties' idealism."

Benjamin remembered that particular collage. It contained peace signs, Beatles memorabilia, and reproductions of drafts cards, all covered by dollar bills stained red.

"It was a simple piece," Seina continued, "but even then your talent shown through and I knew you were an artist to watch. And watch I did for nearly a decade and a half. Until I noticed your work begin to decline in quality, even if only slightly." She held up a hand as he opened his mouth to speak. "No need to protest or make excuses, Benjamin. We both know it's true."

"Yes." It was a soft, painful admission.

"And the decline will continue, slowly but surely. The ideas will come harder, and those that do come will be common, pedestrian. You'll stop searching so hard for just the right objects to create your collages and start using whatever's at hand, because it's easier. You'll find that you complete fewer and fewer pieces, and those you do finish will be farther and farther away from your original vision.

"But it doesn't have to be like that, Benjamin." Seina reached for his hand again, then stopped as if thinking better of it. "I can end this dissipation of your powers, even reverse the degradation which has already taken place. I can ensure that your talent will never die, Benjamin. Never."

Benjamin knew he should stop playing along with Seina's fantasy, that he should get up and leave right now. But he stayed where he was. If it weren't a fantasy, if it were true . . .

"What do you have to look forward to for the rest of your life, Benjamin? You have no family, no real friends. You smoke and drink too much. I can hear your lungs laboring to draw breath, your flabby heart struggling to pump blood. You'll be lucky to live another ten years. Ten years of working odd jobs and watching helplessly as your artistic abilities slowly but surely desert you. Is that what you want, Benjamin?"

It sounded like a worse hell than any Bosch ever depicted. "No, it isn't."

She did take his hand this time, and this time he didn't pull away. "Then allow me to help you. Give yourself to me, Benjamin."

Benjamin looked into her eyes, and what he saw there finally convinced him she was what she said she was, and that she could do what she said she could.

He uttered a single, final word. "Yes."

And then Seina embraced him and her mouth found his throat. There was pain, then warmth, then a coldness which began to seep into his limbs. As he listened to the sucking sounds, he began to feel that more than his blood was being drained. It was as if Seina was taking something else as well, something even more vital than blood.

And then he realized the true meaning of what she had said.

Your talent will never die.

She'd said nothing about him.

He tried to pull away, but by this time he was far too weak. Finally, as he sank into the darkness, he was comforted by one thought: at least the best part of himself would live on. In the end, wasn't that every artist's dream?

∞☉∞

Seina wiped her mouth and watched as the dried husk that had been Benjamin began to crumble and decay. Within an hour it would be nothing more than dust, easily disposed of. She felt his abilities settling within her, alongside the countless others she had preserved over the years.

Her first collage should be something special. Something … and then an idea popped into her head. She would create a memorial to Benjamin. Yes, he'd like that.

She stood and flexed her hands. They felt alive and eager to get to work, ready to help her stave off the boredom of eternity for yet another night.

-A New House-
JOHN L. FRENCH

"It is a fine house," thought the vampire, "well suited to my purpose." He had searched for months for just the right dwelling, similar to that in which he lived in Europe. He did not require a mansion nor any kind of luxury. He was beyond that. He needed a house that no one else wanted, that would not be disturbed in any way. He did not want trespassers stumbling over his resting place or vagrants starting fires that he could not put out. Trespassers and vagrants had their uses, but suspicions were aroused when too many disappeared from the same area. He would not make that mistake again.

But the house could not be too derelict. Then the state would come and tear it down, exposing his secrets. He needed a place that people shunned, where no one wanted to go.

He had briefly tried living among his prey, renting a house in a residential neighborhood, keeping to himself, attracting no attention. The needs of this kind of "life" proved too demanding.

He had to create documents to show to landlords, arrange for utilities he did not need, hire people to maintain the exterior of his dwelling. He also had to show himself to his neighbors on occasion, just to avoid being thought of as "different." It was too much; too many people became aware of his existence. No, it was better to live alone, away from the cattle.

Finally, during his nightly forays throughout the city he learned of a house that fit his needs. There had been a tragedy, a death of some sorts. It had stood vacant for over a year. No one wanted it.

The vampire learned more. There had been a burglary. The owner had confronted the thief before he shot and killed the man as he fled out a window. Despite his pleas of self-defense the owner was imprisoned for manslaughter, and should serve another two years in jail. His family moved away, abandoning the house they were unable to sell. The homeless and drug addicted made use of it for a while, but even they gave it up. They had perhaps been encouraged to leave by community pressure and the police, going on to less visible haunts. The house was his to take.

He waited for the conditions to be right and created a fog that covered his move. He placed his box of earth in the basement, in a corner away from the windows. His trunks of personal possessions he also put in convenient, yet secluded, spots. As additional precautions, he drove heavy nails into the rear basement door and silently collapsed the stairs to the first floor. Even if should someone enter, they would not be likely to disturb his rest by coming into the basement.

His preparations had tired him. He would not hunt this night. He sought his coffin for an early rest.

The noise woke him, the breaking of the glass, the raising of the sash.

"Why tonight?" he asked himself. "I watched this house for a week and no one even glanced at it. Some even avoided it, crossing the street to keep from passing it. And now on my first night someone breaks into my home."

He considered ignoring the intruder, trusting to his preparations. But in the end, anger at the invasion and a hunger from his previous exertions caused him to mist and rise to the first floor.

Reforming, he saw the broken window in what had been the kitchen. He turned and saw the young boy creeping around the living room.

"Don't they ever learn?" he asked as his fangs descended. "Well, this one never will."

He stalked the boy while at the same time he considered what to do with the body. Just as he struck, his quarry turned, staring through him. His fangs entered the boy's neck, and he began to feed.

Too late he realized the nature of his prey. A cold burning pain raced through him. He had never felt agony like this, not even during his conversion. As the boy stepped away from him he was flooded with the youth's last living memories.

Through the boy's mind, the vampire remembered approaching the house, sure that no one was home. Again, there was the breaking of glass and the raising of the window. He got as far as the living room when there was the man with the gun. He fled past the man, but too slowly. There was a gunshot, a sharp pain in his back, and then darkness. Coming back to his own mind, the vampire collapsed on the floor.

Unlike the warmth he received from blood, the chilling he had from the boy did not diminish. Rather, the pain intensified, until it was all he could feel. The ghost watched him for a time and then slowly faded, taking the pain with him. Again, there was darkness.

The vampire found himself reforming on the first floor. He saw the broken kitchen window.

Turning, he saw the young boy in the living room. Trapped now in the cycle of the haunting, he forever stalked his prey.

-The Sabbatarian-
DAVID M. FITZPATRICK

"I need you to help me kill a vampire," the wrinkled old man with the eye patch said. "I'm getting too old for this, and this vamp's too powerful anyway."

Rogan Mallory looked at him with a deadpan gaze, not knowing quite what to think. The street corner was desolate under an overcast sky; a few green leaves and paper scraps blew past them and the rows of houses. "And you're a vampire hunter? You hunt them down and kill them?"

"For sixty-two years," the old man said. "Killed my first at age twelve. Took over for my father, who took over for his."

"So this is a family business?" Rogan pulled his brown duster tightly around his waist and crossed him arms defensively. This guy was a crackpot, and he wanted to finish walking home from the library before Delia worried. He remembered summers not long ago when he'd never have spent a warm summer day at the library, but out tearing up the streets on his motorcycle. Age and marriage had certainly tamed him.

"For more generations than I can recount. But I have no son to carry on the tradition. I fathered six kids, four of them boys, but they have predeceased me."

"So you stop the first man on the street?" Rogan said.

"Not quite. You're special, Rogan Mallory."

Rogan looked at him, leery. "How'd you know my name?"

"A little research. Hired a private investigator."

Rogan stepped away from the man. "Okay, pal, maybe it's time we parted company."

"Please, just let me speak," the man said, and Rogan had the feeling there was something sane and honest in his eyes. He was a crackpot, sure, but he didn't seem dangerous. And there *was* a certain amusement factor to the whole bit. "All right, but it's only because I've always liked horror fiction," he said. "Make it fast, and when you're done, I'm leaving."

"I saw you at your real estate office several months ago, and recognized your capability immediately," the man said without prelude, his one visible eye gleaming in the dim light. "You have the most powerful aura I've ever seen in any Sabbatarian—even more than any other red-haired Sabbatarian."

"Sabbatarian?" Rogan echoed, self-consciously running his hand through his red hair. "Isn't that a Jew who celebrates the Sabbath on Saturday? Or anyone who believes in strict observance of the Sabbath?"

"It came to mean that over time. But more specifically, a Sabbatarian is one who is born on Saturday."

"I don't understand."

"The ancient Macedonians knew that Sabbatarians are blessed with an innate protection from vampires. But it's better than that. Sabbatarians have a power that works *against* vampires. Vampires attempting to mesmerize a Sabbatarian are likely to find it won't work, or the vampires end up mesmerized. A red-haired Sabbatarian, on the other hand, is a far more powerful variety."

"This is silly," Rogan said, suddenly keenly aware of a bat fluttering down to a nearby streetlight to nab a flying insect.

"Not at all. I'm a Sabbatarian, and my power has been instrumental in combating them."

"Then why do you need me?"

"As I said, I'm getting old. But you aren't just any Sabbatarian. Far more important events in your life have transpired on Saturdays than normal people. And those events only escalate a Sabbatarian's power. For instance, you were baptized on a Saturday."

"So are a lot of people," Rogan said.

"Think back on the major events of you life, Rogan. Saturday is a nexus point for you. You were married on a Saturday. You graduated both high school and college on Saturdays."

"I do most things I enjoy on Saturday, because it's the weekend," Rogan said. "There's nothing amazing about it. Hell, I think I lost my virginity on a Saturday."

"I can only confirm what I've researched; you alone can recall the others. But your aura radiates with all the power and color of a

Sabbatarian the likes of which nobody has ever seen."

"Right," Rogan said with a smile. "I think our time is up. I'll be on my way." He sidestepped the old man and strode down the street amidst the growing wind and darkening skies.

"I need your strength, Mr. Mallory," the man called after him. "He's far too powerful for me."

Rogan waved after him and kept on going.

The man hollered, "I'll be dead soon, but he'll still be here. He'll rebuild the vampire presence on this world. You may be the only one who can stop it."

He kept walking, trying to ignore the crazy bastard. Truly, this had been a strange day.

And, come to think of it, it was Saturday.

∞☉∞

Delia was quiet when he returned. He could tell she was mad at him. He tried making small talk but she just ate quietly. He knew the routine, knew the script. He finally sighed and set down his fork. "What's wrong, dear?"

The ensuing discussion where she kept telling him nothing was wrong and he kept demanding to know lasted several minutes. Finally, she gave in and said, "I just thought that, for a change, you'd stay home on a Saturday and we'd spend the day together."

"I had some research to do," he said. "This legal tangle with the Crenshaws' building permit is really mucking things up. We'll spend tomorrow together, hon."

"You work Monday through Friday, twelve hours a day or more," she said dully, as if she were protesting but not really caring. "I'd think you'd give me Saturday."

"I'm sorry," he said, and he really meant it. "But being the designated broker is what gives us this nice house and the food we're eating."

She sighed and nodded. "I know. But it's always about you working. It's never about us being together."

"I'm trying."

"I know." Abruptly, she smiled broadly, all perfect white teeth his job had also paid for. "Hey, my sister called this afternoon. We're going out to the mall in about a half hour."

He looked at her in surprise. "You complain about me never

spending time with you, and then you run off with her to go shopping?"

"I didn't know when you'd be home. They're having a mallwalk sale. Everyone's having big discounts and they're keeping the mall open until midnight. It's not like Sarah and I do this often."

∞☉∞

She was still backing out of the driveway in the BMW when the phone rang. He was only mildly surprised to hear the old man on the other end.

"I assume we can talk a bit more," the man said.

"No, we cannot," Rogan said.

"You're making this hard on both of us," he said. "I need you, and I'm not going to leave you alone until you listen. And it doesn't matter if you go to the police, or get a protection order, or hire security guards. This is more important than any of that."

"Mister, put yourself in my position. You approach me on the street, say you're a vampire hunter, and tell me how some random occurrence of Saturday in my life qualifies me to whip Dracula's ass. How would *you* react?"

"Probably the same, which is why I'm so understanding."

There was still a level of amusement to the whole thing, but he didn't need the guy calling his house when Delia was home. "What do I have to do to make you go away?"

"Just believe what I told you."

"That's not likely."

"I figured as much. That's why I saved such proof for you. I have one I captured—here, at my house. It's a young one, not very powerful. I could almost have wrestled it down. Now I promise you, if you just come here and have a look, and don't believe me, you'll never hear from me again."

∞☉∞

He almost took the motorcycle for a change, but he was nervous enough to prefer four wheels. He took the Mercedes to the remote address, which was outside of town, with no houses for a mile either way, surrounded by wide-open fields. Rogan pulled his Mercedes up next to the two vehicles in the driveway—an old van and a big Chrysler New Yorker. He sat, staring at the well-lit front porch.

He couldn't believe he was doing this. The guy could likely have a wooden stake ready to drive through Rogan's own heart, for all he knew. Yet somehow he got out of the car and headed up the walkway.

The house was a veritable anti-vampire fortress. Strings of garlic decorated the eaves under the roof, surrounded the windows inside and out, and encircled the door. Holy symbols from dozens of religions were displayed on the house, on posts around it, and designed into the brickwork of the walkway. Stranger still, he realized the glass in all the windows was one-way: reflecting mirrors, essentially. As he stood at the bottom of the stairs to the front door, he realized the wooden posts that lined the walkway, on which various symbols were displayed, could easily be yanked up from the grass and used as stakes. Rogan wondered if the flat, open fields that surrounded the property were devoid of trees for a reason. Maybe it was to keep the sun shining on the house as long as possible during the day. Was this guy that entrenched in his beliefs?

The door suddenly flew open, and the eyepatched old man regarded him with a smile. "Welcome, Mr. Mallory. Do come in."

"Are you inviting me in?" Rogan asked. "If I'm actually a vampire, that could be disastrous for you."

The old man laughed loudly. "Stoker and Hollywood, Rogan. Absolutely untrue. Besides, I can spot a vampire a mile away, and you're not it. I read auras, like I told you. Now, won't you come in?"

"I'd guess I'd like to at least know your name first."

The old man looked bemused. "And knowing my name will relieve the danger you believe is here?"

"No. But I'll feel better."

"Okay. It's Jonah William Byrne. Now, please … come in."

"I'm regretting this already," Rogan said, but he mounted the stairs and entered the house.

The interior was more or less like the exterior: holy symbols everywhere. Real mirrors abounded—literally, every wall had multiple mirrors. There was no lack of garlic, either, and the whole place smelled of it.

"He's in the basement," Jonah said, opening a door. Steps led down and out of sight. Rogan regarded them, and Jonah, uneasily.

"Either way, the answer is in that basement," Jonah said. "If I'm crazy, you'll know soon enough."

They descended into a full concrete basement, dimly lit by low-wattage bulbs. An oil tank, a water heater, a furnace, and a washer and dryer were all here.

"He's this way," Jonah said, heading toward the darker end of the cellar. It wasn't until they were melting into the darkness that Rogan saw the large walk-in cooler. It was closed, its stainless steel door gleaming in the dim light, a muffled humming playing out a steady mechanical tune.

"You refrigerated him?" Rogan said.

"They don't like cold much, and the walk-in's soundproof," Jonah said. "Now, it's bound pretty damn tight, but it'll probably make a whole load of noise and thrash around. Don't let it scare you. Like I said, it's young and not too tough."

A thought suddenly occurred to him. Rogan had been assuming Jonah was a nut case with a vivid imagination, but suddenly he wondered if Jonah were a *homicidal* nut case with an actual person in there. Worse, maybe Rogan would become that innocent person.

Jonah snapped the handle down and pulled the door open. Within, all was dark. "Here's your proof," he said, and flipped the light switch.

Rogan blinked and recoiled in shock. There was a naked man spread-eagle on the floor, thin limbs extended in four directions, pulled taut with heavy chains. The chains were wrapped around his wrists and ankles many times, and secured to big hooks in the corners of the otherwise empty walk-in. A thin covering of ghostly white skin was stretched over his ribs and bones like a sheet of latex rubber over a birdcage. He regarded them all with sunken, dark eyes set in a gaunt face framed by stringy, black hair.

Rogan was frozen, looking at the man in horror. Jonah Byrne had evidently kept his prisoner tied up down here, without food, for some time. "How ... how long have you ... had him here?" he stammered.

Jonah waved him off, unconcerned. "Oh, don't let his appearance fool you. He's in better shape than he looks."

"How long?" Rogan said, hearing his own voice quavering.

"About a month. I've been saving him for you."

Rogan backed up quickly, bumped into Jonah, and spun about. He intended to make a run for it. He was sure he could outrun the old bastard, make it to his car, and hoof it out of there—but there was Jonah, backing away from him, gun in his hand. Rogan wasn't a gun expert, but he sure as hell knew how to classify the cannon Jonah had pointed at him. It was *a big fucking gun.*

"Please don't," Rogan begged. "I've got a wife at home ... please ... "

"I expected more of you than whimpering and pleading for your life," Jonah said, "but it doesn't matter. You're not leaving here until you *understand.* Now pick up the three-pound sledge and drive that wooden stake through its heart."

The sledgehammer and stake were leaning against the inside wall, and now Rogan's brain was on the spin cycle. "I ... I can't do that."

"You're not getting it, kid," Jonah said. "It's not human. It's a creature. A *monster.* A goddamn *demon* from *Hell,* I tell you!" He was yelling now, and his voice got louder, and he waved the gun as he hollered. "Now you grab that stake, pick up that sledge, and drive it through his *cold black fucking heart!"*

The gun was certainly big. Rogan backed into the walk-in and numbly picked up the items. Behind him, he heard the captive growling. He turned to see the naked guy struggling vainly against his steel bonds, snarling and hissing at him, eyes wild. A man, yes, but after a month like this, it had truly become a creature.

Then it opened its mouth and bared its teeth and Rogan's jaw dropped.

It had huge fangs, almost like a saber-toothed human.

That kind of alteration is popular these days, he told himself.

"He's scared now," Jonah said gleefully. "He knows the Big Stake is here. And he can see your aura. He knows what you are."

Rogan looked at the creature's face, and their eyes met. The creature ceased its growling and hissing almost immediately and, like a docile puppy, relaxed and went completely blank.

Briefly, Rogan's mind filled with a flurry of disjointed images—people he didn't know, places he'd never been, sounds he'd never heard. It was like a confusing dream replayed at high speed. He shook his head to clear it, but never looked away from the thing's eyes.

"What's wrong with him?" Rogan whispered.

"You're what's wrong with him!" Jonah let out a rollicking laugh. "You're a Sabbatarian of the highest order. He's fallen to you. All you have left is to stake him. It's like pounding a nail; you just line it up and hit it on the head. I'd do it for you, but I don't think you quite believe any of this yet. So I have to keep this gun pointed at your head until you do it. Once you do, you'll see."

The phantasmagoria of images kept flying through his mind. Faces, voices, and smells; things, ideas, and feelings. They weren't his. They made no sense. Rogan shook his head. "I can't do it. You're going to have to kill me."

Behind him, Jonah sighed. "Are you really going to make me threaten you with Delia? Are you really going to make me blow a hole through her belly? I'll do it, Rogan. So save your own ass, save your wife's, and save your unborn child's."

"My unborn child?" Rogan echoed.

"I hired the best private detective. She found out Thursday at Dr. Weatherbee's. I guess you didn't know."

"I didn't," Rogan said. Why hadn't she told him? Why would she have kept it from him? *How* could she have *considered* keeping it from him?

"So stake him now, or I'll fucking kill them both," Jonah snarled, and Rogan heard the hammer cock back on the weapon.

He hadn't separated his eyes from those of the entranced captive. Slowly, he moved forward, on legs of rubbery iron, as if guided by some part of his being not under his conscious control. He dropped to his knees beside the chained man and positioned the stake. All the while, the man watched him.

When Rogan raised he sledgehammer high, the prisoner seemed to break out of his reverie: a light humming sound, less than a growl but more than a whimper, floated up. Rogan wavered, even as the strange, alien pictures in his mind seemed to spiral around crazily.

"Don't let him get to you," Jonah said. "You just imagine Delia with her womb ripped open and your baby without its head, and the rest will be easy."

And it was. Rogan brought the sledge down with a strangely alien might, and in that one strike the stake plunged straight through the man's chest and clear to the concrete beneath. The man let out a gut-twisting howl of pain and tightened against its bonds, arching its back. Rogan leaped up and back, crashing into the wall. At the door to the walk-in, Jonah whooped in celebration.

The man still howled in agony, and as Rogan watched, transfixed like a deer in the headlights, its white skin rapidly darkened, blackening like a pig cooking on a spit. Then, just as suddenly, his body collapsed in on itself. Rogan watched in utter horror, even as the last echo of the creature's howling died off, as the remains crumbled up and turned to gray dust.

"Congratulations, Mr. Mallory," Jonah said, lowering the gun and tucking it in his belt. "Your first vampire kill."

∞⊙∞

Rogan sat, mystified, on the L-shaped sectional sofa in Jonah's spacious living room. "You were telling the truth," he said.

At the adjoining kitchen counter, Jonah was pouring coffee. "I'm not as crazy as I look, you know. For the record, the gun isn't loaded. Regular bullets don't do much against these types, so I have little use for it. And I wouldn't have hurt you or Delia. I just had to make you understand."

"How many vampires are there?" Rogan asked.

He still noticed the garlic smell of the house as Jonah joined him and handed him his coffee, but somehow it was comforting. "Hard to say. They're generally limited to big cities and really remote areas. Makes them harder to track. But they're out there, feeding on us."

"Turning us into vampires," Rogan finished, but Jonah shook his head.

"More Hollywood. It's quite the reverse. To become a vampire, you have to drink *their* blood—and lots of it. If a vamp wants a new child, he force-feeds a regular guy and in a few hours: new bloodsucker. The older the vampire, the faster the process."

"You have my attention," Rogan assured him. "When we first met tonight, you said you needed me. You said 'He's too powerful for me' and that only I could stop him. Why?"

"Remember how it calmed down when you looked into its eyes? First it was terrified, but once you had its gaze, it was entranced." He busily packed tobacco into an ornate wooden pipe as he talked. "You have the power—just as I do, just as my forefathers did. We were all born on Saturday, which is almost a requirement to be a vampire hunter. Without the gift, you're just a badass packing weapons and hoping you'll win. The vampire I speak of won't fall to any badass, and not to just any Sabbatarian."

"Who is he? And if you're a Sabbatarian, why can't *you* handle him?"

Jonah lit his pipe and puffed blue smoke as he settled back on the sectional sofa. "The origins of vampires are unknown—we don't know where they came from or when the first one appeared. Likely it was as a result of renunciation of religion on the part of the first one—for instance, most people think the power of their religion can best a vampire. Truth is, it doesn't matter how powerful your faith is; if you're holding a Christian cross up against a vampire who was Jewish before he was transformed, you'd better go get a Star of David instead. It's about what *his* faith was, not what yours is.

"The older they get, the more powerful they become. Thus, the harder they are to kill, and the harder they are to mesmerize if you're a Sabbatarian. Now this vampire I speak of is called Gantu. He's the oldest I've ever known, and I've dedicated my life to hunting him. We've met fifteen times and I've almost died all fifteen times. It's always been a stalemate. I know, as I approach the close of my life, that I no longer have a chance against him. I've always been a capable Sabbatarian, but he's always withstood my power. Now, as my strength winds down, his is stronger than ever.

"Gantu is incredibly powerful. I've watched him withstand direct sunlight and end up with nothing worse than a few blisters, when other vampires explode into fireballs. It's a wooden stake through the heart or nothing, followed by decapitation and cremation—he won't just crumble to dust like that baby you skewered. The only way I can achieve that is if a Sabbatarian of your caliber helps me. You have the power to mesmerize him, but even you can't hold him *and* attack. But we can take him down together."

At the end of his spiel, his pipe was only smoldering, so he relit it. Rogan said, "Why is it so important that Gantu be killed?"

"It's important that all vampires be killed, but he's the worst. In addition to empowerment with age, they create more vampires the longer they're around. It's a gang mentality—the children follow their sires. Younger vampires start making too many followers; the older ones take them out. Now, to give you an idea of Gantu's capability, the one you staked tonight is a few years old at best. The strongest I've taken out was twelve hundred." He lowered his pipe, leaned toward Rogan, and said, "Gantu is eight thousand years old."

Rogan felt his jaw drop. "How do you know?"

"A Sabbatarian can see it during his mesmerism. You probably had weird images going through your mind when you dealt with the one tonight—yes?"

"Just fleeting pictures, really ... disjointed and confusing."

"Try one who's been around a hundred years. The older they are, the clearer the flurry of information becomes. I've met up with Gantu many times, and although my attempts at mesmerism always failed,

I've gained new insights every time. I've seen memories of him feeding on humans as far back as predating the Great Pyramid of Giza. I'm pretty sure he was in Mesopotamia as early as 6000 B.C."

"Damn," Rogan breathed, shaking his head. "So he's beyond just being really powerful. How do we find him?"

"I know right where he is. I've meshed with his mind enough over the years. I can track him—almost like he's wearing a homing beacon."

Rogan swallowed the lump in his throat. "So what's the plan?"

"I track him. You hold him. I kill him."

He hadn't touched his coffee, and now he tipped it back and downed it. "I need to sleep on this, Mr. Byrne. I need to go home and be with my pregnant wife … and think this through."

Jonah said simply, "The baby thing was bullshit."

He felt his neck heat up with anger. "You son of a bitch."

"Don't get all pissed off. Delia's not worth it. See, that private detective I hired really is the best. I didn't go looking for it, but your wife's been screwing around on you."

He looked at the one-eyed man incredulously and shook his head. "That's impossible."

"I'm not going to play guessing games, Mr. Mallory," Jonah snapped, "and I'm not going to hold your hand. She's banging a guy, does so most weekends. Where do you think she went tonight?"

"Shopping with her sister," Rogan said weakly, even then remembering all the odd excuses she'd had for being late.

"Well, I'll tell you what. On your way home, stop by 1340 East Riverdale Drive. In the meantime, I have all the evidence you need to make sure she doesn't screw you over in divorce court."

∞☉∞

Her BMW was there, right where Jonah had said. He only had to wait forty minutes. She left the house, her fling in tow. They smooched on the front porch, groping each other and probably confessing their mutual love.

He didn't even cry. Somehow, he was anesthetized to the pain after the night's happenings.

When he got home and confronted her, she lied through her teeth until there was no getting around it. Then she cried and bawled and begged forgiveness, and of course tried to blame it on him a half dozen different ways. The evening culminated in her packing her bags and heading to her sister's—or wherever.

So much for perfect Saturdays, he thought.

∞☉∞

He filed for divorce that Monday. A phone call to Jonah had all the pictures and evidence needed sent to his lawyer, so at least that was easy. Jonah called on Friday to check on things.

"I appreciate all you've done for me," Rogan said.

"In all fairness, I was doing it for me," Jonah said. "But I know if someone caught my wife cheating I'd sure as hell want to hear about it."

"It's more than that. You've opened my eyes to a lot of things."

"I'm glad you feel that way. Shall we get together tomorrow?"

"What for?"

"It's Saturday. Our power day. The best day to hunt down an ancient vampire."

It seemed like late night B-moviedom to Rogan, but the excitement was too intense. "Sounds good."

∞☉∞

The house was strangely empty without Delia, but he didn't miss her. He sat alone in his living room, drinking a double Scotch on the rocks, listening to Billy Joel singing that she could ruin your faith with her casual lies and that she only reveals what she wants you to see. That didn't help.

Last weekend, he'd driven a wooden stake through the heart of a vampire and watched its body disintegrate. Tomorrow, he was going hunting for an ancient vampire to attempt the same. He was a real-estate agent; this wasn't his thing. He'd given up partying years ago, most of his life when he'd married Delia, and even his motorcycle when he knew he'd gotten too old for that sort of thing.

The doorbell sounded. It was nine o'clock, too late for company. Delia, perhaps, after more of her things. He sighed and set his drink on the coffee table, strained to get to his feet, and plodded into the foyer. He unlocked the door and threw it open.

The man there was tall, handsome, pale as a ghost, with long, black hair tied back in a ponytail. He wore a black trench coat and black leather boots, and his gloved hands were clasped before him. Rogan felt the coils of terror tightening up in his gut, preparing to spring.

"Good evening, Mr. Mallory," the man said, and Rogan realized the man's eyes were red. "My name is Gantu. We must talk."

He was sure his face had gone as white as Gantu's. He was two rooms away from the nearest phone, and Jonah was a twenty-minute drive at best. As it was, Rogan knew he'd never outrun the ghoulish figure, much less get the door closed.

I'm a Sabbatarian, he thought frantically. *I have the power.*

Boldly, he locked eyes with Gantu, and for a brief moment he thought it was all for nothing, that the ancient vampire was too powerful even for him. But as he stared deep into those red eyes, Gantu faltered, teetered back a half step, and tried to look away. Rogan could feel the vampire's inability to break the gaze.

He can't look away! I'm doing it!

Gantu breathed heavily for a quick breath. "Please, Mr. Mallory … I know who and what you are. The fact is, I concede that you can overwhelm me with your Sabbatarian powers. But you can do no more than hold me. Once you break your concentration, I could kill you in a second."

"Then I'll hold you until dawn," Rogan said through gritted teeth. Images fluttered through his mind, at the periphery of his consciousness. It was starting.

Gantu curled his lips. "Mr. Mallory, I have twenty times your strength and endurance. Your power is great while you're in fine shape, but it's getting late and you're very tired. I, on the other hand, have only been awake a few hours. I can do this all night as well. I am willing to bet you will falter in your concentration before I will—and far before dawn. One slight moment when the shroud of sleep attempts to grab you, and you are mine. And if you do manage to hang on, I'm not quite as worried about the sun in my old age. I suppose I'm overdue for a tan."

Rogan felt panic start to wash over him, but he fought it back. No time to give in. The scattered images were getting stronger, more confusing.

"I could have come in here and simply killed you," Gantu said. "I rang your bell. I come here under a flag of truce. Please, let us stop this for now. You'll want to hear what I have to say."

∞☉∞

The past week had been strange enough; now, the very vampire he was to hunt tomorrow was sitting in his living room, thanking him for the Scotch.

"A very nice place you have," Gantu said. "I suppose a real-estate agent has the pick of the lot."

"I have the most powerful vampire on Earth drinking whiskey in my living room and talking about my architecture," Rogan said. His voice was shaking; he could hear every word warble. His mouth was dry and sticky with nervousness.

Gantu looked down at his drink in surprise. "I'm terribly sorry. If you'd like, I'll stop drinking."

"No, please drink … whiskey," Rogan said hurriedly.

Gantu laughed. "You've certainly been hanging with Jonah Byrne. He has you believing what a terrible bloodsucker I am. Well, he's right, to a point, but there's a lot you don't know. For instance, while we require blood, it need not be human."

"You're saying you don't kill people?"

"Certainly, we do. But not to extreme, and then only those who deserve it."

"How do you come to such judgments?"

"When I find a dozen men gang-raping a woman in an alleyway, a logical judgment presents itself," Gantu said icily. "I am very selective, sir; as are most of us. And I assure you that when a vampire goes off the deep end, we work to end his tenure immediately. It's bad for our kind to have careless vampires on the loose."

Rogan's head swam. He half expected werewolves and zombies to come storming in the house next, followed closely by a warlock or two. "So how do you survive?"

"In addition to blood, I prefer Chinese."

"Chinese … people?"

"No … *food*, Mr. Mallory. Chinese *food.*"

"I thought vampires didn't eat."

"You watch too much television, sir," Gantu said with a smile. "And, I suspect, listen to Jonah Byrne too much. He's not what he claims to be."

"He claims to be a vampire hunter, and so far he looks like exactly that."

"But he claims to be ridding the world of evil vampires. What he is doing is crusading against our kind—obliterating us, one at a time. He's a Sabbatarian, like his ancestors, misguided in his belief that we are all abominations. He believes it's his duty to rid the world of us. We would prefer that not to happen."

"Why are you telling me this?"

Gantu downed his drink. "I want you to simply not help him, for starters. He's not long for this world, you know; soon, the cancer eating at his insides will claim his life, and none of this will matter. His family line will end, and there will be no more Sabbatarians hunting us."

"There will be," Rogan said, with a surprising boldness that confused him.

"He's using you, Mr. Mallory. He's showing you how terrible we're supposed to be—feeding into your mind, which has been plagued by a lifetime of folklore and fiction, and turning you into a crusader for his cause."

"I'm doing nothing of the sort. I'm only helping him destroy *you*— no others."

"But if you succeed, you'll find you enjoy it. You'll want to do it again. Eventually, you'll be a vampire hunter, crusading whether you planned to or not. And for what? To rid the world of your Hollywood perceptions? We're just different, Mr. Mallory—stronger, faster, spookier, but more or less the same. We pay for those advantages with an eternal nightlife. And when we do take human blood, we rarely kill and barely injure—and they never remember. When most of us kill, it's rapists, murderers, and street scum. We help keep the world clean."

"It just isn't right for you to judge and execute people."

"No less so than Byrne's family hunting us to the brink of extinction for ten centuries," Gantu said. "He's not only the last of his line—he's the last of any line. We were hoping that when he went, it would be over. But then, he found you." He cocked his head, surveying Rogan curiously. "And, naturally, he has found the most powerful Sabbatarian I've ever seen. How ironic. Your life must have been filled with a lot of very important Saturdays, Mr. Mallory."

"So it seems."

"Could I have a refill?" Gantu asked, holding out his tumbler glass.

"Uh … sure."

He felt ridiculous, tending bar for this vampire. He felt even stranger when he realized he was standing with his back to Gantu, and in a mild panic his eyes found Gantu in the decorative bar mirror. The vampire sat on the sofa, calmly waiting.

"You reflect," he said suddenly.

Gantu chuckled. "It makes shaving much easier."

"But Jonah's house—"

"Yes, a carnival funhouse of mirrors; a thousand years of superstition at work. That only works on the very young vampires. Garlic, though, that's bad for us. Too bad; I still love the aroma. Younger vampires can't even catch a whiff of it, much less be near it. I can wear the stuff and it won't bother me, but I can't eat it."

"This is crazy," Rogan said.

"Beg pardon?"

"I'm sitting here chatting with you like you're my next-door neighbor," he said. "I don't know who to believe, you or Jonah … but either way, this whole past week has been, by far, the strangest of my life." He returned to the sectional and handed the Scotch to Gantu. "So you're basically telling me I have a choice: help him kill you, or help you kill him."

"I have no such designs. As I said, he'll be gone soon enough."

"So either I help you, or we lock eyes until somebody falters," Rogan amended.

"I have no interest in killing you," Gantu said with a thin-lipped smile, his white fangs shining like polished ivory. "Let me be honest, Mr. Mallory: you impress me. Never has one been able to hold me so easily. But to be frank, the sun won't reach me at all inside this house. I can go for a week without sleep. You can't. But I don't want to do that—and unless you force my position, I won't."

Rogan shook his head. "Just tell me what you want."

"I want you to stay out of this. Let things happen as they will."

"How do I know you won't kill him?"

"I have no need to."

Rogan got up, paced to the fireplace, and turned back, his brow furrowed. "Everything in me says what you and your kind do is wrong—regardless of whether your victims are rapists or whatever."

"At least *we're* selective," Gantu said. "Do you go out of your way to slaughter only the evil cows, or the criminal pigs, or the chickens with bad hearts? Certainly not; worse, you breed them for the sole purpose of having them end up on your plates. Given that comparison, who is the worse vampire?"

"Barnyard animals aren't human beings."

"It could be argued that those we choose to kill aren't, either. They're lower than barnyard animals—abominations to *your* kind. Do you not execute your own when their crimes are terrible enough? When a man rapes and kills a seven-year-old girl, is locking him up for life the wrong thing to do?"

It made sense, and it was true that Gantu probably could wait it out and kill him; certainly, he could have burst into the house and ripped him apart without so much as a hello, but he hadn't. Or maybe he really couldn't and was even afraid. Or maybe he really did want to talk. Or … or maybe Rogan didn't know what to think.

Gantu said, "Let me put this into perspective. I understand you're going through a divorce."

"You use the same private detective as Jonah?"

"Unlikely. Would you say your wife and her lover have devastated your life?"

"Hell, yeah, I'd say that."

"Would you like me to kill them?"

Rogan's heart stopped cold. Images flipped through his mind like illustrations in a book. He envisioned her suffering and dying, her lover right along with her. For a moment, it seemed utterly right and just.

But he blinked and shook his head to clear it. "No."

"But you thought about it, didn't you?"

He regarded Gantu's red eyes with a cold look. "Of course I did."

"Now think of her in bed with him, being pleasured by him," Gantu said firmly. "Of her pleasuring him. Riding him, taking his seed within her, and coming home to your bed with lies and excuses."

Rogan turned his head away. He felt tears brimming. He wasn't about to let Gantu see them.

"Imagine how many times you were inside her after he was." Gantu's voice was harsher now, almost commanding Rogan to heed the words. "Those times when you thought she was wet just for you—but it was his juices in which you basted, my friend."

"Stop it," Rogan hissed.

"There are no secrets here, Sabbatarian," Gantu said. "Say the word, and I shall execute your vengeance on them!"

"No," Rogan said. "Let them have each other. Besides … maybe I could have done more to make her happy. Been home more, worked less. But it doesn't matter. But thanks for offering."

He clambered to his feet and faced Gantu. "And I'm thankful for Jonah, who discovered her affair. It hurts now, but better now than years later, and maybe other lovers, later."

"What are you saying?"

"I'm saying I can't help either of you. If he dies naturally, he dies. But if he comes for you, I can't let you kill him."

"I had hoped you would have thought otherwise," Gantu said.

"I'm sorry." Rogan swallowed hard, starting to sweat again. "Are you going to kill me now? Should we begin the stare-down?"

Gantu sighed and shook his head, coming to his feet. Rogan did so as well as the vampire strode past him towards the foyer. "No, we should not. The truth is, perhaps I'm all talk." He turned when he reached the front door and looked back. "You really *are* the most powerful I've ever seen, Sabbatarian, and I've dealt with your kind for a long time. I don't know if I *could* hold out before you'd overcome me."

"That's a hell of a way to show your hand," Rogan said. "You had me believing I'd lose that stand-off."

"I really don't know. I don't believe I wish to find out. I hope you don't, either."

Rogan smiled. "I guess I don't."

"Good evening, Mr. Mallory."

"Good evening."

Gantu opened the door and, in a sudden flash, was gone in a small hurricane. The potted trees in the foyer blew furiously around and the door suctioned shut with a bang.

∞Θ∞

Jonah showed up at his house late Saturday morning with a loaded double-bolt crossbow. "Are you ready?"

"A little early, isn't it?" Rogan asked. "Not a lot of vampire action at high noon, you know."

"Best time to do it. They're holed up somewhere. Anyway, I've got the gear loaded in the car, so let's get going."

"He came to see me last night."

Jonah looked at him sideways. "Who came to see you?"

"Gantu."

Jonah's face hardened, his good eye squinting. "Son of a bitch.

Thought he'd go a round with you. Since you're still here, I'm guessing he didn't win. What happened?"

"We had a few drinks together."

"Had a few—? You're kidding!"

Rogan was very aware of the deadly weapon Jonah held. It was currently pointing down, a good sign. "I'm not. He came to plead his case."

"Plead his case? What, he tried to talk you into killing me, is that it?"

"Not at all. Just wants me to stay out of it. He knows you're dying, and he knows you're the last of your line—of any Sabbatarian line."

"He knows shit!" Jonah said with a snarl. "The bloodsucking bastard knows he's beat. He knows I'm coming for him, and he knows I found you. He probably came to kill you last night, and found out how fucking powerful you are. Had a few drinks, my ass! He was screwing with you, Mallory—messing with your head to keep you from wasting him!"

"I don't think so," Rogan said. "They're different from us, Jonah, but … maybe not as different as you think."

A look of realization crossed Jonah's face. "Christ, you bought into it. You listened to him. Did anything I said get through to you?"

"Everything."

"But what he said made more sense, is that it?" Jonah backed up suddenly, bringing the crossbow to bear at Rogan's chest. "You bastard … you walk in the sun and you don't drink blood, but you're one of *them!*"

Rogan backed up a step. "Of course I'm not. Put that thing down."

He reached for the edge of the door, intending to throw it shut, but Jonah figured it out. He moved quickly into the foyer, shoving the weapon roughly forward as he backed Rogan up. "What the hell kind of Sabbatarian sides with vampires?" he hollered.

"I'm no kind of Sabbatarian!" Rogan cried out. "I lived my whole life without even knowing what a Sabbatarian was! You find me on the street and tell me all this … of a family dedicated to destroying vampires through the ages. I'm just supposed to accept that everything you and your forefathers believe is the truth?"

"Yes!" Jonah screeched, and now Rogan was against the wall: nowhere to go. He held his breath as the crossbow butted into his sternum, inches below his chin. "For generations, we've dedicated our lives to ridding the world of these monsters. I know what they are! I know what they do!"

"Maybe they're not all evil," Rogan managed, willing his voice not to shake. "Maybe they're no different than men like you with blind purposes—men who never question, who kill without a thought."

"You sniveling pile of shit," Jonah said, showing gritted teeth, his single eye burning with hate. "I'm gonna stake you, right here, just like them. Stake you to your own fucking wall and let you die there."

"Is that the kind of man you are?"

Jonah wavered. "I'm a man who won't allow vampires to rule this world."

"You're a man who has only known one thing all his life," Rogan said. "You're a man who killed his first vampire when he was twelve and he's been crusading ever since. And you've been crusading with a thousand years of anger and vengeance and you don't even know why!"

"I know exactly why!"

"You know what you were told to know! Your entire belief system is based on childhood commands given to you by forty generations of unquestioned tradition! You're no different than a bigot raised to hate blacks, or a Republican to hate Democrats, or a rock and roller to hate country music. You're a robot, Jonah, a mindless robot running programs and you don't even know why!"

Jonah's face was dark and etched in steel. His lips curled back over his teeth. "I know why. Justice. I kill those who must be killed. I kill to bring justice to the human race."

"Gantu said something similar. Maybe you're more alike than you realize."

Jonah shoved the crossbow harder into Rogan's ribs, moved his finger onto the trigger. "Say good-bye, vampire lover," he said, and began to squeeze.

Rogan's mind raced. There was no way out of this. No way—

—unless there was.

He looked into Jonah's good eye with both his own, and the two locked gazes. He didn't know exactly what to do, so he just did whatever felt right. In his mind, he evoked images of fire and electricity, of molten iron burning like a sun and thunderstorms laying waste to everything in their paths. He envisioned his Sabbatarian powers welling up within him like a massive hurricane, and in the same moment saw it compact rapidly into a monstrous cyclone of unbelievable ferocity. Then he envisioned launching that amazing force at Jonah.

Peripherally, he saw Jonah freeze, finger nearly depressing the hair trigger of the crossbow. Jonah's good eye widened.

"What are you doing?" Jonah hissed.

Rogan didn't break concentration. He kept his gaze fixed, kept the invisible cyclone of power spinning out of him, engulfing Jonah. Jonah moved back half a step, and the crossbow went with him. He could sense Jonah's finger trembling on the trigger, feel him trying to contract muscles and tendons to fire the bolt into Rogan's chest.

"Stop," Jonah said. "Stop it!"

Images flickered in Rogan's mind's eye. He saw a man filled with mindless hate imbued upon him in his youth. He saw vampires dying from stakes, garlic juice injections, the blazing sun. He saw holy symbols of every religion, over the decades, driving them back.

"No," Jonah whispered. "How can you do this ... ?"

Jonah moved back a step, then another, but it was under Rogan's power. Rogan moved forward, raising his hands before him. He brought them down, slowly, and as he did, Jonah's crossbow lowered until it pointed at the ground. Jonah grunted, straining, sweating like a cold pipe in a hot basement, but his attempt was nothing to Rogan. It was like an infant struggling against a circus strongman. There was no contest.

"Fire," Rogan said softly, and Jonah's finger yarded on the trigger. The bolt launched into the stone floor of the foyer and bounced away, splintering into pieces. Jonah cursed.

"Again," Rogan commanded, and Jonah's finger moved to the second trigger and released the other bolt to the same results.

"You can't ... stop me!" Jonah howled. "You can't! I must ... do my duty!"

"No more weapons," Rogan said, and he flicked his left hand to the side. The crossbow flew from Jonah's hands as if it had been yanked by an invisible rope. Jonah muttered another hopeless oath. Rogan brought his hands together, before him, and cupped them. Then he lifted them, envisioning the field of power gathering beneath Jonah, and the vampire hunter levitated off the floor.

"Move beyond this hatred before you die this way," Rogan said. "Don't crusade against an enemy you don't even know."

"You're powerful indeed," Jonah said, breathing heavily. "A Sabbatarian with power over other Sabbatarians—what a cruel joke the gods are playing!"

"Leave them alone," Rogan said. "It just isn't worth the rest of your life, Jonah."

"I'll never stop!" Jonah shouted. "I haven't long to live in a godforsaken world crawling with those evil creatures, but I'll hunt them until my dying breath!"

"We'll see," Rogan said, and with a gentle influx of power, he willed Jonah out the door. The old man landed on the porch with a grunt. Rogan released him and broke the gaze.

He tried to will the door to shut, but seemed to have no power over it. He reached out and calmly closed and locked it.

He listened as Jonah returned to his car, screaming foul epithets along the way. The engine roared to life, and Rogan listened as the car squealed off.

He knew what he had to do.

∞☉∞

They called them crotch rockets, because the power between your legs was a lot like that. He hadn't ridden it in several years, beyond just around the block. He'd always told himself—and Delia, and anyone who'd listen—that he was getting too old for that sort of thing. It was always just an excuse for him to wallow deeper in his unfulfilled life.

The bike was black and shined like volcanic glass. There was chrome in all the right places, including a custom-made front wheel featuring multiple lightning bolts. Delia had complained about his childish vanity, spending money on the custom wheel—and the bike itself, for that matter. Back then, he just liked how cool it all was. Now, straddling it felt as if he were preparing to ride into space on some personal launch vehicle.

He wore his black leather jacket and matching pants. Chaps were for the laid-back bikers; pants were for style, speed, and cool. He closed the visor on his shining black helmet and adjusted his gloves. He felt powerful.

He *was* powerful.

He roared the bike to life and tore out of the garage, feeling the beginnings of his rebirth.

∞ ⊙ ∞

He envisioned both Jonah and Gantu in his vivid mind's eye, and it worked as Jonah had described. It was as if he had psychic radar that tracked paranormal homing beacons, and it took him into the city. He didn't know where he was going, but somehow he knew his subconscious did. He laid his faith in that lower mind and moved like the wind. He rode through traffic, snaking around vehicles with all the speed and daring of his youth—but all the care and control of his older years, and maybe with an injection of something else more supernatural.

He headed straight for the east side, taking rights and lefts and shortcuts, guided by his intuition. Before he saw the abandoned factory, he knew he was headed there. It came into view along the edge of the waterfront, old and in need of exterior work but otherwise in decent shape. A massive old parking lot, long out of use, encircled it on all sides the water didn't. The entire place was corralled with a rusted chain-link fence.

Far to the right, near the building's corner, was Jonah's car. Rogan roared the bike through the recently smashed gate and crossed the expansive, cracked asphalt in seconds. He could see the broken headlights, dents, and scratched paint on Jonah's car, as well as the broken-in door leading into the building. He killed the bike, ditched the helmet, and headed inside. The moment he passed through the door, he froze in shock.

He was in a huge warehouse, and he wasn't alone. Gantu and Jonah stood in the middle of the empty room, facing off a dozen feet apart. Jonah looked like an anti-vampire Christmas tree. Belts and bandoliers of garlic were draped all over him, and holy symbols decorated him like bulbs and ornaments: Christian crosses, Jewish stars, Muslim crescents, and many more Rogan didn't know. Jonah held two more crossbows, one in each hand, each with two bolts at the ready.

Gantu faced him, and their eyes were locked. Rogan focused on the two and willed his mind to see them as they truly were. Their forms suddenly became bathed in colors, and Rogan could see the holding effect in three dimensions of light: extending from Jonah, surrounding Gantu, and Gantu's own complex aura of dancing, flowing hues.

But that wasn't what had shocked Rogan into a standstill.

There were about sixty other people surrounding the two in a haphazard circle, like a street audience readying to watch a brawl. In stark contrast to their ghostly complexions, the five dozen attendants wore everything from navy blue to maroon to dark green to brown to black. To Rogan's auravision, they all lit up like fireworks. They all shared certain aspects of Gantu's aura, and given the fact it seemed likely anyway, Rogan knew they were all vampires.

The vampires were tightening their circle. Rogan could feel Jonah's awareness of them closing behind him. The old hunter held his crossbows, one above the other, four armed bolts aimed for Gantu's heart. It was a classic Mexican stand-off. Jonah hadn't realized Gantu was amidst a whole nest of vampires, and if he killed Gantu, there was no way he could hold off sixty more. So long as he kept Gantu in his sights and held him with his Sabbatarian powers, the sixty likely wouldn't attack.

There was no time to think it through.

Rogan let out an attention-getting bellow, and sixty vampires whirled to face him, They growled, teeth bared, red eyes glowing in the dim light. Deadly sunlight filtered in through high windows, but they were well out of harm's way. Gantu and Jonah remained gaze-locked.

"A Sabbatarian!" hissed one of the vampires.

"He's strong," another called out.

"I've never seen such power," said yet another.

Rogan's heart was firing like a semiautomatic, and he fought every instinct to turn and run. "All of you, back away from the hunter," he ordered.

"Leave, Mr. Mallory," Gantu's weakened but clear voice called out. "Leave while I still have a choice to let you live."

"I can't do that, Gantu. Order your vampires back and we'll resolve this peacefully. If you don't, I'll have no choice but to kill you all."

The words were bigger than Rogan was, and he knew it. He heard Gantu chuckling. "I admire you, but there's a fine line between courage and stupidity."

"Run, boy," Jonah's cracking voice came. "This is my fight. Even you can't help me now."

"Release him, Jonah," Rogan said. "As soon as he orders the vampires back."

"Never," Jonah said.

"The vampires stay," Gantu said. "This is your last chance, Mr. Mallory. Don't make me send my vampires after you."

"Bring them on," Rogan said, and struck a sideways martial arts stance he remembered from his younger days. He hoped it conveyed his confidence and power. He was scared, but somehow he felt in control.

Gantu growled out an order to attack, and at least half the vampires launched. Most in the front ran at high speed towards him; the ones to the flanks and rear took to the air above the others' heads and flew. They crossed the distance between them and he in less than a second, a frontal assault of inhuman missiles coming in low, packed tightly together, homing in on him.

In that instant, Rogan visualized his cyclone of power. Instead of focusing it small and tight, he envisioned it roaring wider. In his mind's eye, it became a maelstrom of raw energy, coning out before him on some invisible astral plane, and he felt his mind latch on to each of the sixty torpedoing bodies. He felt as if he were making sixty simultaneous connections on an old-fashioned telephone switchboard. He felt all the power and effects of his supernatural lock with Jonah earlier that day, sixty-fold. It was as if his brain operated as sixty sub-minds, all working independently yet controlled by his higher consciousness.

The vampires hit invisible walls of force and blew backward as fast as they had been coming at him. Five dozen wails of surprise and pain echoed through the warehouse. Bodies bowled across the concrete floor, slammed into walls, banged into steel rafters above. One careened high and left toward a window, and even before he smashed through it, the rays of the sun ignited him in a fury of flames. He fireballed out into the daylight, squealing in agony.

Vampires were still hitting the floor like sacks of potatoes as others staggered to their feet. A half dozen wasted no time, tearing right back toward him at high speed, like rubber balls fired against a wall. Rogan never quite completely detached from the others, but he focused most of his strength on those six.

They were blown back as if kicked by an angry god, two hundred feet or more into the far wall. Blood sprayed everywhere, and the vampires crumpled like fallen angels.

The others had regained their feet, staring at their comrades and Rogan in stunned silence. Gantu and Jonah were still locked together, but Rogan knew Gantu had seen what had happened. He moved toward the duo, and no vampires moved to intercede.

"Stop him!" Gantu called out.

They moved forward, slowly and uncertainly.

"Call them off," Rogan said. "I'll kill them if they come closer."

"You came at him tightly, from the front," Gantu hollered. "All of you, fly wide, and encircle him. Even he cannot fight you all off then."

The tactic made perfect sense, and they all apparently thought so. Vampiric lightning bolts, they hurtled themselves into the air and climbed. Some went straight up over him, others banked to the left or right. No two found the same height, and in moments all fifty-three orbited him, a sphere of destruction, spinning about him faster and faster, closing the radius as they did.

His fear mounted, and he heard Gantu laughing with satisfaction: "You'll fail, old hunter, and your all-powerful Sabbatarian will fall!"

"I'll take you with me!" Jonah roared, and fired off the first two shots from his crossbows. Rogan watched as the wooden bolts thudded like armor piercing rounds into the flesh of Gantu's chest. Unable to break the hold, the ancient vampire could only endure it, and he screamed in agony. The bolts had missed his heart, if barely; one had burrowed into his left shoulder, the other into his right lung.

The spinning sphere of vampires closed on Rogan. In moments, they would be on him, and he'd be out of the game. He was still tuned to each of them, and now he summoned the image of his cyclone and projected it around him, mentally overlaying the spinning vortex of power on their circular flight. He threw his hands above his head and mentally commanded the cyclone to erupt.

It was like fifty-three spinning tops being dropped into a blender. Vampire bodies were torn to ribbons; arms and legs were torn from bodies, heads ripped off, entrails flying. Blood sprayed outward, covering the floor and walls.

Rogan's eyes were closed, but he could still see them as auras in his mind. Their remnants flew everywhere around him, chased by dying screams of pain. As each mind was extinguished, fleeting images flooded his brain. He saw entire lifetimes, some dating back centuries—lifetimes of memories of loving, hating, winning, losing … he saw memories of sunrises long past, of bright days always coveted. He saw loved ones left behind in the wakes of their immortality—parents and children and lovers and friends long since dead and gone. As well, he saw feasting on the blood of animals and humans. He saw some who killed for the sheer pleasure of killing, but mostly he saw as Gantu had said: killing only those who deserved it. He saw feasting on humans who never knew it happened. He saw care and finesse, good judgment and wisdom; he saw pitiful creatures damned to en eternity of moons and stars, of shadows and darkness.

And as the last scream ended, and the last scenes of a life snapped like a film reel in a projector, he realized that he mourned the loss of all those live that had paid such a terrible price for immortality, lives with precious memories spanning countless years. He realized suddenly that the experiences of knowing every one of those minds would have been unequalled. The stories they could have told him! The lessons they could have taught! The wonders they could have related! The mistakes from which they had learned, the successes they had celebrated—it was all gone, in those few moments of Rogan's awesome resistance. While he knew he'd had no choice, he wished otherwise.

The echoes died. He opened his eyes, his face wet with rivulets of tears. All about were the remains of the vampires. It was a gruesome factory of body parts gone mad; blood coated everything around him for fifty feet. Rogan hadn't a drop on him. He took a deep breath and turned back to the locked duo.

Gantu stood solidly, unmoving, the two bolts in his chest and shoulder. He didn't appear to have been seriously damaged. Jonah still had the crossbows, each with a bolt left, aimed at him, and was slowly inching closer, stepping forward with his left foot and dragging his right up, like a policeman in a movie nervous about approaching the downed bad guy for fear the guy might suddenly roll over and open fire.

"Two bolts lost, and your aim is off," Gantu said with a grin.

"Not for long," Jonah said.

Rogan strode across the warehouse toward them. The closer Jonah got to Gantu, the truer his aim was to the vampire's heart. Gantu's smile was fading, and Rogan could see his arms trembling at his sides. He was trying to move, but Jonah had managed to keep him bound there.

"When you squeeze that trigger, I'll be on you," Gantu said. "Your concentration is failing."

"Enough!" Rogan called out, double-timing his steps.

"Stay out of this!" Jonah hollered.

Rogan reached them, stood so they were before him, Gantu to the left and Jonah to the right. "I said enough, Jonah. Lower the crossbow and step away. Release your hold on him."

"The moment I do, he'll have me."

"I'll protect you," Rogan said.

"Your powers are impressive, Sabbatarian," Gantu said. "But now you wish to deprive Byrne of his lifelong dream of killing me, and let him merely watch as you do it yourself. Except for the part about me dying, it's almost worth it, knowing he'll be denied his pleasure."

"That's not happening," Rogan said. "I'm here to protect both of you."

"How can I believe you?" Gantu said. "You've just killed sixty of my kindred."

"You set them against me."

"I thought you were here to assist him."

"I'm here to break this up. Now Jonah, drop the crossbow and release him. And when he does, Gantu … don't try anything."

"It's not happening, Mallory," Jonah said. "You'll have to kill me. Because I'm killing him."

And then Jonah Byrne's focused concentration faltered as he fine-tuned his crossbows' aims and squeezed the triggers.

It happened in the wink of an eye, but to Rogan everything seemed to slow down. Jonah's crossbows leveled out, even as his fingers began pulling back on the triggers. Gantu's own impressive power overcame the weak link in Jonah's supernatural grip and he lunged at speeds beyond the capability of mortal men.

Rogan spun his mind into action, reaching out four ways at once: two narrow dust devils of power for the small stuff, and two dense vortices for the others.

Jonah's right finger squeezed the trigger and the bolt was unleashed from the crossbow as if from a cannon. It cut through the short distance to the heart of the speeding vampire coming at it. Gantu's eyes brightened to fiery burns, his arms reaching for Jonah's throat, over the top of the rocketing wooden stake. Jonah fired the other bolt right behind the other. It was at a slightly different angle, both homing in, straight and true.

Rogan whipped out at the bolts. The first was already piercing Gantu's chest when Rogan kicked it sideways and it pinwheeled away. He slammed the second with another concentrated beam of power and the next bolt, an inch away, exploded into splinters.

Gantu cleared the distance, hands outstretched and claws digging, nearly at Jonah's throat. Jonah had begun to lean back as he fired, but there was no way he could match the vampire's speed.

Rogan grabbed Gantu with a whirling funnel of magic just as Gantu's hands began closing around Jonah's windpipe, even as he kicked Jonah backward and away from Gantu. Jonah tumbled backward to the floor as Rogan threw Gantu up and back.

Time seemed to return to normal as Rogan let up. Jonah landed on his ass with a THUMP and Gantu landed on his feet several feet back.

Nobody said anything. The two combatants simply stared at Rogan.

"Nicely done," Gantu said.

Rogan said, "Are you all right, Jonah?"

Jonah sat, elbows on knees, head down. His face was long and sad. "Of course I'm not. A lifetime of chasing him, and you've taken the hope from me. Those bolts would have killed him. I'd have double-staked him—and they were soaked in my own blood, just for good measure."

"I'd have still ripped your throat out," Gantu said.

"Touché," Jonah said. He glared at Rogan then with his good eye. "You ungrateful shit. You were nothing until I told you what you were. Now you're the perfect Sabbatarian, and you're controlling the outcome of my life? I'm the last of my line, the last chance to end it. This was my last chance to succeed."

"You think killing me will rid the world of vampires?" Gantu laughed loudly. "Hardly. It's a twisted, personal thing for you, that's all."

"Every one of you I take with me betters this world."

"We're not all the way you think we are," Gantu snarled. "I'm sick of hearing about it, but you'll never believe otherwise."

"You're heartless killers!"

"Some perhaps, but not most!" Gantu growled and bared his fangs. "Just hurry up and die, old man, so those of us who aren't heartless killers can get on without you."

"That's not going to happen," Rogan said.

"I think the gods have other plans for him," Gantu said with a sly smile.

"I have other plans."

Gantu and Jonah looked to him curiously. "What are you talking about?" Jonah said.

Rogan pointed to Gantu. "Slice open your wrist."

"What?" Gantu sounded completely bewildered.

"Slice it open. Now."

The vampire's face darkened. "I'll do no such thing—"

Rogan made a motion with his hand as if making a sweeping cut with a machete, at the same time firing out a mental blade. An eight-inch gash sliced open down Gantu's arm, tearing clothing with it. Gantu leaped back in shock. Crimson blood dripped everywhere.

"You fuck!" he hissed. "You've been lucky so far, Mallory—don't make me show you the limits of your power!"

"Feed him," Rogan said.

Gantu blinked in surprise. "What?"

"Feed him." He nodded to Jonah, and then Jonah and Gantu both understood.

"You can't be serious," Gantu said.

"That isn't going to happen," Jonah said, seething.

Rogan moved his hands like an insane conductor and grabbed them both. Gantu shot forward, blood flying everywhere. Jonah came off the floor with a yell as they hurtled toward each other. Rogan stopped them in mid-air, Jonah's face just inches from Gantu's arm.

Rogan worked a little more magic, and in one swift motion, Jonah's right arm snapped straight up in the air and a similar wound opened up on his arm. He hollered in anguish as his own blood went everywhere.

"And *you* feed *him*," Rogan said.

"You can't do this!" Jonah screamed. "A thousand years we've hunted them! You can't dishonor me so! You can't disgrace forty generations of my ancestry!"

"It can't be done," Gantu said, and he was nervous now. "He's a Sabbatarian, like you—he's an antivampire! We're polar opposites. It's never been tried before."

"'Never been tried' is a far cry from 'impossible,'" Rogan said.

He came forward, still in control of the hovering men, and raised his hands. He exuded his power and took complete control over both men's bodies. They screamed in agony until their mouths were full of each other's arms. When he had them firmly in place so they couldn't move, Rogan sped up their hearts and watched as they struggled, kicked, and squirmed up there in the air, all the while being force-fed the lifeblood of the other.

He did it for a hard-pushing five minutes. He knew Gantu could lose a lot of blood and survive, but Jonah might still need some of his for awhile. When he was satisfied, he released them. They collapsed to the floor, hacking and choking and spitting blood everywhere.

Rogan sat on the cold concrete and crossed his legs. Elbows on knees, chin in hands, he said, "Now, we wait."

They hacked and coughed, but were without energy to move.

∞☉∞

They crawled around on the floor for hours, hacking and heaving, trying to stay away from each other but often failing. They swore and threatened each other and Rogan whenever they could manage. Occasionally, one would launch into a brutal seizure and collapse again, rolling violently about, writhing and twisting on the floor, often not breathing and usually not coherent.

By nightfall, both men had stopped moving. Rogan extended his auravision and saw they were still alive. Both had changed, though; neither was what it should have been, and each seemed a mix of the other's.

Jonah woke first, suddenly and with much activity. He was hollering as if in pain, sitting bolt upright and fighting to remove the strands of garlic wrapped around him. It took him some doing, but he finally dislodged himself from the strands and staggered away from them, unsure. It had landed next to his opponent.

Gantu stirred on the floor, turning his head toward the pile of strung garlic. He recoiled when his eyes opened and he growled in anger, rolling away and coming to his feet.

"By the gods," Jonah said, curling his lips back to reveal his fangs, "what have you done?"

"Making history," Rogan said. "I'm guessing there's little difference between vampires and Sabbatarians on a spiritual level. Now you both should easily be able to track and repel vampires. Those of you who have been vampires, and those of you who have been vampire hunters, will find this both extremely advantageous and disadvantageous."

"You bastard," Gantu said. "You've destroyed us both. Whatever hold I had on the rebellious vampires who kill your kind without care, I'll lose now. Likewise will I be hunted by my own kind, who will see me no longer as the master vampire but as a half-breed with the aura of a vampire hunter!"

"Then I suppose it's good that you have Jonah here to help you," Rogan said. "He has a thousand years of family expertise in dealing with vampires."

"I'll never help him," Jonah said, his eyes glowing red.

"I think there will be no better alternative than working together, because you're two of a kind. Gantu, you told me most vampires stick to the rules and only kill when they have to, and then only those who deserve it. Is this true?"

"It is," Gantu conceded.

"And Jonah, you have an undying desire to kill heartless bloodsuckers, right?"

"Damn straight," the old man said.

"Well, your first problem is obvious: do you kill yourself? If not, I give the both of you about a week before you're starting to see each other's side of things." Rogan got up, turned, and headed for the door. "The best part is, I don't have to worry about Jonah getting killed trying to knock you off, Gantu, and I don't have to worry about him succeeding and actually taking you out. So I can sleep tonight, in peace."

"Why would you do such a thing?" Gantu cried.

"Yes!" Jonah called after him. "Why damn us to this?"

"Well, two reasons," Rogan said, stopping at the door and turning back. "First, the attitudes the two of you have about the other make it only poetic justice to make you need each other to survive."

"And the second?" Gantu said.

"Simply put, I like both of you," Rogan said with a smile. "Stop by the house anytime. I'll have drinks waiting."

∞☉∞

They'd have to do the rest themselves. He hoped they *would* come by some night for a drink—not of him, of course. He figured one of three things would happen. First, they'd destroy each other. Second, one would destroy the other, and the destroyer would be a lone outcast hunted by vampires and hunters alike. Or third, they'd somehow team up in order to survive—and maybe work on abolishing the ongoing, secret war between humans and vampires. He hoped it was the latter.

Rogan rode at dangerous speeds through the midnight city, but he was in control—of the bike, of his life, of his destiny. With his newfound powers and the events of the last week, he felt like a comic book hero. But why not?

He popped a wheelie and screamed off into his future.

-Bridges-

ALAN SMALE

The blood brought him, fresh on the wind like tendrils of sweet copper. She was young, under thirty, and her flawless neck and shoulders made him feel dusty and ancient and almost unbearably sad.

Strange to find her here alone, staring through the trees at the moon.

Her eyes widened when she saw him. Her pulse raced and her breathing quickened, but otherwise she stayed calm.

Anton did not attack. They became prey only when they screamed and ran. Her calmness defanged him.

"Oh God," she said. "I'm so stupid."

Her blood still hung in the air and taunted him.

"What is your name?" he asked.

Her car was thirty feet away. "I'm going to leave now," she said, and began to walk. The doors unlocked with a soft electric click as she pressed the button on her key ring. She did not press the alarm button. He followed her out of the trees. The blood was coming from four punctures in the palm of her right hand, made by her fingernails. She had made them before she'd known he was near.

The car now separated them. He knew he would let her drive away. She was too complex.

She hesitated. "Are you all right?"

He looked away.

She got into the car and started the engine. And waited.

Anton slid into the passenger seat, not knowing why he did it, not knowing why she let him. The car was a Saturn, black and modern, more comfortable than the luxury of centuries past.

The woman put the car in drive and pulled away. He wasn't used to traveling so fast without the wind in his face.

"Where do you need to go?"

"Nowhere," he replied.

"Then what do you want?"

She glowed in the moonlight. Her skin was very pale. Her heady essence filled the car.

Anton wondered if his proximity was having a similar effect on her.

"You know what I am?"

"Yes," she said. "Should I be afraid?"

The answer was unclear, even to him.

"You're bleeding," he said, because it was the main thing on his mind.

She looked down at her hand as if seeing it for the first time. Anton recognized it as a social affectation, an acknowledgment of his words, rather than genuine surprise. "I suppose I am. You have good eyes, to see that."

"Eyes?" he said, baffled.

They'd reached a conversational impasse. As the more powerful being, the responsibility to move ahead seemed to be his.

"Tell me about yourself, and why you're not afraid."

"You're not going to attack me as soon as I stop the car?"

He frowned. Her question made no sense.

"You'd have killed me already if you were going to," she said.

Anton wondered why she believed this. Clearly she did not own a cat. He began to say, "Not necessarily," but desisted. Rusty on the social graces, he was beginning to remember tact.

He turned her verbal techniques against her: "You were in the woods because something is bothering you," he said. "You wished to think and be alone."

"My husband is a pig," she said.

The statement alarmed him only temporarily.

She spoke like a child, but with a late-twenties ennui and a maturity seemingly as ancient as his own. "My name is Rachel. I am twenty-eight years old, and I have a severe marital problem that I'm trying to think through. You didn't surprise me because you're just typical of the way my life is going, right about now. Yes, I'm afraid, but somehow I don't think screaming and shouting is going to help me much."

The vampire sat amazed. Rachel turned off the country lane onto the highway, and continued. "So. Ken just told me he's going to give up his job. It sucks. He's going to look for something else, after he's taken a bit of a break. It's time I supported him for a while, after all. Know what that means? It means he's going to sit around and be bored, and we're not going to be able to make the mortgage payments. He's going to be on my case all the time, and we're going to be poor. You know what else? There's this other woman he sees. Giving up his job means he has all these extra afternoons to meet up with her in motel rooms. You know what else? I boss him around too much. I never consider his feelings. Oh dear. What a witch I am."

Anton was drowning, but she continued. "I discovered today that there's even a title for him. He's a *Difficult Husband*. That's a term used by professional counselors for a man who finds fault in everything I do, has antisocial habits, and changes his moods at random. Eighty percent of the time I spend with him I'm angry, depressed, or otherwise unhappy. It's a co-dependency thing." She glanced at him. "In contrast, you're a rather simple problem."

Anton frowned. "Your pig is a simple problem. Leave him."

"I love him."

"Why?"

Rachel sighed. "How old are you?"

"Older than Christ," he replied. His stock answer to a regular question. "But not as good looking."

The joke fell flat. Anton hadn't used the line in a while. Perhaps it didn't make sense any more.

"So I guess you've seen it all?"

He did not answer.

"Do people ever change?"

The conversation was becoming difficult for him. He would have left, but the Saturn was now traveling at sixty-five miles per hour towards the town. He said, "Sometimes people change. But truly bad men do not."

"Ken is not a bad man," she said.

"Perhaps he will leave you."

She shook her head. "He's getting a free ride. I'm his meal ticket. This other woman won't last. They never do. It's me he loves. It's the job thing that's the problem. He gets really mean when he's bored and doesn't have enough money to spend."

"Does he hurt you?"

Her laugh was dry and bitter.

The vampire tried again. "Does he beat you?"

"He's hit me twice. I told him I would leave if it happened a third time. Since then he hasn't laid a finger on me. I don't believe he will again."

A habitual misuser of women himself, Anton said nothing.

"I mean it," she said, misinterpreting his silence. "I'm not stupid, and we've been married ten years. I know him."

They came up on a deserted pull-off. Rachel parked the Saturn and used both hands to massage her temples and forehead. Trees still surrounded them. The night was quiet. Apparently she had forgotten her fear that he would fall upon her as soon as she halted the vehicle.

Anton decided.

"Rachel, I can solve your problem."

"Don't," she said. "If you're going to kill him, or make me like yourself, so that I'm stronger than he is, forget it. That's not what I need."

"I cannot make you into what I am," he said. "At least, it has never happened yet. But I can certainly remove your difficulty."

"I just told you. We love each other. Anything that hurts him hurts me, one way or another. Forget I mentioned it. I'll work it out. Just leave us alone."

The wind rippled the trees around them. Slivers of liquid moonlight glowed in her eyes. The blood was drying.

"You know what helps me?" she said eventually. "It's when people tell me about their own lousy marriages. Because then at least I know I'm not the only one."

He didn't immediately understand her.

Then, he did.

"I've known countless women," he said. "But our—" *What was the word to go with the plush Saturn and the quick self-awareness of modern women?* "—relationships were rather different."

"I see."

"I've known love," he said. "I … "

"What?"

"Never mind," said the vampire. "None of it would help you."

"Ah," said Rachel. "The boundless wisdom of the millennia. I feel better already."

He searched her face.

"I'm not being sarcastic. Knowing there isn't an answer really does make me feel better." She smiled weakly. "Look ... this is me, feeling better."

"There are many answers," he said. "You are intelligent. You are rich. You are holding all the cards. You can leave him, kill him, or change him."

"I'm trying number three," she said.

The vampire's face was expressionless.

Rachel watched him, a woman waiting for a stone to break in two and yield up water. Anton was confused. He must be missing a step in the modern conversational dance. He had nowhere to go.

"Okay," she said. "Your turn."

It was odd, this glance inside the mind of a twenty-eight year old. Once, he had been so young himself.

"Come on," she said. "Tell me what makes a vampire frown."

His eyes looked back over the centuries.

"Maybe I'd understand."

"Nobody has ever asked me before," he said.

Her fingers touched the back of his hand. He jumped. "I'm not just anybody," she said quietly. "I'm good at empathy."

Without knowing why he did, he pushed his sleeves up his arms. Roman tunics left the forearms bare, and he preferred it that way.

"Try," she said.

"I'm a soldier," he said abruptly. "In the Roman army in Gaul. I'm still human. Twenty-one years old and stupidly brave, the way you are. There are Gauls in the hills and we have to wipe them out. We cross the last Roman bridge before the wilderness, over a mountain gorge with a rushing stream hundreds of feet below. Up the trail, there's a cave. The cave mouth is narrow and the earth in front of it trodden flat. We draw straws, and I lose, and I go in with a burning branch, ready to flee or shout if I encounter Gaulish tribesmen, or a bear."

"Oh my God," she said. "You did that?"

"Choice is a recent invention," said Anton. "Hatred is not. I hated them all. They were my comrades, my own tribe if you will, but I left them in hatred because they stayed outside safe in their numbers and sent me alone into the cave. A sacrificial goat."

He laughed.

"I am in the hillside. It is dark and damp and close, but no Gauls have fallen upon me. I think perhaps I will live after all. Then there is a huge rustling and a rush of air, and they are on me. They knock my torch away, and it falls on the floor and goes out before I can even see them. There are hundreds, or thousands, beating into my face and my body. They are biting me and drawing out my blood."

Rachel's hand was over her mouth. "Gauls bit you?"

"Not Gauls. Vampire bats. I awoke eventually, sore in a million places, but the soreness did not even last until I fumbled my way to the cave entrance. I could not find the torch, but the darkness did not seem so dark any more.

"My cohort were all dead. The Gauls massacred them while I was interred in the hillside becoming a vampire. When I returned down the path I found them hanging from the bridge. The Gauls had tied a rope around each neck and thrown each soldier into the gorge in turn. Ninety-nine bodies in Roman armor hung beneath the bridge. They swayed in the breeze, bumping into each other. Ninety-nine men who had died bathed in my hatred, while I became immortal."

Silence filled the car.

Anton discovered her fingers were entwined with his. Her skin was warm. The little scars from her earlier bloodletting felt rough against his palm. It surprised him how comforting her touch was. He squeezed, gently and instinctively, and Rachel squeezed back.

His mind was empty, and full.

"There's nothing you could have done," she said, after a long pause. "If you hadn't been in the cave, you would have died with them."

"I know," said the vampire.

"And you couldn't have escaped the bats."

"I know."

"And you must have ... killed many more people than ninety-nine, over the last two thousand years."

"I have. But they died one by one, and they were not my cohort, and they were not my friends, and I did not hate them, and I was not twenty-one."

"But—"

"You cannot help," he said. "It is complicated, and besides it might not have really happened that way. It was a long time ago. It is just the memory of a memory."

"But you think about it a lot."

Anton looked out at the night.

Rachel sighed, and looked at her watch. "I have to get home. Ken gets suspicious if I'm home late and he doesn't know where I am."

He looked at her. "You are afraid to go home?"

"Sometimes," she said, with reluctance. "When I don't know … whether he's been drinking."

"I could watch from the—"

"No," she said. "He's my problem. Remember, you've only heard my side of it. His might be different."

"You do not believe that."

"It's probably about as true as your memories," said Rachel.

He looked away.

She glanced at him and softened.

"I'm sure they forgive you," she said.

"I doubt it. Anyway, they have been dead for centuries." He paused. "Your Ken will not change, you know. Do not live your whole life hoping that he will."

Rachel closed her eyes. "All right."

"If he does not change … "

"I'll still love him," she said. "There's always the other twenty percent. Sometimes, it's wonderful."

She pressed a button and the car doors unlocked.

"I will be near," he said.

"Don't be. This was enough. It's too dangerous." He wanted to care. He did care.

"I liked it when you held my hand," she said. "It was nice. I don't get much of that."

Her life would go on, and it would get better or it wouldn't.

Ninety-nine men hung beneath a bridge, blackened tongues protruding.

"Fly away home," said Rachel softly, and he opened the door.

The last thing she said to him was thank you.

He had no words for her in return.

The engine purred. The Saturn's red taillights diminished.

On the road, wind against his cheeks, he could still feel the pressure of her fingers against his. He closed his hand to lock their warmth away from the night.

Anton closed his eyes, and did not watch to see which road she took.

-Thirteen Lines-
DON WEBB

Before I encountered the unfinished sonnet of Henry Salt, I would have said that there was nothing on the world that was worth my life. Everything has changed by my reading the thirteen lines. I now know Love and Terror.

My door into the place of damnation was (appropriately enough) the love of money. I work as a research assistant at the Harry Ransom Center at the University of Texas. We've got quite a collection including the fine copy of Bram Stoker's Dracula; you should stop by some time. My job is to aid those scholars and seekers after the mysteries that visit our air-conditioned halls. Sometimes the work is both hard and exhilarating; sometimes there is nothing to do. Being the thrifty sort that I am, I use my free time to produce little gems of independent scholarship that I sell for small recompense. My real name does not matter, but perhaps you know my pseudonym of John Kincaid, who writes lots of articles of the paranormal or just plain weird.

I had an idea for a honey of an article on strange manuscripts and cursed books. I figured I'd cover four or five texts, plus some pictures and I've got a feature. Maybe if I played my cards right Omni or Playboy would be tempted. My formula for success in paranormal writing—what the heck, I can give it to you now that I'm leaving the field—was to cover the same old ground for 75 - 80 percent of the article, and then add one truly new item. This would make my article hot and quotable and ensure that I could sell my next article.

Very, very few people are aware that I am John Kincaid. It would probably make most researchers uncomfortable. Would you want your research assistant to be the man who wrote "Was Lincoln's Father Bigfoot?" No, I didn't think so.

My article on mysterious texts covered the magical papyri of Thebes, the Voynich manuscript, and Dr John Dee's "Enochian" cipher—all well-researched and well-known texts for the occult crowd. I was browsing through the on-line catalog for occult curiosities when I came across Blood Loss and Poetry: An Account of the Inanna Sonnet by Austin O. Emme, London, Dawglish & Son, 1925. "An account of the so-called vampire sonnet, its translators since the Middle Ages, and the discovery of the original text in Sumerian, with especial emphasis on the life of Henry Salt, Esq." Private edition of 333 copies. LOST.

The last word dashed my hopes as much as all the others had raised them. LOST meant that the book had been part of one of the rare book collections, and that most likely it had walked away with some visiting scholar. Our current security system prevents any such thefts, but in a more trusting age—say, thirty years ago—such a stringent system wasn't in place, and the occasional visitor overcome by bibliophilic lust took a book or two. I decided to post queries on a couple of electronic librarian's lists looking for either Blood Loss and Poetry or any information on Henry Salt.

Then I went out to lunch.

∞☉∞

It was a couple of days before I got a response. A couple of postings revealed that Henry Salt had been an undistinguished curator of Egyptian and Mesopotamian antiquities at the Sallust Museum. A third indicated that he had died during a scandal of 1898, and the fourth proved most interesting.

"We too have lost our copy of Austin Emme's book, but one of our grad students in the Sixties had begun a study of "Scarlet Woman Motifs in Ecstatic Poetry" and provides a copy of the vampire sonnet:

'Look into the heart of wind on storm night
and find a sudden black rainbow.' "

Just as I read the first couplet I heard a sudden metallic noise, like a huge wreck, and I ran to my window. Below on Guadalupe Street what had been a small Japanese car and a large four-wheeled Jeep were now one. Three or four other vehicles had hit each other, or parked cars, in an effort not to smash into the central pair. Students, homeless beggars, and street entrepreneurs were pointing and yelling. Amidst the crowd stood the oldest and ugliest woman I had ever seen. She was dressed head to toe in black, Iranian somehow. Sirens sounded, and I could hear my coworkers going to their windows.

I went back to my terminal, but the screen was blank. Goddamit! Had I hit the delete key or otherwise screwed up? I spent several minutes trying to retrieve the missing message, and wound up sending a note to the computer center asking if they could help me.

I worked till dusk. I had gone through a painful divorce a couple of years ago, one of my best defenses against loneliness is overwork.

It was a beautiful warm Texas night and I didn't want to hurry home. I walked through campus. UT has a beautiful campus, full of Spanish buildings and fountains. I sat on the edge of one of them, where hippocampi sported in the backlit foam. Very pretty and the white noise filled my ears as spray soaked my tired face …

And I found myself dancing in an old palace, all soft stone and candlelight. My partner wore a black veil that shimmered like moonlight on a lake and we danced by vast windows, which looked upon a world in perpetual night where the ground outside was white as snow, but I knew it wasn't covered with snow, then my head plopped back and I woke up.

I had fallen asleep by the fountain. I felt dizzy and confused, and very embarrassed. I'm sure I looked drunk or drugged. I stood up, a little bit staggered by my experience. Someone laughed behind my back.

I didn't feel like driving home, so I decided to return to my office. I was there several minutes before it occurred to me that I might need medical attention. Frankly, I was hoping to fall asleep again and regain the sweet feeling of the dream.

As my orientation returned I decided to check my email: two more messages on Salt. One was from a colleague in Denver; after pleasantries he got to the point:

"We have the Emme book. Henry Salt went from respected 'Orientalist' (as they said in those days) to a kind of street person. He had acquired a clay tablet bearing a hymn to Inanna, which he translated and then discovered that it matched a medieval French poem. At first he published this as a historical finding—evidence of a poetic tradition going back to the Euphrates. Then he went through a period of trying to form a 'Cult of Insubstantiability,' which got him fired from the Sallust. Then he had a change of heart and spent all his money

buying every copy of his articles on the hymn. He even snuck into the Sallust and hammered the tablet to bits. He apparently died in front of the museum a few days later, some said of blood loss. To my surprise I discovered that we've never made a microfilm copy of the book. As soon as we have one made up, I'll send it to you. Thanks for the interesting read."

The other was from the Oriental Institute in Chicago. Its message was more to the point.

"Leave the 'Unfinished Hymn to Inanna' SM 10188 alone. It claims a scholar every couple of decades. Stick with something safe like crack cocaine."

Needless to say I was more intrigued than ever. All commercial dreams had vanished. I wanted something that I could know—some Mystery that was for me and me alone. There is nothing that can be possessed as fully as something within one's mind.

I waited daily for the microfilm from Denver, and I continued to have my little dreams. I remembered little of them, save for the slow lovely dance with the veiled woman and the delicious sense of swooning that accompanied each dance. I wanted to have her, take her, but even more than that I wanted to speak with her to know her thoughts and being.

I don't recall ever being so much in love. Certainly not in my marriage to Beth, certainly not in college or high school romances. Never in fiction or movies or fantasy.

My boss called me in and asked what was wrong with me.

How did she mean?

She said that I had been getting really sloppy about finishing assignments. The other day I had been speaking with a man from Utah and that I had just wandered away from him in mid-sentence.

I sort of remembered this, but shrugged it off with a bad joke about Mormons.

She also asked about my health saying that I was looking pale and wan.

I asked if she was worried about expenses for our health plan. It was all in all very unpleasant.

I knew that I could stop, but I wanted to let things go on for a little while at least. I needed a better picture of things, and besides I felt so dreamy.

∞ Θ∞

The microfilm arrived. I'll quote from relevant sections.

"Dr. Salt's initial paper on the clay tablet from Persepolis stressed that it was not a fragment—that the poem was actually incomplete. He speculated that this was perhaps the initial poem to be written first, before being recited—and that the unnamed scribe simply couldn't think of an ending before the clay dried." Pg. 14.

"Salt never revealed his sources for discovering the medieval French, ancient Greek, or seventeenth century English versions of the hymn; although the existence of some (but not all) of these translations has been verified. His published remarks merely say that these were brought to his attention in a "mysterious manner." This probably marks the beginning of his death as a scholar." Pg. 23.

"Little is known of the Church of the Yellow Light. Salt took in members from all races and classes. When I tracked down members some twenty-five years later, most could recall nothing. A few had vague impressions of meeting in a drafty cheap hall that Salt had rented, and watching some sort of magic lantern projections. Fewer still had been so stirred by their experiences to try their hands at Theosophy or various occult practices—but for the most part their whole involvement with the Church had been a particularly obscure dream in their dreary dreamlike existence." Pg. 48

"Salt gave many alternative translations for the Hymn to Inanna. Some alternate opening couplets include:

She is Thunder, the Perfect Mind
Adversity and Advantage is her Name.

Sweeter than my own thoughts is she
She, who invented thinking for me

What cost red blood for golden nectar?
What cost the world for splendor?

Suddenly a black rainbow in the blue night
and in that other world living gold.

Clearly these cannot be objective translations from the Sumerian. Salt's own explanation for the variations (he apparently produced 418 of them!) was that the original had been written in 'an unknown tongue.' " Pg. 52

"The last meeting of the Church of the Yellow Light occurred on October 16, 1898. Salt had been giving one of his lectures on the insubstantial, when he abruptly seemed to change his views. He began shouting, "No! She's mine! Mine alone!" and chasing people from the hall. The rumor that he later set the hall on fire is unsubstantiated, perhaps this was the work of a disillusioned follower or maybe a random vagrant." Pg. 101

"One of the most ingenious theories was that the poem tried to define the indefinable, or as Salt put it, "to make the Unknown Known." Most of the poets or translators had tried to add a word to the poem, some even attempted a whole line. According to Salt, it was the strain of extending the poem that caused the blood loss. The Sumerian version was a mere eight lines long. Salt had located an English language version of 1814 consisting of twelve full lines and the beginning of a thirteenth. Salt's final version of the poem was cast in the form of an unfinished sonnet awaiting its fourteenth line. I have published the verse as APPENDIX B to this volume. Although I find the supposed occult or "vampiric" nature of the sonnet to be utter rubbish, I must admit I find the lines a bit too fascinating. This undoubtedly speaks of the suggestibility of the human mind, and perhaps lends support to the theories of Dr. Freud." Pg.135

"Although Salt's death was rumored to be caused by anemia, no autopsy was performed nor medial report of any kind made. The sheriff attributed the death to exposure. The body was to have been buried in the family vault, but was stolen by person or persons unknown and no doubt performed its last civil service for aspiring medical students. " Pg. 167

The microfilm broke before I could read the thirteen lines of Henry salt. I had to wait and get help to repair the machine, because I didn't want to risk gumming up the works and possibly loosing my chance to read the microfilm for several days.

While I was waiting for the technician to come to fix the microfilm, my boss sent for me.

She told me that my clothes were dirty. She told me that I smelled. She told me that I needed a shave.

She said my eyes looked sunken. Was I on something?

She told me to go home.

"But I'm waiting for some film to be fixed."

"It's five o'clock. You can look at it tomorrow—when you come in clean and shaved. Get some sleep. Take a vitamin for Christ's sake."

"But this is a very important project. I've been working on it since the day of the big wreck."

"What wreck?"

I began to understand. I went home. I would have to make the decision whether or not to read the poem, because I began to see what the implications were.

∞☉∞

The woman came to me in a dream that night.

As I had expected.

I found myself in the vast stone hall whose windows looked upon miles and miles of ground as white as snow. I could see the land clearly now; it was covered in bones. The soft glow inside the hall, which I had attributed to candlelight in all my dreamy dreams of love, had no source. It came from everywhere and cast no shadows. As I pondered this, a voice came from behind me—a voice so sweet that I could feel it make my sleeping body shiver.

"The light is the force of mind. Ultimately it is the only light we have in this darkling universe. It is my light."

I turned to face her. She had removed her veil. I took her in my arms and we began to waltz to silent music. How can I describe her face, a face that has the beauty of a thousand moonlit nights? Or the eyes of a blue not of your earth, for it is such a blue that can only be imagined? Or her hyacinthine black hair, whose luster suggests another spectrum—an anti-light whose unknown colors could only be spread by a prism whose angles are unknown to man?

All of this and so much more was she.

"None of this is real, is it?" I asked.

"No. Not in the way you mean real," she said. "This is imagination alone. This is the insubstantial. Yet alter anything here, and those things in that other world which are symbols of here are altered proportionally."

We waltzed and waltzed, stone walls and dark windows spun.

"I am the goddess of this place. I am the source and the Form of all dream lovers. I am real as long as I am loved."

"You are Inanna?"

"I have any name you want to give me."

"And how long would you keep that name? How long would you be faithful?"

"I will be faithful as long as you live, devoted to you absolutely. My love and lust would be as absolute as could be imagined by anyone, anywhere. For I am the Form of the dream lover."

"And when I died?'

"I would spirit your body here, to lay in the endless lands of insubstantiality. Your bones would join the millions, and I would become the old woman wandering the earth till another was chosen. One that could see me and my illusions."

"Would you remember me, out of your millions of lovers?"

"No." she said, and I could feel my sleeping twitch with agony, but I did not awaken. She continued, "No, but while we loved the rain of inspiration would fall upon your race. While you struggled to add another line to my poem, a thousand poets would be born. While your blood itself boiled away the idea of Love would become more perfect."

I awoke and I thought of her. I pictured myself crazed and bloodless, trying to live one more day so that I could dream one more night.

I could put it aside. I could throw away the microfilm and delete my computer files. I hadn't taken a vacation in a couple of years. I could go to Vegas, blow some of that money I'd socked away since my divorce. I could get drunk and go to a cathouse. I could ...

I wasn't even fooling myself. Tomorrow I'd shave and bathe, and put on a clean suit. I'd get up early so I could catch breakfast at a restaurant downtown where I'd have beef steak and eggs Florentine to build up my blood.

And I would read Henry Salt's unfinished sonnet and start to work on the fourteenth line.

(For Lilith)

-Flotsam-
SCOTT HARPER

I once thought I controlled time, could make it move and flow according to the caprices of my will. Now, time has become an enemy, more cold and brutal and implacable than any I have faced in my long existence.

My limbs feel like iron, cold morning iron that has endured a chilly alpine night complete with frost and snow. Face down, bobbing along in the waves like the jettison I have become, disoriented and imprisoned by the running waters of the ocean. The days are the worst, of course; the unrelenting sun searing through the remnants of my once-fine clothing, crisping the dead skin underneath. The onset of night brings with it some minor relief, but my body weakens and slowly rots with each passing day that I do not feed. My hair has fallen out. The few brief glimpses I catch of my hands and forearms reveal a body reduced to little more than an emaciated patchwork of burnt, leathery skin. Gulls and other carrion feeders have gathered in the waters around me, pecking away small pieces of flesh from my neck and back, while fish nibble away at my stomach from underneath.

I try to scream, but have no breath. Rank seawater fills my mouth, invades my throat and lungs. I attempt to swim, but have no strength. I fancy myself one of the damned in Dante's ninth circle, frozen solid and unmoving in a lake. I can vaguely recall a time when others labeled me damned as well, people I then considered foolish and beneath my notice. Now, as I am tossed about on the waves, I wonder who was the fool really was?

Consciousness ebbs and flows during the day like the tides. An old, familiar hunger not fed in days accompanies the cold. It fills my every waking moment and haunts my dreams …

∞☉∞

I lie back in the bed as she leans over me, her skin so white it glows, absorbing light, an aura of darkness surrounding her. She mounts me with cat-like grace, her tight stomach brushing mine. Her small breasts hang down and rest on my chest, the softness of her touch exciting me. I breathe rapidly, inhaling her scent, almost panting. Her face floats toward me with blue eyes both cold and hungry, her black hair streaming behind. I reach up to satisfy my lust, but she brushes my hands away with casual ease. She is in charge of this moment, my life in her hands.

I hold my breath as she caresses my neck, stroking my fevered pulse with the lightest touch. I feel her kiss, intimate and deep and deadly, on the same place she has been caressing. My eyes flare open and for a brief moment the world becomes more intense, all my senses more heightened than they had been through my whole life of living with them. A final, all-consuming sensory overload. My body is slowly dying, drained of life and blood, and this intensity represents my mind's way of clinging to life's memories. I let it wash over me. Her lips are so cold; not smooth as I expect but more scaly like a fish. They grate on my skin and pull away. I feel it again and jerk away, startled by swarms of silver flashes spinning all around me, diving in again to pick, pick, pick at my flesh. Not my maker, but my reality …

∞☉∞

The gulls scatter as I feebly heave my body about, the blood reveries of a dead man temporarily interrupted. The birds return to their feast as soon as my energy gives out and my struggles cease. My mind wanders, lulled as the sun's heat inexorably cooks my brain. Reality and recollection, substance and dream mix and become one.

∞☉∞

Images flash before me. Some are rapid and easily dismissed. Others I choose to draw out and explore further, turning over and over, looking for new angles of incite, like rereading a familiar book on a lazy Sunday afternoon. I am transformed, physically and emotionally, no longer a discarded, emaciated skeleton bobbing hopelessly on the water. Fine clothing adorns me, indicative of class and breeding. Long, chestnut brown hair flows down over the wide shoulders of a muscular physique. My skin is pale, but neither sallow nor thin, my lips full and red. And my eyes … they burn with a fierce red intensity, a sureness of power no living man could ever duplicate.

She is there as well, of course. She becomes my dark mother, bringing me across the plane of death with care and precision, my heart stilled, lungs empty, my lifeblood coating her lips. She returns the blood to me, mixed with her own, revitalizing a corpse shell, her willpower grasping my departing soul and refusing to let it go.

Her eyes fill my vision as I rise from the bed that has become a grave and embrace her with unnatural fervor, our first blood kiss, a clash of lip and fang and tongue. She pledges between moans to school me in the ways of her night world. I moan in return. My sharp nails tear into the skin of her back as I feel truly alive for the first time.

Time becomes a vast whirlpool, images of unlife tossed about and jumbled together without chronology. I see myself accepting my new form of existence, coping with and reveling in it. Altering my body, taking to the sky with wings as dark as the night, soaring underneath the moon's brilliance. Chasing the slow human prey she finds, more deadly than any African lion, knocking them to the ground with frightening ease and feasting on them. Engaging witch hunters and churchmen in battles of wit and intrigue and mortal pawns spanning decades. Sparring with wolfmen for supremacy of the woods, engaging the fierce beasts in combat, tooth to tooth, talon to talon. Noting her look of approval and pride as I raise high the head of a loup-garou, his animal blood coating my proud fang teeth.

Some of the memories exhilarate me and are welcomed. Others come unsolicited, like a tax collector or a spurned lover at the front door, causing uncertainty and angst.

We are back in the same room, her room, where she sired me. I see her move away from me, rage and disappointment vying for control of her features, her face turning away.

"I'm sorry," I say, but bloody tears have already appeared in her eyes.

"How could you?" she accuses. "I made you to be with me always." She looks at the bed that stands between us, the same bed where we made love for the first time all those years ago. The bed where I gave up my humanity to become something both more and less than a man.

"I no longer need you. I've outgrown you. You limit me." The words come out harshly, but the thing I've become has no compassion, has no care save for his own needs. I feel neither gratitude nor hate toward her. "I'm leaving."

My words enrage her further. She reacts uncharacteristically, striking out, smashing the nightstand like so much kindling. I ignore her outburst.

"I've booked passage on a ship leaving tomorrow. I've made arrangements for my belongings to be delivered prior to my departure. There's no need for any involvement on your part. And you don't need to know where I'm going."

She laughs, her fang teeth unsheathed, the blood tears streaking down her face. "Have you learned nothing in your time with me? You share my blood. I'll always know where you are. The sea is our enemy. We cross it only when we must, and only after taking the necessary precautions. Storms are at their worst at this time of year, and you cannot feed. The shipping companies keep very accurate manifests. Missing passengers will be noticed and cause unrest."

"And still I will leave," I say matter-of-factly.

"And without me you will die. Again," she warns. I laugh and leave.

∞ ⊖ ∞

I never knew what caused the ship to sink. I was awakened in my daytime slumber by a thunderous crash, the movement of the ship smashing my coffin and heaving me out onto the cargo deck floor. I struggled to consciousness underneath a rising mountain of water, being pushed and pulled about by inexorable icy currents. I fought back with all the unnatural strength at my command, but soon found myself exhausted by the elemental purity of the ocean waters. After a short period of time I floated to the surface, weak and spent and unmoving, just another of the hundreds of other carcasses scattered amongst the ship's wreckage, littering the silent sea.

I wait now for the bliss of final obliteration. A dead damned thing, I cannot drown, nor can I burn entirely while half submerged in water. The gulls and fish consume my flesh at an agonizingly slow pace. Only the complete destruction of my remains will free what little remains of my soul.

There was a time when I sought to avoid death at all costs, when I found the concept of my own mortality alarming. I eventually went to the extent of making love to a dead creature in order to avoid that mortality, allowing her to drink my blood and ensnare my soul. Now I would welcome the finality of true death. Perhaps, if there indeed is a deity, it has chosen to extract recompense from me for all the lives of its creations I have snuffed out over these many years. If so, I can only begin to imagine how long this unliving hell will continue.

At first I do not notice the tugging on my boots, caught up as I am in my dazed reveries. A stronger pull wakes me from my languor. I note briefly that the sun has set, the night's coolness slightly invigorating my tired frame. A small measure of comfort, a familiar affinity with the darkness sets in.

A powerful grip attaches to my legs just below the calves and pulls me with astonishing force below the waves. I both feel and hear the bones break. The grip takes me downward for a short period of time, then releases. A sense of the utter, terrifying depth of the ocean below envelops me. I see the colossal form of a shark as it swims out from underneath, its black body large enough to eclipse the moonlight. It rounds with extraordinary swiftness for such a large creature. I see its clown eyes set just above an enormous mouth lined with row after row of deadly teeth. The leviathan's jaws encircle my torso with unerring precision, shattering ribs and puncturing skin. It begins to dive. I feel the crushing pressure of the ocean increase as the beast swims deeper and deeper.

I feel no fear at this point, having died once before already. A portion of the man that remains buried deep within this undead corpse wishes to be consumed, to finally end this nightmare existence. The shark's penetrating teeth remind me of my human death beneath the teeth of my maker. A trail of black ichor seeps from my torso wounds, trailing upward behind the shark's tail. The creature's eyes are closed as it begins to shake me in its immense jaws.

Ancient survival instincts come to the fore, strengthened by a fevered desire to prevent my maker's dire predictions from coming true. Despite my weakness, despite the suffocating weight of the water, I summon the strength to dig my hands, now adorned with black claws, into the fleshy area around the shark's gills. I begin to methodically tear chunks of red flesh from the huge creature.

The shark reacts predictably to the pain, opening wide its massive maw. The wake pushes me out of the beast's jaws. I manage to hang on by one hand to an open wound I have inflicted as the shark dives deeper, attempting to escape. I plant both hands into the wound and pull. The tough hide and muscle give way with frightening ease. Blood fills the water, blinding me. My lips pull back in a mirthless smile, teeth exposed.

I bury my face in the wound, gulping down seawater and the shark's gamy life fluids. My tongue digs deep into the meat and gristle, my throat swallows, greedy for more. The ice that has invaded my body dissipates some as strength returns. I am overcome by a steadily increasing sense of invigoration and repletion as I continue to vacuum out the beast's lifeblood. I fail to notice as the shark eventually slows its dive, stops, then begins to float upside down.

The shark's life energy has become my own. My burnt, emaciated skin has healed and become whole, hair now covering my head. Strength and power flood now muscular limbs and torso. I now am no longer a corpse, but a man. A man with a name.

Zecheriah. My name is Zecheriah.

The knowledge does me little good, for despite my newfound strength the sea still imprisons me. The shark has floated to the surface, now belly up. I manage to push my head out of the water and attempt scramble up onto the top of the corpse, but find little purchase.

Boundless rage fills my heart. Still unable to escape this torment. To have the raw power to tear apart a giant killing machine, but at the same time be unable to pull myself a short distance out of water? Alive, but not truly alive. Such were the inexplicable contradictions of the "life" I had chosen. Still unable to put the lie to my maker's words of warning. I scream again. This time air fills my dead lungs, and my cries travel unanswered into the night.

I begin to wonder if I can truly can die. Perhaps at some point I will sink to the bottom, paralyzed by cold and disoriented, but conscious … forever. The strength of the shark's blood is short-lived, sucked out by the icy running water. Confusion settles in, periods of lucidity become shorter and shorter, intertwined with memories of an undying woman.

I am aroused from my stupors by the thunderous echo of a gunshot. A bloodless wound opens up on the shark's white belly. I hear male voices speaking behind me and attempt to twist my head to see their source. More gunshots. This time my body bucks under the impact, shots tearing through my waterlogged torso. I feel sharp metal slam through my back and push out from my chest. I am hauled unceremoniously away from the dead shark, out of the water and onto the deck of as ship.

I find myself on an antiquated wooden vessel, the planks and railings caked in grime and sea salt. A gibbous moon shines over masts outfitted with flat sails, as there are no drafts in the early evening. Dark, malodorous forms surround me. Their dress and mannerisms suggest they are brigands of some sort. Drawn to carnage like vultures to carrion, they have begun looting the corpses left in the wake of my ship's disaster. Perhaps they were the cause of the wreck.

I make out at least ten of them, armed with an array of knives, swords, clubs, and firearms. A large hook attached to a long wooden pole pierces my torso. I have been gaffed like a common fish.

A massive African with a scarred, heavily muscled physique approaches me. He pins my head to the deck, a boot thrust into my neck, and extracts the gaff with a wet sucking sound. Two of his colleagues approach. Thinking me dead, they rifle through the remains of my clothing.

The fire inside me is rekindled. Anger about my condition. Hatred for my maker. Rage against the recent indignities I'd been forced to endure. These and other frustrations explode at once as I retaliate with inhuman ferocity. Within the span of a heartbeat the throats of the pickpockets are ruptured in a spray of blood and sundered windpipe. The other brigands attack. I feel the impact of blows from fists and clubs, ignore cuts and thrusts from knives and swords. I become a virtual hurricane, sweeping through the pirates in an orgy of shattered skulls, broken necks, and torn-out hearts. One brave soul points a pistol at my head and fires. White-hot pain floods my vision as the shot shatters my skull, sending a mist of black ichor into the air. I stumble but quickly recover as the wound heals almost instantaneously, bones knitting, flesh reforming. Her blood has made me strong, ungodly resilient. I grab the man by the front of his oily shirt, lifting him effortlessly into the air with but a single hand, and sling him over the rail. He screams as he is torn apart by a horde of smaller sharks, newly arrived and feeding on the remains of the one I had killed.

A fearsome cry assaults my ears. I feel the wooden deck shake under the impact of massive booted feet. The giant African slams into me, causing me to stagger back. I almost lose my footing on the slick deck. The pirate's huge, meaty hands encircle my neck and lift me into the air. His hands exert incredible pressure, pressure that would easily have broken the neck of a normal man. I laugh, a full-throated laugh that almost brings tears to my eyes. I relish the challenge this man offers, and respond in kind. His eyes betray disbelief as my own blaze crimson in the night. My clawed hands sweep down and pulp the African's massive forearms. A mixed cry of agony and terror shoots from his lips. We fall to the deck. I bury my mouth into his neck. Rich, powerful, hot blood pulses down my throat, flooding me with energy, dispelling the iciness that had permeated my dead body. Its thickness flows like fire in my veins, and something in me rises up and sings in delight at its flavor. The cold ichor of the shark seems like gruel in comparison. I feed until the man's heart is stilled, the blood run out.

I discard the corpse, casually fingering a remaining button on a once-fine shirt. I survey the carnage. Though still damned, I am imprisoned no more. At least, not physically. I feel the strength of her blood call out to me, across land and sea, offering understanding and forgiveness. I take flight, seeking some form of resolution.

∞☉∞

She waits for me on the bed, her white nightgown open in the front, her pale skin beckoning me.

"*Denn die Todten reiten schnell,*" she comments. *For the dead travel fast.*

"I did not die, as you predicted," I state matter-of-factly.

She rises on her knees and encircles my shoulders with her thin arms. She looks on me, her dark eyes filling my vision.

"I'm glad." She brushes her lips on mine, not kissing, just arousing.

"I have a memento," I say, and dig my fingers through recently healed tissue, deep into my ribcage. I retrieve a serrated shark tooth and place it in her hand. She kisses it and licks my pale blood from it, leaning back to expose her chest. She trails the tooth just below the areola of her right breast, black blood slowly seeping out from the small incision. She guides my head to the cut. I let her. My lips take hold as her head falls back, her back arched in passion. I drink, her cold blood more powerful and delicious than I remember it.

In the end, I realize, blood is stronger. Stronger than will, stronger than hate, stronger than destiny, stronger than time itself. I embrace that knowledge which has cost me so dearly to obtain, and join with her, accepting my eternity and the comfort she offers.

-Moving Lines-
STEVE VERNON

What can I tell you? I'm a gypsy, or at least the sign outside my shop said so.

GYPSY FORTUNE TELLING
BY WALK-IN OR APPOINTMENT ONLY
ASK US ABOUT OUR RAINY DAY SPECIAL!

That was one sign. There was another on the lamppost outside my shop window. It told anyone who cared to read that:

JESUS CHRIST SAVES FROM ALL SINS
PRAY TO JESUS NOW
OBEY THE BIBLE

Lines delivered as directly as a marine drill instructor. They didn't call it the Salvation *Army* for nothing. A Cosa Nostra strong-arm paissano, with biceps the size of bowling balls and tattoos on each arm that read MUDDER and MURDER could not be half so explicit.

There was a basketful of tracts sprouting from beneath the sign. The basket was refilled every couple of weeks. I don't know who refilled it. I've never seen anyone even go near the basket. Maybe it was refilled by night. Maybe the tracts spontaneously procreated. Maybe there was a miniaturized printing press installed inside the lamppost.

Stranger things have happened.

I never see anyone reading any of the tracts. I think a few discerning winos use the tracts to blow their noses on when the weather was cold.

Underneath the basket the motif continued with a few more lines– –DEATH, JUDGMENT, ETERNITY, HEAVEN OR HELL, YOU DECIDE—which kind of reminded me of those guilt-riddled warnings that the government printed on cigarette packages.

Remember, only you can prevent lung cancer.

I've got another sign hung on the wall beside my table that was printed on a sheet of cardboard as neatly as my penmanship allowed, in bright red magic marker; and covered with a thin layer of plastic sandwich wrap.

It almost looked professional.

"The moving finger writes and having writ moves on, nor all your wit shall lure it back to cancel half a line, nor all your tears wash out a word of it."

Omar Khayam.

Now there was a fellow who truly knew his lines.

I'm a palmist. I flip the tarot. I've got a knack for seeing what people want to see in their dreams. I can fake a teacup if the price is right.

Some folks call me Gypsy Jack.

Ha!

The truth is, I don't know jack.

Is it a con? Sure, what isn't? We live in concrete tombs built out of cons and promises and lies. We fill our ears with radio waves and television signals stuffed full of larcenous fantasies. We play bingo and invest in the stock market, and figure its all the way things ought to be.

I'm an honest to Cheiro palmist. One of those crazy guys who actually believes in what he's doing. That was rare, these days.

The believing.

Not the palmistry.

My granny taught me how, much to the undying shame of my poppa. Poppa thinks I should leave the teacups and cards for the women and take up a trade as an honest thief. What can I tell you? Fathers are never happy with their sons. I think it's some kind of immortal law, you know?

God forbid, if I ever have a son I promise to be happy with him.

Unless he disappoints me.

So here I am in my rented storefront with my cot out back. The building code tells me I'm not supposed to sleep here, but I read palms, not codes. What the slumlord doesn't know isn't going to hurt me.

I've been here for six whole months. In six more months this block is scheduled for urban renewal—another sacrifice to the power of progress and the gluttonous juggernaut of endless gentrification. Call it what you will, it's all means the same damn thing. Me and the tattooist upstairs and the lady in the basement who takes in homeless sailors are going to be out on the street.

What can I tell you? Nothing lasted forever. Six months before I was somewhere else. In six months from now I'll just move on. The cheapest buildings were always the ones about to die.

It isn't that vicious of a cycle.

I like what I'm doing most of the time, except every now and then I get to feeling like a priest who's heard one too many lousy confessions.

Like today, for instance.

Today came down like a rain of endless thunder.

I should have seen it coming. The signs were everywhere. A cat moaned under my window. A dog howled under the streetlight even though the moon had its eye poked out for the next three days. I woke up this morning with a mouthful of cobweb and a dead rat at my doorway.

Oh can I hear an omen, please?

I should have seen it coming when she first walked in. I should have seen it in the way she looked at me like a lonely moonlit cave. I should have turned her away. It was nearly night time; I was thinking about frying a couple of sausages with some peppers and onions and garlic and that bottle of plonk I'd saved since Saturday. Then she walked in and all I saw was a customer, and a chance to feed the bills.

"I want to know my future," she said. "Palm or cards, I don't care, just tell me what you see."

"What I tell you depends on what you want to know. The palm tells everything. Birth to death, cradle to grave. Only general, you know? The cards are specific, but short sighted. Two or three months at best. The cards don't see far, but they do see straight."

"I don't know about two or three months," she said. "I just know I'm here, for now, so maybe it better be the palm."

"Sit down."

I've got a card table from a junk shop. It's covered with a black cotton tablecloth an old lady sewed me for a dream I read. There are a couple of chairs—a green plastic lawn chair that she sits in. I found that in an alley that growled at me when I took it. There was also a wooden chair that I'm already sitting in.

The wooden chair came with the rent.

"Are you right handed or left handed?"

"Does it make a difference?"

"In the old days the palmist read your left hand. Closest to the heart tells truth, so they figured. But that's nothing but bullshit. The heart is the biggest liar you ever met. I read the hand you think with, the one you work with. The hand you don't use, that's what you were born with," I tell her. "The hand you use, that's what you made of it."

"What if I'm ambidextrous?"

It was late and my patience was never long lived.

"Then you ought to make up your mind," I said, trying to make my irritability into a joke.

She just stared.

"So, are you?"

"Am I what?"

"Are you ambidextrous?"

"No," she said. "I'm right handed."

So I get her to hold out her right hand.

"You're receptive," I say. "Like a radar dish to life, you take in what it sends you. You lap it up, like a cat licks cream."

The shape of her palm, her splayed out fingers, they tell me this, that, and a pretty good guess. Her grin tells me I guessed right.

I hold her hand, and test it for flexibility. A stiff hand means an inflexible person—someone who doesn't change easily, a control freak, unreceptive to new ideas. Her hand is cold, but it's almost night and there's probably a chill in the air. I could tell her that she had a warm heart, but I don't believe in that old saying: *cold hands, warm heart.*

Next I always turn the hand over and look at the life line. That's the line that fish hooks from between your thumb and index and down towards your wrist. If it's long and strong it means a good healthy life. If it bends away from your thumb, like a linebacker heading out for a lateral pass, it shows a wild spirit, a black sheep, someone who has disappointed their father early on. If there is a second line inside it, it means a strong inner life.

Only this line wasn't like any of those others. This line was like some kind of crazy spiral dance. This line looked like a long skinny worm wrapped around and around her thumb. It just kept running on, wrapping around her thumb and back again, like a string that she'd tied on so as not to forget something.

The line looked like one of those spinning hypnotic discs you used to be able to buy in the back of comic books. You know, the ones right next to the garlic chewing gum, the X - Ray glasses, and the genuine shrunken heads. Do you remember those X-Ray glasses? They were supposed to allow you to hypnotize women into letting you have your way with them.

Believe me, they didn't work.

"What do you see?" she asked.

What do I see? Christ, I don't want to see what I'm seeing.

I try to swallow, but my tongue has swollen to the size of an overstuffed couch.

"What do you see?" she repeated.

This means a lot to her. She really *needs* to know.

Call me Galahad, but there's something about a woman in need I can't resist.

I swallow the couch and find my voice.

"I see a long life. A very, very long life."

I'm not kidding. A life line like this you would expect to see on something like a god. Something that's going to be around for a very long time.

"What else do you see?" she asked impatiently.

What could I tell her? It was like her life line had swallowed everything—heart, head, fate—all gone in a single gulp.

"I see hunger," I say. "A life of endless hunger."

She clears her throat, as if she's tasting something she doesn't like.

"What about happiness? What about children? What about marriage?" she asks.

There is a fistful of unshed tears trembling in her voice, but I can sense that she isn't the kind of woman who cries a lot.

In fact, she isn't any kind of woman at all.

I remember something granny told me about a life line that ran like this; something I had brushed off as old superstition. I was putting pieces together—Verdelak. Nosferatu. Vampire, Count Yorga, Barnabas Collins, Christopher Lee in all those old Hammer movies … only worse.

This was real.

She was real.

She kept asking me questions.

"What about love?" she asked.

"What about it? You might as well ask me which way the wind will blow, three hundred years from tomorrow. It's late. Go home, and come see me in the morning."

"I don't see anyone before sundown," she said.

It figures.

"What about my future?"

"Future is all you got. Future, past, and hunger. Lots of lonely hunger."

Now she's looking at me like I might look at a good tavern steak.

I figured it was time for a little creative self-defense. So I stood up quickly. I kicked over the wooden chair and brought my boot down on it as it hit the ground.

The rungs shattered.

She watched me like a patient diner, waiting for their favorite midnight snack.

I grabbed the broken chair rung and pointed it at her like a knife.

"Get back vampire. There's no future for you today."

She looked at the chair rung. One eyebrow rose up like a black sunrise.

"Not sharp enough. If you're going to stick me, it's got to be sharper than that."

Ha.

Some joke.

If she smiled I was going to scream.

I wished I had time to unsnap my jackknife and whittle a point, but wishing, like my stake, was pointless.

She held up her palm like an Indian in a bad cowboy movie about to say, "How."

Suddenly she was Mandrake, Svengali, and Mesmer rolled into one. I didn't want to look, but I had to. I had to look at her palm only it was like staring at a whirlpool in the ocean and I was falling in to it and it was spinning about me, rising up to entangle me.

It felt a little like falling headfirst into a canyon full of maggots.

I felt the line, *her life line*, wrapping about me. I felt like Tarzan wrestling a giant snake, only this snake was colder than any mere reptile. This snake was cold and unbelievably dead and absolutely hungry. I felt it sucking at me, drawing me inwards. She was amoebic, like one of those creeping vines that strangle sunflowers.

Forget about movies. Vampires, the real ones, they never bite. Vampires suck. Sure, that sounds like the punchline to a bad pun, but I'm not joking here. I'm talking about death by osmosis. A little visceral empathy, if you please.

I've got one hope.

I reached down below me, down through the clinging lines that wrapped about me like I was a virgin in a lounge room, undead pick up artists slinging line after unholy line, to feel the broken wreckage of my wooden chair. I rose up amidst the gut storm of this evil thing's life line, clinging to two chair rungs like a drowning sailor clinging to a couple of match sticks.

I crossed them, and held them outward. I tried my best to think of Van Helsing. I tried to think about the pope. I thought about Mother Theresa and Billy Graham and Evil Knievel.

It's been years since my mother took me to church, but I remembered some of it.

I recited the one prayer from the rosary I remembered.

"I believe in God, the Father Almighty, Creator of heaven and earth; I believe in Jesus Christ, His only Son, our Lord, who was crucified, died, and was buried."

I'm getting some of the lines wrong, but I must be doing something right because the life line about me loosened and I began to feel a kind of hope being born. Like a ninety-year-old deathbed repentant who hasn't seen the inside of a church since his grandmother took him to be baptized, I kept on praying.

"He descended into hell and on the third day He rose again from the dead; He ascended into heaven, and sits at the right hand of God."

I can't remember the last of it, something about communion and resurrection and maybe it wasn't so good a thing to be praying for in the face of what I was facing. Then I remembered a prayer my uncle taught me, the time the neighborhood bully kicked my ass.

"Saint Michael the Archangel, defend us in our day of battle; protect us against the deceit and wickedness of the devil. May God rebuke him, we humbly pray."

St. Michael did the trick. I was free, and I was back in my room, behind the refuge of my overturned card table that had somehow been kicked over in the heat of our struggle, brandishing my make shift crucifix in the face of this hungry she-devil.

What could I do? I kept on praying, falling back on the ever-reliable Lord's Prayer.

"Our father, who art in heaven, hallowed be thy name."

She swatted the card table out of the way. It slammed against the far wall and one of its chrome legs snapped off.

The part of my mind closest to my wallet mourned the loss of a perfectly good card table and my favorite wooden chair.

The sensible part kept on praying.

"Thy kingdom come, thy will be done ... "

She laughed at this, the kind of laugh that crows laugh over the bones of dead men.

I felt a little less than confident, but I kept on praying.

" ... as it is in heaven. Give us this day our daily bread."

She swatted the Tim Allen cross from my hands, and I felt my daily bread grow cold and moldy. So I crossed my fingers and began to chant, *"the power of Christ compels you, the power of Christ compels you,"* but I guess she hadn't seen that movie.

She caught me by my throat, and held me close enough to smell the stink of the graveyard dirt she'd slept in.

"My people are older than your people," she said in a voice that sounded like a toad that had somehow learned to speak. "My people are older than *His* people."

I was scared. I tried not to show it. I figure I did pretty well, seeing how I managed not to soil my pants.

I kept trying to pray.

"Our father, our father ... "

But I guess he wasn't listening as her grip choked the words from me. She knew it was all an act. I hadn't been to church since Jesus was a Jew.

"Little god-boy, you mouth your prayers, yet you have not been to confession in more years than you will admit," she said. "Your words are wind; smoke that slips from the chimney that I will make of your open throat."

"Holy Mary, mother of ... "

She shook me like a dog shakes a dead rat, and then threw me to the floor.

"I spit on you, your father and your mother." she said.

That did it.

That, more than anything else did it.

No one insults my mother.

I was laying face first on the floor, staring at a tarot card that had fallen when she'd knocked over the card table. It was the card they call the hanged man.

I stared at that card and thought of my mother and as that she-demon picked me up again by my throat I found the strength to speak.

"Vampire," I said, spitting the word like a swallow of bad mouthwash. "You mock me, you say my words are empty. Yet last week I slept with a gypsy girl whose piss was warmer than what passes for your pitiful blood. Her laugh was like a gift from heaven and her heart beat like a thunder of roses. You have nothing to match her."

She squeezed tighter, but I was inspired. Out of pure mule stubborn spunk I kept on taunting her.

What the hell did I have to lose?

"You can take my life, and you still have nothing," I told her. "No children, no love, no happiness. I know, I'm a gypsy and I see it in your palm. You live in the grave, and no matter how far you walk by night you will always live in your grave, and that is no life at all."

I thought about dying. I wished I had time to make a will, but what the hell, I had nothing worth bequeathing and no one to bequeath it to. My favorite chair was broken, and I was lying about the gypsy girl.

The truth was I hadn't been laid in months and right about now my future prospects didn't look so hot. I kept on talking, even though the words cut through my damaged throat like razors made of barbed wire.

"As dead as I am about to be I have more future than you. That gypsy girl will someday tell her children about the night I tripped over her father's pig trying to sneak into her camp and was chased away by the hounds, and her children will laugh and I will be reborn in their laughter. Who have you made laugh, bitch? Who has smiled for you? Who will remember you and grin?"

She hissed like an angered snake, slamming my back against the wall and the last breath from my lungs. The room swam. Bright spots of good-bye polka danced about my eyes. I felt her teeth kiss my neck. I felt the weight of her nonexistent breath haunting my skin. Then she screamed, and the room turned over as she threw me to the floor.

I fell beside the wreckage of my broken card table. My arm felt broken, but I didn't have time for pain. I tried to rise. If I were to greet death today, I would do it on my two good feet.

I was my mother's son.

I was a gypsy.

She let me stand.

She stood there, staring at something far beyond me.

I kept waiting for her to finish me, but she did nothing.

I stared at her and she stared at something so unimaginably vast I couldn't begin to tell you what it was.

She began to moan, and the building shook, and if the tattooist upstairs was tattooing an angel on a sailor's back, he probably just gave the angel an extra tit.

And the noise she made, such a noise, I had never heard in my entire lifetime. Just try to imagine the sound that the moon might make as she wailed for her long lost lover on a cold November night in the highest reaches of the Balkan Mountains. Just try to imagine the shrieking of Mary as the Roman centurions nailed her heart to a couple of two by fours.

Then multiply them both by one hundred and ten.

I covered my ears, for fear of going deaf.

Finally she stopped screaming.

The corner of her left eye began to bleed a single tear, blood that was cut with the smallest spectre of sorrow. We stood and stared at each other while I counted time by my heartbeat, until she found the courage to speak.

"Do you know," she asked, with a lopsided grin that was halfway to heart break. "Do you know that I have not seen a sunrise since your grandfather's grandfather first drew breath?"

Her voice was strained, as if I had been strangling her and not the other way around. Her voice cracked and groaned like the door of a long unopened secret.

"What are you going to do about that?" I asked.

She smiled, the kind of smile that blessedly didn't show her teeth.

"I think I will stand alone," she said. "Outside your door, and watch the sun rise one final time."

She walked to the door, opened it, and was gone.

I followed her outside.

I sat down on my front steps.

She stood beside the lamppost with that sign that spoke of redemption and damnation, waiting through the long cold night.

The two of us waited for the sun to rise.

Once a car slowed down to wait beside her, thinking that perhaps that she was the woman who took in homeless sailors. The man in the car spoke. I couldn't hear his line, but I heard her laugh, that once, bitter and sweet and lonely like a very old child.

The car slowly drove away.

We waited some more.

Once she looked at me, and I thought that maybe she was having second thoughts.

Perhaps she was.

She could have had me. I would not have fought. I had fallen in love with that last little laugh of hers, that oh so lonely laugh that sounded so much like a child who had been turned away by her father some thousand years ago.

Loneliness ached within my heart, and love like a moth that flutters beneath the moon was born.

She could have had me, but she didn't.

I could see daylight breaking above the distant horizon, like a knife sliced over hot flesh. I could see the morning sun reaching like the flames of an oncoming forest fire searing the gray distant wait.

The sun rose like a reborn phoenix, roared into the heavens and without looking at me for even once she screamed a long red goodbye.

-Farm Wife-
NANCY KILPATRICK

Noma stationed herself at the back porch and propped the screen door open with her left foot. The sun hadn't set but one hour ago and already the Napanee sky was the color of ashes from the woodburner. Out past the pale tripod fencing and across the dying rye fields she saw Bert shuffling, Dog by his side. The sickness drained him. And left him hungry. Hungry all the time. Lord knows she fed that man a baker's dozen meals a day, but it was never enough. The more he ate, the thinner he got. Wasted. Just this morning she noticed he barely cast a shadow.

A mosquito trying to sneak into the house paused on her meaty upper arm. Yard was swarming with the last of 'em. She watched the bloodsucker poke its snout into a pore. "Want blood you'll get blood," she promised. Her skin began to itch bad but she made herself wait. Easy now. Ball the fist and knot the shoulder like her daddy had showed her. Noma's work developed muscles tensed. She believed she could feel the strong blood forced up that chute.

The sucker went rigid.

Swelled to triple size.

Probably didn't even think about getting away.

She flicked the bloody corpse into the coming night and scratched her wound.

Noma shut the screen door but continued watching Bert make his way slowly toward the house. Sure is a stubborn man, she thought. Had been the forty-odd years she'd known him. Her daddy'd warned her, said it ran in Bert's family, but she wouldn't listen. When Bert first come down with the sickness she tried getting him over to the hospital, but he didn't trust city-trained doctors, didn't trust doctors at all, especially since his sister. Noma couldn't blame him, though.

Seeing Ruby lying like milkweed fluff on those crisp sheets the color of white flour and brittle as dead leaves, eyes shot with blood and sunk back into her head, breath rank, gums shrunk up from the teeth like that … God, what a waste.

The doctors claimed it was some fancy kind of anemia. Gave her stuff but it didn't make the slightest bit of difference that Noma could see. Bert did the right thing in bringing her home. Ruby stayed upstairs in the room next to them, fading day by day, withering to less than nothings, just like Bert was now, until one morning when Noma took up eggs and bacon and found that Ruby had departed. "Best that way," Bert said. Noma had to agree.

And now it's him, she thought. As he reached the vegetable garden, even in the poor light she could see his bones pressuring the skin to set them free. His face wasn't more than a skull, with hardly any flesh for that pale hide to stretch across, and just a tuft of red on top. He lifted an arm and waved; she knew how hard that was for him.

As Bert reached the porch, Noma stepped out, ready to give him a hand up the steps, but he shrugged her off. *You old curmudgeon*, she thought. Even now, when he can use it most, he won't take no help. Well, that's just like a farmer, isn't it?

By the time she'd latched the screen door and closed and locked the inside one, he was at the refrigerator, dragging out the apple pie she'd baked this afternoon. He got a dessert plate from the cupboard and placed a hearty slice on it. That slice went right back into the refrigerator. Out came the cheddar, and pure cream she'd whipped. He plunked himself down in front of the bulk of the pie, helped himself to a wedge of cheese the size of Idaho and scooped seven or eight kitchen spoons of milk fat onto the whole mess. She figured by eating so much he fooled himself he wasn't sick.

"Cuppa coffee?" she asked.

He grunted and nodded but didn't pause.

Noma plugged in the kettle, but before the water got a chance to boil, the pie-tin was empty and he was back for that abandoned slice.

She measured freeze-dried coffee into two mugs, one twice the size of the other, and glanced out the window while she poured water over it. Gonna be cool tonight. October tended to be like that. Leaves on the willow been gone over a week; branches swayed in the breeze like a woman's hair. Might be a harvest moon come up, if the sky stayed clear. Low on tile horizon. And full. She checked the calendar. Nope. Full moon tomorrow night. Be plenty to do come sunrise.

When Bert finished the pie be leaned his skinny self back in the chair and belched loud, then patted his stomach, or what used to be a stomach but had become so bloated he looked like he swallowed a whole watermelon. "Waste not want not," he said, and she agreed. She handed him his coffee and he took it to the living room. She heard the television; sounded like a sports show.

About eleven, Noma put Dog out and they went upstairs. Bert tossed and turned, keeping her awake for a time, but she must have dozed off because she woke when she heard the stairs creak as he stumbled down. The refrigerator door opened and closed. Opened and closed again. Then the back door. The screen door slammed. She turned onto her side and pulled the feather pillow over her ear and went back to sleep.

∞☉∞

Noma got up with the sun. Down in the kitchen she cleared the mess Bert had left. She opened the back door to let Dog in and fed him the scraps. The sky was packed with clouds the color of cow's brains, the air snappy. Farmer's Almanac promised frost tonight.

When breakfast was out of the way and she'd fed the chickens and pigs and milked the cows and turned them out to pasture, Noma harvested as much of the Swiss chard from the garden as she could, two and a half bushel baskets worth. She washed and blanched the iron-rich greens then stuffed them in airtight plastic bags that she sealed for the freezer. Bert hated chard, hated vegetables on principle, he said, but Noma couldn't get enough.

There was bed-making, washing to do, some mending, lunch to get ready and eat, vacuuming, and a call to the feed store to see if that new corn and soya mix for the pigs was in yet. It wasn't.

Around four Noma began supper. Hadn't seen Bert all day. Didn't expect to. Still, she cooked up a mess of chard, and a ton of beef stew, the way she'd made a big lunch and breakfast, just in case.

Around six the cows came back. She locked them up in the barn and on her way to the house looked across the rye. The fields had faded to the color of dry bone. No sign of Bert. Not surprising. Still.

Noma watched reruns of that show with the fat woman but it wasn't very funny this week. She crawled into bed early, not quite ten-thirty. She'd done all she could, all anybody could, but sleep wasn't about to help her out tonight.

The eaves creaked. The wind picked up and howled the way it can. The house her daddy left her was old but solid. Noma grew up here, married here, had her kids, buried her folks. Through every season, lean and plenty, she was used to the sounds.

But when Dog howled at the moon, well; Bert always looked after Dog. She went to the window at the back and was about to warn the mutt to settle himself or else, but stopped. Dog wasn't making a peep now. He stood quivering, scruffy tail between his legs, ears back, about to bolt. And staring at Bert.

A cloud lifted from the bloated moon and Bert turned his face up. The sickness was all over him. Eyes flecked with red like the blood that spurts from a leghorn when you chop the head off. He'd turned into a skeleton and what flesh he had left, the moon showed as a kind of whitewashed blue. "Noma," was all he said. He grinned at her and she saw his gums had receded; his teeth reminded her of the sharp teeth on the combine. But the worst of all was his shadow. It was gone.

"Ain't letting you in," she told him firmly.

His eyes got hard and fiery red like sumac fruit. He stepped up onto the porch, out of her sight. She heard him rattling the back door. "Noma," he called again, so pathetic it got to her.

Despite her better judgment, she went down to the kitchen and opened just the inside, keeping the screen door between them.

"Best you be off," she told him. He cocked his head to one side; that always softened her up. The yellow kitchen light gave him some color. "Noma," he whispered, like they were in bed together.

She shook her head but opened the screen door.

He was on her in a second, pitchfork teeth tearing into her throat. Noma'd always been a big strong woman, but he was stronger, she'd discovered that early in their marriage. This was more so. He stank like the compost heap and his skin rivaled the frosty air. It was plain enough, he was starving, she was supper.

He held her against the kitchen table. She felt the iron blood being drawn from her like milk from a cow. Wasn't but one thing to be done, what her daddy had taught her.

Noma worked slow, tensing the muscles up from her legs, through her privates and stomach, her arms, chest and back. When that was done, she eased up a second. One final overall squeeze did the trick.

Bert looked like he'd been slammed by a bale of hay. Blood gushed from his mouth, nose, and ears. His eyes popped wide. He swelled fast, the way the skin does when you're frying up chicken. A funny sound, kind of a cross between her name and a goose hissing, started to rise out of him but didn't get much of a chance.

Noma shook for a while but figured there wasn't any point to that. The clock over the stove read two thirty. She glanced out the window. Frost had taken the Last of the chard. The waste of it troubled her.

The walls and ceiling were splattered, the floor slime. She cleaned up what she could of the gory mess, then opened the door. Dog bounded in, happy to gobble the scraps.

Noma dabbed alcohol on her neck and checked the clock again. Time to get herself to bed. Sunrise wasn't far off. Tomorrow there'd be plenty to do. Always is for a farm wife.

-About The-
AUTHORS

JAMES ROY DALEY ~ is a writer, editor, and a professional musician. He studied film at the Toronto Film School, music at Humber College, and English at the University of Toronto. He is the author of the hardcore horror novel, *Terror Town*. In 2007 his first novel, *The Dead Parade*, was released in 1,100 bookstores across America. In 2009 he founded a book company called Books of the Dead Press, where he enjoyed immediate success working with many of the biggest names in horror. His first two anthologies, *Best New Zombie Tales Volume One*, and *Best New Zombie Tales Volume Two*, far exceeded sales predictions, leading many of the top horror writers in the world to view his little company as one worth watching.

ROBERT ELROD ~ Award-winning illustrator and graphic designer, Robert Elrod, strives to embrace a variety of styles and genres. He works in acrylics, watercolors, inks, colored-pencils, pencils, and digitally. He's active in local and national art shows and conventions, focusing primarily on images that depict horror, fantasy, and science fiction. His portfolio includes book covers, CD covers, comic books and pinup artwork. Robert's work can be found in *Vincent Price Presents* (Bluewater Comics), *New Horizons* (the British Fantasy Society), and in galleries across America.

MATT HULTS ~ lives in Minneapolis, Minnesota with his wife and two children. His work can be found in *Best New Zombie Tales Volume 1 & 2*. Books of the Dead Press released *Husk*, his first novel, in 2011.

JOHN F.D. TAFF ~ is an author with more than 25 years experience in all sorts of writing...public relations, marketing, sales, journalism and creative. He's a published author with more than 50 short stories and seven novels in print. His latest sales have been to Schrodinger's Mouse, Morpheus Tales, Black Ink Horror, Short-Story.me, PseudoPod and Jack O'Spec. Over the years, four of his short stories have been awarded honorable mentions in Datlow & Windling's *Year's Best Fantasy & Horror.*

RYCKE FOREMAN ~ received the acceptance letter for his first published short story in 1992--on his 21st birthday. He has continued to publish short stories and poetry periodically to date, primarily in the horror/fantasy/slipstream genres. His work has appeared in *Marion Zimmer Bradley's Fantasy Magazine, Arkham Tales, The Writer's Eye, Niteblade, Tales from the Moon-Lit Path, Dark Planet, Crossroads...Where Evil Dwells, Gaslight: Tales of the Unsane, Journal of the Dark* and many other others. He is an award winning editor and part-time publicist, and currently co-edits *69 Flavors of Paranoia* with Miranda. He's written and directed three short films to date, and co-wrote/-directed/-produced one full length feature with longtime friends and associates, Thomas La Rue, Jeremy Orr and George Thomas. In January of 2009, he optioned a script to a small Hollywood production company, and is currently working on an independent horror film titled *Slash.*

FREDRICK OBERMEYER ~ lives in Cooperstown, NY. He enjoys writing science-fiction, horror, crime and fantasy and has had stories published in the *Dead Inn, Alternate Realities, Planet Relish, Fedora, SDO Fantasy,* the *Fifth Di* and *Forgotten Worlds.*

DAVID NIALL WILSON ~ David has been writing and publishing horror, dark fantasy, and science fiction since the mid-eighties. An ordained minister, once President of the Horror Writer's Association and recipient of the Bram Stoker Award for poetry and short fiction, as well as being nominated for long fiction and non-fiction, his novels include *Maelstrom, The Mote in Andrea's Eye, Deep Blue, the Grails Covenant Trilogy, Star Trek Voyager: Chrysalis, Except You Go Through Shadow, This is My Blood, Ancient Eyes* and the upcoming supernatural mystery novel *Vintage Soul: Volume I of the DeChance Chronicles.* The Stargate Atlantis novel *Brimstone,* written with Patricia Lee Macomber was published in 2010. He has over 150 short stories published in anthologies, magazines, and five collections, the most recent of which were *Defining Moments*, published in 2007 by WFC Award winning Sarob Press, and the currently available *Ennui & Other States of Madness*, from Dark Regions Press. His work has appeared in various anthologies and magazines. David lives and loves with Patricia Lee Macomber in the historic William R. White House in Hertford, NC with their children, Billy, Stephanie, and Katie, David's mother Jean, and occasionally his boys Zach and Zane.

WILLIAM MEIKLE ~ is a Scottish writer with ten novels published in the genre press and over 200 short story credits in thirteen countries, and the author of the ongoing Midnight Eye series among others. His work has appeared in a number of anthologies.

JAMES NEWMAN ~ James lives in North Carolina with his wife, Glenda, and their two sons, Jamie and Jacob. James has several published novels to his name, including *Animosity, The Wicked*, and the coming-of-age fan favorite *Midnight Rain.*

JOHN EVERSON ~ John is the Bram Stoker Award-winning author of the novels *Covenant, Sacrifice, The 13th* and *Siren*, and the short story collections *Creeptych, Needles & Sins, Vigilantes of Love* and *Cage of Bones & Other Deadly Obsessions.* He shares a deep purple den in Naperville, Illinois with a cockatoo and cockatiel, a disparate collection of fake skulls, twisted skeletal fairies, Alan Clark illustrations and a large stuffed Eeyore. There's also a mounted Chinese fowling spider named Stoker courtesy of Charlee Jacob, an ever-growing shelf of custom mix CDs and an acoustic guitar that he can't really play but that his son Shaun likes to hear him beat on anyway. Sometimes his wife Geri is surprised to find him shuffling through more public areas of the house, but it's usually only to brew another cup of coffee. In order to avoid the onerous task of writing, he holds down a regular job at a medical association, records pop-rock songs in a hidden home studio, experiments with the insatiable culinary joys of the jalapeno, designs photo collage art book covers for a variety of small presses, loses hours in expanding an array of gardens and chases frequent excursions into the bizarre visual headspace of '70s euro-horror DVDs with a shot of Makers Mark and a tall glass of Newcastle. For information on his fiction, art and music, visit John Everson: Dark Arts at www.JohnEverson.com.

MICHAEL LAIMO ~ Michael's novels include *Atmosphere* (nominated for the Bram Stoker Award in the category of first novel), *Deep In The Darkness* (nominated for the Bram Stoker Award in the 'novel' category) *The Demonologist*, *Dead Souls* and *Fires Rising*, all of which were published by Leisure Books. He is the author of the dark S/F-Suspense novel, *Sleepwalker*, which came out in Limited Edition hardcover from Delirium Books. His short fiction has found its way into the pages of *In Delirium*, *A Walk On The Darkside*, *Lost On The Darkside*, *Hot Blood XII: Strange Bedfellows*, *Surreal Magazine*, *Inhuman Magazine*, *The Best Of Epitaphs*, *The Best Of All Flesh*, *Li Pulse Magazine*, plus many more anthologies and magazines, many of which have been collected in *Demons, Freaks, And Other Abnormalities*, *Dregs of Society*, and *Dark Ride*. He can be contacted at Michael@laimo.com.

JAY CASELBERG ~ is an Australian science fiction/mystery author. As of September 2007, he has published four novels and multiple short stories under his own name. He has also written under the pseudonym James A. Hartley. All of the books published under his own name feature "psychic investigator" Jack Stein, a man whose slight psychic talent (which manifests in dreams and gut feelings) led him from a job in the military to a stint in Intelligence, and later to a job as a private investigator.

COLLEEN ANDERSON ~ is a writer with fiction and poetry that has appeared in over 100 publications, with newer works in *OnSpec Magazine* and *Don Juan & Men*. She is a member of SFWA, SF Canada, the Editors' Association of Canada, and is the assistant poetry editor at *Chizine*. New work will be coming out in *Evolve, Alison's Wonderland* and *Horror Library Vol. 4*.

BARBARA RODEN ~ is a World Fantasy Award-winning editor and publisher, whose short stories have appeared in numerous publications, including *Year's Best Fantasy and Horror: Nineteenth Annual Collection, Horror: Best of the Year 2005, Bound for Evil, Strange Tales 2, Gaslight Grimoire, Gaslight Grotesque, The Year's Best Dark Fantasy and Horror 2010, Best New Horror 21*, and *Poe: 19 New Tales Inspired by Edgar Allan Poe*. Her first collection, *Northwest Passages*, was published in

2009; the title story was nominated for the Stoker, International Horror Guild, and World Fantasy awards, while the book received a World Fantasy Award nomination for Best Collection.

TIM WAGGONER ~ wrote his first story at the age of five, when he created a comic book version of King Kong vs. Godzilla on a stenographer's pad. It took him a few more years until he began selling professionally, though. Overall, he's published over 70 stories of fantasy and horror as well as hundreds of nonfiction articles. In addition to writing fiction, Tim has worked as an editor and a newspaper reporter. He currently teaches creative writing at Sinclair Community College in Dayton, Ohio, and in the MA in Writing Popular Fiction program at Seton Hill University. He has two bright and beautiful daughters. Tim hopes to continue writing and teaching until he keels over dead, after which he wants to be stuffed and mounted, and then placed in front of his computer terminal.

JOHN L. FRENCH ~ is familiar with monsters. Having worked over thirty years for the Baltimore Police Department as a crime scene investigator, he witnessed more than his share of what horrors one person can inflict on another. Working with patrol officers and detectives, John has been involved in putting many of these people behind bars for very long sentences. In 1992 John began writing crime fiction, basing his stories on his experiences on the streets of what some have called one of the most dangerous cities in the country. His books include *The Devil Of Harbor City, Souls On Fire, Past Sins, Here There Be Monsters* and (with Patrick Thomas) *Bullets And Brimstone* and the upcoming *From The Shadows*. He is the editor of *Bad Cop, No Donut,* which features tales of police behaving badly.

ALAN SMALE ~ writes fantasy and horror, alternate and twisted history, urban fantasy and slipstream, with over two-dozen stories published in speculative fiction magazines and original anthologies. Born and raised in England, he lives in Maryland and works as an astrophysicist and data archive manager at NASA's Goddard Space Flight Center. In what is humorously referred to as his 'spare time', he sings bass and serves as Business Manager for high-energy vocal band The Chromatics, and performs occasionally in Community Theater.

DAVID M. FITZPATRICK ~ has 50 short stories have appeared in print magazines and anthologies in the U.S., the U.K., and Canada. He has edited or co-edited several anthologies, with many new titles coming this year. By day, he works as a newspaper writer; by night, he occasionally teaches creative writing. He lives in Brewer, Maine, across the river from Bangor, and he hopes Stephen King's Muse accidentally lands on his house by mistake. No luck yet.

DON WEBB ~ Don's latest book *Webb's Weird Wild West* is a collection of weird surreal westerns. Webb has 14 books out now, with two more due from Wildside Press. His nonfiction deals with esoteric topics ranging from Aleister Crowley to the Greek Magical Papyri, His fiction has worn awards ranging form the Fiction Collective Award to the Death Equinox Idiot Savant Award. He teaches High School English at a rural Texas reform school by day and Creative Writing for UCLA Extension by night. He has a lovely wife Guiniviere and two cats Sascha and Big Pig.

STEVE VERNON has been writing dark fiction for an awful lot of years. You'll find his work in the pages of *Cemetery Dance*, Tor's *Year's Best Horror*, *The Horror Show*, *Flesh & Blood*, *Hot Blood*, *Horror Garage* and many other tastefully titled markets and magazines. Steve's ghost story collections *Wicked Woods*, *Halifax Haunts*, and *Haunted Harbours* (Nimbus) are available in many Maritime bookstores. Steve has been doing a lot of work with e-publisher Crossroad Press. Look for his out-of-print weird west novella *Long Horn, Big Shaggy*, his dark superhero collection *Nothing To Lose* as well as a follow-up volume, and a brand new never-before-published novel of historical horror *Devil Tree* due out in e-book format from Crossroad Press in the year 2011. Finally, Steve's first YA novel, *Sinking Deeper* – a touching tale of sea monsters and caber tossing – will be released in the spring of 2011 from Nimbus Publishing. For more info go to Steve Vernon's website.

SCOTT HARPER ~ works in the waste management system, otherwise known as law enforcement. When he's not at work or in the gym, he dreams of writing the perfect vampire story – sexy, dark and violent. His stories have been published in a number of venues, including *Space and Time Magazine*; his story *Let Loose* is scheduled for publication later this year in an anthology called Groanology. He lives in Huntington Beach, California with his wife, son and dog.

NANCY KILPATRICK ~ Nancy's generational "The Power of the Blood" vampire series includes the novels *Child Of The Night, Near Death, Reborn, Bloodlover* and *Transformation. As One Dead* was a collaboration with Don Bassingthwaite for *White Wolf's Vampire: The Masquerade* series, while *Dracul: A Love Story* was a novelization of a stage play of the same name. Her other novels include *Jason X: Planet Of The Beast* and *Jason X: To The Third Power.* She compiled the non-fiction study *The Goth Bible: A Compendium For The Darkly Inclined* for St. Martin's Press, and co-edited the anthologies *Outsiders: 22 All-New Stories From The Edge* (with Nancy Holder) and *Graven Images And In The Shadow Of The Gargoyle* (both with Thomas Roche). Her short fiction is collected in *Sex And The Single Vampire, Endorphins, The Vampire Stories Of Nancy Kilpatrick* and *Cold Comfort.* Under the pseudonym "Amarantha Knight" she has written a number of erotic novels in *The Darker Passions* series, including *Dracula, Dr. Jekyll And Mr. Hyde, Frankenstein, The Fall Of The House Of Usher, The Portrait Of Dorian Gray, The Pit And The Pendulum, Carmilla* and *Curse Of The Mummy,* as well as editing the anthologies *Love Bites, Flesh Fantastic, Sex Macabre, Seductive Spectres* and *Demon Sex.* Originally published by Masquerade Books, they are currently being reprinted by Circlet Press.

MORE GREAT BOOKS FROM
BOOKS OF THE DEAD

NOVELS
Matt Hults - Husk
James Roy Daley - Terror Town

ANTHOLOGIES
Best New Zombie Tales (Vol. 1)
Best New Zombie Tales (Vol. 2)
Best New Zombie Tales (Vol. 3)
Classic Vampire Tales (Vol.1)

COLLECTIONS
James Roy Daley -13 Drops of Blood